"There's a demon stration up there."

"So what," I growled. "There's a demonstration at that corner about three days a week." Then it sank in. A *demon* stration? I hoped the building would survive. There'd be SWAT teams and God only knows what all else up there, trying to keep the irate Powers from turning the place into an inferno.

It took a while for me to inch close enough to find out that the Powers at this demon stration weren't apt to turn violent. They were all succubi. Pictures don't begin to convey the essence of what succubi are all about. When you see them you can't help but think they're the creatures men were really designed to mate with; they make women look like clumsy makeshifts.

One little devil with a blue dress on happened to catch my eye. The promise on her face, the way she ran an impossibly moist tongue over unbelievably sweet, unbelievably red lips, the sinuousness — When you think about it, you shouldn't be surprised our sexual demons are so strong. They've been evolving right along with us for as long as we've been human, proof of which is how strongly they manifest themselves on This Side. They're used to coming Across; they've been doing it for millions of years. They didn't carry signs or chant slogans. They just paraded; they were their own best message.

HARRY TURTLEDOVE

THE CASE OF THE TOXIC SPELL DUMP

BAEN

THE CASE OF THE TOXIC SPELL DUMP

Copyright © 1993 by Harry Turtledove

A Baen Books Original

Baen Publishing Enterprises
P.O. Box 1403
Riverdale, N.Y. 10471

ISBN: 0-671-72196-8

Cover art by Stephen Hickman

First printing, December 1993

Distributed by
SIMON & SCHUSTER
1230 Avenue of the Americas
New York, N.Y. 10020

Typeset by Windhaven Press, Auburn, N.H.
Printed in the United States of America

ACKNOWLEDGMENTS

At a panel on magic and technology at the 1991 World Fantasy Convention in Tuscon, Alexandra Honigsberg remarked that any means of manipulating the environment, whether through technology or magic, brought a price. That led me to make a crack about toxic spell dumps, which led me to scrawl the phrase down on my pocket program, which led to this book. Thanks, Alexandra.

Thanks to Poul and Karen Anderson, who were in the audience at that panel, for liking the crack and encouraging the book.

Thanks to Jim Brunet for the spellchecker, to Susan Shwartz for sylph abuse, and to John Johnston III for St. Florian.

Somewhere close to half the other strange things in the book come from Laura—thanks to her, too, as always and for the usual excellent reasons.

The rest is my fault.

I

I hate telephones.

For one thing, they have a habit of waking you up at the most inconvenient times. It was still dark outside when the one on my nightstand went off like a bomb. I groaned and tried to turn off the alarm clock. Since it wasn't ringing, it laughed at me. The horrible racket from the phone kept right on.

"What time is it, anyhow?" I mumbled. My mouth tasted like something you'd spread on nasturtiums.

"It's 5:07," the clock said, still giggling. The horological demon in there was supposed to be friendly, not sappy. I'd thought more than once about getting the controlling cantrip fixed, but twenty-five crowns is twenty-five crowns. On a government salary, you learn to put up with things.

I picked up the receiver. That was the cue for the noise elemental in the base of the phone to shut up, which it did—Ma Bell's magic, unlike that from a cheap clock company, does exactly what it's supposed to do, no more, no less.

"Fisher here," I said, hoping I didn't sound as far underwater as I felt.

"Hello, David. This is Kelly, back in D.St.C."

You could have fooled me. After the imp in one phone's mouthpiece relays words through the ether to the one in another phone's earpiece and the second imp passes them on to you, they hardly sound as if they came from a real person, let alone from anyone in particular. That's the other reason I hate phones.

But the cursed things have sprouted like toadstools the past ten years, ever since ectoplasmic cloning let the phone company crank out legions of near-identical speaker imps, and since switching spells got sophisticated enough so you could reliably select the imp you wanted from among those legions.

They say they're going to have an answer to the voice problem real soon. They've been saying that since the day after phones were invented. I'll believe it when I hear it. Some things are even bigger than Ma Bell.

Nondescript voice aside, I was willing to believe this was Charlie Kelly. He'd probably just got to his desk at Environmental Perfection Agency headquarters back in the District of St. Columba, so of course he'd picked up the phone. Three-hour time difference? They don't think that way in D.St.C. The sun revolves around them, not the other way round. St. Ptolemy of Alexandria has to be the patron of the place, no matter what the Church says.

All this flashed through my mind in as much of a hurry as I could muster at 5:07 on a Tuesday morning. I don't think I missed a beat—or not more than one, anyhow—before I said, "So what can I do for you this fine day, Charlie?"

The insulating spell on the phone mouthpiece kept me from having to listen to my imp shouting crosscountry to his imp. I waited for his answer: "We have reports that there might a problem in your neck of the woods worth an unofficial look or two."

"Whereabouts in my neck of the woods?" I asked patiently. Easterners who live in each other's pockets have no feel for how spread out Angels City really is.

The pause that followed was longer than conversations between phone imps would have required; Charlie had to be checking a map or a report or something. At last he said, "It's in a place called Chatsworth. That's just an Angels City district name, isn't it?" He made it sound as if it were just around the corner from me.

It wasn't. Sighing, I answered, "It's up in St. Ferdinand's Valley, Charlie. That's about forty, maybe fifty miles from where I am right now."

"Oh," he said in a small voice. A fifty-mile circle out from Charlie's office dragged in at least four provinces. Fifty miles for me won't even get me out of my barony unless I head straight south, and then I'm only in the one next door. I don't need to head south very often; the Barony of Orange has its own EPA investigators.

"So what's going on in Chatsworth?" I asked. "Especially what's going on that you need to bounce me out of bed?"

"I am sorry about that," he said, so calmly that I knew he'd known what time it was out here before he called. Which meant it was urgent. Which meant I could start worrying. Which I did. He went on, "We may have a problem with a dump in the hills up there."

I riffled through my mental files. "That'd be the Devonshire dump, wouldn't it?"

"Yes, that's the name," he agreed eagerly—too eagerly. Devonshire's been giving Angels City on-and-off problems for years. The trouble with magic is, it's not free. All the good it produces is necessarily balanced by a like amount of evil. Yeah, I know people have understood that since Newton's day: *for every quality, there is an equal and opposite counter-quality*, and all the math that goes with the law. But mostly it's a lip-service understanding, along the lines of, *as long as I don't shit in my yard, who cares about next door?*

That attitude worked fine—or seemed to—as long as next door meant the wide open spaces. If byproducts of magic blighted a forest or poisoned a stream, so what? You just moved on to the next forest or stream. A hundred years ago, the Confederated Provinces seemed to stretch west forever.

But they don't. I ought to know; Angels City, of course, sits on the coast of the Peaceful Ocean. We don't have unlimited unspoiled land and water to exploit any more. And as industrial magic has shown itself ever more capable of marvelous things, its byproducts have turned ever more noxious. You wouldn't want them coming downstream at you, believe me you wouldn't. My job is to make sure they don't.

"What's gone wrong with Devonshire now?" I asked. The answer I really wanted was *nothing*. A lot of local industries dispose of waste at Devonshire, and some of the biggest ones are defense firms. By the very nature of things, the byproducts from their spells are more toxic than anybody else's.

Charlie Kelly said, "We're not really sure there's anything wrong, Dave." That was close to what I wanted to hear, but not close enough. He went on, "Some of the local people"— he didn't say who—"have been complaining more than usual, though."

"They have any reason to?" I said. Local people always complain about toxic spell dumps. They don't like the noise, they don't like the spells, they don't like the flies (can't blame them too much for that; would you want byproducts from dealings with Beelzebub in your back yard?). Most of the time, as Charlie said, nothing is really wrong. But every once in a while . . .

"That's what we want you to find out," he told me.

"Okay," I answered. Then something he'd said a while before clicked in my head; I hadn't been awake enough to pay attention to it till now. "What do you mean, you want me to take a *quiet* look around? Why shouldn't I go up there with flags flying and cornets blaring?" A formal EPA inspection is worth seeing: two exorcists, a thaumaturge, shamans from the Americas, Mongolia, and Africa, the whole nine yards. Sometimes the incense is a toxic hazard all by itself.

"Because I want you to do it this way." He sounded harassed. "I've been asked to handle this unofficially as long as I can. Why do you think I'm calling you at home? Unless and until you find something really out of line, it would be best for everybody if you kept a low profile. Please, Dave?"

"Okay, Charlie." I owed Charlie a couple, and he's a pretty good fellow. "It's politics, isn't it?" I made it into a swear word.

"What's not?" He let it go at that. I didn't blame him; he had a job he wanted to keep. And telephone imps have ears just like anything else. They can be tormented, tricked, or sometimes bribed into blabbing too much. Phone security systems have come a long way, yeah, but not all the devils are out of them yet.

I sighed. "Can you at least tell me who doesn't want me snooping around? Then if anybody tries anything, I'll have some idea why." Just silence in my ear, save for the light breathing of my phone imp. I sighed again. It was that kind of morning. "Okay, Charlie, I'll draw my own conclusions." Those conclusions made for one ugly drawing, let me tell you. After a last sigh for effect, I said, "I'll head up to the Valley right away. God willing, I can get going before St. James' Freeway turns impossible."

"Thanks, David. I appreciate it," Kelly said, coming back to life now that I was doing what he wanted.

"Yeah, sure." I resigned myself to a long, miserable day. "'Bye, Charlie." I hung up the phone. The imp went dormant. I wished I could have done the same.

I grabbed a quick, cold shower—either the salamander for the block of flats wasn't awake yet or somebody had turned it into a toad overnight—a muddy cup of coffee, and a not quite stale sweet roll. Feeling as near human as I was going to get at half past five, I went out to the garage, got on my carpet, and headed for the freeway.

My building has access rules like any other's, I suppose: anybody can use the flyway going out, but to come in you have to make your entry talisman known to the watch demon or else have one of the residents propitiate him for you. Otherwise you come down—with quite a bump, too—outside the wall and the gate.

I rode west along The Second Boulevard (don't ask me why it's The Second and not just Second; it just is) about twenty feet off the ground. Traffic was moving pretty well, actually, even though we all still had our lanterns on so we could see one another in the predawn darkness.

The Watcher who lets carpets onto St. James' Freeway from a feeder road is of a different breed from your average building's watch demon. He holds the barrier closed so many seconds at a time, then opens it just long enough for one carpet to squeeze past. Nobody's ever figured out how to propitiate a Watcher, either. Oh, if you're quick—and stupid—you may be able to squeeze in on somebody else's tail, but if you try it, he'll note down the weave of your carpet, and in a few days, just like magic, a traffic ticket shows up in your mailbox. Not many people are stupid twice.

The freeways need rules like that; otherwise they'd be impossibly jammed. As things were, I got stuck no matter how early I'd left. There was a bad accident a little north of the interdicted zone around the airport, and somebody's carpet had flipped. The damned fool—well, of course I don't actually know the state of his soul, but no denying his foolishness—hadn't been wearing his safety belt, either.

One set of paramedics was down on the ground with the fellow who'd been thrown out. They had a priest with them, too, so that didn't look good. The other Red Cross carpet was parked right in the middle of the flight of way, tending to victims who hadn't been thrown clear—and making everyone detour around it. People gawked as they slid by, so they went even slower. They always do that, and I hate it.

After that, I made pretty good time until I had to slow down again at the junction with St. Monica's Freeway. Merging traffic in three dimensions is a scary business when you think about it. Commuters who do it every day don't think about it any more.

The rush thinned out once I got north of Westwood, and I pretty much sailed into St. Ferdinand's Valley. I slid off the freeway and cruised around for a while, getting closer to the Devonshire dump by easy stages and looking for signs that might tell me whether Charlie Kelly had a right to be worried about it.

At first I didn't see any, which gladdened my heart. A couple of generations ago, the Valley was mostly farms and citrus groves. Then the trees went down and the houses went up. Now the Valley has industry of its own (if it didn't, I wouldn't have had to worry about the toxic spell dump, after all), but in large measure it's still a bedroom community for the rest of Angels City: lots of houses, lots of kids, lots of schools. You don't care to think about anything nasty in a part of town like that.

Before I went out to the dump itself, I headed over to the monastery to do some homework. The Thomas Brothers have chapter houses in cities all across the west; more meticulous record-keeping simply doesn't exist. Even if the Valley looked normal, I had a good chance of finding trouble simply by digging through the numbers they enshrined on parchment.

I've heard the Thomas Brothers have an unwritten rule that no abbot of theirs can ever be named Brother Thomas. I don't know if that's so. I do know the abbot at the Valley chapter house was a big-nosed Armenian named Brother Vahan. We'd met a few times before, though I didn't often work far enough north in Angels City to need his help.

He bowed politely as he let me precede him into his office. Candlelight gleamed from his skull. He was the baldest man I'd ever seen; he didn't need to be tonsured. He waved me to a comfortable chair, then sat down in his own hard one. "What can I do for you today, Inspector Fisher?" he asked.

I was ready for that. "I'd like to do some comparison work on births, birth defects, healings, and exorcisms in the northwest Valley ten years ago and in the past year."

"Ah," was all the abbot said. When viewed against his hairless skull, the big black caterpillars he used for eyebrows seemed even more alive than they might have otherwise. They twitched now. "How big a radius around the Devonshire dump would you like?"

I sighed. I should have expected it. I'm Jewish, but I know enough to realize fools don't generally make it up to abbot's grade. I said, "This is unofficial and confidential, you understand."

He laughed at me. I turned red. Maybe I was the fool,

telling an abbot about confidentiality. He just said, "There are places you would need to be more concerned about that aspect than here, Inspector."

"I suppose so," I mumbled. "Can your data retrieval system handle a five-mile radius?"

The caterpillars drooped; I'd offended him. "I thought you were going to ask for something difficult, Inspector." He got up. "If you'd be so kind as to follow me?"

I followed. We walked past a couple of rooms my eyes refused to see into. I wasn't offended; there are places in the Temple in Jerusalem and even in your ordinary synagogue where gentiles' perceptions are excluded the same way. All faiths have their mysteries. I was just thankful the Thomas Brothers didn't reckon their records too holy for outsiders to view.

The scriptorium was underground, a traditional construction left over from the days when anyone literate was assumed to be a black wizard and when books of any sort needed to be protected from the torches of the ignorant and the fearful. But for its placement, though, the room was thoroughly modern, with St. Elmo's fire glowing smoothly over every cubicle and each of those cubicles with its own ground-glass access screen.

As soon as Brother Vahan and I stepped into a cubicle, the spirit of the scriptorium appeared in the ground glass. The spirit wore spectacles. I had to work to keep my face straight. I'd never imagined folk on the Other Side could look bookish.

I turned to the abbot. "Suppose I'd come in without you or someone else who's authorized to be here?"

"You wouldn't get any information out of our friend there," Brother Vahan said. "You would get caught." He sounded quietly confident. I believed him. The Thomas Brothers probably knew about as much about keeping documents secure as anyone not in government, and what they didn't know, Rome did.

Brother Vahan spoke to the ground-glass screen. "Give this man unlimited access to our files and full aid for . . . will four hours be enough?"

"Should be plenty," I answered.

"For four hours, then," the abbot said. "Treat him in all ways as if he were one of our holy brethren." That was as *blanche* a *carte* as he could give me; I bowed my head in profound appreciation. He flipped a hand back and forth, as if to say, *Think nothing of it.* He could say that if he wanted to (humility is, after all, a monkish virtue), but we both knew I owed him a big one.

"Anything else?" he asked me. I shook my head. "Happy hunting, then," he said as he started out of the scriptorium. "I'll see you later."

The spirit manifesting itself in the access screen turned its nearsighted gaze on me. "How may I serve you, child of Adam given four hours of unlimited access to the files of the Thomas Brothers?"

I told it the same thing I'd told Brother Vahan: "I want to go through births, birth defects, healings, and exorcisms within a five-mile radius of the Devonshire dump, first for the year ending exactly ten years ago and then for the year ending today." Humans can handle approximate data; with spirits you have to spell out every word and make sure you've crossed your *t*'s and dotted your *i*'s (and even your *j*'s).

"I shall gather the data you require. Please wait," the spirit said. The screen went blank.

In the beginning was the Word, and Word was with God, and the Word was God. Yes, I know that's Brother Vahan's theology, not mine. It's a lot older than Christianity, for that matter. In Old Kingdom Egypt, the god Ptah was seen as both the tongue of the primeval god Atum and as the instrument through which Atum created the material world. Of course thought is the instrument through which we perceive and influence the Other Side; without it, we'd be as blind to magic as any dumb animals.

But John 1:1 and its variants in other creeds are also the basis of modern information theory. Because words partake of the divine, they manifest themselves in the spiritual world as well as in our own. Properly directed—ensorceled, if you will—spirits can gather, read, manipulate, and move the essence of words without ever having to handle the physical documents on which they appear. If the Greek and Roman mages had known that trick, their world could have been drowning in information, just as we are now.

I didn't have to wait long; as I'd expected, Brother Vahan used only the best and most thoroughly trained spirits. Ghostly images of documents began flashing onto the access screen, one after another—records from ten years ago. "Hold on!" I said after a few seconds.

The spirit appeared. "I obey your instructions, child of Adam," it said, as if daring me to deny it.

"I know, I know," I told it; the last thing I wanted was to get the heart of the access system mad at me. "I don't need to look at every individual report, though. Let me have the numbers in each category for the two periods. When I know what those are, I'll examine specific documents. That way, I'll be able to see forest and trees both."

The spirit looked out at me over the tops of its spectral spectacles. "You should have no difficulty in maintaining your mental view of both categories," it said reprovingly. That's easy for someone on the Other Side to say, but I have the usual limits of flesh and blood. I just stared back at the spirit. If it kept acting uppity, I'd sic Brother Vahan on it. After a last sniff, it said, "It shall be as you desire."

One by one, the numbers came up on the screen. The Thomas Brothers certainly did have a well-drilled scripto-rium spirit; the creature wrote so its figures ran the right way for me to read them. It hardly needed to have bothered. I'm so used to mirror-image writing that I read it as well as the other kind. Maybe learning Hebrew helped get my eyes used to moving from right to left.

When the final figure faded from view, I looked down at the notes I'd jotted. Births were up in the most recent year as opposed to ten years ago; St. Ferdinand's Valley keeps filling up. Blocks of flats have replaced a lot of what used to be single-family homes. We aren't as crowded as New Jorvik, and I don't think we ever will be, but Angels City is losing the small-town atmosphere it kept for a while even after it became a big city.

The rate of healings hadn't changed significantly over the

past ten years. "Spirit," I said, and waited until it appeared in the access screen. Then I played a hunch: "Please break out for me by type the healings for both periods I'm interested in."

"One moment," it said.

When they came up, the data weren't dramatic. I hadn't expected them to be, not when the overall frequency had stayed pretty much constant. But the increased incidence of elf-shot within the pool of healings was suggestive. Elves tend to be drawn to areas with high concentrations of sorcery. If the Devonshire dump were as clean as it was supposed to be, there shouldn't have been that many elves running around loose shooting their little arrows into people. Elf-arrows aren't like the ones Cupid looses, after all.

Exorcisms were up, too. I asked the access spirit for sample reports for each period. I wasn't after statistical elegance, not yet, just a feel for what was going on. I got the impression that the spirits who'd needed banishing this past year were a nastier bunch, and did more damage before they were expelled, than had been true in the earlier sample.

But the numbers that really leaped off the page at me were the birth defects. Between ten years ago and this past year, they'd almost tripled. I whistled softly under my breath, then called for the scriptorium spirit again. When it reappeared, I said, "May I please have a listing of birth defects by type for each of my two periods?"

"One moment," the spirit said again. The screen went blank. Then the spirit started writing on it. The first set of data it gave me was for the earlier period. Things there looked pretty normal. A few cases of second sight, a changeling whose condition was diagnosed earlier enough to give her remediation and a good chance at living a nearly normal life: nothing at all out of the ordinary.

When the birth defect information for the year just past came up on the ground glass, I almost fell off my chair. In that year alone, the area around the Devonshire dump had seen three vampires, two lycanthropes, and three cases of apsychia: human babies born without any soul at all. That's a truly dreadful defect, one neither priests nor physicians can do a thing about. The poor kids grow up, grow old, die, and they're gone. Forever. Makes me shudder just to think about it.

Three cases of apsychia in one year in a circle with a five-mile radius . . . I shuddered again. Apsychia just doesn't happen except when something unhallowed is leaking into the environment. You might not see three cases of apsychia in a year even in a place like eastern Frankia, where the toxic spells both sides flung around in the First Sorcerous War still poison the ground after three quarters of a century.

I finished writing up my notes, then told the spirit, "Thank you. You've been most helpful. May I ask one more favor of you?"

"That depends on what it is."

"Of course," I said quickly. "Just this: if anyone but brother Vahan tries to learn what I've been doing here, don't tell, him, her, or it." Scriptorium spirits, by their nature, have very literal minds; I wanted to make sure I covered both genders and both Sides.

The spirit considered, then nodded. "I would honor such a request from a monk of the Thomas Brothers, and am instructed to treat you as one for the duration Brother Vahan specified. Let it be as you say, then."

I didn't know how well the spirit would stand up under serious interrogation, but I wasn't too worried about that. Shows how much I knew, doesn't it? I guess I'm naive, but I thought the automatic anathema that falls on anyone who tampers with Church property would be plenty to keep snoops at arm's length. I'm no Christian, but I wouldn't have wanted an organization with a two-thousand-year track record of potent access to the Other Side down on me.

Of course, the veneration of Mammon goes back a lot farther than two thousand years.

I stopped by Brother Vahan's office on the way out so I could thank him for his help, too. He looked up from whatever he was working on—none of my business—and said two words: "That bad?"

He couldn't possibly have picked that up by magic. Along with the standard government-issue charms, I wear a set of my own made for me by a rabbi who's an expert in kabbalistics and other means of navigating on the Other Side. So I knew I was shielded. But abbots operate in this world, too. Even if he couldn't read my mind, he must have read my face.

"Pretty bad," I said. I hesitated before I went on, but after all, I'd just pulled the information from his files. All the same, I lowered my voice: "Three soulless ones born within that circle in the past year."

"Three?" His face went suddenly haggard as he made the sign of the cross. Then he nodded, as if reminding himself. "Yes, there have been that many, haven't there? I talked with the parents each time. That's so hard, knowing they'll never meet their loved ones in eternity. But I hadn't realized they were all so close to that accursed dump."

An abbot does not use words like *accursed* casually; when he says them, he means them. I wasn't surprised he hadn't noticed the apsychia cluster around the dump. That wasn't his job. Comforting bereaved families was a lot more important for him. But the Thomas Brothers collected the data I used to draw my own conclusions.

"Elf-shot is up in the area, too," I said quietly.

"It would be." He got up from behind his desk, set heavy hands on my shoulders. "Go with God, Inspector Fisher. I think you will be about His business today."

I didn't even twit him about turning One into Three, as I might have if I'd come out of his scriptorium with better news. Blessings are blessings, and we're wisely advised to count them. I said, "Thank you, Brother Vahan. I just wish I thought He was the only Power involved."

He didn't answer, from which I inferred he agreed with me. Wishing I could have come to some other conclusion, I went out to my carpet and headed over to the Devonshire dump. I drove around it a couple of times before I set down. Scout first, then attack; the army and the EPA both drill that into you.

Not that I learned much from my circumnavigations. You think dump, you think eyesore. It wasn't like that. From the outside, it didn't look like anything in particular, just a couple of square blocks with nothing built on them, nothing, at least, tall enough to show over the fence. And even that fence wasn't ugly; ivy climbed trellises and spilled over inside. If you wanted to, you could probably climb those trellises yourself, jump right on down.

You'd have to be crazy to try it, though. For one thing, I was certain catchspells would grab you if you did. For another, the ornaments on the perimeter fence weren't just there for decoration. Crosses, *Magen Davids*, crescents, Oriental ideograms I recognized but couldn't read, a bronze alpha and omega, a few kufic letters like the ones that lead off chapters of the *Qu'ran* . . . Things were being controlled in there, Things you wouldn't want to mess with.

They weren't being controlled well enough, though, or babies around the dump wouldn't come into the world without souls. I dribbled a few drops of Passover wine onto my spellchecker, murmured the blessing that thanked the Lord for the fruit of the vine.

The spellchecker duly noted all the apotropaic incantations on the wall . . . and yes, there were catchspells behind them. But it didn't see anything else. I shrugged. I hadn't really expected it to: its magical vocabulary wasn't that large. Besides, if the sorcerous leakage from the dump was so obvious that anybody with a thirty-crown gadget from Spells 'R' Us could spot it, Charlie Kelly wouldn't have needed to send me out to look things over. Still, you'd like things to be easy, just once.

There was a parking lot across the street from the entrance. I set my carpet down there, chanted the antitheft geas before I climbed off it. I do that automatically; Angels City has had big-city crime for a long time. Leave a carpet unwarded for even a few minutes and you're apt to find it's walked with Jesus.

I crossed in the crosswalk. They still call it that here, though in a melting pot like Angels City it also has symbols to let Jews and Muslims, Hindus and Parsees and Buddhists, and several different flavors of pagan (neo and otherwise) get from one side of the street to the other in safety. I don't know what you're supposed to do if you're a Samoan who still worships Tanaroa. Run like hell, I suppose.

The entryway to the Devonshire dump projected out several feet from the rest of the wall. A guard in a neat blue denim uniform came out of a glassed-in cage, tipped his cap to me. "May I help you, sir?" he asked politely, but in a way that still managed to imply I had no legitimate business making him get off his duff and step outside.

I flashed my EPA sigil. At a toxic spell dump, that effectively turns me into St. Peter—I'm the fellow with the power to bind and loose, at least. The guard's eyes widened. "Let me call Mr. Sudakis for you, Inspector, uh, Fisher, sir," he said, and ducked back into his cell. He grabbed the phone, started talking into it, waited for his ear imp to answer, then replaced the handset in its cradle. "You can go in, sir. I'll help you."

Help me he did. The gate was the kind with the little wheel on the bottom that retracted in back of the fence. He pushed it open. Behind it was a single, symbolic strand of barbed wire, with a placard whose message appeared in several languages and almost as many alphabets. The English version read, ALL HOPE ABANDON, YE WHO UNAUTHORIZED ENTER HERE. Dante always makes people sit up and take notice.

The guard moved the wire out of my way, too. Behind it was a thin red line painted on the ground which went across the gap where the two sections of wall came out to form the entryway. The guard picked up a little arched footbridge made of wood, set it down so that one end was outside the red line, the other inside. He was very careful to make sure neither end touched the strip of paint. That would have breached the dump's outer security containment, and doubtless cost him his job no matter how many backup systems the place had.

"Go ahead, sir," he said, tipping his cap again. "Mr. Sudakis is expecting you. Please stay within the confines of the wires and the amber lines inside." He grinned nervously. "I don't know why I'm telling you that—you know more about it than I do."

"You're doing what you're supposed to do," I answered as I mounted the little footbridge. "Too many people don't bother any more."

As soon as I'd got off the bridge, the guard picked it up and put it back on his side. The amber lines on the concrete and the barbed wire strung above them marked the safe path to the administrative office, a low cinderblock building that looked like a citadel in both the military and sorcerous senses of the word.

I looked around as I walked the path. I don't know what I'd expected—blasted heath, maybe. But no, just a couple of acres of weeds, mostly brown now because nobody's spells have been able to bring much rain the past few years. And yet—

For second or two, the fence around the dump seemed very far away, with a whole lot of Nothing stretching the dirt and brush the same way you'd use bread crumbs to make hamburger go farther. Astrologers babble about the nearly infinite distances between the stars. I had the bad feeling I was looking at more infinity than I ever cared to meet, plopped down there in the middle of Chatsworth. Magic, especially byproducts of magic, can do things to space and time that the mathematicians are still trying to figure out. Then I looked again, and everything seemed normal.

I hoped the wards the amber lines symbolized were as potent as the ones the red line had continued. By the data I'd taken from the Thomas Brothers' chapter house, even those weren't as good as they should have been.

A stocky fellow in shirt, tie, and hard hat came out of the cinderblock building and up the path toward me. He had his hand out and a professionally friendly smile plastered across his face. "Inspector—Fisher, is it? Pleased to meet you. I'm Antanas Sudakis; my job title is sorcerous containment area manager. Call me Tony—I'm the guy who runs the dump."

We shook hands. His grip showed controlled strength. I was at least six inches taller than he; I could look down on the top of his little helmet. Just the same, I got the feeling he could break me in half if he decided to—I'm a beanpole, while he was built like somebody who'd been a good high school linebacker and might have played college ball if only he'd been taller.

He wasn't hostile now, though. "Why don't you come into my office, Inspector Fisher—"

"Call me Dave," I said, thinking I ought to keep things friendly as long as I could.

"Okay, Dave, come on with me and then you can let me know what this is all about. All our inspection parchments are properly signed, sealed, blessed, fumigated, what have you. I keep the originals on file in my desk; I know you government folks are never satisfied with copies called up in the ground glass."

"What sorcery summons, sorcery may shift," I said, making it sound as if I was quoting official EPA policy. And I was. Still, I believed him. If his parchmentwork wasn't in order, he wouldn't brag about it. Besides, if his parchmentwork wasn't in order, he'd have more to fret about than a surprise visit from an EPA inspector. He'd be worrying about the wrath of God, both from bosses who didn't pay him to screw up and maybe from On High, too. A lot of things in the dump were unholy in the worst way.

His office didn't feel like a citadel, even if it had no windows. The diffuse glow of St. Elmo's fire across the ceiling gave the room the cool, even light of a cloudy day. The air was cool to breathe, too, though St. Ferdinand's Valley, which like the rest of Angels City was essentially a desert before it got built up, still has desertly weather.

Sudakis noticed me visibly not toasting. He grinned. "We're on a circuit with one of the frozen water elementals up in Greenland. A section of tile here"—he pointed to the wall behind his desk—"touched the elemental once, and now it keeps the place cool thanks to the law of contagion."

"Once in contact, always in contact," I quoted. "Modern as next week." A lot of buildings in Angels City cool themselves by contagious contact with ice elementals. That wasn't what I meant by modern; the law of contagion may be the oldest magical principle known. But regulating the effect so people feel comfortable, not stuck on an ice floe themselves, is a new process—and an expensive one. The people who made a profit off the dump didn't stint their employees; I

wondered how the leak had happened if they had money like
this to throw around.

Once his secretary had brought coffee for both of us,
Sudakis settled back in his chair. It creaked. He said, "What
can I do for you, Dave? I gather this is an unofficial visit: you
haven't shown me a warrant, you haven't served a subpoena,
you don't have a priest or an exorcist or even a lawyer with
you. So what's up?"

"You're right—this is unofficial." I sipped my coffee. It
was delicious, nothing like the reconstituted stuff that makes
a liar of the law of similarity. "I'd like to talk about your containment scheme here, if you don't mind."

His air of affability turned to stone as abruptly as if he'd
gazed on a cockatrice. By his expression, he'd sooner have
had me ask him about a social disease. "We're tight," he said.
"Absolutely no question we're tight. Maybe we'd both better
have priests and lawyers here. I don't like 'unofficial' visits
that hit me where I live, Inspector Fisher." I wasn't Dave any
more.

"You may not be as tight as you think," I told him. "That's
what I'm here to talk about."

"Talk is cheap." He was hard-nosed as a linebacker, too. "I
don't want talk. I want evidence if you try and come here to
say things like that to me."

"Elf-shot around the dump is up a lot from ten years ago
till now," I said.

"Yes, I've seen those numbers. We've got a lot of new
immigrants in the area, too, and they bring their troubles
with them when they come to this country. We have a case of
jaguaranthropy, if that's a word, a couple of years ago. Try
telling me *that* would have happened when all the neighbors
sprang from northwest Europe."

He was right about the neighborhood changing. I'd gone
past a couple of houses that had signs saying *Curandero*
tacked out front. If you ask me, *curanderos* are frauds who
prey on the ignorant, but nobody asked me. A basic principle
of magic is that if you believe in something, it'll be true—for
you.

I'll tell you something I believed. I believed that if the

EPA took Devonshire dump to court just on the strength of an increase in elf-shot around the area, the lawyers Sudakis' people would throw at us would leave us so much not-too-lean ground beef. I had no doubt Tony Sudakis believed it, too.

So I hit him with something bigger and harder. "Are you going to blame the immigrants for the three cases of apsychia around here in the past year?"

He didn't even blink. "Coincidence," he said flatly. One hand, though, tugged at the silver chain he wore around his neck. Out popped the ornament on the end of it. I'd expected a crucifix, but instead it was a polished piece of amber with something embedded inside—a pretty piece, and one that probably cost a pretty copper.

"Speaking off the record, Mr. Sudakis, you know as well as I do that three soulless births in one area in one year isn't coincidence," I answered. "It's an epidemic."

He let the amber amulet slide back under his shirt. "I deny that, off the record or on it." His voice was so loud and ringing that I would have bet something was Listening to every word we said, ready to spit it back in case we did end up in court. *Interesting*, I thought. Sudakis went on. "Besides, Inspector, think of it like this: if I didn't think this place was safe, why would I keep coming to work every day?"

I raised what I hoped was a placating hand. "Mr. Sudakis—Tony, if I may—I'm not, repeat not, claiming you're personally responsible for anything. I want you to understand that. But evidence of what may be a problem here has come to my attention, and I wouldn't be doing my job if I ignored it."

"Okay," he said, nodding. "I can deal with that. Look, maybe I can clear this up if I show you the containment scheme. *You* find any holes in it, Dave"—I was *Dave* again, so I guess he'd calmed down—"and I will personally shit in my hat and wear it backwards. I swear it."

"You're not under oath," I said hastily. If he turned out to be wrong, I didn't want to leave him the choice of doing something disgusting or facing the wrath of the Other Side for not following through.

"You heard me." He got up from his desk, went over to a file cabinet off to one side, started pulling out folders. "Here, look." He unrolled a parchment in front of me. "Here's the outer perimeter. You'll have seen some of that; here's what all really goes into it. And here's the protection scheme for the complex we're sitting in."

I was already pretty much convinced the outer perimeter of the dump was tight; that's what the spellchecker had indicated, anyhow. And a cursory glance at the plans to keep the blockhouse safe told me Sudakis didn't need to be afraid when he came to his job. Satan himself might have forced his way through those wards, or possibly Babylonian Tiamat if her cult were still alive, but the lesser Powers would only get headaches if they tried.

"Now here's the underground setup." Sudakis stuck another parchment in front of my face. "You look this over, Dave. You tell me if it's not as tight as a Vestal's—"

Unlike the other two plans, this one really did demand a careful onceover. Proper underground containment is the Balder's mistletoe of almost any toxic spell dump. The ideal solution, of course, would be to float the dump on top of a pool of alkahest, which would dissolve any evil that percolated through to it. But alkahest is a *quis custodiet ipsos custodes?* phenomenon—being a universal solvent, it dissolves *everything* it touches, which would in short order include the dumping grounds themselves.

Some of the wilder journal articles suggest using either lodestone levitation or sylphs of the air to raise the dump above the ground and to keep it separated from the alkahest below. I think anybody who'd try such a scheme ought to be made to live in the dump office. Lodelev is a purely physical process, and, like any physical process, vulnerable to magical interference. And sylphs of the air really are just as flighty as their reputation makes them out to be. They'd get bored or playful or whatever and forget what they were supposed to be doing.

That wouldn't be good, not where alkahest is involved. They used it in the First Sorcerous War, but not in the Second. It's just too potent, even as a weapon. As it eats its way straight toward the center of the earth, it's liable to bring up magma or ancient buried Powers through the channels it cuts. Nobody even stockpiles it—how could you?

So, no alkahest under the Devonshire dump. Instead, the designers had put in the usual makeshifts: blessings and relics and holy texts from every faith known to mankind, and elaborate spells renewed twice a year to use the law of contagion to extend their effect to the places where they weren't actually buried.

"It looks like a good arrangement on parchment," I said grudgingly. "I presume you rigidly adhere to the resanctification schedule." I made it sound as if I assumed nothing of the sort.

Tony Sudakis set more parchments in front of me. "Certification under canon law, the ordnances of the Baron of Angels, and national secular law."

I examined them. They looked like what they were supposed to be. The dump management outfit might have forged the secular documents; the worst the Baron of Angels can do is send you to jail, the worst the secular power can do is leave you short a head. But you'd have to be pretty bold to forge a canon lawyer's hand or seal. The punishment for that kind of offense could go on forever.

I shoved the pile of parchments back at Sudakis. Now my tone of voice was different: "I have to admit, I don't know what to tell you. This really does look good on parchment. But something's not right hereabouts; I know that, too." I told him about the rest of the birth defects I'd spotted, the vampirism and lycanthropy.

He frowned. "You're not making that up?"

"Not a word of it. I'll swear by *Adonai Elohaynu*, if you like." I am, God knows, an imperfect Jew. But you'd have to be a lot more imperfect than I am to falsify that oath. People who would risk their souls by falsely calling on the Lord won't make it past the EPA spiritual background checks, and a good thing, too, if you ask me.

Sudakis' beefy face set in the frown as if it were made of quick-drying cement. "Our attorneys will still maintain that the effects you cite are just a statistical quirk and have nothing to do with the Devonshire dump, its contents, or its activities. If we go to court, we'll win."

"Probably." I wanted to hit him. The certain knowledge that he'd murder me wasn't what stopped me. Getting in a good shot or two would have made that worthwhile. Far as I'm concerned, people who hide "it's wrong" behind "it's legal" deserve whatever happens to them. The only thing that held me back was knowing I'd bring discredit to the EPA.

Then Sudakis pulled out that little amber charm again. He licked a fingertip, ran it over the smooth surface of the amulet, and murmured something in a language I not only didn't know but didn't come close to recognizing. Then he put the amulet back and said, "Now we can talk privately for a little while."

"Can we?" I had no reason to trust him, every reason to think he was trying to trap me in an indiscretion. The lawyers he'd been throwing at me would have loved that.

But he said, "Yeah, and I think we'd better, too. I don't like the numbers you laid out for me, I don't like 'em at all. This place is supposed to be safe, it's been safe ever since I took over here, and I want it to keep on being safe. That's what they pay me for, after all."

"Why do you have to turn aside the Listener if that's so?" I asked. Come to that, I didn't know his outré little ritual really had turned aside anything.

He said, "Because the company basically just wants me to run this place so it makes them money. I want to run it right."

All I could think was, *Hell of a note when a man has to deafen the Listener before he says he wants to do a proper job.* But he'd convinced me. Too many top corporate managers hide dorsal fins under expensive imported suits. If one of those types got wind of what Sudakis had said, let alone what he'd done, he'd be out on the street with a big dusty footprint on his behind.

"How'd you get word there was trouble here, anyhow?" he asked. "Did you paw through the Thomas Brothers' files hoping you'd stumble over something you could use to curse us?"

His bosses wouldn't have let him manage the dump if he was stupid. I answered, "No, as a matter of fact, I didn't. I got a call from the District of St. Columba this morning, telling me I ought to check things out. So I did, and now you know what I found."

"That's—interesting." He stuck out his chin. "How'd Charlie Kelly know back there that something was up when you hadn't heard anything out here?" No, he wasn't stupid at all, not if he knew the fellow at the EPA who was likeliest to give me orders.

"His job is to hear things like that," I answered, suspicious again. Not all the ways Sudakis might have learned about Kelly were savory ones.

"Yeah, sure, sure. But how?" If he was acting, he could have given lessons. He looked down at his wrist, said something scatological. That's a safer way to work off your feelings than swearing or cursing. "My stinking watch says it's day before yesterday. Must be eddy currents from the garbage outside."

"You ought to wear something better than that cheap mechanical," I said. I touched the tail of the timekeeper that coiled round my wrist. It's a better-behaved little demon than the one that sits on my nightstand at home. It yawned, stretched, piped, "Eleven forty-two," and went back to sleep.

Sudakis scatologized again. "The Listener will go back on duty any minute now. I can't put it out two times running; the magic doesn't work. I hate doing it even once: too much magic loose here as is. That's why I don't wear a fancy watch like yours. Mechanicals are all right. When one gets bollixed, I just buy another one: no need to worry about rites or anything like that."

I shrugged; it wasn't my business. But I have as little to do with mechanicals as I can. If the Other Side weren't as real as this one, they might be all right. But as Atheling the Wise put it, though, most forces are also Persons, and mechanicals have no Personalities of their own to withstand the slings and arrows of outrageous fortune—to say nothing of outraged (or sometimes just mischievous) Forces. That's why you'll never see lodestone levitation under an alkahest pool.

Sometimes, when I'm in the mood for utopian flights of fancy, I think about how smoothly the world would run if all natural forces were as inanimate as the ones that let mechanicals operate. We'd never have to screen against megasalamanders launched on the wings of supersylphs to incinerate cities anywhere in the world. Neither of the Sorcerous Wars that devastated whole countries could have happened. For that matter, I wouldn't have had to worry about toxic spell dumps or the ever-growing pollution of the environment. Things would be simpler all around.

Yeah, I know it's a dream from the gate of ivory. Without magic, the world would probably have farmers, maybe towns, but surely not the great civilization we know. Can you imagine mass production without the law of similarity, or any kind of communications network without the law of contagion?

And medicine? I shiver to think of it. Without ectoplasmic beings to see and reach inside the body, how would medicine be possible at all? If you got sick, you'd bloody well die, just like one of Tony Sudakis' cheap watches when magic touched its works.

I pulled my mind back to business and asked him, "Can you give me a list of the firms whose spells you're storing at this containment facility?" That was a question I could legitimately ask him, regardless of whether the Listener was conscious.

He said, "Inspector Fisher, in view of the unofficial nature of your visit, I have to tell you no. If you bring me a warrant, I will of course cooperate to the degree required by civil and canon law." He thought he was being heard again—he tipped me a wink as he spoke.

"Such a list is a matter of public record," I argued, both because it was something I really wanted to have and because I still wasn't sure I could trust him.

"And I will surrender it to properly constituted authority, but only to such authority," he said. "But it could also give competitors important information on the spells and charms we use at this facility. Limited access to magical secrets is one of the oldest principles of both canon and civil law."

He might have been playing it to the hilt for the sake of the Listener, but he had me and I knew it. Sophisticated magic has to be kept secret or else everyone starts using it and the originator gains no benefit from hard and often dangerous research work. People who want to socialize sorcery don't realize there wouldn't be much sorcery to socialize if they took away the incentive for devising new spells.

"I shall return with that warrant, Mr. Sudakis," I said formally.

He grinned and gave me a silent thumbs-up the Listener wouldn't notice, so he was either really on my side or one fine con man. "Will there be anything else, Inspector?" he asked.

I started to shake my head, then changed my mind. "Is there a safe spot in this building where I can look out at the whole dump?"

"Sure is. Why don't you come with me?" Sudakis looked happy for any excuse to get up from behind his desk. My guess was that he'd been promoted for outstanding work in the field—he probably liked the money from his administrative job but not a whole lot of other things about it.

Our shoes rang on the spiral stairway that led to the roof of the cinderblock office. Steps and rail alike were cold iron, a sensible precaution in a building surrounded by such nasty magic. The trapdoor through which we climbed was also of iron, heavily greased against the rains Angels City wasn't seeing lately. Sudakis effortlessly pushed it out of the way.

"Here you are," he said waving. "You're about as safe here as you are indoors; topologically, we're still inside the same shielding system. But it doesn't feel the same out in the open air, does it?"

"No," I admitted. I felt exposed to I didn't know what. I wondered if the air itself was bad somehow. I imagined tiny demons I couldn't even see crawling down into my lungs and relieving themselves among my bronchial passages. An unpleasant thought—I scuttled it as fast as I could.

The dump still looked like a couple of acres of overgrown, underwatered ground. If it had been paved over, it would have been a perfect used carpet lot. I don't know what I'd expected from a panoramic view: maybe that I could spot boxes or barrels with corporate names on them. I didn't see anything, though. The most interesting thing I did see was a little patch of ground about fifty yards from the office building that seemed to be moving of its own accord. I pointed. "What's over there?"

Tony Sudakis' eyes followed my finger. "Oh, that. It'll be a while before decon does much with that area, I'm afraid. Byproducts from a defense plant—I can say that much. Those are flies you see stirring around."

"Oh." I dropped the subject, at once and completely. I'd thought about the Lord of the Flies on the way over to the dump. He's such a potent demon prince that even saying his name can be dangerous. *Speak of the devil*, as everyone knows, is not a joke, and the same applies to his great captain, the prince of the descending hierarchy.

I didn't care for the notion of the Defense Department dealing with Beelzebub, either. I know the Pentagram has the best wizards in the world, but they're only human. Leave out a single line—by God, misplace a single comma—and you're liable to have hell on earth.

I looked back toward the place where I'd seen a whole lot of Nothing when I was coming up the protected (I hoped) walk toward Sudakis' office. From this angle, it didn't look any different from the rest of the dump. I thought about mentioning it to Sudakis, but didn't bother; he probably saw enough weird things in the course of a week to last an ordinary chap with an ordinary job a lifetime or two.

Besides, that thought gave rise to another: "How often do you run across synergistic reactions among the spells that get dumped here?"

"It does happen sometimes, and sometimes it's no fun at all when it does." He rolled his eyes to show how big an understatement that was. "Persian spells are particularly bad for that, for some reason, and there's a large Persian community here in the Valley—refugees from the latest secularist takeover, most of them. When their spiritual elements fused with some from a Baghdadi candy-maker's preservation charm, of all the unlikely things—"

I drew my own picture. It wasn't pleasant. Shia and Sunni magic are starkly different but argue from the same premises. That makes the minglings worse when they happen: as if Papists and Protestants used the same dump in Ireland. The Confederation is a melting pot, all right, but sometimes the pot wants to melt down.

I didn't see anything else about which to question Sudakis, so I went back down the spiral stairs. He followed, pausing only to shut the trap door over our heads. As we walked back to his office, I said, "I'll be back with the warrant as soon as I can: in the next couple of days, anyhow."

"Whatever you say, Inspector Fisher." He winked again to show he was really on my side. I wondered if he was. He sounded very much like a man speaking for the Listener when he said, "I'm happy to cooperate informally with an informal investigation, but I do need the formal parchment before I can exceed the scope of my instructions from management."

He went out to the entrance with me. I craned my neck to see if the Nothing reappeared as I passed the place where I'd seen it before. For an instant I thought it did, but when I blinked it was gone.

"What's there?" Sudakis asked when I turned my head.

"Nothing," I said, but I meant—I guessed I meant—it with a small *n*. I laughed a little nervously. "A figleaf of my imagination."

"You work here a while, you'll get those for sure." He nodded, hard. I wondered what all he'd seen—or maybe not seen—since he started working here.

When we got out to the front gate, the security guard again carefully placed the footbridge so it straddled the red line. I felt like a free man as soon as I was on the outside of the dump site. Sudakis waved across from his side, then went back to his citadel.

It wasn't until I'd crossed the crosswalk, chanted the phrase that unlocked the antitheft geas on my carpet, and actually gotten into the air that I remembered the vampires, the werewolves, the kids born without souls, all the other birth defects around the Devonshire dump. Getting outside the site didn't necessarily free you from it. Were that so, I wouldn't have had to make this trip in the first place.

Midday traffic was a lot thinner than the usual morning madness. I was more than twice as far from my Westwood office in the Confederal Building as I was when I left from my flat, but I didn't need any more time to get there than I do on my normal commute. I slid into my reserved parking space (penalty for unauthorized use, a hundred crowns or an extra year for your soul in purgatory, or both—judge's discretion: if he thinks you won't rate purgatory, he'll just fine you), then walked inside.

The elevator shaft smelt of almond oil. At the bottom was a virgin parchment inscribed with the words GOMERT and KAILOETH and the sigil of the demon Khil, who has control over some of the spirits of the air (he can also cause earthquakes, and so is a useful spirit to know in Angels City). The almond oil is part of the paste that summons him, the other ingredients being olive oil, dust from close by a coffin, and the brain of a dunghill cock. "Seventh floor," I said, and was lifted up.

As soon as I got into the office, I called Charlie Kelly. He listened while I told him what I'd found, then said, "Nice piece of work, Dave. That confirms and amplifies the information I'd already received. Go to work on that warrant right away."

"I will," I promised. "I know just the judge: I'll take the information over to *qadi* Ruhollah. He's about the strictest man in A.C. when it comes to environmental damage." I chuckled. "For that matter, he's a rigorist on just about every-thing—Maximum Ruhollah, we call him out here."

"Sounds like the fellow we need, all right," Kelly said. "Anything else?"

I started to say no, but had to think better of it. "There is one other thing, as a matter of fact. Sudakis—the dump manager—wondered how you'd heard something new might be wrong at his place when no one out here had a clue. I couldn't give him an answer, but it made me curious, too."

As it had once or twice when he'd called me at home, the

silence stretched longer than imp relay could account for by itself. Finally Charlie said, "A bird told me, you might say."

"A little bird, right?" I started to laugh. "Charlie, I stopped believing in that little bird about the same time I found out the stork only brings changelings."

"However you want it," he said. "That's all I can tell you, and more than I ought to."

I thought about pushing some more, but decided not to. People back in D.C. are supposed to have good sources; they justify the fancy salaries that come out of your purse and mine by knowing what's going on all over the country and how to find out about it even if the people who are doing it don't want it found out. But I was still moderately graveled that somebody a continent away had picked up on something I hadn't heard the first thing about right in my own back yard.

"Get the warrant, Dave," Charlie said. "We'll go from there, depending on what we learn."

"Right," I said, and hung up. Then I grabbed a sandwich and a cup of coffee at the little cafeteria in the building. They perfectly balanced virtue and vice: they were lousy but cheap. Lousy or not, my stomach stopped growling. I made another phone call.

The phone on the other end must have yammered for quite a while, because I listened to my imp drumming his fingers on the inside of the handset until at last I got an answer: "Hand-of-Glory Press, Judith Adler speaking."

"Hi, Judy—it's Dave."

"Oh, hi, Dave." I thought her voice went from businesslike to warm, but with two phone imps between us I had a hard time being sure. "Sorry I took so long to pick up there. I was in the middle of a tough passage, and I wanted to get to the end of a sentence so I could be sure I wouldn't miss even a single word when I went back to it."

"Don't apologize," I said. "Doing what you do, you have to be careful."

Hand-of-Glory Press, as you'd guess from the name, publishes grimoires of all sorts, from simple ones on carpet maintenance up to the special secret sort with olive-drab covers. Judy's their number one proofreader and copy editor. She's the most intensely detail-minded person I know, and she needs to be. An error in a grimoire on flying carpets might end you up in Boston, Oregon, instead of Boston, Mass. An error in a military magic manual might leave you dead, or worse.

She said, "So what's up?"

"Feel like going out to dinner with me tonight?" I asked. "I ran into something interesting today, and I wouldn't mind hearing what you think of it." Knowing someone who can see not only forest and trees but also count leaves is wonderful. Being in love with her is even better.

"Sure," she said. "Meet at your place after work? I ought to be able to get there before six."

"You'll probably beat me there, then, the way traffic on St. James' has been lately," I told her.

"Sounds good."

"There's a new Hanese place a few blocks away that I want to try."

"Sounds good to me, too. You know how much I like Hanese food."

"See you tonight, then. Now I'll let you get back to what you were doing. 'Bye."

I went back to work, too, although my mind wasn't really on the main project that currently infested my desk. A couple of days before, a big carpet carrying fumigants had overturned in an accident, spilling finely ground linseed, psellium seed, violet and wild parsley root, aloes, mace, and storax. Because they're materials used in conjurations, I had to draft the environmental impact statement.

I could have just written *no impact* and let it go at that: the fumigants were harmless in and of themselves, and required combustion and ritual to become magically significant. A two-word report, however, would not have made my boss happy, and might have given people outside the EPA the idea that we didn't take seriously the job we were doing.

So, instead, I wasted taxpayers' time and parchment writing five leaves that ended up saying *no impact* but did it in a bureaucratically acceptable way. I do sometimes wonder why governmental agencies have to act like that, but it seems as universal as the law of contagion.

Suffused in virtue, I dropped the draft of my statement on my boss' desk for her changes, then went down the slide, out to my carpet, and onto the freeway. Sure enough, traffic was beastly, especially down by the airport. Not only was everybody getting on and off there, but the flight lanes for the big international carrier really cramp air space for local travelers.

Judy was waiting for me when I got home, as I'd thought she would be. We'd been seeing each other for about two and a half years, then; I'd gotten her a spare entry talisman and given her the unlocking Word for my door pretty early in that time, and she'd done the same for me.

She greeted me with a pucker on her lips and a cold beer in her hand. "Wonderful woman," I told her, which might have helped heat the kiss a little. She got a beer for herself, too. We sat down to drink them before we went out.

Judy's a big tall brunette with hazel eyes and a mass of wavy brown hair that falls halfway down her back. She doesn't walk, exactly; when she moves, it's more like flowing. She looked too feline ever to seem quite at home on my angular apartment-house furniture. I enjoyed watching her all the same.

"So what did you come across today?" she asked.

I finished my beer and said, "Let's talk about it at the restaurant. If I start explaining it now, we won't get to the restaurant, and then you'll think I invited you over just to lure you into bed."

"It is nice to know you occasionally have other things on your mind," she admitted, upending her own bottle. "Let's go, then."

We rode on my carpet; the safety belts held us companionably close. The restaurant parking lot had a sign with a big Hanese dragon breathing ornately stylized fire and a blunt warning: TRESPASSERS WILL BE INCINERATED. Judith smiled when she saw it. I didn't. I live in a moderately tough part of town, and I figured there was at least one chance in three the sign was no joke.

Wonderful smells greeted us just inside the entrance. The only trouble with Hanese restaurants is that so much of what they serve is forbidden to those who observe the Law. Sea cucumbers I can live without, but I've heard so much about scallops and lobster that I'm always tempted to try them. But how can a man who'd break what he sees as God's Law be trusted to uphold the laws of men? I was good again. So was Judy, whose job and whose life also took discipline.

Still, you can't really complain about hot and sour soup, beef with black mushrooms, crispy duck, and crystal-boiled chicken with spicy sauces. Everything was good, too; this was a place I'd visit again. While Judy and I ate, I told her about the Devonshire dump.

"*Three* cases of apsychia this year?" she said. Her eyebrows went way up, and stayed way up. "Something's badly wrong there."

"I think so, too, and so does the dump administrator—fellow named Tony Sudakis—even though he won't say so where a Listener can hear him." I sipped my tea. "You deal with magic more intimately than I do, maybe even more intimately than Sudakis: intimately in a way different from his, anyhow. I'm glad you're worried; it tells me I'm right to feel the same way."

"You certainly are." She nodded so vigorously, her hair flew out in a cloud around her head. Then her eyes filled with tears. "Just think of those poor babies—"

"I know." I'd thought about them a lot. I couldn't help it. Vampires and lycanthropes have their problems, heaven knows, but what hope is there for a kid with no soul? None, zero, zip. I drank more tea, hoping it would cleanse my mind along with my palate. No such luck. Then I told Judy what Charlie Kelly had said about a bird telling him something might be amiss at the dump. "He wouldn't give me any details—he *wanted* to be coy. What do you suppose he meant?"

"A bird? *Not* a little bird?" She waited for me to shake my head, then started ticking off possibilities on her fingers. "First thing that occurs to me is something to do with Quetzalcoatl."

"You just made dinner worth putting on the expense account," I said, beaming. "I hadn't thought of that."

I felt stupid for not thinking of it, too, for no sooner had I spoken than a busboy stopped at the table to clear away some dirty dishes. Unlike our waiter, he wasn't Hanese; he was stockier, a little darker, and spoke his little Anglo-Saxon with a strong Spanish accent. A lot of the scutwork in Angels City gets done by people from the south. As Sudakis had said, more of them come here every year, too. Times are so hard, people so poor, down in the Empire that even scutwork looks good to a lot of people.

Angels City, much of the Confederation's southwest, used to belong to the Empire of Azteca. The nobles, some of them, still plot revenge after a century and a half. For that matter, though most people in the Empire speak Spainish these days, some of the old families there, the ones that go back before the Spaniards came, go right on worshiping their own gods in secret, even though they go to Mass, too. Quetzalcoatl, the Feathered Serpent, is much the nicest of those gods, believe me.

The old families crave the Empire's old borders, too, even if their own ancestors never ruled hereabouts. They call our southwest Aztlan, and dream it's theirs. The way immigration is headed, in a couple of generations that may be true in all but name. Some people, though, might not want to wait. So, Quetzalcoatl.

Judy asked, "What ideas have you had yourself?" Thinking is hard work. She didn't want to do it all herself, for which I couldn't blame her.

I seized a big, meaty mushroom on my chopsticks, then said, "The Peacock Throne crossed my mind."

Judy was chewing, too. She held up a finger, swallowed, then said, "Yes, I can see that, especially since—didn't you say?—you know some Persian firms use that dump?"

"That's right. Sudakis told me so." The Peacock Throne is the one which was warmed by the fundament of the Shahan-Shah of Persia until the secularists threw him out a few years ago. St. Ferdinand's Valley has a large Persian refugee community. And if Persians had been whispering in Charlie

Kelly's ear, I wouldn't have any trouble getting a warrant from old Maximum Ruhollah, either. He was *plus royal que le roi*, if you know what I mean.

"After the Peacock Throne, the next possibility I thought of was the Garuda Bird project," I went on. "Aerospace and defense are Siamese twins, and a lot of defense outfits use the Devonshire dump."

Judy nodded, slowly. Her eyes caught fire. So did mine whenever I thought about the Garuda Bird. Up till now, no one's ever found a sorcerous way to get us off Earth and physically into space. People have even talked about trying to do it with pure mechanicals, though anybody who'd fly a mechanical in a universe full of mystic forces is crazier than any three people I want to deal with.

But the Garuda Bird project links the ancient Hindu Bird with the most modern western spell-casting techniques. Before long, if everything goes as planned, we'll try visiting the moon and the worlds in person, not just by astral projection.

"There's a good-sized Hind community up in the Valley, too," Judy said.

"That's true." It was, but I didn't know how much it meant. Angels City and its metropolitan area are so big, they have good-sized communities from just about every nation on earth. If God decided to build the Tower of Babel now, he'd put it right here: the schools, for instance, have to try to teach kids who speak close to a hundred different languages, and some towns have laws that signs have to be at least partly in the Roman alphabet so police, firefighters, and exorcists can find the places in case of emergency.

I ate another mushroom, then said, "Any more ideas?"

"I didn't have any others until you mentioned the Peacock Throne," Judy said, "but that made me think of something else." She didn't go on; she didn't look as if she wanted to.

"Well?" I asked at last.

She looked around and lowered her voice before she spoke; maybe she didn't want anybody but me hearing. "There's the Peacock Throne, but there's also the Peacock Angel."

Not everybody, especially in this part of the world, would have taken her meaning. But while neither one of us is a sorcerer, we both deal with the Other Side as much as a lot of people who make a good living at wizardry. I felt a chill run up my back. The Peacock Angel is a euphemism the Persians use for Satan.

"Judy, I hope you're wrong," I told her.

"So do I," she said. "Believe me, so do I."

I remembered the knot of stirring flies I'd seen in the dump—Beelzebub is very high up (or low down, depending on how you look at things) in the infernal hierarchy. And that Nothing—had I really seen it, or was it just jitters at being in a—literally—spooky place? If it was real, what, or Who, caused it? Those were interesting thoughts. I didn't like any of them.

Suddenly a little bit of Nothing seemed to fall like a cloak over the warm, comfortable restaurant. I didn't want to be there any more. I waved for the bill, pulled money from my wallet to cover it, and left in a hurry. Judy didn't argue. Even euphemisms can bring trouble in their wake.

My flat felt like a fortress against our gloom. As soon as I'd locked the door and touched the mezuzah that warded it, Judy came into my arms. We hugged, hard, just holding each other for a long time. Then she said, "Why don't you bring me another bottle of beer?"

When I got back from the icebox with it, she'd taken from her purse two small alabaster cups, thin to the point of translucency. Into each she poured a little powder from a vial she carried. I'd once asked the ingredients of the "cup of roots," and she'd told me gum of Alexandria, liquid alum, and garden crocus. Mixed with beer, it was a contraceptive that dated back to the ancient Egyptians. I was convinced it worked: not only had it never failed us, how many ancient Egyptians have you seen lately?

Just to be safe, though, I also followed Pliny's advice and kept the testicles and blood of a dunghill cock under my bed. Unlike the old Roman's, mine were sealed in glass so they wouldn't prove contraceptive merely by stinking prospective partners out of the bedroom.

If you ask me, making love, especially with someone you do love, is the most sympathetic magic of all. Afterwards, I asked Judy, "Do you want to stay the night?" I admit I had an ulterior motive; she's different from most of the women I've known in that she often feels frisky in the morning.

But that night she shook her head. "I'd better not. I'd have to take the cup of roots again if you wanted me, and I don't want to drink beer and then steer a carpet through rush-hour traffic."

"Okay." I hope I gave in with good grace. If you love somebody not least for having a good head on her shoulders, you'd better not get annoyed when she uses it.

She went into the bathroom, came back and started to get dressed, then stopped and looked over at me. "Could we try again tonight?"

" 'Try' is probably the operative word." But I was off the bed like a shot and heading for the kitchen. "Woman, you'll run me out of beer and make me go up with the window shade, but you're nice to have around."

"Good," she said, a smile in her voice. Beer in hand, I hurried back toward the bedroom. Her nice, sensible head was not the only reason I loved her. No indeed.

II

Judy did end up staying the night, because she didn't feel like flying after two rounds of the cup of roots. (In case you're wondering how we did the second time, it's none of your business.) No hanky-panky in the morning, though. We were both up early, her to go back to her place and change before she headed for work, me to to the parchmentwork I'd need to get a warrant from Judge Ruhollah.

After a fast breakfast, I walked her out to her carpet (as I said, I don't live in the best neighborhood), then went back to my own and headed for the Criminal and Magical Courts building downtown.

The commute downtown wasn't too bad, but parking in the heart of Angels City is outrageously expensive, even though they stack carpets up higher than you'd see in a rug merchants' bazaar. I was almost as upset as if I'd had to pay with my own money, not the EPA's.

You want to see every kind of human being any kind of God ever made, go the the Criminal and Magical Courts building: secular judges in black robes, canon law judges in red ones, bailiffs and constabulary and sheriffs looking more like soldiers than anything else, defendants sometimes looking guilty of everything in the world (regardless of whether they're only charged with flying a carpet too fast) and others who from the outside might be candidates for sainthood, witnesses, doctors, rabbis, wizards . . . If you like people-watching, you won't find better entertainment.

Judge Ruhollah's bailiff was a big Swede named Eric something-or-other—I never can remember his last name, though I'd dealt with him before. He said, "I'm sorry, Inspector Fisher, but the judge won't be able to see you till about eleven. Something's come up."

I sighed, but what could I do about it? I went over to the bank of pay phones across the hall from the courtrooms. When I told the mouthpiece imp what number I wanted, it squawked back, "Forty-five coppers, please." I pushed change into the outstretched hand of the little pay phone demon, which must be descended from Mammon by way of the Gadarene swine. If I'd turned my back on it, I'm sure it would have tried to pick my pocket.

After I called in at the office to say I'd be late, I bought some coffee (and a Danish I didn't really need) and cooled my heels in the cafeteria, looking with one eye at the data I'd be giving the *qadi* and with the other at people going past. Two cups and another Danish later (I promised myself I wouldn't eat lunch), it was a quarter to eleven. I threw the parchments back into my briefcase and presented myself to Eric again.

He picked up a phone, spoke into it, then nodded to me. "Go on in." I went.

How do I describe Judge Ruhollah? If you're Christian (which he wasn't), think of God the Father when He's had a lousy eon. I don't know how old Ruhollah is, not even to the nearest decade. Long white beard, nose like a promontory, eyes that have seen everything and disapproved of most of it. If you're up before him and you're innocent, you're all right. But if you're even a little bit guilty, you'd better run for cover.

He glowered at me as I approached the bench. Had this been the first time I'd come before him, I'd've been tempted to pack it in as a bad job: either fall on my knees and pray for mercy (not something Maximum Ruhollah handed out in big doses) or else turn around and run for my life (for who's not a little bit guilty of something?). But I knew he glowered most of the time anyhow, so he didn't intimidate me . . . much.

I began as etiquette prescribed—"May it please your honor"—though I knew it was just a polite phrase in his case. I set forth the reasons the Environmental Perfection Agency, and I as its representative, wanted to examine the records of the Devonshire Land Management Consortium.

"You have supporting documents to show probable cause?" he asked. He didn't have an old man's voice. He'd been in the Confederation for close to forty years (he was expelled from Persia the last time the secularists there seized power for a while), but he'd never lost his accent.

I passed him the documents. He put on reading glasses to inspect them. Just for a second, he reminded me of the scriptorium spirit at the Thomas Brothers monastery. Before I could even think of smiling, though, his hard old face became so terrible that I wanted to look away. I had a pretty good idea what he'd come across, and I was right.

He stabbed at the parchment with a forefinger shaking with fury. "It is an abomination before God the Compassionate, the Merciful," he ground out, "the birthing of children without souls. All should have the chance to be judged, to delight with God the great in heaven or to eat offal and drink boiling water forever in hell. This dump is causing the birth of soulless ones?"

"That's what we're trying to learn, your honor," I answered. "Finding out just who dumps there—which is what the warrant seeks—will help us determine that."

"This cause is worthy and just," Judge Ruhollah declared.

"Pursue it wherever it may lead." He inked a quill and wrote out the warrant in his own hand, signing it at the bottom in both our own alphabet and the Arabic pothooks and squiggles he'd grown up with.

I thanked him and got out of there in a hurry; his wrath was frightening to behold. As I went back to where my carpet was parked, I skimmed through the document he'd given me. When I was finished, I whistled softly under my breath. If I'd wanted to, I could have closed down the Devonshire dump with that warrant. Of course, if I'd tried it, the consortium's lawyers would have descended on me like a flock of vampires and gotten the whole thing thrown out. I didn't want that, so I planned on carrying out the strictly limited search I'd already had in mind.

Rather to my own surprise, I was virtuous enough to skip lunch. I just headed straight for the Valley; the sooner I served the warrant, the sooner I could—I hoped—start finding answers.

Thanks to a stupid publicity stunt, I got stuck in traffic in Hollywood. If you ask me, stunts by the side of the freeway ought to be illegal; it goes slow enough without them. But no. One of the light and magic companies was releasing a spectacular called *St. George and the Dragon*, so nothing would do but to have one of their tame dragons roast a sword-swinging stunt man right where everybody could stop and stare and ooh and ahh. People who actually had to go someplace—me, for instance—got stuck right along with the rubbernecking fools.

Behind the stunt man in his flame-retardant chain mail stood a blonde who wasn't wearing enough to retard flames. The dragon was well trained; he didn't breathe fire anywhere near her. Even so, I wondered what she was doing there. She wasn't the sort of maiden *I* pictured St. George rescuing. If they'd been making *Perseus and Andromeda*, maybe—but St. George?

Well, that's Hollywood for you.

I made good time after I finally put dragon, stunt man, and bimbo behind me. I parked in the lot across from the Devonshire dump I'd used the day before. This time the security guard was on the phone before I got across the street. He came out of his cage, started wheeling back the gate. "Mr. Sudakis is expecting you, sir," he said.

"Thanks." I crossed the wooden footbridge, went into the dump site. Sure enough, Tony Sudakis was already on his way out to greet me. I still wasn't sure whose side he was on, but he brought a lot of energy to whichever one it was.

"How may I be of assistance to you today, Inspector Fisher?" he asked in a loud, formal voice that said he knew what was coming.

I produced the parchment and did my best to speak in ringing tones myself: "Mr. Sudakis, I have in my possession and hereby serve you with this warrant of search issued by Judge Ruhollah authorizing me to examine certain records of your business."

"Let me see this warrant," he said. I passed it to him. I thought his scrutiny would be purely *pro forma*, but he read every word. When he spoke again, he didn't sound formal at all: "You do everything this parchment says you can do and you'll break us to bits. Maybe I'd better call our legal team."

I held up a hasty hand. "I don't intend to do or seek any more than we talked about yesterday. Is that still agreeable to you?" Light the candle or cast the spell, Mr. Sudakis.

"Let's go to my office," he said after a pause like the ones I'd been hearing from Charlie Kelly. "I'll show you where the client lists are stored."

By the time I thought to look for the Nothing I might have seen the day before, I was already past the place on the walk where I'd noticed it. I had more concrete things on my mind, anyhow.

Sudakis pulled open a file drawer. "Here are clients who have used our facility in the past three years, Inspector Fisher."

I started pulling out folders. "I will copy these parchments and return the originals to you as soon as possible, Mr. Sudakis." We were both talking with half a mind for the Listener in his office. I asked, "Does this list also include the spells and thaumaturgical byproducts each of the consortia and individuals stated were assigned for containment here?"

"No, not all of them. That's a separate form, you know." He glanced down at the warrant he was still holding. "We didn't discuss those lists yesterday. This thing"—he waved the warrant—"gives you the authority to go fishing . . . until and unless our people try to quash it. Shall I make the phone call now?"

I pointed to the amber amulet he wore—it made a small lump under his shirt. He nodded, pulled it out, went through his little ritual. I wondered again what language he was using. As soon as he nodded a second time, I said, "Look, Tony, you know as well as I do that finding out what's in here will help us learn what's leaking."

"Yeah, but we didn't talk about it yesterday." He looked stubborn.

I talked fast. "I know we didn't. If you want to play all consortiate, you can lick me on this one. For a while. But how will you feel when you read the next little story in the Valley section of the *Times* about a kid who's going to vanish out of the universe forever some time in the next fifty or seventy or ninety years?"

"You fight dirty," he said with a fierce scowl.

"Only if I have to," I answered. "You're the one who told me you wanted to keep this site safe. Did you mean it, or was it so much Fairy gold?"

He looked at his watch. It must have been a new one, because he didn't ask me what time it was. After about a minute and a half (my guess; I didn't bother checking), he said, "Very well, Inspector Fisher, I shall comply with your demand." Clearly we were out from under the rose.

More folders followed, too many for me to carry. Having decided to be helpful, Tony was very helpful: he got me a wheeled cart so I could trundle them down the path and out to my carpet. I said, "I hope losing these won't inconvenience your operation."

"I wouldn't give 'em to you if it did," he said. "I have copies of everything. They're magically made, of course, so they aren't acceptable to you, but they'll keep this place running until I get the originals back."

I didn't say that might be a while. If we ended up going to

court again to seek a closure order, the parchments would be sequestered for months, maybe for years if the dump's legal staff used all the appeals they were entitled to. Sudakis had to know that, too. But he seemed satisfied he could go on doing what he needed to do, so I didn't push him.

He even trundled the cart out to the entrance for me. When we got there, a slight hitch developed: the cart was too wide to go over the footbridge. "Can't I just stand on one side of the line and you on the other?" I asked. "You can pass the documents out to me."

"It's not that simple," Sudakis said. "Go on outside; I'll show you." I crossed the bridge, stepped a couple of feet to one side of it. Sudakis made as if to pass me a folder; I made as if to reach for it. Our hands came closer and closer to one another, but wouldn't touch. Sudakis chuckled. "Asymptotic zone, you see? The footbridge is insulated, so it cleaves a path right on through. We do take containment seriously, Dave."

"So I notice." Even if Anything was on the rampage in the dump, that zone would go a long way toward keeping it inside where it belonged. When I leaned toward Sudakis above the footbridge, he had no trouble passing me the files. I turned to the security guard. "Do you have twine? I don't want these blowing away after I load them onto my carpet."

"Lemme look." He went back into his cage and came back out with not only a ball of twine but also a scissors. I hadn't expected even that much cooperation, so I was doubly glad to get it.

Sudakis watched me tie parcels for a minute or two, then said, "I'm going back to work. Now that you've officially taken these documents, you understand I'm going to have to notify my superiors about what you've done."

"Yes, of course," I said. Decent of him to remind me, though. I thought he really might be on my side, or at least not altogether on the side of his company.

I carted the documents across the street to my carpet; I needed three trips. Like anybody, I had storage pockets sewn on, but the great pile of parchments overwhelmed them. I don't know what I would have done if the guard hadn't had any twine. Sat on some of the folders and hung onto others, I suppose, until I flew by a sundries store where I could buy some for myself. You see people doing that every day, but it's neither elegant nor what you'd call safe.

Back to my Westwood office, then. When I got there, I discovered the elevator shaft was out of order. Some idiot had managed to spill a cup of coffee on the Words and sigil that controlled Khil. A mage stood in the shaft readying a new compact with the demon, but *readying* didn't mean *ready*. I had to haul my parchments up the fire stairs (*you* wouldn't want to be in an elevator shaft when the controlling parchment burns, would you?), slide back down, and then climb the stairs again with the other half of my load. I was not pleased with the world when I finally plopped the last parcel down by my desk.

I was even less pleased when I saw what lurked on that desk: my report about the spilled fumigants, all covered over with red scribbles. That meant I wasn't going to get to the documents I'd so laboriously lugged upstairs by quitting time. I thought they were a lot more important than the report, but my boss didn't see things that way. Sometimes I wish I were triplets. Then I might keep my desk clean. Maybe.

The office access spirit appeared in the ground glass when I called it. I held up the pages one by one so it saw all the changes, then said, "Write me out a fresh version on parchment, if you please."

"Very well," the spirit said grumpily. It likes playing with words, but has the attitude that actually dealing with the material world and getting them down in permanent form is somehow beneath it. It asked me, "Shall I then forget the version you had me memorize yesterday?"

"Don't you dare," I said, and then, because it was literal-minded, I added a simple, "No."

My boss had the habit of making changes and then going back and deciding she'd rather have things the first way after all. Yes, I know it's a female cliche, but she really was a woman and she really was like that. Judy, now, Judy is more decisive than I'll ever be.

After the spirit promised it would indeed remember both versions of the report, I waited for it to finish setting down the new one. When that finally wafted over to my desk, I read it through to make sure all the alterations were accurately transcribed, then set it in my boss' in-basket for the next round of changes. And then, it being about the time it was, I went out to my carpet and headed home.

I took with me the list of firms that used the Devonshire dump. I left behind the forms that showed what they'd dumped there; those would be more secure behind the office's wards than the cheap ones my block of flats uses. But I figured I could do some useful work at the kitchen table, just grouping the firms by type. That would also give me at last a start on knowing what sort of toxic spells were in there.

After a dinner I'd rather not remember—certainly nothing to compare to the lush Hanese spread I'd enjoyed with Judy the night before—I piled dishes in the sink, gave the table a couple of haphazard wipes, took out a sheet of parchment and inked a pen, then buckled down to it.

The first thing that hit me was just how many defense firms dumped at the Devonshire site. All the big aerospace consortia that have kept the Angels City economy booming for decades used the place: Confederated Voodoo (it's Convoo these days, what with the stupid and paranoid mania for clipping consortiate names into meaningless syllables: who'd waste time with name magic against as diffuse an entity as a consortium?), North American Aviation and Levitation, Demondyne, Loki (I wondered if byproducts from Loki's famous Cobold Works were trying to trickle through the wards around the dumps; some of them might be very bad news indeed), all the other famous names.

Along with them were a host of smaller outfits, subcontractors mostly, that nobody's ever heard of except their mothers: firms with names like Bakhtiar's Precision Burins, Portentous Potions, and Essence Extractions, Inc. I looked at that last one for a while, trying to figure out in which square it belonged: my transmogrified list had evolved into a chart. Finally I stuck it in almost at random: with a name like that, it could have done just about anything (another modern trend I despise).

Along with the defense outfits were several of the Hollywood light and magic companies. When I thought about it, that made sense; Hollywood has always been a magic-intensive business. I wished I remembered which outfit had made the St. George epic that had snarled traffic this morning—I might have been tempted to try some name magic on it myself, more because I knew it would be useless than for any other reason.

I was a little more surprised to find how many hospitals were on the list. Layfolk see only the benefits medicine brings; they don't think much about the costs involved (except the ones that come from their purses). But healing bodies—and especially working with diseased souls—takes its toll on the environment like any high-tech enterprise.

There's only one major carpet plant left in Angels City—the General Movers looms in Van Nuys. They dumped at Devonshire, too. The GM plant wasn't high on my list of probable culprits, though. For one thing, I had a solid notion of the kinds of spells it used. For another, it's likely to close down in the next year or two: too much competition from less expensive Oriental rugs.

And what was I supposed to make of outfits called Gall Divided, Slow Jinn Fizz, and Red Phoenix? Until I got back to the office to see what they were dumping, I was as much in the dark about what they actually did as I was with Essence Extractions, Inc. They sounded more interesting, though, I must say.

After a moment, my eyes came back to Red Phoenix. I underline the name, just on the off chance. The phoenix was a bird neither Judy nor I had thought of the night before. It would be worth checking out, at any rate.

I started to call Judy to tell her about it, then remembered Wednesday was her night for theoretical goetics. She's only a couple of classes away from her master's initiation. One day before too long I expect her to be writing grimoires instead of copy-editing them.

Having done as much on the list as I could do, I tossed it

back in my attaché case, read for a while, and then got ready for bed. Through the thin wall of my flat, I heard the fellow next door howling with laughter at whatever ethernet program he was listening to.

One of these days soon, I figured I'd break down and buy an ethernet set for myself. They're based on a variant of the cloning technique that's put telephones all over lately. In the ethernet, though, they clone thousands of imps identical to a few masters. Whatever one of the masters hears, each clone repeats exactly—provided you've chosen to rouse that particular imp from dormancy.

You can buy plug-in imp modules that let you choose from up to eighty or a hundred different ethernet offerings at any one time. More and more people all over the country are listening to the same shows, admiring the same performers, telling the same jokes. Unity isn't bad, especially in a country as big as the Confederation, and I don't deny the advantages of being able to pass on news, for instance, quickly.

So why didn't I have an ethernet set of my own? I guess the basic reason is that too much of what they spread is, pardon my Latin, crap. Not to put too fine a point on it, I'd sooner think for myself than get my entertainment premasticated. Go ahead, call me old-fashioned.

When I got to the office the next morning, the wizard was still working on the elevator shaft. No, I take it back; more likely, the wizard was working on the elevator shaft again. What with everybody's budget being tight these days, the government isn't enthusiastic about overtime. I walked up to my office. Yes, I know it's good exercise. It also wasted the shower I'd taken just before I left home.

And on my desk waiting for me, just as I'd known it would be, was my second draft of the report on the spilled load of fumigants. I gave it a quick look-through. Not only had my boss changed about half of her revisions back to what I originally wrote, she'd added a whole new set, something she didn't often do on a second pass. And on the last page, in green ink that looked as if it would be good for pacts with demons, she'd written, "Please give me final copy this afternoon."

I felt like pounding my head on the desktop. That cursed silly report, which could have been and should have been two words long, was going to keep me from getting any useful work done that morning. Then the phone started yelling at me, and the report turned into the least of my worries.

"Environmental Perfection Agency, Fisher speaking," I said, sounding as brisk and businesslike as I could before I'd had my second cup of coffee.

Just as if I hadn't spoken, my phone asked me, "You are Inspector David Fisher of the Environmental Perfection Agency?"—and I knew I was talking to a lawyer. When I admitted it again, the fellow on the other end said, "I am Samuel Dill, of the firm of Elworthy, Frazer, and Waite, representing the interests of the Devonshire Land Management Consortium. I am given to understand that yesterday you absconded with certain proprietary documents of the aforesaid Consortium."

Even through two phone imps, I could hear that capital "C" thud into place. I could also hear Mr. Dill building himself a case. I said, "Counselor, please let me correct you right at the outset. I did not 'abscond with' any documents. I did take certain parchments, as I was authorized to do under a search warrant granted in Confederal court yesterday."

"Inspector Fisher, that warrant was a farce, which you must realize as well as I. Had you fully implemented all its provisions—"

"But I didn't," I answered sharply. "And, in case you have a Listener on this call, I make no such admission about the warrant. It was duly issued in reaction to a perceived threat to the environment from the Devonshire dump. And surely *you*, sir, must admit examining dump records is not unreasonable in light of evidence showing, among other things, increased birth defects in the community surrounding the dump."

"I deny the land management consortium is in any way responsible for this statistical aberration," Dill replied, as I'd known he would.

I pressed him: "Do you deny the need to investigate the matter?" When he didn't answer right away, I pressed harder: "Do you deny that the EPA has the authority to check records to evaluate possible safety hazards?"

By now, I ought to be old enough to know better than to expect straight answers from lawyers. What I got instead was about a five-minute speech. No, Dill didn't deny our right to investigate, but he did deny that the dump (not that he ever called it a dump, not even once) could possibly be responsible for anything, even, it sounded like, the shadow the containment fence cast. He also kept coming back to the scope of the warrant under which I'd conducted the search.

Blast Maximum Ruhollah. That warrant was the juristic equivalent of performing necromancy to get someone to tie your shoelaces for you. I said, "Counselor, let me ask you again: do you think my taking the documents I took was in any way exceptionable?"

I got back another speech, but what it boiled down to was *no*. Dill finished, "I want to put you on notice that the Devonshire Land Management Consortium will not under any circumstances tolerate your use of that outrageous warrant to conduct fishing expeditions through our records."

"I understand your concern," I said, which shut him up without conceding anything. He finally got off the phone, and I put the second-generation changes into that worthless Hydra-headed report. I was about halfway through letting the access spirit scan it when the phone yowled again.

I said something I hoped nobody (and Nobody) noticed before I answered it. Turned out to be Tony Sudakis. He said, "I just wanted to let you know my people aren't too happy about my turning records over to you yesterday."

"They've made me aware of that already, as a matter of fact," I said, and told him about the phone call from the Consortium's lawyer. "I hope I haven't gotten you into a pickle over this."

"I'll survive," he said. "However much they want to, they can't send me to perdition for obeying the law. If you push that warrant too hard, though, things'll get more complicated than anybody really wants."

"Yeah," I said, still puzzled about where he was coming

from. The contemptuous way he dismissed higher management made me guess he'd worked his little charm with the amulet again, but the message he delivered wasn't that different from Dill's. I'd got somewhere pushing Dill, so I decided to push Sudakis a little, too: "You aren't having any kind of trouble out there, are you?"

But Sudakis didn't push. "Perkunas, no!" he exclaimed, an oath I didn't recognize. "Everything's fine here . . . except for your ugly numbers."

"Believe me, I don't like those any better than you do," I said, "but they're there, and we need to find out why."

"Yeah, okay." He suddenly turned abrupt. "Listen, I gotta go. 'Bye." He probably had done his little charm, then, and run out of time on it.

I pulled out my *Handbook of Goetics and Metapsychics* to see what it had to say about Perkunas. I found out he was a Lithuanian thunder-god. Was Sudakis a Lithuanian name? I didn't know. The Lithuanians, I read, had been about the last European people to come to terms with Christianity, and a lot of them also remained on familiar terms with their old gods. Tony Sudakis certainly sounded as if he was.

Grunting, I put the handbook back on the shelf. Anybody who uses it a lot develops shoulders like an Olympiadic weightlifter's—if you hung two copies on opposite ends of a barbell, you could sure train with 'em.

I'd just started my third stab at revising that blinking report when the phone went off again. I thought hard about ordering the imp to answer that I wasn't there, but integrity won. A moment later, I wished it hadn't: "Inspector Fisher? Pleased to make your acquaintance, sir. I am Colleen Pfeiffer, of the legal staff of the Demondyne Consortium."

"Yes?" I said, not wanting to give her any more rope than she had already.

"Inspector Fisher, I have been informed that you are investigating the sorcerous byproducts Demondyne deposits in the Devonshire containment area."

"Among others, that's correct, Counselor. May I ask who told you?" I'd expected calls from some of the consortia that dumped at Devonshire (I'd also expected nobody's lawyer would say anything so bald as that), but I hadn't expected to get the first one by half past nine of the morning after I searched.

Like any lawyer worth a prayer, Mistress Pfeiffer was better at asking questions than answering them. She went on as if I hadn't spoken: "I want you to note two areas of concern of Demondyne's, Inspector Fisher. First, as you must be aware, byproduct information can be valuable to competitors. Second, much of our work is defense-related. Some of the information you have in your possession might prove of great interest to foreign governments. An appropriate security regime is indicated by both these considerations."

"Thank you for expressing your concern, Counselor," I said. "I have never had any reason to believe the EPA's security precautions don't do the job. The parchments to which you refer have not left my office."

"I am relieved to hear that," she said. "May I assume your policy will remain unchanged, and make note of this for the rest of the legal staff and other consortium officials?"

Such an innocent-sounding question, to have so many teeth in it. I answered cautiously: "You can assume I'll do my best to keep your parchments safe and confidential. I'm not in a position to make promises about where they'll be at any given moment."

"Your response is not altogether satisfactory," she said.

Too bad, I thought. Out loud, I said, "Counselor, I'm afraid it's the best I can do, given my own responsibilities and oaths." Let her make something of that.

My phone imp reproduced a sigh. Maybe I wasn't the only one who thought I was having a bad day. Colleen Pfeiffer said, "I will transmit what you say, Inspector Fisher. Thank you for your time."

I'd just reached for the fumigants report—I still hadn't had the chance to let our access spirit finish looking at it—when the phone yarped again. I took in vain the names of several Christian saints in whose intercession I don't believe. Then I lifted the handset. It was, after all, part of my job, even if I was growing ever more convinced I wasn't going to get around to any other parts today.

No, you're wrong—it wasn't another lawyer. It was the owner of Slow Jinn Fizz, an excitable fellow named Ramzan Durani. I'd noted that as one of the smaller companies that used the Devonshire dump; evidently it wasn't big enough to keep lawyers on staff just to sic them on people. But the owner had the same concerns the woman from Demondyne and the fellow from the Devonshire Land Management Consortium had had. For some reason or other, I began to suspect a trend.

Then I found myself with another irate proprietor trying to scream in my ear, this one a certain Jorge Vasquez, who ran an outfit called Chocolate Weasel. I tried to distract him by asking—out of genuine curiosity, I assure you—just what Chocolate Weasel did, but he was in no mood to be distracted. He seemed sure every secret he had was about to be published in the dailies and put out over the ethernet.

Calming him down, getting him to believe his secrets could stay safe for all of me, took another twenty minutes. I still wanted to know why he called his business Chocolate Weasel and what sort of magic he did in connection with it, but I didn't want to know bad enough to listen to him for twenty minutes more, so I didn't ask. I figured I could make a fair guess from the dump records anyhow.

When I got around to them. If I ever got around to them. That all began to look extremely unlikely. Just as I was about to let the spirit start moving with the report again, someone came into my office. I felt like screaming, "Go away and let me work!" But it was my boss, so I couldn't.

Despite my grumblings, Beatrice Cartwright isn't a bad person. She's not even a bad boss, most ways. She's a black lady about my age, maybe twenty-five pounds heavier than she ought to be (she says forty pounds, but she dreams of being built like a light-and-magic celeb, which I'm afraid ain't gonna happen). She's usually good about keeping higher-ups off her troops' backs, but she can't do much when Charlie Kelly calls you (or, more to the point, me) at home at five in the morning.

"David, I need to talk with you," she said. I must have looked as harassed as I felt, because she added hastily, "I hope it won't take up too much of your time." Even talking business, her voice had a touch of gospel choir in it. She never hit people over the head with her faith, though. I liked her for that.

I said, "Bea, I'll have that fumigants report for you as soon as the bloody phone stops squawking at me for three minutes at a stretch." I looked at it, expecting it to go off on cue. But it kept quiet.

"Never mind the report." She sat down in the chair by my desk. "What I want to know is why I've gotten calls from Loki and Convoo and Portentous Products this morning, all of them screaming for me to have you pulled away from the Devonshire dump. I didn't even know you were working on anything connected with the Devonshire dump." She gave me her more-in-sorrow-than-in-anger look, the one calculated to make even an eighth-circle sinner get the guilts.

More-in-sorrow-than-in-anger disappeared when I explained how Charlie had gone around her to call me. Real anger replaced it. If she'd been white, she'd have turned red. She said, "I am sick to death of people playing these stupid games. Mr. Kelly will hear from me, and that is a promise. Doesn't he have any idea what channels are for?" She took a deep breath and deliberately calmed down. "All right, so that's how you got involved with the Devonshire dump. Why are these people phoning me and screaming blue murder?"

"Because something really is wrong there." By now, I could rattle off the numbers from the Thomas Brothers' scriptorium in my sleep. "And because I'm trying to find out what, and—I think—because the Devonshire Land Management Consortium honchos aren't very happy about that."

"It does seem so, doesn't it?" Bea thought for maybe half a minute. "I still am going to talk to Mr. Charles Kelly, don't you doubt it for a minute. But I would say that, however you got this project, David, you are going to have to see it through."

"I thought the same thing the minute I first saw those birth defect statistics up at the monastery," I answered.

"All right. I'm glad we understand each other about that,

then. From now on, though, I expect to be kept fully informed on what you're doing. Do I make myself clear?"

I almost sprained my neck nodding. Even if she weren't my boss, Bea wouldn't be a good person to argue with. And she was dead right here. I said, "I was going to tell you as soon as I got the chance—Monday morning staff meeting at the latest. It's just that"—I waved at the chaos eating my desk—"I've been busy."

"I understand that. You're supposed to be busy. That's what they pay you for." Bea stood up to go, then turned back for a Parthian shot: "In spite of all this, I do still want the revisions on that spilled fumigants report finished before you go home tonight." She swept away, long skirt trailing regally after her.

I groaned. Before I had the chance to let the access spirit finish scanning the secondary revisions (and, let us not forget, the primary revisions about which Bea had later changed her mind), the phone yelled for attention again.

After Judy and I went to synagogue Friday night, we flew back to my place. I've already remarked that my orthodoxy is imperfect. Really observant Jews won't use carpets or any other magic on the Sabbath, though some will have a sprite trained to do things for them that they aren't allowed to do themselves—a shabbas devil, they call it.

But such fine scruples weren't part of my upbringing, so I don't feel sinful in behaving as I do. Judy's attitude is close to mine. Otherwise, she would have called me on the carpet instead of getting on one with me.

When we were settled with cold drinks in the front room, she said, "So what's the latest on the Devonshire dump?"

I took a sip of *aqua vitae*, let it char its way down to my belly. Then, my voice huskier than it had been before, I explained how all the consortia that dumped at Devonshire were so delighted to have their records examined.

"How do they know their records are being examined?" Judy, as I've noted, does not miss details. She spotted this one well before I needed to point it out to her.

"Good question," I said approvingly. "I wish I had a good answer. The people who've been calling me, though, sound like they've been rehearsing for a chorus." My voice, to put it charitably, is less than operatic. I burst into song anyhow: "It has come to my attention that—" I gave it about enough vibrato to fly a carpet through.

Judy winced, for which I didn't blame her. She tossed back the rest of her drink, then got out those two little porcelain cups. I would have been more flattered if I hadn't had the nagging suspicion she was trying to get me to shut up.

Whatever her reasons, though, I was happy to let her use up some of my beer. And, not too long afterwards, we were both pretty happy. Later, she got up to use the toilet and the spare toothbrush in the nostrums cabinet. Then she came back to bed. Neither of us had to go to work in the morning. Except for Saturday morning services, we'd have the day to ourselves.

I thought.

We were sound asleep, half tangled up with each other as if we'd been married for years, when the phone started screaming. We both thrashed in horror. She bumped my nose and kneed me in a more tender place than that, and I doubt I was any more gallant to her. I had to scramble over her to answer the phone; my flat's laid out to suit me when I'm there by myself, which is most of the time.

I spoke my first coherent thought aloud: "I'm going to kill Charlie Kelly." Who else, I figured, would call me at whatever o'clock in the dark this was?

But it wasn't Charlie. When I mumbled "Hullo?" the response was a crisp question: "Is this Inspector David Fisher of the Environmental Perfection Agency?"

"Yeah, that's me," I said. "Who the—who are you?" I wasn't quite ready to start swearing until I knew who my target was.

"Inspector Fisher, I am Legate Shiro Kawaguchi, of the Angels City Constabulary." That made me sit up straighter. I was beginning to be fully conscious. Having Judy pressed all warm and silky against my left side didn't hurt there, either. But what Kawaguchi said next made me forget even the sweet presence of the woman I loved: "Inspector Fisher, Brother Vahan of the Thomas Brothers monastery requested that I notify you immediately."

"Notify me of what?" I said, while little ice lizards slithered up my back. Judy made a questioning noise. I flapped my free hand to show her I couldn't fill her in yet. "Of what?" I repeated.

"I regret to inform you, Inspector Fisher, that Brother Vahan's monastery is now in the final stages of burning down. Brother Vahan has forcefully expressed the opinion that this may be related to an investigation you are pursuing."

"God, I hope not," I told him. But I was already getting out of bed. "Does he—do you—want me to come up there now?"

"If that would not be too inconvenient," Kawaguchi answered.

"I'm on my way," I said, and put the handset back in its cradle.

"On your way *where?*" Judy asked indignantly, mashing her pretty face into the pillow against the glare of the St. Elmo's fire I called up so I could find my pants. "What time is it, anyhow?"

"Two fifty-three," said the horological demon in my alarm clock.

"I'm going up to St. Ferdinand's Valley." I rummaged in my drawer for a sweater; Angels City nights can be chilly. As I pulled the sweater over my head, I went on, "The Thomas Brothers monastery up there, the one with all the damning data about the Devonshire dump, just burned down."

Judy sat bolt upright, the best argument I'd seen for staying home. "It wasn't an accident, or they wouldn't have called you." Her voice was flat. She started getting dressed, too.

By then I was buckling my sandals. "Brother Vahan doesn't seem to think so, from what the cop I talked with told me. And the timing of the fire is—well, suggestive is the word that comes to mind." No, I wasn't looking at her. Besides, by that time she already had on skirt and blouse and headscarf. "You don't really need to bother with all that," I said. "Sleep here, if you like. I'll be back eventually."

"Back?" If she'd sounded indignant before, now she was furious. "Who care when you'll be back? I'm coming with you."

Procedurally, that was all wrong, and I knew it. But if you think I argued, think again. It wasn't just that I was in love with Judy, though I'd be lying if I said that didn't enter into it. But procedure aside, I was glad to have her eyes along. She was likely to notice something I'd miss. And as far as investigating arson went, I'd be pretty useless up there myself. That's a job for the constabulary, not the EPA.

The freeway flight corridors were almost empty, so I pushed my carpet harder than I could have during the day. All the same, some people shot by me as if I was standing still. And one maniac almost flew right into me, then darted away like a bat out of hell. I hate drunks. The one advantage of being a regular commuter is that you don't see a lot of drunks out flying during regular commuting hours. It's not much of an advantage, but commuters have to take what they can get.

One of these days, the wizards keep promising, they'll be able to train the sylphic spirits in new carpets not to fly for drunks. This is another one I wouldn't stake my soul on. Sylphic spirits are naturally flighty themselves, and they hardly ever get hurt in accidents. So why should they care about the state of the people who ride their rugs?

I pulled off the freeway and darted north up almost deserted flight lanes toward the Thomas Brothers monastery. Toward what had been the Thomas Brothers monastery, I should say. It was still smoldering when I stopped at the edge of the zone the constabulary and firecrews had cordoned off.

Fighting fires in Angels City is anything but easy. Undines are weak and unreliable here: simply not enough underground water to support them. Firecrews use sand when they can, and the dust devils which keep it under control. For big fires, though, only water will do, and it has to come through the cooperation of the Other Side: the Angeles City firecrew mages have pacts with Elelogap, Focalor, and Vepar, the demons whose power is over water. Most of the time, that just means keeping the infernal spirits from harassing the mechanical system of dams and pipes and pumps that fetch our water from far away.

But sometimes, like tonight, the crews need more than sand can do, more than pipes can give. I was just showing my sigil to a worn-looking constable when one of the monastery towers flared anew. A wizard in firecrew crimson gestured with his wand to the spirit held inside a hastily drawn pentacle. I saw the mermaid-shape within writhe: he'd summoned Vepar, then.

That mage had a job I wouldn't want. Incanting always in a desperate hurry, drawing a new pentacle in the first open space you find, never daring to take the time to do a thorough job of checking it for gaps the summoned spirit could use to destroy you . . . only military magic takes a tougher toll on the operator.

But this fellow was cool as an ice elemental. He called on Vepar in a clear and piercing voice: "I conjure thee, Vepar, by the living God, by the true God, by the holy and all-ruling God, Who created from nothingness the heavens, the earth, the sea, and all things that are therein, Adonai, Jehovah, Tetragrammeton, to pour your waters upon the blaze there in such quantity and placement as to be most efficacious in extinguishing it and least damaging to life and property, in this place, before this pentacle, without grievance, deformity, noise, murmuring, or deceit. Obey, obey, obey!"

"It pains me to cease the destruction of the monastics housed therein." I felt Vepar's voice rather than hearing it. Like the demon's visible form, it was sensuous enough to make me want to forget from what sort of creature it really came.

The wizard didn't forget. "Obey, lest I cast thy name and seal into this brazier and consume them with sulphurous and stinking substances, and in so doing bind thee in the Bottomless Pit, in the Lake of Fire and Brimstone prepared for rebellious spirits, remembered no more before the face of God. Obey, obey, obey!" He held his closed hand above the brazier, as if to drop into the coals whatever he held.

I wouldn't have ignored a threat like that, and I'm a material creature. To Vepar, who was all of spirit, it had to be doubly frightening. Water suddenly saturated the air around the burning tower; you could see fog turn to mist and then to rain. The same thing had to be happening inside, too. The flames went out.

"Give me leave to get hence," Vepar said sullenly. "Am I now sufficiently humiliated to satisfy thee?"

The mage from the firecrew was too smart to let the demon lure him into that kind of debate. Without replying directly, he granted Vepar permission to go: "O Spirit Vepar, because thou hast diligently answered my demands, I do hereby license thee to depart, without injury to man or beast. Depart, I say, but be thou willing and ready to come whenever duly conjured by the sacred rites of magic. I adjure thee to withdraw peaceably and quietly, and may the peace of God continue forever between us. Amen."

He stayed in his own circle until the mermaid-shape vanished from the pentacle. Then he stepped—staggered, actually—out. I hoped the fire truly had a stake through its heart; that mage didn't look as if he could summon up ten coppers for a cup of tea.

A slim, Asian-looking man in constabulary uniform came up to me. "Inspector Fisher?" He waited for me to nod before he stuck out a hand. "I'm Legate Kawaguchi. As I said, Brother Vahan asked for your presence here." He affected to notice Judy for the first time. His face went from impassive to cold. "Who is your, ah, companion here?"

What are you doing bringing your girlfriend along on business? he meant. I said, "Legate, allow me to present my fiancée, Judith Adler." Before he could blow up at me, I added, coldly myself, "Mistress Adler is on the staff of Hand-of-Glory Publishing. As I feared magic might well be involved in this fire, I judged her expertise valuable." I gave him back an unspoken question of my own: *Want to make something of it?*

He didn't. He bowed slightly to Judy, who returned the courtesy. Kawaguchi turned back to me. "Your fears, it seems, are well-founded. This indeed appears to be a case of arson and homicide by sorcery."

I gulped. "Homicide?"

"So it would appear, Inspector. Brother Vahan informs me that eleven of the monks cannot be accounted for. Firecrew have already discovered three sets of mortal remains; as the site cools further, more such are to be expected."

"May their souls be judged kindly," I whispered. Beside me, Judy nodded. Until it happens, you don't want to imagine men of God, men who worked for nothing but good, snuffed out like so many tapers. Murder of a religious of any creed carries not just a secular death sentence but the strongest curse the sect can lay on, which strikes me as only right.

Kawaguchi pulled out a note tablet and stylus. "Inspector Fisher, I'd be grateful if you'd explain to me in your own words why Brother Vahan believes your recent work to be connected with this unfortunate occurrence."

Before I could answer, Brother Vahan himself came up. I might have known nothing, not even magical fire, could make the abbot lose his composure. He bowed gravely to me, even managed a hint of gallantry when I introduced Judy to him. But his eyes were black pools of anguish; as he stepped closer to one of the firecrew's St. Elmo's lamps, I saw he had a nasty burn across half his bald pate.

I explained to Kawaguchi what I'd been investigating, and why. His stylus raced over the wax. He hardly looked at what he was writing. Later, back at the constabulary station, he'd use a depalimpsestation spell to separate different strata of notes.

When I was through, he nodded slowly. "You are of the opinion, then, that one of the firms in some way involved with the Devonshire dump was responsible for this act of incendiarism?"

"Yes, Legate, I am," I answered.

Brother Vahan nodded heavily. "It is as I told you, Legate Kawaguchi. So much loss here; enormous profit to someone must be at stake."

"So I see," Kawaguchi said. "You must understand, though, sir, that your statement about Inspector Fisher's investigations is hearsay, while one directly from him may be used as evidence."

"I do understand that, Legate," the abbot answered. "Every calling has its own rituals." I didn't really think of the secular law, as opposed to that of the Holy Scriptures, as a ritual system, but Brother Vahan had a point.

A firecrewman with the crystal ball of a forensics specialist on his collar tabs stood waiting for Kawaguchi to notice him. When Kawaguchi did, the fellow said, "Legate, I have determined the point of origin of the fire." He waited again, this time just long enough to let Kawaguchi raise a questioning eyebrow. "The blaze appears to have broken out below ground, in the scriptorium chamber."

I started. So did Brother Vahan. Even in the half-dark and in the midst of confusion, Kawaguchi noticed. Judy would have, too; I wasn't so sure about myself. The legate said, "This has significance, gentlemen?"

The abbot and I looked at each other. He deferred to me with a graceful gesture that showed me his arm was burned, too. I said, "I drew the information alerting me to a problem around the Devonshire dump from the scriptorium. Now, I gather, any further evidence that might have been there is gone."

"The actual parchments from which you made your conclusions, and from which you might have gone on to draw other inferences, are surely perished," Brother Vahan said heavily. "I confess I have given them little thought, being more concerned with trying to save such brethren as I could. Too few, too few." I thought he was going to break down and weep, but he was made of stern stuff. He not only rallied but returned to the business at hand: "The data, as opposed to the physical residuum on which they resided, may yet be preserved. Much depends on whether Erasmus survived the conflagration."

"Erasmus?" Legate Kawaguchi and I asked together.

"The scriptorium spirit," Brother Vahan explained. He hadn't named the spirit for me when I was down there, but that had been strictly business.

Kawaguchi, Judy, and I turned as one to look at the smoking ruin which was all that remained of the Thomas Brothers monastery. Gently, Judy said, "How likely is that?"

"If the spirit betook itself wholly to the Other Side when the fire started, there may be some hope," the abbot said.

"The monastery is—was—consecrated ground, after all, and thereby to some degree protected from the impact of the physical world upon the spiritual."

Kawaguchi looked thoughtful. "That's so," he admitted. "Let me talk to the firecrew. If they think it's safe, we'll send a sorce-and-rescue team down into the scriptorium and see if we can't save that spirit. It may be able to give vital evidence."

"Without the corroborating physical presence of the parchments, evidence taken from a spirit is not admissible in court," Judy reminded him.

"Thank you for noting that, Mistress Adler. I was aware of it," the legate said. He didn't sound annoyed, though; my guess was, Judy had just proved to him she knew what she was talking about. He went on, "My thought was not so much for your fiancée's investigation as for the facts relating to the tragic fire here. For that, the spirit's testimony may very well be allowed."

"You're right, of course," Judy said. One of the many remarkable things about her is that when she has to concede a point (which isn't all that often), she concedes it completely and graciously. Most people go on fighting battles long after they're lost.

Kawaguchi went off to consult with the firecrew. I turned to Brother Vahan. "I'm sorry, sir, more sorry than I could say. I never imagined anyone could be mad enough to attack a monastery."

"Nor did I," he answered. "Do not blame yourself, my son. You uncovered a great evil at that dump; that I knew when you spoke to me of what you'd found. Now it has proved greater than either of us dreamt. But that is no reason to draw back from it. Rather, it is more reason to work to root it out."

I had nothing to say to that. I just dipped my head, the way you do when you hear the truth. Rather to my relief, Kawaguchi came back just then. A couple of men in red dashed into the ruins. My eye followed them. Seeing my head twist, Kawaguchi nodded. "They will make the effort, Inspector Fisher. They have, of course, no guarantee of success."

"Of course." I noted the understatement. After a moment, I went on with a question: "Did you call me up here just to take my information, or can I help you with what you're doing?"

"The former, I fear, unless you have resources concealed in your carpet which are not immediately obvious." Did the legate's eyes twinkle? I wasn't sure. If he had a sense of humor, it was drier than Angels City in the middle of one of our droughts.

"Well, then," I said, "do you mind my asking you for as much as you can give me of what you've found out here? The more I learn about how this fire started and the magics that went into it, the better my chance of correlating those data with one or more of the consortia that use the Devonshire dump. That'll help me figure out whose spells are leaking, which ought to help you figure out who's to blame for this burning."

I've worked with constabularies before. Constables are always chary about telling anybody anything, even if the person who wants to know is on the same side they are. Kawaguchi visibly wrestled with himself; under other circumstances, it would have been funny.

Finally he said, "That is a reasonable request." Which didn't mean he was happy about it. "Come with me, then. You may accompany us if you like, Mistress Adler."

"How generous of you," Judy said. I knew she'd have accompanied us whether Kawaguchi liked it or not, and gone off like a demon out of its pentacle if he tried to stop her. The irony in her voice was thick enough to slice. If the legate noticed it, though, he didn't let on. I wondered if the Angels City constabulary wizards had perfected an anti-sarcasm amulet. If they had, I wanted to buy one.

Such foolishness vanished as the legate took Judy and me over to his command post (Brother Vahan tagged along, without, I noticed, any formal invitation). The firecrew forensics man was talking with his opposite number in the constabulary, a skinny blond woman who had a spellchecker that made my little portable look like a three-year-old's toy.

I stared at it with honest envy. As soon as Kawaguchi introduced me to her—she was Chief Thaumatechnician Bornholm—I asked, "How many megageists in that thing, anyway?"

She must have heard me salivating, because she smiled, which made her look a little younger and a lot less tough. "Four meg active, eighty meg correlative," she answered.

"Wow," I said; beside me, Judy whistled softly. I wondered when the EPA would get a portable spellchecker with that kind of power. Probably some time in the new millennium; it would just about take the Millennium for us to have the tools we need to do the job right. The next century shouldn't be more than two or three decades old before we're ready to deal with this one.

"So what do we have in there?" Kawaguchi asked.

Bornholm was a good constable; she glanced over to him and got his nod before she started talking in front of us civilian types. Then she said, "Even with the spellchecker, this won't be as easy as I'd like; on hallowed ground, sorcerous evidence has a way of evanescing in a hurry." She turned her head in Brother Vahan's direction. "The abbot here has a most holy establishment: good for his monks and a credit to him, but hard on the constabulary."

"All right, I won't expect you to hand me the case all sealed up with a papal chrysobull," the legate said, "though I wouldn't have been sorry if you did. Tell me what you know."

"About what you'd expect in an arson case," Bornholm said: "strong traces of salamander, rather weaker ones from the use of a blasting rod."

"Uh-huh," Kawaguchi said. "Any special characteristics of the salamander that would help us trace it back to a particular source on the Other Side?" Different rituals summon different strains of salamander; had this been one of the unusual ones, it could have told a lot about who called the creature to the monastery.

But the thaumatech shook her head. "As generic a spell as you can find. Ten thousand campers use it out in the woods every day to get their fires going. Of course, they tack a dismissal onto it, too, and that didn't happen here. Just the opposite, in fact; it was encouraged. Same with the blasting rod: very ordinary magic."

"Hellfire," Kawaguchi said, which wasn't literally true—salamanders are morally neutral creatures—but summed things up well enough.

Bornholm hesitated, then went on, "When I first set up, I thought something else might be there, too. I wanted to stake down the certain arson traces before anything else, though, and by the time I came back to the other, it was gone. Hallowed ground, like I said. I'll take the rap for it—it was my choice."

"That's what free will is about," Kawaguchi said. "You did what you thought was best. I presume you ordered the spirit to remember, not just analyze. We can do further evaluation later."

"Certainly," Bornholm answered, with a *What do you think I am, an idiot?* look tacked on for good measure. I didn't blame her, not one bit. She added, "The trouble is, you can't evaluate what just isn't there."

"I understand that." Kawaguchi smacked right fist into left palm in frustration. I didn't blame him, either. There was the spellchecker, with access and correlation capability on relations with the Other Side for everybody from Achaeans to Zulus and all stops in between, with hordes of microimps inside to do the thinking faster and more thoroughly than any mere man could manage—but, as the thaumatech had said, you can't analyze what isn't there.

"Legate!" The shout rang through the smoky night. Kawaguchi spun round (so did all of us, as a matter of fact). One of the guys from the sorce-and-rescue crew had emerged from the ruined scriptorium. His boots thumped on the pavement as he walked over to us. He was sooty and sweaty and looked about half beaten to death, but his eyes held triumph. "We made contact with that access spirit, Legate."

"Good news!" Kawaguchi exclaimed. "That's the first piece of good news I've heard tonight. What sort of shape is the spirit in?"

"I was just getting to that, Legate," the sorce-and-rescue

man said, and some of the sudden hopes I'd got up came crashing down again—he didn't sound what you'd call upbeat. "The spirit's here—it's manifested enough so we can move it—but it's not in good shape, not even slightly. Preliminary diagnosis is that whoever set the fire went after the poor creature on the Other Side, too."

"Poor Erasmus," Brother Vahan said, with as much concern as if he were talking about one of his monks.

"Erasmus? Oh," the sorce-and-rescue man said; then: "I don't think it'll perish, but it's had a rough time. Hard to characterize torments on the Other Side, but—did it used to manifest itself with its spectacles cracked?"

"No," Brother Vahan said, and started to weep as if that was to him the crowning tragedy of all those which had befallen the Thomas Brothers monastery tonight. I remembered the fussy, precise spirit and the neat little pair of glasses it had worn. How could you crack lenses that weren't really there? I suppose there are ways, but I got queasy thinking about them.

"We can run the spellchecker on this access spirit," Thaumatech Bornholm said. "Maybe we'll learn just what hit the monastery by finding out how the spirit was tormented."

"For that matter, simple questioning may yield the same information," said Kawaguchi, who sounded ready to start asking poor abused Erasmus questions right then and there if the sorce-and-rescue man would summon the spirit onto a ground-glass screen.

But the sorce-and-rescue man shook his head. "Nobody's going to run a spellchecker on that spirit any time soon. Any sorcerous nudge right now, before it has a chance to regain some strength, and it'll be gone for good. I'm not kidding—a sorcerous nudge right now *will* destroy, uh, Erasmus, and I'll set that down on parchment. The same goes for interrogation. If that spirit were a material being, it would've gotten last rites. Because it's not material, it has a better chance of recovering than thee or me, but I warn you: you'll lose it if you push."

"I shall pray for Erasmus' recovery along with the recovery of my brethren who took hurt in the fire," Brother Vahan

said, "and for the souls of the brethren who lost their lives."
He spoke slowly and with great dignity, partly because he
was that kind of man and partly to hold the tears back from
his voice.

Judy stepped up to him and put a hand on his shoulder.
He twitched a little; you could see how unused he was to
having a woman touch him. But after a couple of seconds, he
realized she meant only to comfort him. He eased, as much
as you can when everything that matters to you is gone.

I wished I'd thought to make the gesture Judy had. I suspect the trouble is that I think too much. Judy felt what she
ought to do and she did it. I'm not saying she doesn't think—
oh my, no. But it's nice to be in touch with This Side and the
Other Side of yourself, so to speak.

I turned to Legate Kawaguchi. "Do you need us for anything more here, sir?"

He shook his head. "No, you may go, Inspector Fisher.
Thank you for your statement. I expect we will be in touch
with each other about aspects of this matter of mutual concern." I expected that, too. Then Kawaguchi unbent a little;
maybe a human being really did lurk behind the constabulary uniform. "A pleasure also to meet your fiancée,
Inspector. A pity to drag you out of doors at such an unholy
hour, Mistress Adler, especially on dark, grim business like
this."

"I asked David to let me come along," Judy said. "And
you're right—this business is dark and grim. If I can do anything to help you catch whoever did it, let me know. I'm no
mage, but I'm an expert on sorcerous applications."

"I shall bear that in mind," Kawaguchi said, and sounded
as if he meant it.

Judy and I ducked under the tape the constabulary had
put around the Thomas Brothers monastery and walked
back toward my carpet. The sun was just starting to paint the
sky above the hills to the east with pink. I asked my watch
what time it was and found out it was heading toward six. By
my body, it could have been anywhere from midmorning to
midnight.

We fastened our safety belts and headed back toward the

freeway. A couple of minutes before we got there, Judy said, "I didn't know I was your fiancée."

"Huh?" I answered brilliantly.

"The way you introduced me to Legate Kawaguchi," she said.

"Oh. That." I'd just done it because it seemed the easiest way to explain what she was doing over at my place at two-something of a morning. I thought about it for a few seconds, then said, "Well, do you want to be?"

"Do I want to be what?" Now Judy was confused.

"My fiancée."

"Sure!" she said, and her smile was brighter than the sun which just that moment poked itself into the sky. It wasn't the traditional way to answer a proposal of marriage, but then I hadn't proposed the way I'd intended to, either. I really had intended to get around to it, but I didn't know just when. Now seemed as good a time as any.

We held hands on St. James' Freeway all the way back to my block of flats. After a black night, morning sun felt very fine indeed.

III

When I got to work Monday morning, somebody ambushed me in the parking lot. No, it's not what you think; this fellow standing outside the entrance to my building called out, "Are you EPA Inspector David Fisher?" When I said I was, he came trotting over to me, stuck a glass globe in front of my face, and said, "I'm Joe Forbes, Angels City Ethernet Station One News. I want to ask you some questions about the tragic Thomas Brothers fire Friday night."

"Go ahead," I said, peering cross-eyed into the globe. The imp inside had enormous ears, mournful little eyes, and a mouth that stretched all the way across its face. I'd never seen an ethernet imp before.

Forbes shifted the globe back toward his own mouth. "How are you involved with the Thomas Brothers, and why were you called to the scene of the fire shortly after it occurred?" He held the globe out to me again.

"I'd been using some Thomas Brothers records in an ongoing EPA investigation, and the constabulary were trying to find out if there was any connection between that investigation and the fire," I answered, truthful enough but not what you'd call forthcoming.

As I talked, I watched the little imp in the globe. Its ears twitched with every syllable I spoke. Its mouth moved in a rather exaggerated parody of human speech. I've never had any reason to learn to read lips, but I didn't need long to notice it was echoing what I said, about half a beat behind me. It was transmitting my words back to Ethernet Station One, either to one of its own clones that would relay what I said on to the master broadcasting imp so all the master's clones in people's sets could hear, or else to a Listener that would speak them in front of the master imp at a time more convenient for the station crew.

Joe Forbes took back the globe. "Do I understand correctly, Inspector Fisher, that an immaterial witness survived the fire and may yet provide important information about the case?"

I'd talked to Kawaguchi the afternoon before. From what he said, Erasmus was probably going to pull through its ordeal, though the access spirit wouldn't be in any shape to answer questions for a while yet. Actually, Erasmus didn't have any shape at all, but you know what I mean.

I started to tell Forbes as much, but had second thoughts. I didn't know how many people listened to the ethernet news, but could I afford to assume none of the people who'd burned the monastery did? And if those bastards were listening, could I afford to tell them they'd botched the job on Erasmus? They might try again, and they might do it right the next time.

All this went through my mind in about the time it took to finish exhaling, inhale, and begin to talk. If Forbes had caught me on an inhale, I must have just started talking before I stopped to think. As it was, I said, "I really think that's something you ought to take up with the constabulary. They know more about it than I do."

Forbes looked unhappy; I guess he saw from my answers that he wasn't going to get any exciting revelations from me. He asked a couple of innocuous questions, then tried once more with something substantive: "What sort of Thomas Brothers records were you using in your own investigation?"

Maybe he'd hoped I'd not notice that one was charmed, and would blab away. But I didn't; I answered, "I'd rather not comment, since the investigation is still under way." The fellow's laziness irked me as much as anything else. If he'd known This Side from the Other, he could have gone down to the Criminal and Magical Courts Building and found the parchments I'd filed to get my search warrant. But no—he wanted me to do his work for him.

Well, I had enough work of my own. I said as much: "I'm sorry, Mr. Forbes, but I really have to get upstairs now."

"Thank you, Inspector David Fisher of the Environmental Perfection Agency," Forbes boomed, just as if I'd told him something worth knowing. I pitied his poor imp. It didn't look very bright, but I wouldn't have been very bright after listening to and transmitting the mind-numbing stream of chatter Forbes turned out.

I'd hoped to start getting some serious work done on the sorcerous contamination at the Devonshire dump itself, but I hadn't taken into account its being Monday morning. Monday morning under Beatrice Cartwright is a ritual that, while not as old as the Mass or synagogue Sabbath rite, is every bit as sacred: the staff meeting.

Monday morning, everybody in the department sits around for two, two and a half hours listening to what everybody else is doing. About ninety-nine times out of a hundred, what everybody else is doing is, to put it mildly, irrelevant to what you're doing yourself, and you could better spend the time actually doing whatever it is you can't do while you're sitting around in staff meeting (thank God we're an Agency, not a Department, the way some people back in D.St.C. want; if we were a Department we'd probably meet twice a week, not just once).

I mean, in an abstract kind of way I was glad to hear that Phyllis Kaminsky was working closely with the constabulary to make several Angels City streets less congenial to succubi; vice of that sort does need to be combated. But even if her report did earn Phyllis a pat on the fanny from Bea, I didn't need to know all the ichor-filled details.

And I didn't need to know about the aerial garlic spraying Jose Franco was working on with some of the horticulture people at UCAC to try to slow down the little vegetable vampires that have played such havoc with the local citrus crop over the past few years, ever since they got here in a cargo of imperfectly exorcised lemons from Greece. It wasn't that I had anything against Jose or his project; I don't want to have to pay three crowns for an orange any more than anyone else. But just the same, Medvamps aren't my biggest worry in the world.

For that matter, even though people looked more interested than usual (which isn't saying much) when I talked about the Devonshire mess, it didn't have a whole lot to do with their lives or their jobs. But Bea likes to soak it all in, so every Monday morning we meet. World without end, amen, or so it seems in the middle of a staff meeting, anyhow.

At last we were released; I felt as if I were upward bound from purgatory (no, not a Jewish concept, but useful all the same). I staggered off to the jakes with the staff graphic artist. "At least here I know what I'm doing," I said as we stood side by side. Martín laughed and nodded; he's about as fond of staff meetings as I am.

Having accomplished at least one worthwhile thing that morning, I went back to my desk to see if I could make it two. I wished the thaumatech had been able to catch more about the incendiary sorcery that had torched the Thomas Brothers monastery; it might have given me a better notion of which toxic spell components to be alert for, and from that which consortia to suspect. But if magic were just wishing, life would be too simple to stand.

I made myself a new chart, an expanded version of the one I'd done on my kitchen table the week before. This one broke things out not just by consortium and type of business, but also by specific type of contaminant. In lieu of turning the chart three-dimensional, I assembled a neat battle line of quills, each in an inkstand of a different color (to be sure I had enough, I'd borrowed some from Martín's immense supply).

Just when I was ready to buckle down to some serious work, the phone yammered at me. I didn't say what I thought, but I thought it real loud. That, of course, didn't make the phone shut up. I spoke to the mouthpiece imp: "David Fisher, Environmental Perfection Agency."

"Good morning, Dave—Tony Sudakis calling."

"Good morning, Tony. How are you?" Half my annoyance went away; at least the call had something to do with the case I was working on. "What's up?"

"I heard about the Thomas Brothers fire over the weekend. Terrible thing. Those are good people there. We need more like 'em."

"That's certainly true. But there are less like them now—eleven less, I understand."

"Yeah, I know." A pause. I was getting used to pauses from people I talked with, which is not to say I liked them any too well. Once Tony was finally done with his, he went on, "I just want you to know that the Devonshire Land Management Consortium didn't have thing one to do with this fire."

I chewed on that, found I didn't care for the taste. As politely as I could, I pointed out, "Tony, you can speak for yourself, but how can you go about declaring your whole consortium innocent?" Oh, he could declare it, sure, but how was he supposed to make me believe it?

He surprised me—he found a way that sort of worked: "The consortium management staff is contributing twenty-five thousand crowns to the constabulary's reward fund for the capture and conviction of whoever fired the place."

"Interesting," I said, and it was; interesting enough to write down, in fact. Figuring out exactly what it meant wasn't so simple. The most obvious interpretation was that management staff was innocent. The other possibility was that somebody up there was guilty as sin and had found a particularly devious way to cover his—or even her—tracks. In the absence of further data, I just had to note it and go on.

Sudakis was dealing with my pause now. Into it, he said, "You don't take anything on trust, do you, Dave?"

"I trust in God," I answered. "He has a more reliable record than most of the people I know."

"Life must be easy if you can honestly give all your allegiance to one omniscient, omnipotent deity," Sudakis said. "But I didn't call you up to talk theology with you. I wouldn't mind doing that over some beer one day, but now now. I've said what I needed to say, and I've got the usual swamp full of alligators here."

He meant that more literally than most people who use the line—and his particular swamp held worse things than mere alligators. We said our goodbyes and hung up. I looked at the phone for a few seconds afterwards. Maybe Sudakis never had reconciled himself to Christianity, or to monotheism generally. That last comment of his made me wonder. Well, the Confederacy is a free country. He could believe whatever he wanted, as long as the didn't go burning down monasteries to make his point.

"Interesting," I said again, to nobody in particular, and started squeezing the undines out of my own swamp.

I'd decided to note the contaminants from the smaller companies first, before I tackled the light-and-magic outfits and the aerospace consortia. If one of the little guys was dumping something spectacularly illicit, my hopes was that it would stand out like a mullah in the College of Cardinals.

I was amazed to see just how much nasty stuff some of the little guys messed around with. Take the outfit called Slow Jinn Fizz, for instance. Heaven help me, they were using things there I wouldn't have expected to find coming out of Loki's Cobold Works. I mean, they were stowing stove-in Solomon's Seals at Devonshire. You think for a while about the thaumaturgical pressure it takes to deform one of those things, and the likely effect on the surrounding countryside when you try it, and you'll have some idea why I noted that in red.

Chocolate Weasel had just as many nastinesses, things EPA men in most of the Confederation wouldn't see once in a thousand years—Aztecian stuff, almost exclusively. My stomach did a slow flipflop when I saw one neatly written item on their dumping manifesto: flayed human skin substitute.

As I think I've said before, human sacrifice is—officially—banned within the Aztecian Empire these days. But it used to be a central part of the Aztecian cult. One whole twenty-day month of their old calendar, Tlaxipeualiztli (say it three times fast—I dare you), means "boning of the men," and almost all of it had parades where priests capered around wearing the skins of sacrificial victims.

Obviously, death magic is some of the strongest sorcery there is. But modern technology has eliminated the need that was formerly perceived for it. Proper application of the law of similarity lets the Aztecians produce by less blood-thirsty means the same effect they used to get from ripping the hearts out of victims. But it's still a daunting item to find on a form.

There are also rumors that some of the flayed skin substitute isn't created through the law of similarity, but rather through the law of contagion. Yes, I'm afraid that means what you think it does: the substitute material gains its effectiveness by touching a real flayed human skin, one hidden away since the days when such sacrifices were not only legal but required.

The Aztecians spend a lot of time denying those rumors. The EPA spends a lot of time checking them—we don't want that kind of sorcery getting loose in this country. Nothing's ever been proved. But the rumors persist.

I noted that one down in red ink, too. Chocolate Weasel, I thought, would get a visit from some inspector soon; if not me, then someone else. Properly manufactured flayed skin substitute isn't illegal, but it is one of the things we like to keep an eye on.

None of the other little firms that used the Devonshire dump put anything quite so ferocious in it, though I did raise an eyebrow to see how many roosters' eggshells Essence Extractions was getting rid of. "Cockatrices," I said out loud. The little creatures are dangerous and always have been ferociously expensive because they're so rare, but I wondered if these folks hadn't found a way to turn them out in quantity.

I looked thoughtfully at that manifest before I went on to

the next one. If Essence Extractions had found a way to produce lots of cockatrices, they were sitting on the goose that laid the golden egg. Pardon the botched ornithological metaphor, but it's true. And the dumping records gave some good clues on how they were going about it. Tony Sudakis hadn't worried about confidentiality for nothing.

Seeing the folks who are trying to thwart you as people just like yourself rather than The Enemy (in Satanic red sometimes, not just capital letters) isn't easy. You're better off dealing with them that way, though, because it's surprising (or revolting, depending on how you look it at) how often they have a point.

I knocked off at five, slid down to the ground. Pickets were marking on the sidewalk off to one side of the parking lot. Pickets marched outside the Confederal Building about three days out of five, touting one cause or another (sometimes the people touting one cause run into those touting another, and then there can be trouble).

These particular pickets weren't just marching; they were chanting, too: "Hey, hey, waddaya say, let's throw out the EPA!"

That flicked my curiosity. I wandered over to see what they were upset about. Their signs spoke for themselves: SAVE OUR STRAWBERRIES! was one. Another said, STOP AERIAL GARLIC SPRAYING! And a third—BETTER MEDVAMPS THAN TURNING MY BACK YARD INTO AN ITALIAN DELI! I liked that, actually, even if I couldn't agree with it.

Sometimes protesters will listen to reason. I decided to give it a try, remarking to a fellow with a blond beard, "You know, if we let Medvamps establish themselves here, they'll wipe out a good part of our agriculture. Look what they've done to the Sandwich Islands."

"I don't care about the Sandwich Islands, pal," Blond Beard answered. "All I know is that as far as I'm concerned, garlic stinks. I have to smell it every hour of the day and night, and I think it's making me sick. *And* it's gotten into my flying carpet, and the sylphs don't like it any better than I do. I may have to trade the stupid thing in, and with the performance shot, I won't get near what it's worth. So there!"

"But—" I started. Blond Beard had stopped paying attention to me; he was chanting again. I gave up and headed back to my own carpet. Reminding him that all the people in the spraying area had been warned to cover up their carpets or bring them indoors wouldn't have changed his mind, it would just have made him angrier than he was already. Some people might as well be zombies, for all the constructive use they get out of their free will.

As I started to fly toward the freeway, I noticed a familiar-looking man holding a glass glove up to the mouth of one of the picketers. It was Joe Forbes of Ethernet Station One. "Thanks a lot, Joe," I muttered. Thousands of people, I had no doubt, would hear about the imaginary evils of garlic spraying just as if they were thaumaturgically established.

I hoped he'd have the integrity to interview an EPA sorcerer or somebody from the citrus business, too. But even if he did, the views of people who didn't know anything except what they didn't like would in effect get equal weight with those of folks who'd been studying the problem since it first bared its teeth. I sighed. What could I do about it? People out picketing and raising a ruckus were "news," regardless of whether they had any facts to back them up.

The freeway was jammed, too, which didn't do anything to improve my mood by the time I finally got home.

Next morning, I started adding to my chart some of the toxic spell components the aerospace firms dumped at Devonshire. I hadn't been at it for more than a couple of hours before I saw I'd have to talk with my boss.

Bea was on the phone when I went up to her office. Sometimes I think she's had that imp permanently implanted in her ear. As soon as she laid down the handset, I scurried in. Before the phone could go off again, I tossed my still only half-done chart on the desk in front of her.

Her eyes followed it down. When she saw some of the things I'd written in red, she gave a real live theatrical gasp. "Good God in heaven, are we actually storing these things inside a populated area?" she exclaimed, raising a shocked hand. Her gaze lingered on the flayed human skin substitute. Even though it's legal, it's appalling to contemplate.

"Looks that way," I said, "and this isn't all of it, by any means. I wanted to ask you to let me do some afternoon fieldwork this week, maybe talk to some of the people who use this stuff and see if there aren't substitutes. Or even substitutes for the substitutes," I added, wondering if a second-generation *ersatz* skin would be magically efficacious.

"Go ahead," she told me without hesitation; she really is a pretty good boss. "Do one other thing first, though: call Mr. Charles Kelly and let him know what sort of mess he's landed this office in. I've already had words with him about that, but you can emphasize it, too. If we have to holler for help from the District of St. Columba, I don't want him to be able to say he wasn't warned in advance."

Burning brimstone makes you think of demons. Bureaucratic finagling has a smell of its own, too. I went back to my desk and made the call. When I got through to Charlie, he sounded jovially wary, a combination implausible only to someone who's never taken his crowns from the government. "What can I do for you this afternoon, David?" he boomed. I'd expected him not to bother remembering it was still morning for me, so I wasn't disappointed when he didn't.

"You've hear about what happened out here over the weekend?" I asked. It wasn't really a question.

For a second, though, he sounded as if it was. "Only news out of Angels City I've heard is that monastery fire." He hesitated, just for a second. I could almost see the ball of St. Elmo's fire pop into being above his head. "Wait a minute. Are you telling me that's connected to the Devonshire case?"

"I sure am, Charlie. Eleven monks dead of arson, in case all the news didn't make it back East." Without giving him a chance to rally, I pushed ahead: "My boss Bea says she's already spoken to you about the way I got this case. It's bigger than you thought, it's bigger than I imagined when I dropped it on me. You should be aware that we may have to have help from D.St.C."

"If you do, you'll get it. Eleven monks. Jesus, Mary, and

Joseph." Charlie being of the Erse persuasion, I thought that would hit him where he lived.

"Something else," I said: "Don't you think it's time to level with me and stop playing coy about the 'bird' who tipped you to the trouble at the Devonshire dump?"

This time, Kelly's pause lasted a lot longer than a second. Even through two phone imps and three thousand miles of ether, he sounded unhappy as he answered, "Dave, I'd tell you if I could, but I swear I can't. I'm sorry."

I blew exasperated air out my nose, hard enough to stir the hairs of my mustache against my upper lip. "Okay, Charlie. Play a game with me, then. Is your feathered friend from groups involved with any of these . . . ?" I named the Garuda Bird, Quetzalcoatl, the Peacock Throne, (hesitantly) the Peacock Angel, and, as an afterthought, the phoenix.

More silence from Charlie. Finally he said, "Yeah, the bird's in there somewhere. Believe me, I'm taking a chance telling you even that much. So long." And he was gone, faster than a Medvamp out of a Korean restaurant.

Nice to know one of the ideas Judy and I had come up with was the right one. It would have been nicer still, of course, to know which. I thought about what he'd said and, as well as I could tell over the phone, how he'd said it. Maybe politics wasn't what sealed his lips. Maybe it was fear. That was the first time I started getting a little bit fearful myself.

Well, onward—no help for it unless I felt like quitting. And if I did that, not only would I not want to look at myself in the mirror but Judy would drop me like something just up from the Pit. So off I went to Slow Jinn Fizz, the closest outfit I'd yet found that had a red-letter contaminant on my chart.

The carpet ride up into St. Ferdinand's Valley took about twenty minutes. Slow Jinn Fizz was on the chief business flyway of the Valley, Venture Boulevard. The address itself was enough to tell me the outfit had money. The building argued for that, too: an elegant gray stucco structure with SLOW JINN FIZZ in neat gold letters on the plate glass window by the entry door. Underneath, in smaller (but just as gold) letters, it added, A JINNETIC ENGINEERING CONSORTIUM.

"Aha!" I said before I walked in. The combination of the name and the Solomon's Seals discarded at the Devonshire dump had made me figure jinnetic engineering was what Slow Jinn Fizz was all about. Nice to be right every so often.

A dazzling blond receptionist, as expensive-looking and probably as carefully chosen as the rest of the decor, gave me a dazzling white smile. "How may I help you, sir?" she asked in the kind of voice that suggested she'd do *anything* I asked.

I reminded myself I was engaged. The smile congealed on her face when I pulled out my EPA sigil. "I'd like to see Mr. Durani, please, in connection with some of your firm's recent dumping activities."

"One moment, Inspector, uh, Fishman," she said, and disappeared into the back of the building.

Ramzan Durani came out a couple of minutes later, in person. He was a plump, medium-brown fellow in his midforties who wore a white lab robe of Persian cut and an equally white turban. "Inspector Fisher, yes?" he said as we shook hands. I gave him a point for getting it right even though his receptionist hadn't. "We spoke on the phone last week, did we not?"

"That's right, sir. In a way, this is about the same matter."

"I thought it might be." He didn't seem as volatile in person as he had over the phone, for which I was duly grateful. "Please come with me to my office, and we shall discuss this further."

The only thing I'll say about his office is that it made Tony Sudakis' look like a slum, and Tony's beats mine seven ways from Sunday. He poured mint tea, gave me sweetmeats, sat me down, and generally fussed over me until I felt as if I'd gone back to my mom's for Rosh Hashanah dinner. I don't care for the feeling at my mom's and I didn't care for it here, either.

I answered it with bluntness: "Devonshire dump is under investigation for leaking toxic spell components into the surrounding environment. We haven't learned exactly what's getting out yet, but I can give you an idea of how serious the problem is by telling you there have been three cases of apsychia in the area over the past year alone."

"And you think *we* are to blame? Slow Jinn Fizz?" Durani bounced—no, flew—out of his chair. His volatility was still there, all right; I just hadn't conjured it up in polite greetings. "No, no, ten thousand times no!" he cried. I thought he was going to rend his garment. He didn't; he contented himself with grabbing his turban in both hands, as if he feared his head would fall off. "How can you accuse us of such an outrage? How dare you, sir!"

"Calm yourself, Mr. Durani, please." I made a little placating gesture, hoping he'd sit down again. It didn't work. I went on quickly, before he threw the samovar at me. "Nobody's accusing Slow Jinn Fizz of anything. I'm just trying to find out what's going on at the dump site."

"You dare accuse Slow Jinn Fizz of causing apsychia!" He extravagantly wasn't listening.

"I haven't accused you," I said, louder this time. "Have— not. I'm just investigating. And you must admit that Solomon's Seals are very potent magic, with a strong potential for polluting the environment."

Durani cast his eyes up to the ceiling and, presumably, past it toward Allah. "They think I am destroying souls," he said—not to me. He glared my way a moment later. "You wretched bureaucratic fool, Slow Jinn Fizz does not cause apsychia. I—we—this consortium—am—are—is on the edge of curing this dreadful defect."

I started to get angry at him, then stopped when I realized what he'd just said. "You are?" I exclaimed. "How, in God's name?"

"In God's name indeed—in the name of the Compassionate, the Merciful." Durani calmed down again, so fast that I wondered how much of his rage was real temper and how much for show. But that didn't matter, either, not if he really was on the edge of beating apsychia. If he could do that, I didn't mind him chewing me out every day—and twice on Fridays.

"Tell me what you're doing here," I said. "Please." People have been trying to cure apsychia since the dawn of civilization, and probably long before that. Modern goetic technology can work plenty of marvels, but that . . .

"Jinnetic engineering can accomplish things no one would have imagined possible only a generation ago," Durani said. "Combining the raw strength of the jinn with the rigor and precision of Western sorcery—"

"That much I know," I said. Jinnetic engineering outfits have fueled a lot of the big boom on the Bourse the past few years, and with reason. The only way their profit margins could be bigger would be for the jinni to fetch bags of gold from the Other Side.

But Durani had found something else for them to do Over There: jinn-splicing, he called it. What he had in mind was for the jinni to take a tiny fraction of the spiritual packet that made up a disembodied human soul, bring it back to This Side, and, using recombinant techniques he didn't— wouldn't—describe, join it with a bunch of other tiny fragments to produce what was in essence a synthesized soul, which could then be transplanted into some poor little apsychic kid.

"So you see," he said, gesturing violently, "it is impossible—impossible, I tell you!—for Slow Jinn Fizz or any of our byproducts to cause apsychia. We aim to prevent this tragedy, to make it as if it never was, not to cause it."

Whether what he aimed at was what he accomplished, I couldn't have said. For that matter, neither could he, not with any confidence. Sorcerous byproducts have a way of taking on lives of their own.

But that wasn't what was really on my mind. "Have you actually transplanted one of these, uh, synthesized souls into an apsychic human being?" I knew there was awe in my voice, the same sort of awe the Garuda Bird program raises in me: I felt I was at the very edge of something bigger than I'd ever imagined, and if I reached out just a little, I could touch it.

"We have transplanted three so far," he answered with quiet pride.

"And?" I wanted to reach out, all right, reach out and pull the answer from him.

"The transplants appear to have taken: that is to say, the synthesized souls bond to the body, giving the apsychic a true spirituality he has never before known." Durani held up a warning hand. "The true test, the test of Judgment, however, has not yet arisen—all three individuals who have undergone the transplant procedure remain alive. Theory indicates a risk that the synthesized soul may break up into its constituent fragments when its connection to the body is severed at death. We shall research that when the time arises."

"Yes, I'd think so," I said. A soul, after all, exists in eternity: it lives here for a while, but it's primarily concerned with the Other Side. What a tragedy it would be to give a living man a soul, only to have him lack one when he died and needed it most. Worse than if he'd never had one, if you ask me—and till that moment, I'd never imagined anything worse than apsychia.

Something else struck me: "What happens to the souls from which you're taking out your little packets? Are they damaged? Can they still enspirit a human being?"

"This is why we take so little from each one," Durani answered. "To the limits of our experimental techniques, no measurable damage occurs. Nor should it, for is not God not only compassionate and merciful but also loving and able to forgive us our imperfections?"

"Maybe so, but do your artificial imperfections leave these, hmm, sampled souls more vulnerable to evil influence from the Other Side?" The further I got into the case of the Devonshire dump, the more hot potatoes it handed me. This new technique of Durani's was astonishing, but what would its environmental impact be? The lawsuits I saw coming would tie up the ecclesiastical courts for the next hundred years.

You may think I'm exaggerating, but I mean that literally. For instance, suppose somebody does something really horrible: oh, suppose he burns down a monastery. And suppose he's able to convince a court that, on account of the Durani technique, he's been deprived of 1% or 0.1% or 0.001% of the soul he would have had otherwise. Is he fully responsible for what he did, or is it partly Durani's fault? A smart canon lawyer could make a good case for blaming Slow Jinn Fizz.

Or suppose somebody does something horrible, and then *claims* as a defense that he's been deprived of part of his soul by the Durani technique. How do you go about proving him wrong, if he is? I'm no prophet, but I foresaw the sons of a lot of canon lawyers (and the nephews of Catholic canonists) heading for fine collegia on the profits of that argument alone.

And here's another one: let's suppose the Durani technique is as safe as he says it is, and doesn't do irreparable harm to anybody's soul. Let's suppose again that his synthesized souls have even been passing the test of Judgment. But nothing manmade can hope to match God's perfection. What happens if a misassembled soul does break apart on death, leaving a poor apsychic all dressed up with no place to go? To what sort of recompense is his family entitled?

All at once, I wished again that magic were impossible, that we just lived in a mechanical world. Yes, I know life would be a lot harder, but it would be a lot simpler, too. The trouble with technology is that, as soon as it solves a problem, the alleged solution presents two new ones.

But the trouble with no technology, of course, is that problems don't get solved. I don't suppose apsychics, suddenly offered the chance for a better hereafter, would worry about risks. I wouldn't, in their shoes.

I guess nothing is ever simple. Maybe it's just as well. If things were simple, we wouldn't need an Environmental Perfection Agency and I'd be out of a job.

Caught in my own brown study, I'd missed a couple of sentences. When my ears woke up again, Durani was saying, "—may develop a sampling technique to bring back components only from what you might term *mahatmas*, great souls, those who have spirit to spare."

"Very interesting," I answered, and so it was, though not altogether in the way he'd intended it. Sounded to me as though he had some concerns over safety himself. I wondered who *his* lawyers were. I hoped he had a good team, because I had the feeling—the strong feeling—he'd need one.

"Is there anything further, Inspector Fisher?" he asked.

He'd relaxed now; I guess he only got vehement when he thought his interests were endangered. A lot of people are like that.

"That's about it for now," I told him, whereupon he relaxed even further. He thought the operative phrase there was *that's about it*; I thought it was *for now*. He'd done something new and splendid, all right, but I wasn't sure he'd ever realize any profit from it. He hadn't had a lawyer at his beck and call the week before. He'd need one soon, or more likely a whole swarm of them.

Remembering his call reminded me how many I—and Bea—had fielded all at once. I asked my watch what time it was, found out it was a few minutes before three. I decided to go over to the Devonshire Land Management Consortium offices and find out just how so many of their clients found out about the EPA investigation so fast.

My sigil got me into the office of a markgraf in charge of consortiate relations, a redheaded chap with hairy ears whose name was Peabody. He showed a full set of teeth undoubtedly kept so snowy white by sympathetic magic (I wondered what would happen if a forest fire spilled soot all over the snow to which those teeth were attuned).

I give him credit: he didn't try to cast any spells over me. "Of course we notified our clients," he said when I asked him my question. "Their interests were impacted by your search of files at the containment site, so we might have been liable to civil penalty had we kept silent."

"All right, Mr. Peabody, thanks for your time," I said. Put that way, he had a point. I might have thought better of him if he'd talked about loyalty instead of liability, but how much can you expect from a mercenary in a fancy suit?

After that, I headed for home. I picked up a daily once I got off the freeway, for the sake of the sport more than anything else. Over in Japan, I saw, the Giants had beaten the Dragons for their league title. And closer to home, the Angels and Blue Devils played to a scoreless tie.

"Might as well be real life," I muttered when I saw that. Then I shook my head. In real life, the Cardinals would never have been higher in the standings than the Angels.

But looking at the score gave me an idea. I called Judy. "Feel like a Zoroastrian lunch tomorrow?" I asked her.

She giggled. "Sounds good. But to make it perfect, I ought to fly my carpet. After all, it's an Ahura-Mazda."

"That's right, you did buy an import last year, didn't you?" I said. "But let me pick you up instead afterwards anyhow." I explained what I was doing with my red-letter list.

"That'll be fine," Judy said. "Nice you get a chance to be away from the office part of your day. Too bad it couldn't be mornings, though." She knows how much I hate staff meetings.

I smacked myself in the forehead. "I should have thought of that. But listen to what I came across today—" I told her about Ramzan Durani and Slow Jinn Fizz.

"That's exciting!" she breathed. "To give those poor people hope . . . Have they worked all the gremlins out of the process?"

"I couldn't tell you. Durani talks like he has, but it's his operation, so you'd expect him to."

"Yes," Judy said. "Of course, even if he has, the moment anything goes wrong the lawyers will say he hasn't. The spiritual implications are—overwhelming is the word that comes to mind."

"You know one of the reasons I love you?" I said. She didn't answer, just waited for me to go on, so I did: "You see implications. So many people don't; they just go 'Oh, how marvelous!' without stopping to think what their marvels end up costing them."

"Thank you," she said, her voice surprisingly serious. "That doesn't sound anywhere near as romantic as something like 'You have beautiful eyes,' but I think it gives us a much better promise of lasting. I feel the same way about you, just so you know."

"What, that I have beautiful eyes?" I said. She snorted. I added, "Besides, I told you that was just one of the reasons. I wish you were here right now, so we could try one of the others."

"Now what might that be?" She sounded so perfectly innocent, she was perfectly unbelievable. She didn't even believe herself: "I wish I were over there, too, honey, but I've got to finish working out this astrology problem for my class. Reconciling western and Hanese systems is a bitch and a half. I'll see you tomorrow for lunch."

"Twelve-thirty all right?"

"Sounds good. 'Bye."

Judy works in a part of East A.C. where you hear Spainish spoken in the streets about as often as English. The rage for Zoroastrian diners has reached even there, though. Next year, no doubt, they'll be passé; right now, they're fun.

The one trouble with those places is that Judy and I can't enjoy them to the fullest, because a lot of their dishes feature deviled ham. We managed, though. I ate angel-hair pasta and devil's-food cake, while she had a deviled-egg-salad sandwich and angelfood cake. Just names, sure, but names have power.

"So where are you going this afternoon?" Judy asked while we waited for the waitress to bring us our lunches.

"Up to Loki, in Burbank," I said. "I have the feeling their parchmentwork didn't report half of what they're dumping. They have a real reputation for secrecy; nobody except them and the military knows what goes on at the Cobold Works up in the desert, and nobody at all, it looks like, knows—or will say—what comes out of the Cobold Works."

"They're working in the Garuda Bird project, too, aren't they?" Judy said.

"That's right—and if you think I'm going up there partly so I can learn more about that, you're right," I admitted. Space travel has fascinated me ever since the first magic mirror let us see the far side of the moon back when I was a kid.

The girl carried our plates over to us just then. "Thanks," I said as she set them down. Because she looked as if she'd understand it better, I added, "*Gracias.*"

"*De nada, señor,*" she answered, smiling. She hardly seemed old enough to be working full time. Maybe she wasn't. People who come up to Angels City to get away from Azteca find out soon enough that the sidewalks aren't paved with gold here, either. They do what they can to get by, same as my great-grandparents did a hundred years ago. Most of them will.

It was a pleasant lunch. Any time with Judy was pleasant, but the good food and the chance to be out and about in the middle of the day (she'd been right about that the night before) just added to it. I hated to leave, but she had to get back to work and I needed to be at the Loki plant early enough in the afternoon to do some useful work.

I parked my carpet in the loading zone in front of Hand-of-Glory's office, kissed Judy goodbye before I took off. It was a pretty thorough kiss, if I say say myself. This ten-year-old who should have been in school made disgusted noises as he walked by. I didn't care. Give him a few more years and he'd find out about the sweet magic between man and woman.

I waited there till I saw Judy safe indoors, then headed up the Golden Province Freeway to Burbank. The Loki works weren't far from the little airport there. They were big and sprawled-out enough to have separate buildings and lots for each of the consortium's many projects; I flew around till I found a sign that said SPACE DIVISION and had a stylized Garuda bird under it. I parked my carpet as close to the sign as I could, then walked off some of my lunch hiking toward the entrance.

Inside, where they didn't show from the parking lot, were guards armed with pistols and holy water sprayers. I presented my EPA sigil. Even though I'd phoned ahead in the morning, I could see how little ice it cut here. The guards were ready to take on major foes, from This Side or the Other. One bureaucrat wasn't worth getting excited about.

Which is not to say they weren't thorough. They turned a spellchecker on my sigil, to make sure it wasn't forged and hadn't been tampered with. One of them carefully compared the image on my flying license to my face. The other waited till the first was done, then called my office to confirm I really did work there. He didn't ask me for the number; he looked it up himself.

Only when they were satisfied did they phone deeper into the building. "Magister Arnold will come to escort you shortly, sir," one of them said. "Here is your visitor's talisman." He pinned it on me, then added, "Once you pass through that door, the demon in the talisman will be roused and will sting you if you get more than fifteen feet away from Magister Arnold. Just so you know, sir."

"What happens if I need to use a toilet?" I asked.

"Magister Arnold must accompany you to the facility, sir," he answered, unsmiling. The guy outside the Devonshire dump had billed himself as a security guard. This Loki fellow really was one.

I found another question: "Suppose I ditch the talisman once I go inside?"

"First, sir, any attempt to do so would rouse the demon. Second, once inside the door there, the talisman will weld itself to your clothing and remain bonded to it until you emerge. If you're a good enough sorcerer, sir, you can beat the talisman, but you'll set off a great many alarms in the process, and will be apprehended in short order."

"I don't want to beat it and I don't want to be apprehended," I said. "I was just curious." The guard nodded, polite but unconvinced. His job was being unconvinced, and he was real good at it.

Magister Arnold came out a couple of minutes later. He was a big, rangy fellow in his mid-fifties, in a lab robe almost as fancy as Ramzan Durani's. "Call me Matt," he said after we shook hands. "Come along with me now."

I came along. The door closed behind us. I gave the talisman a surreptitious yank. Sure enough, it was stuck to the front of my shirt. I'd figured it would be. Loki took security seriously.

I found out just how seriously when we got to the door of Arnold's office: it was hermetically sealed. Now I grant you that Hermes is a good choice of protector for an aerospace office—in his wingfoot aspect, he's naturally related to flight sciences, and who better to propitiate in a security system than the patron deity of thieves?

But merciful heavens, the expense! A security system isn't just a seal; the backup is a lot more important. Maintaining a whole cult at a level sufficient to keep its god active and alert will kill you with priests' fees, fanes, sacrifices, what have you. I wondered how much of the bill Loki was paying itself and how much it was passing on to the taxpayer. Somehow cost overruns never turn out to be anybody's fault. They're just *there*, like crabgrass, and about as hard to weed out.

Be that as it may, Magister Arnold rubbed the toggle that served as the door Herm's erect phallus. The Herm must have recognized his touch, for it smiled and the door came open.

It closed behind us with a definitive-sounding *snick*. "Coffee?" Arnold asked, waving to a pot that sat on top of a little asbestos salamander cage.

"No, thanks," I answered; I'd just as soon drink vitriol as muck that was reheating all day. And besides— "You really don't feel like following me down the hall if I have to use the men's room, do you?"

"Oh, yes, of course. That's right, you're wearing a visitor's talisman, aren't you? I hope you don't mind if I have a cup?" At my inviting wave, Arnold poured himself one. It looked as thick and dark and oily as I'd figured it would. Even the fumes were enough to make my nostrils twitch. When he set the cup down, he asked, "So what have we done that's brought the EPA down on us?" He didn't say *this time*, but you could hear it behind his words.

"I don't know that you've done anything," I answered. "I do know that somebody's spells are leaking out of the Devonshire dump, and I also know that whoever that somebody is, he's murdered monks to keep his secret."

That got Arnold's instant and complete attention. His eyes gripped me like the Romanian giants Eastern European sorcerers use to handle magical apparatus they wouldn't touch with a ten-foot Pole. He was quick on the uptake. "The Thomas Brothers fire is connected to this affair, is it?" he said. "A bad business, very bad."

"Yes." I let it go at that; no need for him to know I was personally involved with the monastery fire. I pulled out my chart. "As near as I can tell from this, Magister Arnold, Loki puts more toxic spells into Devonshire than anybody else— and the ones I have here are those you admit to publicly."

"For the record," Arnold said loudly, "I deny there are any others." His tone was just as sincere as Tony Sudakis', and told me (in case I hadn't been sure already) a Listener was in there with us.

I liked that tone even less from the magister, because I knew he wasn't on my side while I hoped Sudakis was. All Arnold wanted to do was play with his projects, whatever they happened to be. It wasn't that I doubted their worth. I didn't; as I've said, I'm demons for the space program myself. But nobody has any business fouling the nest and then pretending his hands are clean.

"For the record," I answered, just as loudly and just as snottily, "I don't believe you." Arnold glared; my guess was that nobody'd talked to him like that for a while. I let him steam for a few seconds, then said, "Are you seriously telling me nothing too secret to get into your EPA forms goes on at the Cobold Works?"

"What Cobold Works?" he said, but he couldn't keep a twinkle from his eye. That the establishment in the desert exists is an open secret. But his smile disappeared in a hurry. "If it's too secret to go into the forms, Inspector Fisher, it's also too secret to talk about with you. No offense, but you need to understand that."

"I'm not out to betray our secrets to the Hanese or the Ukrainians," I said. "You need to understand that, and to understand that the situation around the Devonshire dump is serious." I tossed him the report on birth defects around the site. As he read it, his face screwed up as if he'd bitten into an unripe medlar. "You see what I mean, magister."

"Yes, I do. You have a problem there, absolutely. But I don't believe the Loki Space Division, at least, is responsible for it. If you'll give me a chance, I'll tell you why."

"Go ahead," I said. Nobody I'd talked to would even entertain the idea that he could be responsible for the leaks. Well, I didn't find the idea entertaining, either.

"Thanks." Arnold steepled his fingers, more a thoughtful gesture, I judged, than a prayerful one. He went on. "I gather this toxic spell leak is believed to be through the dump's containment system rather than airborne."

"Yes, I believe that's true," I said cautiously. "So?"

He nodded as if he'd scored a point. "Thought as much. I'm not breaking security to tell you that Space Division spells are universally volatile in nature, with byproducts to match. That's not surprising, is it, considering what we do?"

"I suppose not," I said. "What exactly is your consortium's role in getting the Garuda Bird out of the atmosphere?"

That did it. He started rolling like the Juggernaut's car, which, considering the project we were talking about, isn't the worst of comparisons. Loki was in charge of two project phases, the second of which (presumably because it dealt with air elementals) had been split into two elements.

"First, we handle the new spells pertaining to the Garuda Bird itself." Arnold pointed to a picture tacked onto the wall behind him: an artist's conception of the Bird lifting a cargo into low orbit, with the curve of the Earth and the black of space behind it. Even in a painting, the Bird is something to see. Think of a roc squared and then square that again— well, the Bird could turn a roc into a pebble. For a second, I forgot about being an investigator and felt like a kid with a new kite.

"The Bird is magic-intensive anyway," Arnold went on. "Has to be, or else that big bulk would never get off the ground. But we've had to upgrade all the spell systems and develop a whole new set for upper-atmospheric and exatmospheric work. They do fine in similarity modeling; pretty soon we'll get to see what the models are worth. You with me so far?"

"Pretty much so, yeah," I answered. "What's this other phase you were talking about? Something to do with sylphs?"

"That's right. Turns out our models show that max-Q—"

"What?"

"Maximum dynamic pressure on the Bird," he explained grudgingly, and then, because I still didn't get it, added more grudgingly still, "Maximum air buffeting."

"Oh."

I'd distracted him. He gave me a dirty look, as if he were a wizard who'd forgotten the key word of an invocation just as his demon was about to appear in the pentacle. When I didn't rip off his head or swallow him whole, he pulled himself together. "As I was saying, max-Q on the Garuda Bird occurs relatively low in the atmosphere, due to sylphic action on the traveler through the aery realm."

"Sylphs are like that," I agreed. "Always have been. How do you propose to get them to act any different?"

"As I said before, we have a two-element approach to the problem—"

He pulled a chart out of his top desk drawer and showed me what he meant. If he hadn't been an aerospace thaumaturge, he would have called it the carrot-and-stick approach. As it was, he talked about sylph-esteem and sylph-discipline.

Sylph-esteem, I gathered, involved making the sylphs above the Garuda Bird launch site so happy they wouldn't think about blowing the Bird around as it flew past them. Like a lot of half-smart plans, it looked good on parchment. Trouble is, sylphs by their very nature are happy-go-lucky already, and also changeable as the weather. How do you go about not only making them even more cheerful than they were already but also making them stay that way?

If you ask me (which Magister Arnold didn't), sylph-discipline is a better way to go. Putting the fear of higher Powers into the sylphs might well make the air elementals behave themselves long enough to let the Garuda Bird get through. True, you couldn't keep it up long, sylphs being as they are, but then, you wouldn't need to.

"For sylph-discipline to be effective, timing is of the essence," Arnold said. "Implement your deterrence activity too soon and the elementals forget the brief intimidation; implement it too late and it is useless. We are still in the process of developing the sorcerous systems that will enable us to ensure minimal sylphic disturbance as the Garuda Bird proceeds on its mission."

"If you're still developing them, am I correct in assuming that no byproducts from that element of your project would appear on my list of contaminants from Loki?"

"Let me check, if I may," he said. He looked at my chart,

just as I'd looked at his. "No, that's not correct. Some of this activity with Beelzebub comes from our shop."

I remembered the patch of flies at the Devonshire dump and shivered a little. Dealing with Beelzebub involves some of the most potent, most dangerous sorcery there is. I said, "Sounds like overkill to me. Why pick such a mighty potentate of the Descending Hierarchy to overawe the air elementals?"

My guess was that asking the question would prove a waste of time, that Arnold would baffle me with technical jargon till I gave up and went away. But he fooled me, saying, "It's really quite straightforward, at least in broad outline. We shall require the Lord of the Flies to inflict a plague of his creatures on the sylphs to distract them from the passage of the Garuda Bird."

"You don't think small," I said. Then something else occurred to me: "But what's to keep the flies from tormenting the Garuda Bird along with the air elementals?"

Magister Arnold smiled thinly. "As I said, it's straightforward in broad outline. Details of the negotiations with the demon are anything but simple, as you may imagine. He is, if you will forgive me, hellishly clever."

"Yes." I let it go at that; if it were up to me, I'd have come up with some other way of distracting the sylphs. After a couple of seconds, I said, "Don't byproducts from a conjuration involving Beelzebub have a chance of sliding through the underground containment scheme at the dump? They aren't all volatile, as you claimed before."

"I suppose that's true." Arnold sounded anything but happy about supposing that was true, but he did it anyhow. I give him credit for that. He tried to put the best face on it: "You haven't alluded to these particular byproducts as being the ones which are leaking, however, Inspector Fisher. Until you show me evidence that they are, I hope you will forgive my doubts."

"Okay, fair enough," I said. Going around the edges of the dump with a sensitive spellchecker, checking air and earth, fire and water for sorcerous pollutants would blow Charlie Kelly's request for discretion further into space than the

Garuda Bird could carry it, but that couldn't be helped, not now.

I got up and started to leave. I'd just about made it to the door when I remembered the demon imprisoned in my visitor's talisman. I turned around and headed right back toward Magister Arnold. He was coming after me.

"Thanks," I said.

"Don't mention it." His voice was dry. "My own peace of mind is involved in keeping you healthy till you get out the door, you know. Just think of all the parchmentwork I'd have to fill out if an Environmental Perfection Agency inspector got stung to death by the Loki security system. I wouldn't get any real work done for weeks."

Knowing the EPA bureaucratic procedures as I do, I was sure he was right about that. Then a couple of casually uttered words sank in. "Stung to *death*, Magister Arnold?" I said, gulping. "The security guard didn't mention that little detail."

"Well, he should have," Arnold answered testily. He must have noticed my face chance expression. "Before you ask, Inspector, we do have a permit to incorporate deadly force into our security setup because of the sensitive nature of so much of what we do here. If you like, I will be happy to show you a copy, complete with chrysobull, of that permit."

"No, never mind." The assurance in his voice said he wasn't bluffing. And if I wanted to check, I could do it at the Criminal and Magical Courts building. "But visitors should be warned before they enter the secure area, sir. They'd have more of an incentive for following instructions carefully."

"Oh, it seems to work out all right. We haven't lost one in a couple of weeks." The aerospace man had a perfect deadpan delivery. At first I accepted what he'd said without thinking about it, then did a double take, and only then noticed the very corners of his mouth curling up. I snorted. He'd got me good.

He led me out to the door by which I'd entered. As soon as I was on the far side of it, I took off the talisman (now I could) and all but threw it at the security guard. "You didn't tell me it was lethal," I snarled.

"If your intentions were good, sir, you didn't need to know," he answered. "And if they were bad, you also didn't need to know."

He should have been a Jesuit. After I got done gasping for air, I slunk out toward my carpet, then headed for home. It was still early, but if I'd gone someplace else and done my song and dance, I'd have been late. I was late the day before. Put the two days together, I figured, and they'd come out even. It was the sort of logic you'd expect after a Zoroastrian lunch, but it satisfied me for the moment.

Because I was early, I made good time on the way back down to Hawthorne. Of course, that left me rattling around my flat for a chunk of the afternoon. I'm usually good at just being there by myself, but it wasn't working that day. I didn't feel like going out and going shopping; besides, with next payday getting close and the last one only a ghostly memory, the ghouls had been chewing on my checking account.

I decided to do something to put crowns into my pocket, not take them out. I had three or four sacks of aluminum cans rattling around under the sink and in my closet; I took 'em out (which freed up space to put in more), carried 'em down to my carpet, and headed for the local recycling center.

SAVE THE ENVIRONMENT AND SAVE ENERGY, said the sign outside: RECYCLE ALUMINUM. I nodded approvingly as I lugged the cans over. Some programs sell themselves as being good for the environment when they're not, but recycling isn't one of them.

The fellow at the center tossed the cans on the scale, looked back at a little chart on the wall behind him. "Give you two crowns sixty," he said, and proceeded to do just that.

The small change went into my pocket, the two-crown note into my wallet. "Thank you, friend," I told him.

"Any time," he answered. "See you again soon, I hope. You're making some sorcerer's life easier."

I let that go with a nod. Since I work for the EPA, I would have bet I knew more about it than he did. Recycled aluminum lets magicians use the law of similarity to extract more of the metal directly from the ore; it's a lot cheaper and more energy efficient than the alchemy they have to resort to when they're working without any aluminum source . . . to say nothing of the preposterous and expensive mechanical processes you have to use to coax aluminum free of the minerals that contain it. Were it not for sorcery, I doubt we'd ever have learned what a wonderfully useful metal aluminum is.

Two crowns sixty wouldn't come close to paying the bill from the Department of Water and Powers I'd found in my mailbox. The bill was up from last month, too; the Department, a little clipped-on notice said, had gained approval for a three percent increase in salamander propitiation fees. Everything costs more these days.

The money I'd got for the aluminum cans would just about cover a hamburger, though not the fries that went with it. A Golden Steeples was right around the corner from the recycling center. I went in there, spent my dividend and a bit more besides. It was a long way from a gourmet treat, but when you're eating by yourself, a lot of the time you don't care.

A newspaper rack stood just outside the Golden Steeples: it used the same kind of greedy little imp that dwells in pay phones. I stuck in the right change, pulled out a *Times*. If I'd tried to take more than one, the imp would have screamed blue murder. I think it's a shame the racks have to resort to measures like that, but they do. Life in the big city.

Back in my flat, I opened a beer and drank it down while I read the daily. One of the page-nine stories directly concerned me: Brother Vahan was appealing to the Cardinal of Angels City for a dispensation to allow cosmetic sorcery for one of the monks badly burned in the Thomas Brothers fire.

I prayed that the Cardinal would grant the dispensation. Cosmetic sorcery can do marvelous things these days. If the doctors and wizards have a recent portrait of someone before he was burned, they can use the law of similarity to bring his appearance back to what it used to be. Function doesn't follow superficial form, of course, but a burn victim gains so much by not becoming a walking horror show.

Trouble is, the Cardinal of Angels City is a stiff-necked

Erseman who takes the mortification of the flesh and God's will seriously. The story said he was considering Brother Vahan's appeal, "but the issuance of a dispensation cannot be guaranteed." He was liable to decide God wanted that monk disfigured, and who were we to argue with Him?

That sort of attitude never made sense to me. Far as I can see, if God wanted burn victims to stay ugly forever, He wouldn't have made cosmetic sorcery possible. But then, I'm just an EPA man, not a theologian (and especially not a Catholic theologian). What do I know?

St. George and the Dragon was splashed all over the entertainment section (and I wondered what the Cardinal thought about *that*). I hadn't gotten a good enough look at the blonde by the Hollywood Freeway to tell if she was the one falling out of her minitunic in the ads. I wasn't about to go to the light-and-magic show to find out, either. That miserable publicity stunt had cost them at least one cash customer.

When I got to work the next morning, more pickets were marching out alongside the Confederal Building to protest the aerial spraying for Medvamps. I shook my head as I went up the elevator to work. Some people simply cannot weigh short-term inconvenience against long-term benefit.

As soon as I got to my desk, I started working like a man possessed; had a priest wandered by, he probably would have wanted to perform an exorcism on me. But I banged through the routine parts of my job as fast as I could so I'd have time to investigate the Devonshire case properly. I wanted to get out to Chocolate Weasel that afternoon.

The best-laid plans—

I'd just managed to get the wood on top of my desk out from under the usual sea of parchments and visible to the naked eye once more when the phone started yelling at me. Unlike some people I know, I don't usually have premonitions, but I did this time. What I smelled was trouble. The phone hadn't given me much else lately.

"David Fisher, Environmental Perfection Agency."

"Mr. Fisher, this is Susan Kuznetsov, of the Barony's Bureau of Physical and Spiritual Health . . ."

"Yes?" I'd never heard of her.

"Mr. Fisher, I'm calling from Chatsworth Memorial Hospital. I was going to notify the St. Ferdinand's chapter of the Thomas Brothers, as is usual in such cases, but due to the recent tragedy there, that was impossible. When I called the East Angels City Thomas Brothers monastery, I was referred to you."

"Why?" I asked. My mind wasn't on the Devonshire dump, not that minute. But then, before she could answer, I put together whom she worked for, where she was calling from, her likeliest reason for wanting to get hold of the Thomas Brothers, and their likeliest reason for passing her on to me. "Don't tell me, Mistress Kuznetsov—"

"I'm afraid so, Mr. Fisher. We've just had an apsychic baby born here."

IV

I don't know much about babies: call it lack of practical experience. Give Judy and me a few years and I expect we'll do something about that, but not now. Oh, my brother up in Portland has a two-year-old girl and I have some little cousins up there, too, but I can count on the smelly fingers of both hands the number of diapers I've changed.

So poor little Jesus Cordero (the irony of the name struck me as soon as I heard it) didn't look much different from any other new-minted kid to me. He lay on his tummy in the cradle, wriggling in a sort of random way, as if he didn't really understand he had arms and legs and could do things with them. The only thing in the least remarkable about him to the eye was an astonishingly thick head of black, black hair.

His mother sat on the side of the bed by the cradle. She

101

was nineteen, twenty, something like that; she might have been pretty if she hadn't looked so wrung out from giving birth. Her husband had a hand on her shoulder. He was about her age, dressed like a day laborer. They talked back and forth in Spanish. I wondered if they'd entered the Confederation legally, and wondered even more if they truly understood what had happened to little baby Jesus.

In the room with them were Susan Kuznetsov—a middle-aged woman, no-nonsense variety, built like a crate—and a priest. He was a tubby little redheaded fellow named Father Flanagan, but he proved to speak fluent Spanish himself. In Angels City, that's a practical necessity for a priest these days.

"Any question about the diagnosis, Father?" I asked him.

"Not a bit of it, worse luck for the poor boy," he answered. Listening to him, I wondered if you could speak Spanish with a brogue. But all such frivolous thoughts vanished as he went on: "I was going through the nursery last night the way I always do, blessing the newborns of my creed. I came to this little fellow and—well, see for your own self, Inspector."

He took off the crucifix from around his neck, set it against the baby's cheek, murmured a few words of Latin. That's not my ritual, of course, but I knew what was supposed to happen: because babies, being new to the world, are uncorrupt, the cross should have glowed for a moment, symbolic of the linkage between goodness on the Other Side and the innocence of the baby's soul. Not for nothing did Scandinavian converts speak of the White Christ.

But nothing was all we saw here. The crucifix might have been merely metal and wood, not one of the most potent mystical symbols on This Side. At its touch, little Jesus twisted his head in the hope that it was a milk-filled breast.

Gently, his face sad, the priest redonned the crucifix. Susan Kuznetsov said, "Father Flanagan called me first thing this morning. Of course, I came out immediately. He repeated the test in my presence then, and I made others so as to be absolutely certain. This baby, though otherwise healthy and normal, possesses no soul."

Tears stung my eyes. Having something so dreadful happen to a poor tiny kid who'd never even had the chance to commit a sin struck me as horribly unjust. Not even Satan got anything out of it, either, because when Jesus Cordero died, he'd just be *gone*. What did it mean? Far as I could tell, it meant only that we don't understand the way things work as well as we'd like to.

"Sir," I said to the baby's father (his name was Ramón; his wife was Lupe), "I'd like to ask you some questions, if I may, to see if I can learn how this unfortunate thing happened to your son."

"*Sí*, ask," he said. He understood English, even if he didn't speak it too well. His wife nodded to show she also followed what I'd said.

The first thing I asked was their address. I wasn't surprised to learn they lived within a couple of miles of the Devonshire dump; we were only five or six miles away there at the hospital. Then I tried to find out if Lupe Cordero had used any potent sorcerous products during her pregnancy. She shook her head. "*Nada*," she said.

"Nothing at all?" I persisted; contact with magic is such a part of everyone's everyday life that sometimes we don't even think about it. "Your medical treatments were all of the ordinary sort?"

She answered in rapid-fire Spainish. Father Flanagan did the honors for me: "She says she had no medical treatments till birth; she could not afford them." I nodded glumly; that's the story with so many poor immigrants these days. Through the priest, Lupe went on, "The only thing even a little different was that I had morning sickness, so I went to the *curandero* for help."

Speaking for himself, Father Flanagan said, "Probably something on the order of camomile tea; few *curanderos* traffic with Anything important."

"Probably," I agreed, "but I have to be thorough. Mrs. Cordero, can you give me the name and address of this person?"

"I don' remember," she answered in English. Her face closed up. I could guess what that meant: it was bound to be somebody from her home village back in Aztecia, somebody she didn't want to see in trouble.

I tried again. "Mrs. Cordero, it's possible the medicine you received had something to do with your giving birth to an apsychic child. We have to check that out, to make sure the same misfortune doesn't happen to someone else."

"I don' remember," she repeated. Her face might have been cast in bronze. I knew I wasn't going to get any answers out of her. I caught Father Flanagan's eye. He nodded almost imperceptibly. Maybe he'd try to talk some more with her later, maybe he'd just ask around in the neighborhood. One way or another, I figured before too long I'd find out what I needed to know.

Ramón Cordero bent over the cradle, picked up his son. By the smooth way he held the baby in the crook of his elbow, I guessed it wasn't his first. "*Niño lindo*," he said softly. Even more softly, Father Flanagan translated: "Beautiful boy."

Little Jesus was a nice-looking baby. "Enjoy him all you can, Mr. Cordero," I said. "Love him a lot. This is all he has. He'll have to make the best of it."

"That's good advice," Susan Kuznetsov said. She dropped into Spanish at least as fluent as Father Flanagan's, then returned to English for me: "I told him that many apsychics live extraordinary lives on This Side, maybe to help compensate for not going on after they die. Artists, writers, thaumaturges—"

What she said was true, though she'd just mentioned the good half. There's pretty fair evidence that the Leader of the Alemans during the Second Sorcerous War was an apsychic, and that he promoted the massacres and other horrors of the war exactly because he wasn't afraid of what would happen to him on the Other Side: once he was gone, he was gone permanently. That wasn't the sort of thing you wanted to mention to an apsychic's parents, though.

The baby wiggled, thrashed, woke up with a squall about like what you'd expect from a minor demon who doesn't care to be conjured up. Lupe held out her arms; her husband set Jesus in them. I glanced down at my toes while she adjusted her hospital robe so she could nurse him. The squalls subsided, to be replaced by intent slurping noises.

"Tiene mucho hambre," Lupe said— "He's very hungry." She seemed pleased and proud, as a new mother should. No, little Jesus' tragic lack hadn't fully registered with her.

I stood there for a couple of more minutes, wondering all the while if I ought to say something about Slow Jinn Fizz. Maybe—God willing—Ramzan Durani and his outfit could fill the vacuum at the center of little Jesus Cordero. From what Durani had said, he *could* fill it. What troubled me was whether he was creating similar but smaller vacuums in other souls. He said not, but even he'd admitted his procedure was still experimental.

In the end, I kept my mouth shut. Part of that was not wanting to raise the adult Corderos' hopes too much. The rest was simple pragmatism: even though baby Jesus had no hope for eternal life, odds were he wasn't going to shuffle off this mortal coil tomorrow or next year, either. He had the time to wait while the gremlins were exorcised from Durani's jinnetic engineering scheme.

I wonder what I would have done if I'd been dealing with a seventy-year-old apsychic in poor health, someone facing imminent oblivion. Would gaining that person a soul (assuming the procedure worked) outweigh the harm inflicted on other souls in the process (assuming it didn't work as well as Durani claimed)?

I decided I was awful glad Jesus was just a baby.

Lupe raised the little fellow to her shoulder, patted him on the back. After a few seconds, he let out a burp about an octave deeper than you'd think could come from anything so small.

"When will you be going home from the hospital?" I asked her.

"Mañana," she said.

"I'd like to come by your home that afternoon, if I could," I said. "I have a portable spellchecker, so I can begin investigating for toxic spells in the local environment, and I'd also like a look at whatever potion you got from your *curandero*." I saw from her face that she didn't understand everything I'd said. So did Father Flanagan. He translated for me.

Lupe and Ramón looked at each other. "No questions about nothing else?" he asked.

They were illegals, then. "None," I promised. That wasn't my business. Trying to find out why their son had been born without a soul was. "I swear it in God's name."

"You don' make no cross," Ramón said suspiciously.

Father Flanagan was giving me a questioning look, too. "Tell them I'm Jewish," I said. His face cleared. I was sure he didn't care much for my beliefs, but that's okay: I wasn't fond of all of his, either. But we acknowledged each other's sincerity. He spoke way too rapidly for me to follow what he said to the Corderos, but they nodded when he was through.

Lupe said, "You go, you look, you find out. We trus' you, the *padre* say we can trus' you. He better be right."

"He is," I said, and let it go at that. If I'd taken another oath, the Corderos might have thought the first one wasn't to be trusted. Father Flanagan nodded slowly, understanding what I'd done.

Susan Kuznetsov said, "Besides, Jesus there is a native-born citizen of the Confederation, and entitled to all the protection of our laws." When she turned that into Spanish, the Corderos beamed; they liked the idea. The woman from the Bureau of Physical and Spiritual Health quietly added, "I just wish our laws could do more for the poor little guy." Neither she nor Father Flanagan translated that.

I said my goodbyes, collected Mistress Kuznetsov's *carte de visite*, and flew back to the office. The elves hadn't magically cleaned up my desk while I was gone. I didn't care. It could stay dirty a while longer. I picked up the phone and called Charlie Kelly.

The yammering at the other end went on for so long that I wondered if he was back from lunch yet. It was well past two back in D.St.C.; where the demons did those confounded Confederal bureaucrats get the nerve to keep swilling at the public sty like that? All I needed was a minute of no answer on the phone to swell up and bellow like an enraged bull taxpayer, when after all I was a confounded Confederal bureaucrat my very own self.

"Environmental Perfection Agency, Charles Kelly speaking." Finally!

"Charlie, this is Dave Fisher in Angels City. We just had another apsychic birth close by the Devonshire dump. That makes four in a little more than a year. This isn't going to be a quiet investigation any more, Charlie. I'm going to find out what's leaking and why, no matter how noisy I have to get."

He kind of grunted. "Do what you think necessary."

"Shit, Charlie, you're the one who sicced me onto this." I'm not usually vulgar on the phone and I'm not usually vulgar in the office, but I was steaming. "Now you're making it a lot harder than it has to be."

"In what way?" he asked, as if he hadn't the slightest idea.

When Charlie Kelly goes all innocent on you, check how many fingers and toes you're wearing. The odds are real good they'll add up to a number smaller than twenty. I can't imagine how I kept from screaming at him. "You know perfectly well. Tell me about the bloody bird that keeps singing in your ear."

"I'm sorry, David, but I can't," he said. "I never should have mentioned that to you in the first place."

"Well, you did and now you're stuck with it," I said savagely. "There's something rotten in the area of that dump. People are being born without souls. People are dying, too, if you'll remember the Thomas Brothers fire. You started me on this and now you won't give with what you know? That's—damnable."

"I have to pray you're wrong," Charlie answered. "But whether you are or not, I can't give you what you're asking. This whole matter is bigger than what you seem to grasp— bigger than I thought, too. If I could, I'd shut down your whole investigation."

This, from a high-powered EPA man? "Good God, Charlie? What are we talking about here, the Third Sorcerous War?"

"If we were, I couldn't tell you so," Kelly said. "Goodbye, David. I'm afraid you're on your own in this one." My imp stopped reproducing his imp's breathing; he'd hung up on me.

I don't know how long I stared at my own phone before I hung up, too. Jose Franco walked past my office door. I think he was just going to nod at me, the way he usually does, but he stopped in his tracks when he saw my face. "What's the matter, Dave?" he asked, real concern in his voice. He's a good guy, Jose is. "You look like you just saw your own ghost."

"Maybe I did," I said, which left him shaking his head.

Why in God's name was Charlie Kelly acting altogether too serious about a Third Sorcerous War? The first two were disasters beyond anything imaginable even in nightmares before this century. A third one? If mankind was stupid enough to start a Third Sorcerous War, we'd probably never have to worry about a fourth one, because nobody'd be left to fight it.

And Charlie wouldn't even tell me who the enemy was liable to be. You ever look back on your life and notice just how many sins you've committed to get where you are, how everything that always seemed solid all at once starts to crumble under your feet until you're peering straight down into the Pit? That was what I felt like after I got off the phone with Kelly. The hair stood up on the back of my neck. No wonder I'd alarmed Jose.

Afterwards, I needed to give myself a good hard shake before I went back to work. When you've spent a while contemplating Armageddon, environmental concerns don't look as big as they did. If the Third Sorcerous War comes along, there won't be any environment left to protect, anyhow.

I drowned my sorrows in a cup of coffee, wishing it were something stronger. Then, more or less by main force, I made myself call Legate Kawaguchi to find out how Erasmus was doing. People are like that: the world may be going to hell around them (and the Third Sorcerous War would be a reasonable approximation, believe me), but they try to keep their own little pieces of it tidy.

"Ah, Inspector Fisher," Kawaguchi said after I'd made it through the maze of constabulary operators to his phone. "I was going to phone you in the next few days. We expect that access spirit to become accessible to interrogation within that time frame."

"That's good," I said, both because I hoped I'd learn something that would help my case (and, presumably, Kawaguchi's) and because I was glad Erasmus would make it. "What other news do you have about the fire?"

"Investigations are continuing," he answered, which meant he had no news.

Or maybe it meant he just didn't feel like telling me anything. Constables are like that sometimes. I decided to give him a nudge, see if I could shake something loose: "Have your forensic sorcerers made any progress in analyzing those strange traces the thaumatech picked up at the scene, the ones the consecrated ground erased before she could fully get them into her spellchecker?"

"You have a retentive memory, Inspector." Kawaguchi did not make it sound like a compliment: more as if he'd hoped I'd forgotten. Yet another phone pause, this one, I suppose, while he figured out whether to try to lie to me. Interesting choice for him. Sure, I was a civilian, but a civilian who worked for a Confederal agency. If he did lie and I found out about it, my bosses could make things unpleasant for his bosses, who would make things unpleasant for him.

He finally said, "The traces remain vanishingly faint, but enhancement techniques seem to indicate some sorceries of Persian origin."

"Do they?" I said. Slow Jinn Fizz moved up a few notches on the suspect list. So did Bakhtiar's Precision Burins, an outfit I hadn't yet got around to visiting. I asked him, "What enhancement techniques do the Angels City constabulary use?" I hoped my own shop could learn something new and useful.

But he answered, "Nothing out of the ordinary, I'm afraid. We had our best results with an albite lens focusing the rays of the full moon on the spellchecker chamber that holds the memory microimps."

"Yes, that's pretty much standard," I agreed. Only a constable would call it albite; the more usual name is moonstone. Because it's opaque, a moonstone lens removes moonshine from moonbeams, thereby improving recollections.

"Is there anything else, Inspector Fisher?" Kawaguchi asked.

I wondered if I ought to tell him one of my superiors was afraid the case was connected with the Third Sorcerous War. He'd probably think I was moonstruck—or lunatic, if you prefer the Latin. I hoped he'd be right. Better that than Charlie being right. Besides, Kawaguchi had enough worries of his own; a constable's job is neither easy nor pleasant.

"Anything else?" the legate repeated, more sharply this time.

"No, not really. Thanks for your time. Please do keep me informed on how your investigation is going, and let me know the moment Erasmus becomes available for questioning."

"I will do that, Inspector. Good day to you."

The work I'd meant to do that morning took up the afternoon instead. I had to keep up with it somehow, which meant I didn't get out to Chocolate Weasel as I'd planned to do. I wouldn't manage to do it tomorrow, either, because I was going to take my little portable spellchecker over to the Corderos' house to see what it could find there. And after that, I figured Bakhtiar's Precision Burins had moved ahead of it on my list if Persian magic was involved in the Thomas Brothers fire.

People complain that bureaucracies never accomplish anything. I mean, *I* complain when a bureaucracy I'm not part of succumbs to inertia. Half the time, though, the problem is too few people trying to do too many things in not enough time. I felt like Sisyphus, except getting over to Chocolate Weasel was just one of the stones I had to try to shove to the top of the hill. I kept running back and forth between them, keeping them all from rolling down to the bottom again but not moving any up very far. And every so often, whether I got one of the old stones to the crest of the hill or not, new ones appeared.

All in all, the image was enough to get a man down on ancient Greek religion.

I shoved stones around till it was time to go home. After supper, I called Judy. One of the things that makes troubles smaller is talking about them. Actually, I suppose the troubles stay the same size, but when they're spread between two people they *seem* smaller. I told her about poor little Jesus Cordero, and also about what Charlie Kelly had had to say.

"Maybe one of these days Ramzan Durani can synthesize a soul for the little boy," she said. She has a knack for remembering names and other details that slip through my fingers like sand. Now she went on, "But this other . . . My God, David, was he serious?"

"Who, Charlie? He sure sounded that way to me. What really frosts me is knowing how much he knows that he's not telling."

"I understand," she said. "But what are we supposed to do while he's not telling? Just go on with our lives as if we didn't know anything was wrong? That's not just hard, that's impossible."

"I know, but what choice do we have?" I answered. "People have been doing it as long as there have been people: carrying on inside their own little circles and holding their affairs together as best they could no matter what was going on around them. If they didn't, I've got a feeling the world would have torn itself to pieces a long time ago."

"Maybe you're right," she said, and then, suddenly, "Come over, David, would you? I don't want to be alone, not tonight, not after what you just told me."

"Be there in half an hour," I promised.

I made it, too, with a good five minutes to spare. Judy lives in a flat down in Long Beach, in a neighborhood marginally better than mine. The Guardian at the outer entrance to her building knows me by now, so I didn't have any trouble getting in. Fair enough; I went there about as often as she came to see me.

I liked her place. It was in an older block of flats than mine, so it had occasional plumbing problems, no ice elemental connection for hot summer days, and a wheezy excuse for a salamander that couldn't keep the place warm in winter, but there were compensations. The main one, I think, was decently thick walls: you didn't find out everything your neighbors were up to as if you watched them in a crystal ball.

She'd lived there for five years, and the flat had the stamp of her personality on it. It was crammed with books, maybe even more than mine. The knickknacks (aside from the menorah and brass candlesticks for the Sabbath) were museum copies of Greek and Roman sorcerous apparatus, all mellow clay and greened bronze. The prints on the wall were by Arcimboldo—you know, the fellow who made portraits out of interlocked fish or fruit or imps. They're endlessly fascinating to look at, and you never can decide just how far out of his tree old Arcimboldo was.

If you think I'm building up to a tale of lurid lovemaking, I'm sorry—it wasn't like that. We hugged each other, she made some coffee, we talked later than we should have, and when we slept together, that's all we did: we slept together. If you're under twenty-five you probably won't believe me, but sometimes that's better—and more intimate, too—than twitches and moans. Not, believe me, that I have anything against twitches and moans, but to every thing its season.

My sleep season ended too soon the next morning; the horological demon in Judy's alarm clock bounced me out of her bed with a bloodcurdling ululation. I hurried back to my place (which luckily wasn't far out of my way), showered, changed clothes, grabbed a Danish and my portable spellchecker, and headed for the office.

What I had in mind was racing through business in the morning and heading up to the Corderos' house in the afternoon to take some readings with the spellchecker. That's what I ended up doing, too, but it wasn't as simple as I'd had in mind. Something large and unpleasant landed on my desk with a thud.

I don't quite mean that literally, but the report I was going to have to produce would be fat enough to thud down somewhere. I've mentioned that Angels City is in the middle of a drought. The note Bea passed to me explained that some sorcerers up in the north end of the Barony of Angels tried to bring rain with Chumash Indian charmstones, perhaps in the hope that native spirits would have more effect on the local weather than imported white man's magic.

They got nothing. I don't mean they didn't get rain. Nobody's been able to get much in the way of rain for Angels City the past few years. I mean they got nothing—no sign that the Powers linked to those charmstones were still there to be summoned. What Bea wanted me to do was determine whether the Chumash Powers were in fact extinct.

That's always a melancholy job. Extinction means something wonderful going out of the world forever, whether from This Side or the Other. The poor Chumash, though, have been so thoroughly dispossessed and assimilated over the last couple of hundred years that no one believes any more in the Powers they once revered. Not only does no one believe in them, hardly anybody even knows they exist. And Powers without believers will die. Even the great Pan is two thousand years dead now.

Heavens, before I could get started, I had to go to the reference library to look up Chumash charmstones and how they fit into the rest of the Indians' cult. I found out they were used not only for making rain, but also in war (they could make you invisible to arrows), in medicine, and in general sorcery. They tied in with other talismans—'atishwin, the Chumash called those—and with the Powers who helped the Chumash shamans. And now, by what Bea had passed to me, they were just little carved chunks of steatite, as inert as if they'd never had any magical intent at all.

I went up to Bea's office, shot the breeze with her secretary (Rose really runs that place; if she ever quit, we'd fall apart) until she got off the phone, then ducked in fast before it made noise again. "What's my priority on this Chumash thing?" I asked her. "The Devonshire project is taking up a lot of my time right now."

"I know," she answered. "It still comes first—it's active, while if the Chumash Powers really are extinct, there's no

hurry about saying so. You'll want to get a more formal investigation going to check that out one way or the other, have
the thaumaturges see if the Chumash gods of the Upper
World, the First People, or the *Nunashish* of the Lower
World are still accessible to invocation."

"You've been reading up on this," I said; up until a couple
of minutes before, I'd never heard of the dark, misshapen
Nunashish.

She grinned at me. "Of course I have. If I knew about
these spirits off the top of my head, they wouldn't be on the
edge of extinction, would they? If it turns out they haven't
gone over the edge, report back to me right away, because
we'll need to try to arrange a preservation scheme—assuming we can afford one."

Doing a cost-benefit analysis to figure out whether it's
worthwhile to save an endangered deity is so coldblooded
that it's one of my least favorite parts of the job. It is, unfortunately, also all too often necessary. As I noted when I saw
Matt Arnold's door Herm, maintaining a cult for a supernatural being who would otherwise be gone is expensive: it's
the Other Side's equivalent of a captive breeding program
for an animal that's vanished from the wild.

If the Chumash Powers were still alive, somebody—me,
most likely—would have to figure out their role in the local
thecosystem, and whether that role justified the money to
provide worshipers and whatever else they needed. I'd never
been part of the God Squad before. It's an awesome responsibility, when you think about it.

Bea must have seen the look on my face. "Don't get yourself in an uproar, David. The odds are that these Powers
have just faded away, like so many others the Indians rever-
enced before white folks—and black—settled here. If that's
so, all you'll have to do is write up the report. It's only if the
Nunashish and the rest are still around that you'll have any
bigger worries."

"I know that," I answered. "Actually, I hope they do survive. But if they do, and if they're very much
enfeebled—which they will be—"

"Yes, I know. Holding a Power's fate in your hands isn't

easy. In the old days, they were proud of ridding the world of gods in whom they didn't believe—some of the early Christian writings, the ones from the time of the Great Extinctions in Europe, will sicken you with their gloating. But our ideas are different now; we know everything has its place in Creation, to be preserved if possible."

"But to be the one who decides if it's possible, and then to have to live with myself afterwards . . . it won't be easy, Bea."

"If you wanted a job that was easy all the time, you wouldn't be here," she said. "Anything else? No? All right, thank you, David."

I went back to my office and made a couple of calls, got the ball rolling on the Chumash charmstones. Then I plowed through as much of the more routine stuff as I could before lunch. If I'd known how bad lunch was going to be, I'd have worked straight through it. The cafeteria must have assembled the unappetizing glop on my plate with help from the law of contagion: some time a long while ago, it might have been in contact with real food. Two crowns ninety-five shot to—well, you get the idea.

I slid down to my carpet with my spellchecker in my lap. My stomach made small unhappy noises. Hoping they wouldn't turn into large unhappy noises, I flew on up into St. Ferdinand's Valley. The brown dirt and yellow-brown dry brush of the pass were getting to look very familiar.

The Corderos lived in a neighborhood that had been upper middle class maybe thirty years before. A lot of the houses still looked pretty nice, but it wasn't upper middle class any more. Gang symbols and tags, mostly in Spanish, were scrawled on too many walls, sometimes on top of one another. And the houses, even the nice-looking ones, often held three, four, or more families, because that was the only way the new immigrants could afford to pay the rent.

The house the Corderos lived in was like that. Three women and a herd of kids not old enough for school watched me while I set up the spellchecker. All the men, including Ramón Cordero, were out working. Lupe held poor little Jesus and nursed him while she tried to keep track of a toddler who looked just like her.

One of the women—her name was Magdalena—spoke good English. She translated for me when I said, "First things first. Let me check that bottle of tonic you were telling me about, Mrs. Cordero."

Lupe Cordero rattled off something in Spanish. The woman who wasn't Magdalena disappeared into the back part of the house. She came back a minute later with a jar that had started out life holding tartar sauce. It was half full of a murky brown liquid. Lupe made a face. "Don' taste good," she said.

I actuated the spellchecker with Passover wine and a Hebrew blessing. My rite was close enough to what the women were used to—a Latin prayer and communion wine—that they didn't remark on it, not even to say I'd omitted the sign of the cross. I was almost disappointed. "*Soy judío*" is one of the Spanish phrases I do know.

I unscrewed the lid of the ex-tartar-sauce jar, sniffed the current contents myself. The brown liquid didn't smell like anything in particular. I reminded myself that Lupe had drunk it without ill effect, and that Father Flanagan had told me few *curanderos* trafficked in—or with—anything dangerous. That reminded me: I asked Lupe, "Want to tell me the name of the person you got this from?"

She shook her head. "Don' remember," she said stubbornly. I shrugged; I hadn't expected anything different.

I started to stick the spellchecker's probe right into the liquid, but the microimps inside the unit started screaming as soon as I got the end of the probe over the rim of the jar. The women exclaimed bilingually. I decided I'd better not put the probe in until I saw what the spellchecker was screaming about.

Words started showing up on the ground glass as the microimps tried to tell me what was wrong. They'd been programmed to write in what was mirror image for them, but they were so agitated that they kept forgetting. It didn't matter; I could follow either style well enough.

The ingredient listing came first: *octli* (maguey beer to you), ocelot blood, ferret flesh, dragon blood—I blinked a little at that one, but the Aztecans have dragons, too. Then the spellchecker's imps started writing UNIDENTIFIED—FORBIDDEN over and over and over. I'd never seen the spellchecker do that before. I never wanted to see it again, either.

"Gevalt," I muttered under my breath; sometimes English lacks the words you need. I almost wished Judaism had a convenient gesture like the sign of the cross. I could have used one just then. To say I was flummoxed is to put it mildly.

"Let's try it again," I said, as much to steady myself as for any other reason. I tried again, from square one, shutting down the spellchecker and reactivating it. You have to be careful if you do that more than once in a short time: the spirits inside can take on too many spirits from the wine and lose memory. But it did make them stop screaming.

This time I reversed the normal order and had them analyze the sorcerous component of the tonic, not the physical ingredients that went into making the complete magic. That's what I tried to do, at any rate. The screaming started again as soon as the probe got anywhere near the jar.

I looked at the ground glass to see what the microimps had to say. They expressed their opinion in two words: UNIDENTIFIED—FORBIDDEN. They wrote those two words until the whole screen was full, then started underlining them. Whatever had gone into that tonic, in analyzing it I'd sent a boy to do a man's, or maybe a giant's, job.

Even moving the probe away didn't calm the spellchecker imps. They stopped underlining only when I closed the jar as tight as I could. Even then, none of the usual commands or invocations would clear the ground glass or make them stop screaming. I had to shut down the spellchecker to get them to shut up.

"Mrs. Cordero, whatever is in this potion, it's very strong magic and very dark magic," I said. Magdalena translated for me. "My spellchecker won't even confront it, you see. I want two things from you, please." She nodded. I went on, "First, I want to take this jar to a proper thaumaturgical laboratory for full analysis."

"*Sí*, take it," she said.

"The other thing I want is the name of the *curandero* who sold it to you," I said. "Mrs. Cordero, this stuff is dangerous. Do you want another mother to have a baby born like Jesus?"

"*Madre de Dios*, no," she exclaimed.

"Good," I answered, more abstractedly than I should have. I was wondering if the hellbrew in the tartar-sauce jar had caused all the apsychic births around the Devonshire dump. If it had, then the biggest part of the case for leaks against the dump had just collapsed. But if the dump and everybody using it were innocent, who'd torched the Thomas Brothers monastery, and why? All at once, nothing made sense.

I pulled my attention back to the tacky little living room in which I stood (I'm sorry, but an image of the Virgin of Guadalupe, while undoubtedly effective as an apotropaic, is not to my mind a work of art if it's painted on black velvet in luridly phosphorescent colors). Lupe Cordero still hadn't said who the *curandero* was. I realized she was waiting to be coaxed. Okay, I'd coax her. "Please, Mrs. Cordero, this information is very important."

"You don' tell him who you hear it from?" she asked anxiously.

I hedged. "I'll try not to."

To my relief, that was good enough for her. "Okay," she said. "He call himself Cuauhtémoc Hernandez, and he have his house up near Van Nuys Boulevard and O'Melveny." I noted the irony of a *curandero* operating by a Dutch and Erse corner; Angels City is changing. Lupe went on, "His sign, it say *curandero* in letters red an' green."

"Thanks very much, Mrs. Cordero," I said, and meant every word of it. I wrote down what she'd told me so I wouldn't forget it, then left the house and started flying around looking for a public pay phone. I finally found one outside a liquor store whose front window said CERVEZA FRIA in letters three times the size of the ones that advertised COLD BEER.

I called the office from there, and got Rose. When I asked

to talk to Bea, she said, "I'm sorry, Dave, she's already on the phone with someone."

"Could you ask her to come out to your desk, please?" I said. "This is important."

One of Rose's many wonderful attributes is her almost occult sense of knowing when somebody really means something like that (and if there's a spell to produce the same effect, way too many secretaries have never heard of it). Half a minute later, Bea said, "What is it, David?" *It had better be interesting* lurked behind her words.

When I'd told her what the spellchecker had done with Lupe Cordero's potion, she sighed and said, "Well, you were right: that is important. Bring it in to the laboratory right away, David, and we'll see what really is in it. Then we and the constabulary will drop on Mr.—Hernandez, did you say his name was?—like a ton of bricks. Most of the time these *curanderos* are only guilty of venial sin, but desouling a baby isn't even slightly venial."

"If that's what did it," I said cautiously. "But yeah, I'm on my way. I'm just glad the lab survived last year's budget cuts."

"So am I," Bea answered.

Farming things out to private alchemists and wizards would have eaten up just as much budget as maintaining our own analysis unit: specialists, naturally, charge plenty for their expertise. You're not just paying for what they know now, but for what learning it cost them. And besides, this way we didn't have to stand in a queue in case we needed results in a hurry.

As soon as I got back to the Westwood Confederal building, I took the jar over to the lab. It's on the same floor as the rest of the EPA offices, but tucked into a corner and hedged around with protective charms not much different from the ones on the fence outside the Devonshire dump.

Our principal thaumaturgic analyst (bureaucratese for wizard, in case you're wondering) is a balding blond fellow named Michael (*not* Mike) Manstein. He's very good at what he does; he brings an Alemanic sense of precision and order to what's too often a chaotic art. That he makes me want to stand at attention and click my heels every time I go in to talk with him is by comparison a detail.

"Hello, David," he said, looking up from the table where he was inscribing a circle with his black-handled knife. "What can I do for you this afternoon?"

I gave him the tartar-sauce bottle and explained where I'd got it and how my spellchecker had reacted to it. His eyebrows came together as he listened; a little vertical crease appeared just above his nose. I finished, "So I'd like you to find out what really is in the jar here and what spells made it strong enough to set off my spellchecker like that. I may have to exorcise it before I can use it again."

"Interesting." Michael took the jar from me, wrapped it in a green silk cloth with several magical symbols inscribed on it in pigeon's blood. "When must you have results from the analysis?"

"Yesterday would be good," I said. He laughed the small, polite laugh of a man who not only doesn't have the best sense of humor ever hatched but also has been besieged by importunate clients more times than he cares to remember. I went on, "Seriously, if I can have this tomorrow some time, that would be great. The stuff is suspected of being involved in an apsychia case, and may be linked to several others up in the Valley."

"Ah, I see. This tells me what I need to set my priorities for the coming work." Michael Manstein is too compulsively precise to get sloppy with the language and say things like *prioritize*.

"That's nice," I said. Whatever his priorities were, the potion wasn't at the top of them. He went back to scribing his circle. I turned to go; trying to hurry Manstein is like trying to make the sun rise faster. Then I had an afterthought. "Whose sorcerer's tools do you use, Michael?"

He finished the circle before he answered; one thing at a time with Michael Manstein. "I order them from Bakhtiar's," he said at last. "They've always given me good results."

Back before the Industrial Revolution, a wizard had to be his own smith, his own woodworker, his own tanner. If he didn't make his instruments himself—sometimes right down to refining the ore from which a metal would be drawn—

they wouldn't be properly attuned to him and would give weak results or none at all.

Modern technology has changed all that. Correct application of the law of contagion allows thaumaturgical tools to keep the mystic links to their original manufacturer even when someone else uses them, while the law of similarity permits their attunement to any wizard because of his likeness to the mage who made them. Some firms take one approach, some the other, some seek to combine the two.

Michael asked, "Why do you want to know that?"

"Because I thought you used Bakhtiar's tools," I answered, "and because Bakhtiar's may be somehow connected to the jar of potion I just gave you. What I know is that Bakhtiar's dumps at Devonshire, and there may be an involvement between the Devonshire dump case and this stuff. It's a circumstantial link if it's there at all, but I figured you ought to know about it."

"You're right. Thank you," Manstein said. "I have a spare set my father brought with him when he came here from Alemania after the First Sorcerous War. I'll use that to make sure there's no conflict of sorcerous interest."

"Makes sense," I said. "And Michael—"

"Yes?"

"Be careful of what's in that jar. I have the bad feeling it's really vicious."

"I'm always careful," Manstein said.

The phone yelled at me. I felt like yelling right back. I'd spend most of the morning trying to put together a panel to investigate the thecological status of the Chumash Indian Powers, and I wasn't having much luck. Half the people I'd talked to seemed convinced in advance that the Powers were extinct and good riddance to them. If you listened to the other half, you'd move eight million people out of the Barony of Angels so the Powers could have free rein as they did in the days when the Chumash lived here.

"David Fisher, Environmental Perfection Agency."

It wasn't any of the thecologists, for which I heartily thanked God. It was Michael Manstein. He said, "David, could you come down to the laboratory, please? I'd like to discuss the specimen you brought me for analysis."

"Okay, if you want me to." As soon as I'd heard his voice, I'd picked up a leadstick and a pad of foolscap. "But can't you just tell me what's in it over the phone?"

"I'd really rather not," he said. Judging somebody's tone on the phone is always risky, and Michael wouldn't be anything but mild and serious even if the world started coming to an end around him. But I didn't think he sounded cheerful.

Some new safety symbols were up around the lab, but I didn't pay them any particular attention. Like any wizard worth his lab robe, Manstein was always fiddling with his protective setup. Technology changes all the time; if you don't keep up, it's your soul you're risking. Michael Manstein wasn't a man to take risks he could avoid.

"What do you have for me?" I asked as I came through the door. He'd arranged more amulets inside the lab, too; a lot of them featured the feathered serpent. I made the connection. "Is it as bad as that?"

He stared at me. His eyes had a slightly unfocused look I'd never seen in them before, as if he'd gone fishing for minnows and hooked the Midgard Serpent. On his lab table stood the ex-tartar-sauce jar I'd given him. Around it was scribed a sevenfold circle. Let me put it like this: they only protect the intercontinental megasalamander launch sites with eight. It wasn't "as bad as that," it was worse.

He said, "David, I have been a practicing thaumaturge for twenty-seven years now." Utterly characteristic of him to be exact; had it been me, I'd've said something like *going on thirty*. He went on, "In that entire period, I do not believe I have ever seen an abomination of this magnitude."

"Enough to cause apsychia in a fetus?" I asked.

"I'm surprised it didn't desoul the mother," he answered. From anyone else, that would have been exaggeration for conversational effect. Michael doesn't talk that way. He handed me a sheet of parchment. "Here are the preliminary results of the analysis."

My eyes swept down the list. For a few seconds, they

didn't believe what they were seeing, just as at first you refuse to draw meaning from pictures of camp survivors—and camp victims—of the Second Sorcerous War. Some horrors are too big to take in all at once.

I went back for a second look. The words, curse them, did not change. I made my mouth utter them: "Human blood, Michael? Flayed human skin? Are you sure your techniques distinguish between the substitute and the real thing? Maybe it was a substitute made through contagion rather than similarity?" That would be bad enough, but— I was grasping at straws and I knew it.

But Manstein shook his head. "Probability zero, I'm afraid. I hoped the same thing, but I didn't just use sorcerous tests: I also employed mechanical forensic analysis. There can be no doubt of the actual human component of this elixir."

I gulped. What he'd just told me meant that Lupe Cordero, a very nice girl, was also an unwitting cannibal. I wondered how anybody was supposed to break that to her. Poor kid—all she'd wanted to do was keep her breakfast down. As if she didn't have troubles enough.

I looked at the thaumaturgical column on the parchment. Most of it was innocuous, even beneficial: Manstein had found invocations of the Virgin, the Son (I remembered the name of Lupe's son), several saints from Aztecia, a couple of minor demons related (his neatly printed note said) to childbirth. But there in the middle of them, standing out like a dragon in a fairy ring: "Huitzilopochtli," I said.

"Yes." Michael's understated agreement held a world of meaning.

Why, I wondered, couldn't the Aztecian war god have been teetering on the edge of extinction? No one, not even the sort of people who march to save Medvamps, would have shed a tear to see him leave the Other Side for wherever gods go when they die. His influence on This Side has always been baleful, his power fueled by hearts ripped from human victims. What maniac, I wondered, had imagined he should be summoned to strengthen a potion that exalted life, not gore?

But I knew the answer to that: Cuauhtémoc Hernandez. I

must have said the name out loud, for one of Michael Manstein's butter-colored eyebrows rose an eighth of an inch or so. "The *curandero* who made this stuff," I explained.

"Ah," Michael said. The eyebrow went down.

"Have you called the constabulary about this yet?" I asked.

"No; I thought it appropriate that you be the first to know."

"Thanks." I added, "Thanks twice, in fact. I don't think I'll eat any lunch today, so my waistline thanks you, too."

"Heh, heh," he said, just like that. I'm afraid he really is as straitlaced as that makes him sound.

"We're going to be involved in nailing this *curandero* along with the constables," I said. "I don't remember the last time anything so nasty got loose in the environment, and God only knows how many jars are still sitting on shelves in the nostrums cabinet or next to the sink. If we're real lucky, Hernandez will have kept records on the women he's sold it to so he can try and poison them again with something else. Odds are, though, we'll have to spread the word through the dailies and the churches."

"Hernandez may not even be totally responsible," Manstein said.

"How's that?" I asked indignantly.

"The tests I performed seem to me to indicate that the mild beneficial influences in the potion were overlain on top of the already present summoning of Huitzilopochtli," he answered. "The *curandero* may not have been aware that the latter was present."

"If he didn't know it was there, then he's responsible for being a damned fool," I snapped, and I meant it literally. "He certainly shouldn't be allowed to run around loose practicing thaumaturgy and inflicting this garbage"—I pointed at the tartar-sauce jar—"on innocent, ignorant immigrant women."

"There I cannot disagree with you," Michael said. "Do you want to call the constabulary, or shall I?"

"I'll do it," I said after a few seconds' thought. "I'll want to fly up there with them and be in on the arrest, make sure however much of this potion Hernandez has is sealed and then properly disposed of." I wished Solomon had heard of Huitzilopochtli; that would have made the problem of sealing the vicious stuff simple. But however effective the great king's design is with jinni, baalim, and other Middle Eastern denizens of the Other Side, it's useless against New World Powers, except those largely subsumed into a Christian matrix. And Huitzilopochtli, as Manstein's analysis had shown all too clearly, still had a great deal of independent potency.

Then something else occurred to me: Hernandez's horrible nostrum might end up in the Devonshire toxic spell dump. Tasting the irony of that, I went back to my office and got on the phone.

The first constable I talked to was a fellow named Joaquin Garcia. *"Madre de Dios!"* he burst out when I told him what I'd run into. Being of Aztecan descent, he had a culturally ingrained understanding of just how nasty a power Huitzilopochtli was. I knew it in my head; he felt it in his gut. He bumped me up to his superior, a sublegate called Higgins, and he must have given him an earful, too, because Higgins was the soul of cooperation.

"We'll get going on a warrant for this right away, Inspector Fisher," he promised. "Any time we get a chance to put one like that out of business, we leap on it."

He didn't argue when I said I wanted to go along, either; sometimes constables get stuffy about things like that. I added, "Better make sure your people are well warded, Sublegate: with one potion like that around, who knows what else Hernandez has in there with him?"

"We'll send out the Special Wizards and Thaumaturges team," Higgins said. "If they can't handle it, nobody this side of D.St.C. can. I'll call you back as soon as we have the warrant. Thanks for passing on the information."

"My pleasure," I told him. "I want this guy shut down at least as much as you do."

After I got off the ether with Higgins, I went back through my files and found the names and addresses of the other three apsychic kids born near the Devonshire dump in the past year. Then I checked in the phone grimoire; two of the families were listed. I called both those houses and, by luck, got an answer each time. What I wanted to know was whether the mothers had bought any potions from Cuauhtémoc Hernandez.

Both women I talked to answered no. I thanked them and added the data to my notes, then spent a while scratching my head. The *curandero*'s nostrum was certainly vile enough to have caused Jesus Cordero to be born without a soul, but just because it could have didn't necessarily mean it had. I kicked myself for not doing a more thorough job around the Corderos' house, but I didn't kick too hard. When the microimps in your spellchecker start going berserk, you'd better pay attention to that.

More nearly routine stuff kept me busy the rest of the day. When Bea walked by my office door in the middle of the afternoon and saw me there, she raised an eyebrow and said, "I expected you'd be in the field now."

I'd hoped to get to Bakhtiar's Precision Burins myself, but it just wasn't working. I said, "I'll probably be out tomorrow or the next day," and explained what Manstein had found in the potion I'd brought back from Lupe Cordero's house.

"That's—revolting," she said. "You're right, we need to clamp down on that as hard as we can. With the enormous Aztecian population in Angels City, the last thing we need here is a large-scale flareup of Huitzilopochtlism."

"It would make worries over Medvamps rather small potatoes, wouldn't it?" I said.

"I do admire your talent for understatement, David." Bea headed on down the hall.

Understatement was an understatement. If Huitzilopochtli got established in Angels City, it wouldn't be fruit trees drained dry, it would be people. I thought about hearts torn out on secret altars, necromancy, ritual cannibalism a lot less refined than the genteel Christian variety.

I also thought about all the other bloodthirsty Powers that would be drawn to the area. The act of human sacrifice is so powerful a magical instrument that it reverberates through the Other Side. All sorts of hungry Things would head this way, wanting their share: "When the gods smelled the sweet savor, they gathered like flies above the sacrifice." What Utnapishtim told Gilgamesh five thousand years ago remains true today.

They say that's how the horror happened in Alemania. But the Leader didn't try to throw the Powers out. Oh, no. He welcomed them with open arms and fed them, I dare say, beyond their wildest dreams.

The whole world has seen what came of that. *Not here*, I thought. *Never again.*

Courts in Angels City open at half past nine. At exactly 9:37 the next morning (I asked my watch afterwards), I got a call from Sublegate Higgins. "We have the warrant," he said. It was so fast, I wondered if he'd used Maximum Ruhollah. Maybe not; he operated out of the St. Ferdinand's Valley substation, and he'd be sure to have a local judge up there under his spell. He went on, "We're moving out at ten-thirty. If you're not here by then, you'll be late."

"I'll be there," I said, and got off the phone. *Miserable cowboy*, I thought: everything had to be his way. But I headed for my carpet as fast as I could; when you're dealing with people like that, you don't want to give them any excuse to mess you up.

Just as well I did, too—I made it to the substation with only about three minutes to spare. Traffic up through the pass was just ghastly. Don't ask me how, but when a big longhaul transport carpet broke down and had to land, a unicorn got out of its cage. People on carpets and others riding pegasi were trying to herd it back to where it belonged, and weren't having much luck.

As my carpet crawled through the gawkers' block, I wondered if they'd have to go to a nunnery to find someone who could calm the beautiful beast. Given Angels City's reputation, they might have had a tough time finding a virgin outside of one. Catching the unicorn, thank God, was not my worry.

When I finally did get to the constabulary station, Higgins gave me a disapproving look so perfectly flinty he must have practiced it in the mirror. He introduced me to the SWAT team, who looked more like combat soldiers than highly trained mages. I nodded to the thaumatech. "We've met before."

"So we have." It was Bornholm. "You came up to the Thomas Brothers fire."

"That's right. I still envy you your spellchecker."

"Enough chitchat," Higgins said. "Let's fly."

I'd never ridden on a black-and-white carpet before. Let me tell you, those things are *hot*. As we shot up the flyways to the *curandero*'s place, I reflected that the sylphs in the constabulary carpet could have used a little discipline themselves. A couple of turns would have tossed me off on my ear if I hadn't been wearing my belt. But we got there in a hurry.

Hernandez's house was on O'Melveny, a couple of lots east of Van Nuys. I hadn't known whether he had a storefront for his death shop, but no, it was just a little old house with a hand-lettered sign—in green and red, as Lupe Cordero had told me—that said CURANDERO nailed onto the front porch.

Watching the SWAT team operate was something else, too. Police carpets aren't bound by the governing spells that restrict ordinary vehicles to their flyways. The mages drew an aerial ward circle around Hernandez's establishment from above before anybody landed. Whatever he had in there, they weren't about to give him a chance to use it. Constables don't live to enjoy their grandchildren by taking risks they don't have to.

Sublegate Higgins used an insulated umbrella (same principle as the footbridge at the Devonshire dump, but applied upside down) to penetrate the circle. With him came four of the SWAT team wizards, Bornholm the thaumatech with her fancy spellchecker, and, bringing up the rear, yours truly. All the firepower that preceded me—the constables were armed for any sort of combat, physical as well as magical—made me wish I was one of the mild-mannered bureaucrats the public imagines all government workers to be; I wouldn't have minded falling asleep at my desk just then.

Bornholm said, "The spellchecker's already sniffing something nasty up ahead."

Higgins rapped on the door. Now the boys from the SWAT team stood on either side of him, ready to kick it down. But it opened. I don't know what I'd expected Cuauhtémoc Hernandez to look like, but an Aztecan version of your well-loved grandfather wasn't it. He had white hair, spectacles, and, until he took in the crowd on his front porch, a very pleasant expression.

That faded in a hurry, to be replaced by bewilderment. "What you want?" he asked in accented English.

"You are Cuauhtémoc Hernandez, the *curandero*?" Higgins said formally.

"*Sí*, but—" The old man smiled. "You need what I got, *señor*? Maybe you have trouble keeping your woman happy?"

From the way the back of Higgins' neck went purple and then white, maybe he did have trouble keeping his woman happy. But he was a professional; his voice didn't change as he went on, "Mr. Hernandez, I have here a warrant permitting the Angels City Constabulary to search these premises for substances contravening various sections of city, provincial, and Confederal ordinances dealing with controlled sorcerous materials, and another warrant for your arrest on a charge of dispensing such materials. You are under arrest, sir. Anything you say may be used against you."

Hernandez stared as if he couldn't believe his ears. "*Señor*, you must be mistaken," he said with considerable dignity. "I am just a *curandero*; I don't hardly do no magic worth the name."

"Did you sell a potion to a pregnant woman named Lupe Cordero a few months ago?" I asked: "One that was supposed to fight morning sickness and keep the baby healthy?"

"I sell lots of these potions," he said, shrugging. "It could be."

"Lupe Cordero's baby was born without a soul," I told him.

He went pale under his swarthy skin; had he started off fair, he would have ended up the color of his shining hair. He crossed himself violently. "No!" he cried. "It cannot be!"

"I'm afraid it is, Mr. Hernandez," I said, remembering Michael Manstein's speculation that the *curandero* might not even know what all was going into his nostrums. I went on, "Sorcerous analysis of your potion shows that part of its power comes from ingredients and spells consecrated to Huitzilopochtli."

Like any Aztecans, he knew of the gods his people had worshiped before the Spanish came to the New World. He got paler still; he reminded me of a cup of coffee into which you kept pouring more cream. "In the name of the Father, the Son, and the Holy Spirit, *señor*, I did not use this, this poison of blood."

"But it was there," I said.

"It's still there," Bornholm the thaumatech added. "I can detect it inside the house. Nasty stuff."

"Stand aside, Mr. Hernandez," Higgins said in a voice like doom. The *curandero* stood aside, as if caught in a nightmare from which he couldn't wake up. One of the fellows from the SWAT team took charge of him. The rest of us walked past them into the house.

It was none too neat in there; my guess was that he lived alone. A black-framed picture of a gray-haired woman on the mantle put more force behind the guess.

If he followed Huitzilopochtli, he sure didn't let it show. The front room had enough garish Catholic images to stock a couple of churches, assuming you put quality ahead of quantity. Candles flickered in front of a carved wooden statuette of the Virgin. I glanced at Bornholm. She nodded; the little shrine was what it appeared to be.

One of the bedrooms was messy; it got a lot messier after the boys from the SWAT team finished trashing it. The kitchen was pretty bad, too: Hernandez was not what you'd call the neat kind of widower. The SWAT team started in there as soon as they were done with the bedroom.

What had been the den was the *curandero*'s laboratory these days. A lot of the things in there were about what you'd expect to find in an Aztecian healer's workroom: *peyotl* mushrooms (few more effective aids in reaching the Other

Side), bark of the *oloiuhqu* plant (which has similar effects but isn't as potent: it's related to jimsonweed), a potion of *xiuh-amolli* root and dog urine that was supposed to prevent hair loss. Personally, I'd rather be bald.

Hernandez had had his triumphs, too: a glass bowl held dozens of what looked like tiny obsidian arrow points. Either they were a fraud to impress his patients or he'd been pretty good at curing elf-shot (from which the Aztecans suffer as badly as the Alemans, although Alemanian elves generally make their arrowheads out of flint).

We also found an infusion for invoking Tlazol-teteo, the demon of desire: not, apparently, to provoke lust, but rather to put it down. The infusion had a label written in Spainish on it. Bornholm the thaumatech translated it for us: " 'To be used together with a hot steam bath.' " She laughed. "I wouldn't be horny after a steam bath anyhow, I don't think."

If that had been all the curandero was up to, the visit by the SWAT team would have been a waste of taxpayers' hard-earned crowns. But it wasn't. Bornholm went over to a table in one corner of the room. She looked at her spellchecker in growing concern. "It's here somewhere, in amongst this gynecological stuff," she muttered.

Again, a lot of the stuff you could find at any *curandero's*: leaves for rubbing against a new mother's back to relive afterpangs, herbs to stimulate milk in women with new babies, a douche of *ayo nelhuatl* herb and eagle dung for pregnant women: all more or less harmless. But with them—

"Bingo!" Bornholm said when she opened a jar of clear liquid. I already knew her spellchecker was more sensitive and powerful than mine; now she showed that, being a constabulary model, it was also better protected against malign influences. Her face twisted as she read from the ground glass: "The microimps are reporting human blood and flayed human skin, all right. Disgusting."

"Bring Hernandez in here," Sublegate Higgins ordered. As soon as a couple of fellows from the SWAT team had done so, Higgins pointed at the jar and said, "What's in there, you?"

"In that jar?" Hernandez said. "Is ferret blood and a little bit dragon's blood. Is for mostly the ladies who are going to have babies. They get the—" He ran out of English and said something in Spainish.

"Hemorrhoids," Bornholm translated. "Yeah, I've heard of that one." She gave the *curandero* a look on whose receiving end I wouldn't have wanted to be. "Brew this up yourself, did you?"

"No, no." Hernandez shook his head vehemently. "Dragon blood is *muy caro*—very expensive. I buy this mix from another man—he say he is a *curandero*, too—at one of the, how you say, swap meets they have here. He give me good price, better than I get from anybody else ever."

"I believe that," I told him. "The reason you got such a good price is that it's not what he told you it was. Tell us about this fellow. Is he young? Old? Does he come to the swap meets often?"

You can find just about anything at a swap meet, and cheap. Sometimes it's even what the dealer says it is. But a lot of the time the fairy gold ring you got will turn to brass or lead in a few days, the horological demon in your watch will go dormant or escape—or what you think is medicine will turn out to be poison. The constabulary and the EPA do their best to keep the meets honest, but it's another case of not enough men spread way too thin.

Hernandez said, "He calls himself Jose. He's not young, not old. Just a man. I see him a few times. He is not regular there."

Sublegate Higgins and I looked at each other. He looked disgusted. I didn't blame him. An ordinary guy named Jose who showed up at swap meets when he felt like it . . . what were the odds of dropping on him? About the same as the odds of the High Priest in Jerusalem turning Hindu.

That's what I thought, anyhow. But Bornholm said, "If we can put a spellchecker at the dealers' gates at a few of these places, I'll bet they'll pick this stuff up—it's that strong. I'll work weekends without overtime to try, and I'll be shocked if some other thaumatechs don't say the same thing. Everybody knows about Huitzilopochtli; no one wants him loose here."

Greater love hath no public servant than volunteering for

extra work with no extra pay. Folks who carp about the constabulary and about bureaucracy in general have a way of forgetting people like Bornholm, and they shouldn't, because there are quite a few of them.

I said, "If you'll lend me one of these fancy spellcheckers, I'll take a Sunday shift myself. I know a lot of people would rather worship than work then, but that's not a problem for me."

"I think I'll take you up on that," Higgins said after a few seconds' thought. I'd figured he would; the constabulary doesn't draw a whole lot of Jews. I wrote down my home phone number and gave it to him. "You'll hear from me," he promised.

"I hope I do." I have to confess: I had an ulterior motive, or at least part of one. The dealers at a swap meet get in early, so they can set up. I figured I'd bring Judy along, and after we were done with the checking (assuming we didn't find anything), we could spend the rest of the day shopping. Like I said, you can find just about anything at a swap meet.

V

A couple of days after we put Cuauhtémoc Hernandez out of business, Sublegate Higgins did indeed call me to set up Sunday surveillance at one of the Valley swap meets. That evening, I called Judy to see if she could come along with me. As I'd hoped, she could. After we'd made the date, we kept on talking about the whole expanding case for a while.

I was saying, "If Hernandez can show he gave Lupe Cordero that vile potion out of ignorance rather than malice, he'll get a lighter sentence than he would otherwise."

"I don't think ignorance is a proper defense in case like that," Judy said. "If a *curandero* doesn't know what he's doing, he has no business trying to do it." Dealing with grimoires every day, she takes an exacting view of magic and its abuses.

"I'm not sure I agree with you," I said. "Intent counts for a great deal in sorcery. It—" I heard a noise from the front part of the flat and broke off. "Listen, let me call you back. I think somebody's at the door."

I went out to see who it was: most likely one of my neighbors wanting to borrow the proverbial cup of sugar, I figured. But somebody wasn't at the door, he was already inside, sitting on a living room chair. I could still see the chair through him, too, so it was somedisembody.

"How'd you get in here?" I demanded; as I may have said, I have more than the usual line of home security cantrips. I gave fair warning: "I forbid thee, spirit, in the name of God—Adonai, Elohim, Jehovah—to enter within this house. Depart now, lest I smite thee with the consecrated blasting rod of power." You don't (or you'd better not) bluff when you say you're packing a rod; mine was in the hall closet behind me.

But the spirit didn't move. Calm as could be, he said, "I think you'll want to reconsider that." He traced a glowing symbol in the air.

If you've ever been to a light-and-magic thrillshow, you probably think you know that symbol. As a matter of fact, the one you think you know isn't the genuine article: close, but not quite. Only specially authorized beings may sketch the true symbol and have it take fire for them. I happen to know the difference. My eyes got wide. An ordinary Joe like me never expects to meet a real spook from Central Intelligence.

"What do you want with me?" I asked hoarsely.

The CI spook looked me over. "We take an interest in Huitzilopochtli," he said. "Maybe you'll tell me what you know about the recent manifestation you uncovered."

So I told him. And as I talked, I found myself wondering just what the devil I was getting into. Every step into the toxic spell dump case seemed to drag me deeper into a polluted ooze from which I feared I'd be lucky to escape with my soul intact.

After I was through, the spook sat there for quite a while without saying anything. I watched him, I watched the chair through him, and I tried to figure out how the puzzle pieces fit together. Evidently my visitor from Central Intelligence was doing the same thing, because he finally said, "In your opinion, what, if anything, is the relationship between the various elements you have outlined: the leaking spell dump, the monastery arson, the possibilities inherent in the Garuda Bird project, the decline of the local Powers, and this trouble with the *curandero* and his potions?"

"I didn't think there was any connection between the Chumash and the rest of the mess," I exclaimed; that hadn't even occurred to me. "As for the other things, I'm still digging, and so is the Angels City constabulary. If you want my gut feeling, I think some of the other things will prove tied together, but I don't see how right now—and I don't have any sort of evidence to back me up."

"Never underestimate the value of gut feelings," the spook said seriously. "You ignore them at your peril. The finding at Central Intelligence is essentially the same as yours; otherwise they would not have sent out a spectral operative"—that's spook-talk for spook—"to bring an overview back to D.St.C."

Etheric transport is of course a lot quicker than the fastest carpet: the spook could just cut directly through the Other Side from the District of St. Columba and back, a privilege denied to all mere mortals save a handful of saints, dervishes, and boddhisatvas, none of whom, for various good reasons, was likely to be in the employ of Central Intelligence.

I said, "Since you've come crosscountry to interview me"—that seemed a politer phrase than *interrogate me*— "maybe you'll tell me something, too." When the spook didn't say no, I went on, "Is this case somehow connected with worries about the Third Sorcerous War?"

The spook got up from the chair, took a couple of steps toward me. "How did you make that connection?"

His voice was quiet, and cold as hemlock moving up toward the heart. He took another step in my direction. I don't have a big front room; he was already halfway across it. Three more steps and he could do— I didn't know what, but I'd read enough spy thrillers to make some guesses: reach inside my head and pinch off an artery, maybe. Unless a good forensic sorcerer helped do my autopsy, I'd go into the Thomas Brothers' demographic records as just another case of apoplexy, younger than most.

I skipped backward, yanked open the closet door, whipped out the blasting rod, and pointed it at the spook's midsection. "Back off!" I told him. "This rod is primed and ready—all I have to do is say the Word and you're cooked." Of course, my flat would be cooked, too; a rod operates on This Side as well as the Other. But I figured I had a better chance of escaping from a burning flat than from a CI spook.

He stood very still. He didn't come forward, but he didn't move back, not even when I thrust the rod out toward him. As he had before, he said, "I think you'll want to reconsider that. Unless you're packing something very much out of the ordinary, you'll hurt your books and furniture much more than me."

I knew the military had developed some high-level protection for their own spectral operatives; it seemed reasonable that a Central Intelligence spook would enjoy the same shielding. Come to that, some of the goetic technology has trickled down to the Underworld, which makes constables unhappy. On the other hand—

"This is a Mage Abramelin *Magen David* Special," I said. "I don't care how well you're warded against Christian or Muslim magic: this is the fire that dealt with Sodom and Gomorrah."

Now the spook backed up. Being transparent, his features were hard to make out, but I thought he looked thoughtful. "You could be bluffing," he said.

"So could you."

"Impasse." He went back to the chair, sat down again. I lowered the rod, but I didn't let go of it. The spook said, "Since we are uncertain of each other's powers, shall we proceed as if the recent unpleasantness had not taken place? Let me ask you again, with no threat intended or implied, why you believe this case my be connected to national security issues."

"Well, for one thing, why would you have walked through my door if it weren't?" I said.

The spook grimaced mistily. "Heisenberg's Thaumaturgic Principle: the mere act of observation magically affects that which is being observed. I console myself by remembering I'm not the first to fall victim to it, nor shall I be the last."

I didn't want any kind of spook, not even a philosophical one, in my front room. I went on, "If it makes you feel any better, I was worried about it before I ever set eyes on you. Too many big Powers involved: Beelzebub, the whole Persian mess I haven't got to the bottom of yet, now Huitzilopochtli." I didn't mention Charlie Kelly. I wasn't sure he deserved my loyalty, not any more, but he still had it.

"I must advise you to keep your suspicions to yourself," the spook said after a longish pause (*he might as well have been on the telephone* ran through my mind—one of those maddening bursts of irrelevance that will pop up no matter what you do). "Reaching the wrong ears, your prophecy could become self-fulfilling."

"It might help if you'd tell me which ears are the wrong ones." If I sounded plaintive, can you blame me?

He shook his murky head. "No, for two reasons. First, the information is classified and therefore not to be casually disseminated under any circumstances. And second, the more you know, the more apt you are to betray yourself to those who may have reason to be interested in your knowledge. Your basic assumption should be that no one may be privy to your speculations. If anyone with whom you come into contact shows undue interest in this area, summon me at once from Central Intelligence headquarters in D.St.C."

"How do I get hold of you in particular?" I asked—I mean, Central Intelligence has a lot of spooks on the payroll.

"My name is Legion," he said. "Henry Legion." He turned around, walked out through my chair and wall, and was gone.

Next day, thank God, was Friday. Traffic was light going in, as it often is on Friday mornings. I wasn't fooled; I knew I'd have the usual devilish time getting home. I tried not to think about that. Maybe, I told myself as I floated up the elevator shaft, I'd have myself a nice easy day, knock off early, and beat the weekend crunch on St. James' Freeway.

I walked into my office, took one look at the IN basket, and screamed. Sitting there was one of the ugliest Confederal forms ever designed. In big block letters, the cover said, REQUEST FOR ENVIRONMENTAL IMPACT REPORT. Slightly smaller letters added, PROPOSED IMPORTATION OF NEW SPECIES INTO BARONY OF ANGELS.

Having got the scream out of my system, I merely moaned as I sank into my chair. Who, I wondered, wanted to bring what into Angels City, and why? I just wished Huitzilopochtli had to fill out all the forms he'd need to establish himself here legally: we'd be free of him till Doomsday, or maybe twenty minutes longer.

Huitzilopochtli and his minions, unfortunately, didn't bother with forms. With trembling fingers, I picked up the report request and opened it. Somebody, it seemed, was proposing to schlep leprechauns over from the Auld Sod in hibernation, revive them once they got here, and establish a colony in Angels City.

At first glance it looked reasonable. We have a good number of Erse here, and a lot more who pretend they are when St. Padraig's Day rolls around. The leprechauns wouldn't have any trouble feeling at home in Angels City. Tracking the little critters to their pots of gold would help a few poor folk pay off the mortgage. The odds were about like winning the lottery, but who doesn't plunk down a few crowns on the lottery every now and again?

The way of environmental issues, though, is to get more complicated the longer you look at them. Figuring out how leprechauns would affect the local thecology wasn't going to be easy: tracing the interactions of beings from This Side is complicated enough, but when you start having Powers involved—

I moaned again, medium loud. One of the things I'd have to examine was the impact importing leprechauns would have on the Chumash Powers (assuming those weren't extinct). If the Chumash Powers were still around, hanging by a metaphorical fingernail, would bringing in leprechauns rob them of the tiny measure of devotion they needed to survive?

Bea walked by the open door just in time to hear that moan. She stuck her head into the office. "Why, David, whatever is the matter?" she asked, as if she didn't know.

"This," I said, pointing to the orange cover of the environmental impact report request. "Do you by any chance have a spell for making days forty-eight hours long so I can do everything I'm supposed to?"

"If I did, I'd use it myself," she said, "but I don't think God's been in the habit of holding back the sun since Joshua's day."

"This is going to be a bear to handle," I said, "especially on top of the Devonshire dump case and the Chumash extinction study—" St. Elmo's fire came on above my head, just like you see in the cartoons. "That's why you passed it on to me: so I could run it parallel to the Chumash project."

"That's right, David." She smiled sweetly. Bea isn't what you'd call pretty, but she can look almost angelic sometimes: being sure you're on the right path will do that for you, I guess. She went on, "I figured it would be better to have both of them in your hands than to make two people run back and forth checking with each other all the time and maybe working at cross purposes."

"Okay," I said; put that way, it made sense. Bea didn't get to be boss of my unit on the strength of an angelic smile; she has a head on her shoulders.

"The easiest way to handle the issue would be to work up two scenarios," she said: "one for the leprechauns' environmental effects without worrying about the Chumash powers, the other assuming those Powers do still manifest themselves here."

"Yeah, that makes sense." I scribbled a note on a scrap of foolscap on my desk. "Thanks, Bea."

"Any time," she said, sweetly still, and went off to inflict impossible amounts of work on someone else. To be fair, I have to admit she worked like a team of Percherons herself.

And she had put her finger on the most efficient way to handle the two studies side by side. They still wouldn't be easy or quick. I'd have to design simulations approximating the immediate effect of leprechauns on the thecology of Angels City with and without taking into account the Chumash Powers. Then an EPA wizard would animate the simulations and follow them under the crystal ball as far into the future as he could, noting changes every year or two until the images faded into uncertainty.

I'd have to justify every assumption I used in my initial simulations, too. The people who wanted to import leprechauns in carpetload lots and the folk who were convinced bringing in even one wee fellow would disrupt the local thecosystem would both be preparing their own models and running them under crystal balls. I'd need to demonstrate that mine were the most accurate representations of what was likely to happen.

All of which meant that I didn't get out to Bakhtiar's Precision Burins that afternoon, let alone Chocolate Weasel. And neither I nor anybody else did any fancy spellchecker sniffing around the Devonshire dump to try to find out just what (if anything) was leaking out.

People long for the days (or at least they say they do) when the king ruled instead of reigning, when the power of the barons was undiluted, when the prime minister kept quiet and did what he was told. They say the government's gotten too big, too complex.

Maybe they're right some of the time. I couldn't tell you for sure; politics is a brand of theology that never excited me. But I will tell you this: some important EPA work wasn't getting done because my department didn't have enough people to deal with projects as fast as they came up. Am I supposed to assume we're the only government outfit with that problem?

I know I worked overtime that night; I made it to the synagogue with bare minutes to spare before the rabbi started singing *L'khah dodi* to welcome in the Sabbath. Judy was sitting so close to the front on the women's side that she didn't even see me come in. I didn't manage to nod at her—let alone say hello—until the service was done.

"I was afraid you weren't coming," she said after we hugged.

"Work." I made it sound like the four-letter word it was. "Listen, have you eaten yet?" I grimaced when she nodded. "All right, you want to come along with me anyhow? I'll get you pie and coffee or something. I flew straight here from the office."

"Sure," she said. "Where do you want to go?"

We ended up at a Lenny's not far from the synagogue: a step up from the Golden Steeples, a step down from a real restaurant. I just wanted to feed my face—and they *do* have pretty fair pie.

And besides, I thought, remembering Henry Legion, it wasn't a place that was likely to have a Listener planted in it.

I hadn't called Judy back to tell her about the spook: by the time he got out of my flat, I was imagining people (and Things) listening to my phone calls. When I was through, she stared at me for a few seconds. Then she said, "You're not making that up," in a tone of voice that meant she'd been wondering right up to the end.

"Not a bit of it." I was a little hurt she had trouble believing me, but only a little, because I would have had trouble believing a story like that from anybody else. I mean, people don't just start having visits from spooks with threatening manners . . . except I did. I added, "From what he said, maybe I shouldn't be telling you any of this."

"David Fisher, if you even thought of keeping me in the dark, I'd show your picture to a mirror and then break the mirror," she said indignantly.

"I sort of expected as much," I said. "Thing is, from what Henry Legion said, it's liable to get dangerous."

"You didn't worry about that when you took me to the Thomas Brothers fire—"

I tried to interrupt: "I didn't take you there; you invited yourself."

She rode over me like the demon horses of the Wild Hunt. "—and you invited me to the swap meet with you day after tomorrow."

"I did that before the spook showed up," I muttered.

"Do you want me not to come?" she said. "Do you want me not to go back to your flat with you tonight? Do you want me not to bother going ahead with the arrangements for the wedding? Do you think I'm afraid? Don't you see I want to get to the bottom of this as badly as you do?"

I did the only thing I could possible do at that particular moment: I surrendered. I did it literally—I took a white handkerchief out of my pocket and waved it in the air between us. Judy, bless her, went from furious to giggling in the space of a second and a half. The waitress who'd been about to refill my coffee cup undoubtedly figured I'd gone out of my mind, but that was a small price to pay for keeping my fiancée happy.

Only trouble was, I was kind of afraid myself.

After sunset Saturday, I flew up to St. Ferdinand's Valley to pick up the heavy-duty constabulary spellchecker. An advantage of dealing with the constabulary is that they never close (given human nature, they'd better not). A disadvantage is that their parchmentwork is even more cumbersome than what the EPA uses (and if you didn't think that was possible, you're not the only one). By the language of their forms, they figured I'd abscond with the gadget the second their backs were turned unless I promised not to in writing ahead of time.

"Why don't you just lay a geas on me?" I asked sarcastically.

"Oh no, sir," said the clerk who kept shoving parchments at me. "That would be a violation of your rights." Apparently signing away my life wasn't.

Because I spent so long signing forms, I didn't get back to my place until going on ten. I lugged the spellchecker upstairs (it was nominally portable, but being part troll didn't hurt if you wanted to carry it more than a few feet), put it down so I could open the door, picked it up again with a grunt, and set it down in the middle of the front room.

"It's about time you got back," Judy said. "I was starting to worry about you."

"Forms," I said, and tried to make it sound as blasphemous as one of your more usual maledictions. I must have managed, because Judy laughed. I stretched. Something in my back went *pop*. It felt good. I suspected I'd lost about half an inch of height manhandling the spellchecker up to my flat. Maybe the *pop* meant I was getting it back again. I glared at the gadget. "Miserable thing."

"Twenty years ago, there weren't any portables," Judy reminded me. "Ten years ago, one with the capacity of the 'checker in your closet would have been bigger and heavier than this beast. Ten years from now, they'll probably pack even more microimps into a case you can carry around in your hip pocket."

"Too bad they haven't done it yet," I grumbled, and stretched some more.

Judy gave me a sidelong look. "Are you trying to tell me you want me to get on top tonight?"

"If that's what you'd like," I said. Far as I can see, it's wonderful either way, or any others your imagination conjures up.

She asked her watch what time it was. A tiny vertical frown line appeared between her eyes.

"Whatever we do, let's do it soon. We're going to have to get up early to make it to the Valley when the swap meet dealers start coming in."

So we did it soon, and it was fine. Judy is one of the most thoroughly pragmatic people I've ever met, but that doesn't keep her from being able to enjoy herself. It just means she makes sure she blocks out the time in which to enjoy herself.

My alarm clock woke us up much too early on an otherwise perfectly good Sunday morning, then laughed at us as we staggered around like a couple of the not-quite-living dead. I swore I'd have to get a new clock one day soon. I think I've said that before, but this time I really meant it.

I showered, then shaved while Judy went in after me. I was dressed by the time she came out, and fixed breakfast while she got that thick, wavy hair of hers dry. Scrambled eggs, toast, coffee—very basic. I threw the dishes in the sink for later, did my he-man weightlifting routine with the constabulary spellchecker, and off we went.

They hold the Sunday morning swap meet at the Mason

Fly-In. By night it's the biggest outdoor light-and-magic house in the Valley. By day it's just an enormous parking lot, so they get some extra use—and some extra crowns—out of the space.

Because we were good and early, we got to park close to the dealers' entrance, for which my overworked back was heartily grateful. The only people there were a couple of guards drinking coffee from a big jug. They looked like (and turned out to be) sunlighting off-duty constables.

Their names were Luke and Pete; I had trouble remembering which one was which. They both had the same short, dark hair, the same watchful eyes, the same big shoulders. They'd been told we were coming—somebody was on the ball there. They helped set up the spellchecker at the side of the gate, then poured more coffee for Judy and me. It was nice and hot; the jug must have had a tiny salamander in the base.

Some of the new storage vessels have a salamander on one side and an ice elemental on the other, so they can keep hot things hot and cold things cold. The only problem is, you don't want to drop them. If the partition between the two elementals breaks, they fight like cats and dogs.

I explained what I was looking for, and why. Both guards looked grim. Pete—or maybe it was Luke—said, "I hope you nail the bastard. I got three kids at home; I don't like thinking about anything like that happening to one of 'em."

Luke—or was it Pete?—pointed to the spellchecker and said, "I wish that thing could spot theft along with sorcery. It would sure make the department's life a lot easier."

Pete(?)—anyway, the other one—said, "I was at a briefing about theft detectors a couple of weeks ago. From what I heard, they operate by spotting guilt in a perpetrator's soul. Trouble is, most perpetrators don't feel enough guilt to set 'em off."

Judy said, "I understand they've recently identified the sorcerous component of intent. That may make some new kinds of anti-theft magic possible, provided the discrimination spell routines are sensitive enough to tell real larceny from a merchant's legitimate appetite for profit."

The guards had given her the usual looks a man gives an attractive woman. They were polite about it—nothing to bother her or me. Now they looked at her in a different way. I'd seen that happen a lot of times before, when people realized how sharp she was. I just smiled; I've known it for years.

"I sure hope they make something like that work," Pete said. "An awful lot of stuff you see here is stolen. Everybody knows it, but how do you prove it? If you could—"

"It'll happen," Judy said. "Not tomorrow, probably not the day after, either, but it'll happen. The principles are there. The gremlins are in engineering the actuating sorcery and the support systems."

"By God, I'd cheer for anything that made my job easier for once," Pete said.

"I'd cheer louder if I thought the techniques would just be used for tracking down thieves, but I've got a bad feeling they won't," Judy said. "The more effective magic becomes, the more the powers that be will use it to poke into ordinary people's lives. That's the way things seem to work, anyhow."

Pete and Luke represented the powers that be. Now they looked at each other, but neither of them said anything—I told you they were polite. For that matter, I'm part of the powers that be, too, but I stood with Judy on this one. People often don't realize how precious just being left alone is.

Even if the guards had decided to argue, we'd have been too busy to carry it very far: dealers started showing up. Pete and Luke checked their permits and made sure they'd paid for their stall space. Judy and I monitored the spellchecker as they came through the gateway. Some of them had their goods and stall setups on carts that they pushed or pulled, others piled them onto little carpets. That sort isn't flyway-legal, but it's awfully handy for hauling things around.

Quite a few dealers weren't happy about passing in front of a spellchecker. "What is this, the airport?" one of them grumbled.

So many dealers asked questions that my spiel got real smooth real fast. By the time the first four or five had gone by, I'd taken out my EPA sigil and set it on top of the spellchecker. I'd point to it and say, "We're looking for a very specific contaminant that we have reason to believe is being sold at swap meets, perhaps unwittingly. Nothing else we notice will get cited."

That probably wasn't quite true; if somebody'd come by with something as conspicuously illegal as a crate of black lotuses (better known as Kali's flowers), for instance, we wouldn't have let him take them in. But, to my relief, nothing like that happened, and the explanation kept the dealers from getting antsy.

Heavens, what a lot of stuff there was! Clothes, food, jewelry, nostrums (the microimps in the spellchecker seemed dubious a few times, but not dubious enough to make me stop anybody), ethernet receiver imp modules (I wondered how many of those were stolen), toys both mechanical and sorcerous, guitars, grimoires (Judy looked more than scornful at the quality)—I could go on for a lot longer.

The dealers were as varied as the stuff they sold: men, women, blonds, blacks, Aztecians, Persians, Hanese, Samoans, Indians in dhotis and saris, the other flavor Indians in feathers. I watched one bronze-skinned fellow slip out of his work shirt and put on a feather bonnet. He noticed me watching him, grinned kind of sheepishly. "Gotta look authentic if you want the people to buy your medicine, man," he said as he pushed his cart past me.

"Why not?" I answered agreeably. I glanced down at the spellchecker. From what the microimps had to say about them, the medicines weren't strong enough to be worth buying. I wondered if the alleged Indian was even as genuine as the stuff he sold.

The next fellows through were a pair of Aztecans. The had a rug with their stuff on it, and were chatting with each other in Spanish.

Judy gave me a hard shot in the ribs with her elbow. "Huh?" I said. Then I looked at the ground glass in the spellchecker. If they hadn't been trained to tell what they were sensing, the little imps would have run and hid. As it was— My stomach lurched when I saw what they reported. "Hold on there, you two," I said sharply.

They hadn't noticed me or the spellchecker. "What's the

matter?" one of them asked at the same time as the other one said, "Who are you?"

I picked up my sigil. "Environmental Perfection Agency," I said. "What do you have in those boxes?"

"Nostrums," one of them answered. "I got a friend, his brother-in-law hunts dragons down in Aztecia. He gets the blood, sells some to us, we dilute it, sell some here. Everybody makes some money."

He didn't sound like a crook, just a fellow doing a job. That's what he looked like, too, he and his friend both: ordinary guys in work shoes and jeans, cotton tunics and caps. The first thing you learn is, you can't tell by looking. Pete and Luke came alert. They didn't move toward us, not yet, but they quivered like lycanthropes just before the full moon rises.

"Which one of you is Jose?" Judy asked suddenly.

The one in the red cap jerked in surprise. "How'd you know that, lady?"

I unreeled the long probe from the spellchecker (actually, I wished I had one of those eleven-foot Rumanians). "I'm going to have to ask you to open one of those jars of dragon blood for me," I said.

Jose shrugged. "Sure. Why not?" He flipped the lid off one of the boxes. The jars inside looked like the ones Cuauhtémoc Hernandez kept in his workroom. Once upon a time, they'd held mayonnaise. Now . . . As soon as Jose unscrewed a top, I knew what they held: Judy, who was at the spellchecker, made a small, strangled noise. I'd told her what kind of stuff was in there, but hearing about it doesn't pack the same punch as seeing it in the ground glass.

I waved to Pete and Luke. They came trotting over. The fellow in the blue cap, who'd kept pretty quiet up till now, saw them and said, "What the hell's going on?"

"That's just what I want to know," I snapped. Considering what was in the jars, I meant it literally. I turned back to Jose. "You ever sell any of this, ah, 'dragon blood' to a *curandero* named Cuauhtémoc Hernandez?"

"I sell to lots of people, man," he answered. "They pay cash. I don't ask who they are. You know how that goes." He spread his hands and looked at me, one man of the world to another.

I knew how it went, all right. It meant he didn't pay taxes on the money he made at the swap meets. It's theoretically possible for the Crown to keep track of all the crowns in the Confederation. The financial wizards in the gray flannel suits back in D.St.C. would love to do it, too. Trouble is, of course, that the sorcery involved is so complex that it makes getting the Garuda Bird off the ground look like tossing a roc by comparison. And so people like Jose will go on cheating on what they owe, and people like you and me will end up footing the bill for them.

Except now Jose was facing some time at public expense of an altogether different sort. I said, "By what the spell-checker shows me, sir, there isn't any dragon blood in here. There's human blood, and human skin, and"—I looked back at Judy, who nodded—"a godawful strong stink of Huitz-ilopochtli."

Jose and blue-cap (I found out later his name was Car-los, so I'll call him that) looked at each other. If they weren't utterly appalled, they should have been making their money at the light-and-magic shows, not swap meets. They wouldn't have gotten it in cash, but they'd have made enough to keep from complaining.

As soon as he heard *Huitzilopochtli*, Pete (or maybe Luke) said, "You gentlemen are under arrest. Anything you say may be used against you."

The off-duty constable who hadn't arrested the nostrums peddlers—whichever one he was—headed for the office. "I'll call the station, get 'em to send a squad carpet over here."

As soon as he'd gone maybe twenty feet toward the door, Jose and Carlos tried to run for it. Being off duty, Pete car-ried only a club. He yanked it out and pounded after Jose. That left me with Carlos. "Be careful, Dave!" Judy yelled at my back. It was good advice. It would have been even better had I been in a position to take it.

Carlos was a little wiry guy, and shifty as a jackrabbit. But every one of my strides ate up twice as much ground as his.

He looked over his shoulder, saw I was gaining, and didn't watch where his feet were going. He fell splat on his face. I jumped on him.

His hand darted for one of the pockets in his jeans. I didn't know what he had in there: maybe something as simple as a knife, maybe a talisman like the ones at Loki, except with a demon ordered to attack whoever was bothering him. Whatever he had, I didn't care to find out the hard way, either. I grabbed his wrist and hung on for dear life.

"Don't be stupid," I panted. "You won't get away, and you will get yourself in more trouble."

"*Chinga tu madre*," he said: no doubt sincere, but less than germane. Then he tried to knee me in a place which would have interfered with my carrying out his instructions.

I managed to twist away so I took it in the side of the hip. It still hurt, but not the way it would have. As if from very far away, I heard people shouting back and forth, the way they do when they have no idea what's going on and just get more confused trying to find out. Carlos took another shot at refaceting my family jewels.

Then, from right above us, somebody yelled, "Freeze, asshole!" Somewhere in his past, Carlos must have painfully found out what happened when you disobeyed that particular command. He went limp.

Very cautiously, I looked back over my shoulder. There was (I think) Luke with his club upraised to do some serious facial rearrangement on anybody who felt like arguing with him. "He's all yours," I croaked, and got to my feet.

I hadn't noticed till then that I'd torn my pants, ripped a chunk of hide off one knee, and scraped an elbow, too—not quite as bad. Things started to hurt, all at the same time. I felt shaky, the way you do in the first few seconds after a traffic accident.

Pete had hold of Jose. Luke was frisking Carlos: turned out he'd had a blade in his pocket, maybe two inches long. Not exactly a terror weapon, but not something I'd have wanted sliding along—or maybe between—my ribs.

Judy ran up. "Are you all right, Dave?"

"Yeah, I think so," I said, taking stock one piece at a time.

I hadn't been in a fight since I was in high school; I'd forgotten the way you could taste fear and fury in your mouth, the way even your sweat suddenly smelled different.

I'd sort of hoped she'd throw her arms around me and exclaim, "Oh, you wonderful man!" Something like that, anyhow. As I've remarked, however, Judy is a very practical person. She said, "You're lucky you weren't badly hurt, you know that?" So much for large dumb masculine hopes.

A little man with a big mustache burst out of the office Luke had been heading for when the fun and games started. By then Luke had Carlos handcuffed. He pointed to me and said, "Here, Iosef, fix this guy up, would you? Unless I miss my guess, he's been working harder than he's used to at the EPA."

Iosef looked at my elbow, my knee, and my pants. "You're right," he told Luke. His accent—seems everybody has an accent in Angels City these days—was one I couldn't place. He reached up, patted me on the shoulder. "You come with me, my friend. We fix you up."

I came with him. He fixed me up, all right. He sat me down in the office (an amazing collection of pictures of girls and succubi filled one wall; I was glad Judy hadn't come along, even if she wouldn't have done anything more than sniff), bustled out, and returned a couple of minutes later with a fellow who toted a black bag.

The doctor—his name was Mkhinvari—had the same odd accent as Iosef. He looked at my elbow, said, "Roll up your pants," looked at my knee. "Is not too bad," he said, which was about what I thought.

He cleaned the scrapes (though, being a doctor, he called them abrasions) with spirits, which hurt worse than getting them had. Then he touched each one with a bloodstone to make it stop oozing, slapped on a couple of bandages, and went his way.

Iosef said, "Now we fix trousers. You wait here." I dutifully waited there. This time he came back with a gray-haired woman. "This is Carlotta. She's best in the business."

Carlotta nodded to me, but she was more interested in my pants. She touched the two edges of the hole together, murmured under her breath. Yes, I know you'll say any tailor's shop has somebody who specializes in repairing rips. It's easy to apply the law of similarity because the torn material is in essence like the untorn cloth around it, and to use the law of contagion to spread that cloth over the area with which it was formerly in contact.

But on most repairs you'll be able to see, if you look closely, the seam between the real cloth and the whole cloth from which the fix was made. Not with Carlotta's work, though. As far as I could tell, the pants might never have been torn. I even got the crease back.

That left a fair-sized bloodstain. Carlotta turned to Iosef and said, "Shut the door, please." After he did, she reached into her sewing bag and pulled out a little nightbox, of the sort that are made so carefully no light can get in. When she opened it, a small pallid fuzzy creature crawled out. "Vampire hamster," he explained. "They are drawn to cloth and—well, you will see."

The vampster didn't like even the tiny bit of day sliding under the bottom of the door; it made a snuffly noise of complaint. Before Carlotta could tell him to, Iosef went over and shoved a throw rug into the crack. The vampster relaxed. Carefully—any undead, even a rodent, needs to be handled with respect—Carlotta picked it up by the scruff of the neck and set it on my pants leg.

I sat very still; I didn't want the creature going after blood I hadn't already spilled. But it was well trained. It sniffed around till it found the stain on my trousers, then stuck out a pale, pale tongue and began to lap the blood right out of the cloth. When it was finished, not a trace of the stain was left . . . and the vampire hamster's tongue had turned noticeably pinker as my blood began to enter its circulation.

When Carlotta plucked it off me, it wiggled and hissed; it was feeling frisky now. She plopped it back into the nightbox, closed the lid, and touched a crucifix to the latch so the vampster couldn't get out by itself.

My pants didn't even feel damp. I guess vampire hamsters don't have spit. And the stain was all gone. "Thanks very much," I said to Carlotta. "That's beautiful work."

"For a friend of Iosef's, it's a pleasure. Of course"—she waved at the wall of succubi and girls—"Iosef has lots of friends."

I'd have shriveled up and died (or at least looked for a nightbox to hide in) after a crack like that, but Iosef must have been shriven against embarrassment. "Oh, if only they were," he said, rumbling laughter. "I would die young, but I would die happy." He turned to me. "You are all right?"

"I am all right," I answered. "Thanks for taking care of me."

I went back outside, blinking against the daylight as if I were undead myself. The black-and-white constabulary carpet had just flown in. One of the constables (he looked just like Pete and Luke, except he was blond) took my statement. "You'll hear from us, Inspector Fisher," he promised.

"Good enough." I looked over to where his partner was transferring the vile potion from Jose and Carlos' rug to the squad carpet. "Handle that stuff with extreme respect. You don't want it spilling."

"So we've been warned." He nodded back toward Luke and Pete, then touched the brim of his cap. "God give you good day."

He went back to the carpet to keep an eye on Carlos and Jose. Judy walked over to me. She inspected the bandage on my elbow, then the knee of my trousers. She felt the material. I winced, anticipating she'd poke the raw meat under there, but she didn't. "That's a wonderful patch job," she said.

"Iosef has connections," I said. "I just wish people were as easy to repair as clothes." The elbow and knee were throbbing again.

Luke ambled up and said, "Now that we've dropped on the guys you were looking for, shall we let the rest of the dealers in without running 'em past the spellchecker?" He pointed outside the gates. Nobody had gone through since the dustup with Jose and Carlos started. Now they were lined up like carpets on St. James' Freeway on Friday night, and not moving much slower.

"Sure, go ahead," I told him. "Like you said, we caught

the people we wanted." Glad cries came from the dealers when Luke started waving them through. I stuck my head into Iosef's office and asked if I could store the spellchecker there so Judy and I could do some shopping. When he said yes, I cut across the incoming stream of dealers and lugged the gadget back across. I wondered for a moment if it would react to the pictures of succubi, but it didn't. Iosef sure seemed to, though.

Judy said, "I'm glad we caught them. Now we can enjoy our own Sunday knowing they won't be spreading their poisons to anyone else."

"That pair won't, anyhow," I agreed, but I wondered how much other contraband would get sold right here at this swap meet, and at all the others around Angels City. A lot, unless I missed my guess. I tried not to think about that.

The dealers who'd been delayed were all setting up their stalls in a tearing hurry. When you try to rush things, a lot of the time you end up doing them wrong. Some of the dealers seemed as if they were doing music hall comedy turns: poles and awnings and signs would go up, then a second later they'd fall down again. One guy had his sign fall over three times in a row. After the third time, he gave it a good kick. Maybe that knocked the gremlins loose, because on the fourth try it stayed where he put it.

A couple of minutes later—right at ten—I found out why the dealers were in such a frantic rush. The customer gates opened then, right on time, and never mind that the dealers had been delayed. Iosef was not about to waste a chance: if he'd held up the customers, some of them might have gotten miffed and gone home.

And customers he had aplenty: Jews, Persians, Hanese and Japanese, and Indians, none of whose Sabbath rituals were disturbed by getting there on Sunday and spending money. Along with them were a goodly—but not godly—number of folks I'd have guessed to be Christian, both of Aztecan descent and every other variety. Some people of any faith feel more attachment to money than to any other god.

It may seem crazy, but every once in a while I wish the

Confederation were a little less prosperous, a little less secure. In flush times, people think of themselves, and the devil with anybody and anything else. They sometimes need reminding that what's happening now isn't Forever.

Which probably sounds like sour grapes, since I was out there shopping right alongside everybody else. But you wouldn't—I don't think—have found me there on a Saturday.

Judy and I wandered up one asphalt aisle and down the next, pausing at one stall here, another one there. Judy picked up a green silk scarf that went well with her red-brown hair. I bought a new alarm clock; I was sick of the shrieking horror I had at home, and even sicker of it laughing at me. This one was made in Siam, with a native horological demon. It cost less than five crowns. If I didn't like it, I'd toss it, too, and try one more time.

We both got sausages on buns from a Persian fellow's pushcart. Given his own faith, he wasn't one who'd sell pork.

I think I mentioned that one of the dealers had brought in a load of grimoires. Getting a scarf or a clock at a place like that is one thing, but it never ceases to amaze me that people think you can acquire sorcerous skill and power on the cheap. As with anything important, you need to learn from the one who's best, not the one with the best price.

Naturally, Judy paused at the display. She flipped through a couple of volumes, turned away shaking her head. The fellow who was hawking them scowled in disappointment; he thought he'd found another sucker.

"That bad?" I asked.

"Worse," she said. "The fatter book there is one of those compendia of spells in the public domain, and they're in the public domain because they weren't very good to begin with. The other one, the one in the blue binding, is one of those teach-yourself-to-be-a-mage-in-three-weeks books. I spotted a couple of typos toward the end. They might be dangerous under other circumstances."

"Why not now?"

"Because ninety-nine people out of a hundred won't get far enough in the course to stumble across them and the odd one, the one who does stick to it, will have learned enough to spot them before he does something stupid."

"Okay, I see what you're saying. That makes sense."

But once she got rolling, Judy wasn't one who stopped easily: "The folks who buy those things are the same women who'll plunk down fifty crowns for a 'magic' cream to make their breasts bigger—or men who'll pay a couple of hundred for 'magic' to make something else bigger. The only magic there is the one that the people who sell this kind of junk have for spotting fools."

She didn't bother to keep her voice down; a couple of middle-aged ladies who'd been about to inspect the grimoires took off for another stall as if they'd been caught looking at something blasphemous. "Lady, please," whined the guy who was peddling the junk. "I'm trying to make a living."

"So why don't you try to make an honest one?" she said, but then she threw her hands in the air. "What's the use?"

I'd seen her in those moods before. The only thing to do is get her interested in something new. I said, "Look over there at the jewelry that woman is selling. It isn't something you see every day."

All I'd aimed at was distracting Judy, but by sheer luck I turned out to be right. Some of the pieces from the jeweler—TAMARISK'S GEMS, her sign said—were of the modern sort, clunky with crystals, but even those were in finer settings than you usually find at a fancy store, let alone a swap meet. And the rest—

Judy is enamored of things Greco-Roman. A lot of the necklaces, bracelets, rings, and other pieces were copies so skillful that, but for their obvious newness and their profusion, they might have been museum pieces. And Tamarisk, a sharp-faced brunette who wore her hair tied up in a kerchief—knew her business, too.

Her eyes lit up when Judy pointed at what looked to me like a gold safety pin and called it a fibula, and she practically glowed when Judy identified a little pendant head dangling from a necklace as a bulla. They lost me after that; as far as I knew, they might have been incanting when they started throwing around terms like *repoussé* and *lost wax*.

I saw how Judy's eye kept coming back to a Roman-style ring with an eagle in low relief on a wide, flat gold bezel. It was in profile; a tiny emerald highlighted its visible eye. Normally I would have said it was a man's ring . . . but Judy's last name is Adler, after all, and *Adler* means *eagle*.

In the most speculative voice I could come up with, I remarked, "You know, hon, I haven't found you an engagement ring yet."

Every once in a while, you say the right thing. Judy, as you will have gathered, is a steady, serious person—more so than I am, and I lean in that direction myself. Making her face light up as if the sun had just risen behind her eyes isn't easy. Watching it happen made me light up, too.

Then I got hugged, and then I got kissed, and all the while Tamarisk was just standing there, patient as the Sphinx, and I figure every smooch I got upped the asking price of that ring about another fifteen crowns, but so it goes—some things are more important than money. That's what I told myself, anyhow.

We haggled for a while; considering that Tamarisk knew she had me where she wanted me, she was more merciful than she might have been—but not much. When we finally agreed on a price, she said, "And how will you pay? Cash?"

"No; I don't like to carry that much on me. Do you take MasterImp?"

"Certainly, sir. I'd lose half my business if I didn't."

I dug into my hip pocket, pulled out my wallet and from it the card. Tamarisk took a receiver plate out from under her display table. When I was a kid, credit was a complicated business, full of solemn oaths and threats of vengeance from the Other Side on renegers and much default anyhow because so many people find gold and God easy words to confuse.

It's not that way any more. A lot of the mystique is gone, but so is a lot of the risk. Modern technology again: as with the burgeoning phone system, ectoplasmic cloning has made all the difference. I put my thumb on the card to show I was its rightful possessor. Tamarisk did the same with the receiver plate. Together we declared how many crowns we'd agreed to transfer from my account to hers.

The conjoined microimps in the card and the plate completed the circuit by etherically contacting the accounting spirits at my bank, which confirmed that I did have the crowns to transfer. As soon as the transaction was complete, the card started sliding around on the plate as if it were on a ouija board. I picked it up and stuck it back in my wallet.

Then, with Tamarisk smiling the smile of a businessperson who's just had a good day, I picked up the ring and set it on Judy's finger. Because I'd found the style a little masculine, I was afraid it would be big. Tamarisk said, "I'll size that for you if you need me to."

But Judy held up her hand and showed both of us that it fit well. She and I grinned, liking the omen. "It's wonderful," she said. "Thank you, David." I got kissed again, which couldn't help but improve things.

"I'm always glad to see my customers happy," Tamarisk said, beaming, "and I hope you won't take it amiss if I tell you I also do wedding rings."

"I think we may just make a note of that," I said in my most solemn voice as I pocketed one of her *cartes de visite*. Judy nodded. With a last backward look at the other lovelies on display, we wandered off to have a look at the rest of the swap meet."

Judy kept murmuring, "It's wonderful," over and over. She'd hold up her hand so the ring would sparkle in the sun and the little emerald catch fire as if it were the eye of a living bird.

I said, "First chance you get—maybe tomorrow evening—you ought to take it to a jeweler you trust. I know it looks good and I know Tamarisk seems fine, but I want to make sure you only have the best."

"I'll do that," she said, and then, a moment later, "or maybe I won't have to. We've got a constabulary-quality spellchecker sitting in the office waiting for us. If it won't tell us whether we've just bought fairy gold, what good is it?"

"True enough," I admitted. "And if anything is wrong—not that I think there will be—Mistress Tamarisk will have a visit from Pete and Luke when she sets up here next week."

"Which one of them is which?" Judy asked.

"Oh, good!" I exclaimed. "I'm not the only one who couldn't tell, then." And when somebody like Judy has trouble telling two people apart, you know there isn't much to choose between them.

Before long, we went back to the dealers' gate: after Tamarisk's stall, the rest of the meet was strictly a downhill slide. I manhandled the spellchecker out of Iosef's office, poured out a little wine to enspirit the microimps, and touched the probe to Judy's ring.

Physically it was gold and copper in a ration of three to one: it had an 18-karat stamp, and lived up to it. The little emerald was a real little emerald. That was plenty to satisfy me, but as long as the microimps were looking at the ring, I let them examine its magical component as well.

I wouldn't have been surprised if they'd drawn a blank: jewelry is a trade you can, if you so choose, carry on largely without sorcerous aid. But no—Tamarisk had worked a small spell of fidelity on it, by analogy with the legionary's faithfulness to his Eagle as a symbol of Rome. That just made me happier: what better enchantment to find on an engagement ring?

Judy was reading the ground glass upside down. When she saw that, she squeezed my hand, hard. I shut down the spellchecker, hauled it to my carpet, and took it back to the constabulary station. I got a round of applause when I brought it in. "Sign him up!" somebody shouted, which made me grin like a fool.

We flew back to my block of flats after that. When we got back up to my place . . . well, I won't say I got molested, because I didn't feel in the least that it was a molestation, but it was something on that order. Judy and I liked pleasing each other in lots of different ways, which also augured well for the days that would come after we stood under the *khuppah* together.

After Sunday, worse luck, comes Monday. With Monday, worse luck, would come the weekly office staff meeting. As if that weren't enough to start things off on the wrong foot, congealed was the only word that fit traffic on St. James'

Freeway. What with my weekend peregrinations, I was starting to think I lived on that miserable freeway. It's a curse of Angels City life.

When at last I got up to my desk, I discovered somebody had put a toy constabulary badge on top of the papers in my IN basket. "What's this about?" I said loudly, carrying the souvenir out into the hall.

Several people heard me squawk and stuck their heads of out their offices to see what was going on. "We didn't know till yesterday that we had a real live hero here in the office," Phyllis Kaminsky said. She batted her eyes at me in a way she'd evidently borrowed from the succubi she was trying to control. From her it came off as more sardonic than seductive.

"That's right," Jose Franco chimed in. "I wish my garlic-spraying program would get as much good ethernet publicity as Dave pulled in last night."

"Oh, God," I said, and meant every word of it. "What have they been saying about me?" I didn't really want to know. One more argument against having an ethernet receiver: that way you don't have to listen to what reporters do to things you were involved in.

"We heard what a brave fellow you were, breaking up this contraband ring and capturing the leader singlehanded," Martín Sandoval said. The graphic artist paused before he stuck the gaff in me: "So we all clubbed together to buy you that symbol of our appreciation."

I looked down at the little tin badge. If it cost half a crown, whoever bought it got cheated. "I do hope it won't bankrupt you generous people"

Bea swept into the office just then. "What won't bankrupt whom?" she asked, which meant everybody had to tell the story all over again. I resigned myself to getting ribbed worse than Adam until people got tired of the joke. Bea said, "I know a better way to commemorate the occasion: David can lead off at the meeting this morning."

"Thank you, Bea," I intoned. If she'd told me I could leave after I'd given my report, that would have been worthwhile. As it was, I figured I'd taken the early lead in the running for the dubious achievement of the week award.

I went back into my office and did as much as I could till half past nine, which was meeting time. Just to make sure we couldn't pretend to forget and so accomplish something worth doing before lunch, Rose called everyone to remind us all to come on up to Bea's office. Even Michael Manstein was there, looking out of place in his white lab robe among all the business clothes and Martin's casual getup (since he doesn't go out in the field, he can dress as he pleases, the lucky so and so).

"Good morning, everyone," Bea said when we'd all assembled, bright and not too eager, before her. "I think we'll begin with David this morning. By all accounts, he's had the most exciting week of any of us."

I flashed the little tin badge and growled, "Now listen up, everybody, or else."

Actually, my report went pretty well. Michael backed me up on the sorcerous details of the potion I'd found at Lupe Cordero's, and everyone looked suitably grim on hearing them. I told about the arrest of the *curandero* who'd sold Lupe the stuff, and about being lucky enough to come across Jose and Carlos on Sunday.

"Your diligence does you and the EPA credit, David," Bea said, which was enough of a brownie point to make me want to set out a bowl of milk.

The other nice thing about having been so busy with all that stuff was that I didn't get in trouble for the too numerous things I hadn't managed to accomplish during the week. The toxic spell dump investigation *per se* was stalled; I hadn't managed to get out to Bakhtiar's Precision Burins, let alone Chocolate Weasel or the light-and-magic outfits. I still didn't know whether the Chumash Powers were coming or going. And as for the leprechauns, well, the environmental impact survey hadn't started going anywhere, either.

All of which meant, of course, that for the next several days I'd be running around like acephalous poultry, trying to catch up on those projects and whatever else landed on me in the interim. Not a pleasant prospect to contemplate of a Monday morning.

Bea said, "Jose, you and Martín are going to report together, am I right?"

They did. Martn produced the mockup for a poster of an ugly little green fellow sinking his fangs into an orange. The text said, HE'S NOT YOUR FRIEND—DON'T GIVE HIM A RIDE in English and Spainish.

"That's very good," Bea said, "very good indeed. It ought to make a lot of people who have been raising the roof about garlic spraying see Medvamps in a whole new light. You can start reproducing it right away, as far as I'm concerned. Comments, anyone? Am I missing something?"

With a lot of bosses, you'd better not dislike something after they said they loved it. Bea, bless her, isn't like that. Michael Manstein stuck up his hand and said, "The poster does not accurately reflect the appearance of the Mediterranean fruit vampire."

He was right, of course. Medvamps (not that Michael would use such a colloquialism) are as pale as any other undead creatures, and the sap they suck from fruits and vegetables is commonly clear, too. But Bea said patiently, "We don't need to be precisely accurate here, Michael. We want to get across the notion that the Medvamp is a dangerous pest, not something that ought to survive and flourish in Angels City. Does the poster meet that objective?"

Manstein shrugged. "It should be obvious in any case." And it would be obvious, too, if everyone were as rational as Michael. The general run of people being what they are, though, rationality needs all the help it can get.

The poster was passed by acclamation and we went on to Phyllis. By then it was getting close to eleven o'clock, and my stomach was starting to rumble. But Phyllis had landed a project even uglier than my intertwined investigations of the Chumash Powers and the wisdom of naturalizing leprechauns: she'd started doing a study on the pros and cons of changing the way Angels City handles its sewage.

Not to put too fine a point on it, Angels City produces a whole lot of shit. For the last many years—Phyllis, who is a very thorough person, said how many, but I forget—we've used the demon Vepar to process all this waste. Vepar's provinces are the sea and putrefaction, so the arrangement has always seemed logical enough.

The trouble is, members of the Descending Hierarchy just aren't reliable. Lately, as the population of Angeles City has grown, so have the number of sewage spills and the number of days the water in St. Monica's Bay is too foul for swimming or fishing or anything else.

And so there's been some serious discussion of transferring the job to Poseidon. If anyone on the Other Side has a vested interest in keeping the ocean clean, he's the One. Not only that, he also has power over earthquakes. In Angels City, that matters. Having one Power in charge of both those aspects of local life might well save the taxpayer some crowns.

Or it might not. Poseidon's cult, like that of Hermes, is artificially maintained these days. Angels City would have to pay into the fund that municipalities and organizations which use the sea god's services have set up to provide for his worship. That wouldn't be cheap. Vepar, like any Judeo-Christian demon, has enough genuine believers to keep him active without any expense the city would have to assume.

Bea asked, "What communities are currently using Poseidon to handle their sewage, and what sort of results have they gotten?"

"There are several," Phyllis said. "The first one that occurs to me is Athenai/Piraievs over in Ellas—"

"Not a fair comparison," Michael Manstein put in. "In Ellas the god comes much closer to having a continuous tradition of worship than he would in Angels City, and is likely to be significantly more efficacious. I will be happy to provide documentation to support this assertion."

Phyllis glared at him; no doubt he'd just undercut the example she was going to use. But when Michael says a comparison isn't appropriate, he *will* have evidence to back him up. Fumbling a little, Phyllis talked about Carthage instead (I watched Michael stir in his seat, but he kept quiet).

The real trick, I gathered from what she had to say, was keeping Poseidon happy about getting his hands dirty, so to speak. Some Powers with artificially maintained cults are pathetically eager to do anything at all, as long as they keep their last handful of worshipers. Others have more pride. Poseidon seemed to be part of the second group.

"But he does do a satisfactory job when properly incentivized?" Bea persisted. Michael visibly flinched when he heard that, but again held his tongue. Bea *was* a bureaucrat, after all; every so often, she went and talked like one.

"That is my impression," Phyllis answered. "Let me remind you: if Vepar were perfectly reliable, we'd have no reason for contemplating a change. And there's the added benefit of increased earthquake protection."

"Or increased earthquake risk, if the deity is angered," Michael said. Phyllis glared at him again, but I think he was right to point out the problem. Environmental issues are the most complicated ones this side of theology, and reading the text of the world is often (though not always) more prone to ambiguity than interpreting a sacred scripture.

Bea said, "Thank you for the presentation, Phyllis. Do you think you'll be able to give a preliminary recommendation on whether to pursue making this change in, hmm, two weeks' time?"

"May I have three?" Phyllis asked.

Bea scribbled something on her calendar. "Three weeks it is." She looked around at the rest of us. "Does anyone have anything more?" I sat very still, willing silence on everybody around me. Sometimes that works and sometimes it doesn't. Today, to my vast relief, it did; nobody said anything. Bea looked around again, just in case she'd missed someone on her first check. Then she shrugged. "Thank you all." That was the signal for us to get up and head for the door as fast as we could without being out-and-out rude. "Oh, and David—" Bea called after me.

Caught! I turned around. "Yes?" I said, as innocently as I could.

"I do hope you'll have more progress to report on your other projects at our next meeting," Bea said.

"I'll do my best," I promised, thinking that if I had fewer projects I could get more done on each of them. I also made a note to myself, not for the first time, that Bea didn't miss much. And, I thought but didn't dare say, I could also get more done if I didn't have to spend close to half a day every week in staff meeting.

The papers on my desk were starting to create a rampart effect, as if I were going in for trench warfare, *à la* the First Sorcerous War. I was just getting ready for a serious assault on them when the phone delivered a sneak attack from the flank.

"Environmental Perfection Agency, David Fisher," I said, hoping the switching imps had misspelled and given me a wrong number.

But they hadn't. "Inspector Fisher? This is Legate Kawaguchi, of the Angels City Constabulary Department."

I sat up straighter. "What can I do for you, Legate?" I stopped feeling guilty about getting interrupted: after all, the call involved one of the other projects I was working on. Bea would be pleased.

"Can you come up to the Valley substation, please, Inspector?" Kawaguchi said. "The scriptorium spirit Erasmus now appears capable of communicating."

I wanted to whoop with glee, right in his ear. I don't know how I stopped myself. "I'm on my way, Legate," I chortled. The ramparts on my desk would undoubtedly get higher while I was out of the office. *So what?* I told myself: *this is more important.*

Which was true, but sooner or later I'd have to catch up with the other stuff anyhow. I tried not to think about that as I hurried toward the slide.

VI

My stomach was making little plaintive grumbles by the time I got up into St. Ferdinand's Valley. Even without too many addenda, Bea's meeting ran long, and Kawaguchi had called before I got a chance to think about lunch. I grabbed a dachshund sausage at the first mom-and-pop joint I came to once I got off the freeway, and I must confess that I walked into the constabulary substation smelling of mustard.

Some of the people who'd seen me on Sunday looked surprised to find me back again. "What is this, Fisher? You want to move in?" Bornholm the thaumatech called to me. Offhand, I couldn't think of a notion I liked less.

Legate Kawaguchi's office was a musty little cell, smaller than a monk would live in and messier than an abbot would tolerate. I'm not exaggerating; Brother Vahan was in there when I walked through the door and, by the look on his face, he would have given Kawaguchi a really nasty penance if he'd thought he could get away with it.

"How are you faring?" I asked him after we shook hands. "Did the cardinal ever grant that dispensation so your burned monks could get cosmetic sorcery?"

"No," he said. With that one word, his heavy face closed down completely, so that he looked like nothing so much as one of those alarmingly realistic portrait busts from Republican Rome. The St. Elmo's fire from the ceiling gleamed off his bare pate as if it were polished marble.

Kawaguchi said, "The scriptorium spirit—Erasmus—was more severely harmed in the fire than we realized. Even now, a couple of weeks after the arson was perpetrated, we've needed a team of specialists to establish contact with it. I was just explaining this to the abbot when you came in, Inspector Fisher."

"Please go on, then," I answered. "If I find myself lost, I hope you won't mind me interrupting with a question or two."

"Certainly," Kawaguchi said. "As I was telling Brother Vahan, Madame Ruth and Mr. Cholmondeley"—he pronounced it, correctly, as if it were spelled *Chumlee*—"combine to facilitate communication between This Side and the Other. She is a medium and he a channeler; by pooling their talents and infusing new technology into their work, they've achieved some remarkable results. We have every reason to hope for another success here today."

"Let us hope you are correct, Legate," Brother Vahan said, and I nodded, too.

"They are waiting for us in Interrogation Room Two," Kawaguchi said. "Nominally, since the scriptorium spirit is on the Other Side, it could be manifested anywhere. However, evoking it in an interrogation room will hopefully add to the weight of the questions being asked. And"—the legate coughed—"the chamber in question has more space available than this office, which might otherwise have been suitable."

"Take us to Interrogation Room Two, then," I said.

Brother Vahan got up from his chair. The fire and its aftermath had taken a lot out of him. His stride had been strong and vigorous, but now he walked like an old man, thinking about where he'd plant each foot before it came down.

Interrogation Room Two lay halfway down a long, gloomy hall that seemed especially designed to put the fear of God into miscreants brought there. Kawaguchi opened the door, waved Brother Vahan and me through ahead of him. Introductions took up the next couple of minutes.

Madame Ruth was a tall, swarthy woman with a gold-capped tooth. She was also enormously fat; her bright print dress would have been a tent on anyone else, but had to stretch to cover all of her. "Pleased t'meetchuz," she said. When she shook hands with me, she had a grip like a long-shoreman's.

Her partner Nigel Cholmondeley couldn't have been more different from her if he'd spent his whole life deliberately trying. He was as Britannic as his name: elegant accent; long, thin, red-cheeked face complete with a little brush of sandy mustache; old school cravat . . . Let me put it this way: if he'd been born under a caul, it would have been a tweed one.

Legate Kawaguchi said, "Before we begin, would you care to give the holy abbot and the inspector a notion of the techniques you will utilize?"

The large medium and the English channeler looked at each other for a moment before Cholmondeley said, "Allow me." Madame Ruth shrugged massively. I tried not to show how relieved I was; I'd sooner have listened to him than her any day.

He said, "While communication with the Other Side is as old as mankind, techniques have recently taken several steps forward. As you'll notice, much of the equipment we employ would have been unfamiliar to the practitioners of only a few decades ago."

He pointed to the battered table shoved off to one side of the interrogation chamber. On it were five of the strangest-looking helmets I'd ever seen. They looked as if they'd been made to cover the whole top of the head, from the middle of the nose on up. I didn't see any eyeholes for them, and they had long, blunt projections out from where your ears would go. With one on, you'd look something like an insect and something like a man who'd just had a length of tree trunk pounded in one ear and out the other.

After giving Brother Vahan and me a few seconds to examine those curious artifacts, Cholmondeley resumed: "By your expressions, gentlemen, I should venture to say this is your first experience with virtuous reality."

He waited again, maybe to let us deny it. If he'd kept on waiting for that, he'd have had a long wait.

He saw as much himself and smiled, exposing a formidable mouthful of yellowish teeth. "Virtuous reality, my friends, lets us simulate the best of the world; it creates a plane neither fully of This Side nor of the Other, whereon, for example, a wounded spirit may meet and communicate with us while not having to return fully to the locus of its misfortune."

"How do we go about reaching this, uh, virtuous reality?" I asked.

"Madame Ruth and I shall be your guides." Cholmondeley smiled again, even more toothily than before. "If you will just come over to the table there, sit around it, and place a helmet over your head—"

The prospect did not fill me with enthusiasm, but I went over to the table anyhow. As I sat down on one of the hard Constabulary Department chairs, Madame Ruth said, "Once you put on your helmet, take the hands of the people to either side of you. We'll need an accomplished circle to access virtuous reality."

I reached for the helmet nearest me. It was heavier than I'd expected; maybe the weight lay in those ridiculous earpieces. I slipped it on. It seemed to conform to my face. I'd expected to be blind; I hadn't expected to be deaf as well. But the helmet seemed to suck away all my senses, leaving me a void waiting to be filled.

Distantly, I remembered what Madame Ruth had told us to do. I was sitting between Brother Vahan and Nigel Cholmondeley. I made myself reach out to take their hands, though I could hardly tell if my own were moving.

I found Brother Vahan's hand first. His grip was warm and strong; it helped remind me I still needed to get hold of Cholmondeley. I fought against the apathy the helmet imposed on me. At last, after what seemed a very long time, my fingers brushed his. His bones were thin, delicate, almost birdlike; I was afraid I'd hurt him if I put any pressure on them.

Then I waited another long-seeming while. I'd expected things to start happening as soon as my hands joined my neighbors', but it didn't work that way. I still lingered, my senses vitiated by the helmet. After a while, I began to wonder whether I was still touching the abbot and the channeler. I thought so, but it was hard to be sure.

All at once, color and sound and touch and all my other senses came flooding back. I found out later that that was the instant in which the last two of us finally took each other's hands, completing the circle, as Madame Ruth had said. At the time, I was just relieved to return to . . . well, where had I returned to?

Wherever it was, it wasn't dingy old Interrogation Room Two. It was a garden, the most beautiful I'd ever seen. Colors seemed brighter than life, sounds clearer and sweeter, smells as sharp and informative as if they came through a cat's nose instead of my own.

"Welcome, friends, to the world of virtuous reality," Nigel Cholmondeley said. Suddenly I could see him, though he hadn't been there a moment before. He still looked like himself, but somehow he was handsome now instead of horsefaced.

"This will be a new experience for you, so look around," Madame Ruth chimed in. She too appeared when she spoke. The big city had vanished from her accent, as had the cap from her tooth, and I saw that about sixty percent of the rest of her had disappeared, too. She was still Madame Ruth, as Cholmondeley was still Cholmondeley, but now she looked good.

"Amazing," Legate Kawaguchi murmured softly, which made him spring into view. While remaining himself, he also looked like a recruiting poster for the Angels City

Constabulary Department: no cynicism was left on his face, and no tiredness, either.

"This is—remarkable," I said. I presume that let me become visible to the others, but not to myself: as far as I could tell, I remained a disembodied viewpoint. Too bad; I would have liked finding out what an idealized version of me looked like.

"Let us proceed," Brother Vahan said. Now I saw him, too.

"He doesn't look any different!" I exclaimed, which was true: the abbot remained a careworn man in a dark robe.

Nigel Cholmondeley spoke with enormous respect: "In virtuous reality, only those who are themselves truly virtuous before the experience have their seeming unchanged during it." Suddenly I wondered how much I'd altered to my companions in this strange place. Maybe I didn't want to be idealized after all.

Then all such petty concerns faded into insignificance. You see, I saw a serpent in the garden, and—I don't quite know how to explain this, but it's true—*the serpent wasn't crawling on its belly.* "This isn't just a garden," I said, awe in my voice as the realization crashed over me. "This is *The* Garden."

"That's right—very good." Madame Ruth sounded pleased I'd caught on so fast. "Virtuous reality has translated you to a simulacrum of the place mankind enjoyed before the Original Sin, while we were truly virtuous ourselves."

"I am not sure I approve," Brother Vahan said heavily. "The theological implications are—troubling."

"It's only a thaumaturgical simulation, a symbol, if you will," Cholmondeley assure him. "We don't pretend otherwise. The test of a symbol is its utility, and we have found this one to be of enormous value. On that basis, will you bear with us?"

"On that basis, yes," the abbot said, but if he was happy about it, he concealed the fact very well.

"Good. Without the willing consent of the participants, the simulation is all too likely to break down, which would precipitate us back into the mundane world where, sadly, virtue is less manifest," Cholmondeley said. "And, as I said, virtuous reality can be valuable—as you see." He pointed.

Coming through the trees was Erasmus. In the strange space of virtuous reality, the scriptorium spirit seemed as real and solid as any of the rest of us—more real and solid than I seemed to myself. Brother Vahan made a choked noise and ran toward the spirit. Erasmus ran toward the abbot, too; they embraced.

"I can feel him!" Brother Vahan exclaimed. Finding his old friend palpable seemed to wipe away his reservations about virtuous reality at a stroke.

While Brother Vahan greeted Erasmus, I took a longer look at the trees from which the scriptorium spirit had emerged. I recognized some of them: orange and lemon, pomegranate and date palm. But others were strange to me, both in appearance and in the scents that wafted from their fruits and flowers to my nose.

I wondered if the Tree of Knowledge grew in this version of the Garden, and what would happen if I tasted of it. *Have to ask that serpent*, I thought, but when I looked around for it, it was gone. Just as well, I suppose.

"I grieve that you were wounded," Brother Vahan was saying. We all gathered around him and Erasmus. The abbot went on, "Never in my worst nightmare did I imagine evil being so bold as to assail our peaceful monastery."

"Nor I," Erasmus answered mournfully. I'd never heard him speak till that moment; on This Side, he'd manifested himself only with written words on the ground glass. His apparent voice perfectly fit his studious appearance and the spectacles he affected: it was dry, serious, on the pedantic side. If you imagine Michael Manstein as a scriptorium spirit, you're close.

"Are you in pain now?" Brother Vahan asked anxiously.

"No. Pain, I think, is impermissible in this remarkable place." Erasmus peered from one of us to the next. "I recognize here Inspector Fisher of the Environmental Perfection Agency, and this other gentleman's semblance is also somehow familiar to me, although I do not know his name."

"I am Legate Shiro Kawaguchi of the Angels City

Constabulary Department," Kawaguchi said when Erasmus looked his way. "Perhaps you sensed my aura during the fire; officers under my command helped rescue you."

"That must account for it," Erasmus agreed. "I fear I have not yet made the acquaintance of the other two individuals here."

"Madame Ruth and Mr. Cholmondeley have made it possible for us to use what they term virtuous reality as a meeting ground with you," Brother Vahan explained.

"Yes, I have encountered the concept in recent journal issues"—Erasmus' voice suddenly grew sad again—"now without doubt lost to the flames. Intriguing to observe an application of it."

"Speaking of the flames," Legate Kawaguchi broke in, "I would be grateful for your account of what took place during the evening on which the Thomas Brothers monastery fire took place."

"Must I recount it?" Even in virtuous reality, Erasmus looked scared. "So close came I to being extinguished forever."

"If you want the perpetrators apprehended, we must have your statement," Kawaguchi answered. "Yours, I think, is the only reliable testimony as to what occurred on the Other Side during the commission of the felony."

Brother Vahan added, "You should also know, old friend, that eleven of the brethren lost their lives in the fire, and many others were badly burned." His face twisted. I thought about the stiff-necked Cardinal of Angels City and his doubts about cosmetic sorcery.

"I did not know," Erasmus whispered. His pale, thin visage twisted, too. Remembered pain? Fear? I couldn't tell. "They warned me it would be folly of the purest ray serene to speak of what they did to me, even assuming I was thereafter able to manifest myself, which they found unlikely. But eleven of the holy brethren— Very well, abbot, Legate: I shall speak in praise of folly."

Legate Kawaguchi held a stylus and note tablet in his hands. I don't know where they came from; they hadn't been there an instant before. Maybe it was just the nature of virtuous reality to accommodate itself to the wills and desires of those who occupied it. Being a constable, Kawaguchi felt he needed written documentation when he questioned a witness. Since he needed it, he got it. Or maybe I'm altogether off base; I don't pretend to be a thaumaturge.

At any rate, note tablet poised, the legate asked, "What do you mean by 'they,' Erasmus?"

"The individuals who tormented me on the night of the fire," the scriptorium spirit answered.

Kawaguchi scribbled a note. Then he said, "Let us take that night in chronological order, if possible. That may be the clearest method of ascertaining the facts in this matter. Is that a reasonable request?"

"For many denizens of the Other Side, beings not so bound up in Time as you humans, the answer would be no," Erasmus said. "But as a scriptorium spirit, concerned not only with order in my records but also with regular access to those records by the holy brethren and other researchers"— he looked toward me—"I have a clear sense of duration and sequence, yes."

"Go ahead, then." Kawaguchi poised his stylus.

Erasmus took him literally. Beginning with the monks' celebration of vespers, he began to give a minute-by-minute account of everything that had happened within range of his sensorium. At first, everything was both tedious and altogether irrelevant. If he kept up in that vein, I began to fear we'd stay in virtuous reality forever. It would certainly feel like forever.

Nigel Cholmondeley held up a hand. "Forgive me, Erasmus," he broke in, "but could you perhaps skip to that portion of the evening when you first noticed something amiss?"

"Ah." Erasmus gave Kawaguchi a why-didn't-you-say-what-you-wanted? look, then took up the tale anew: "At 12:04 in the morning, two unauthorized persons entered the scriptorium. I attempted to give the alarm, but was prevented."

Before Erasmus could answer, Brother Vahan put in, "We

noted nothing out of the ordinary, Legate, as I told you on the night of the fire. That evildoers should trespass upon hallowed ground without drawing the notice of anyone within, and that they should overcome alarm spells lain down with the authority of the Holy Catholic Church . . . they had no small power behind them. Till the day, I would not have thought it possible."

Like any other major faith, the Catholic Church maintains that its connections with the Other Side are the most potent around (I'd say the most omnipotent, but purists like Michael Manstein and Erasmus wouldn't approve). With the powers the Church has Over There, it's not easy even for a Jew like me to disagree very loudly. Having his holy protection fail must have been a dreadful shock for Brother Vahan.

"I cannot answer the question with certainty," Erasmus said. "I know only that I was silenced, as the holy abbot has suggested, by a spell of great force."

"What flavor did it have?" I asked. "Was it some strong ancient ritual revived specially for this purpose, or did it carry the precision of modern magic?"

"Again, I cannot say," the scriptorium spirit answered. "If I may use an analogy from your Side, as well ask a mouse crushed by a boulder in a landslide whether it was granite or sandstone."

"Very well, we are to understand you were forcibly silenced and prevented from alerting the brethren," Kawaguchi said, trying to keep Erasmus moving in the right direction. "What transpired subsequently?"

"I was interrogated," Erasmus answered. "My questioners sought to learn what Inspector Fisher here had gleaned from our records. I tried to refuse, I tried to resist; the holy abbot had ordered me to treat the inspector in all ways as if he were one of the brethren, and I should never have betrayed their secrets who came into the scriptorium like—or rather, as—thieves in the night. Then they began to torment me."

So much for virtuous reality. I didn't feel virtue, not after I heard that—what I felt was guilt. I didn't need to ask that disappearing serpent where the Tree of Knowledge grew; I'd already eaten of it at the Thomas Brothers monastery. And because I had, Erasmus had suffered.

Brother Vahan made a noise that said he was suffering, too. He embraced the scriptorium spirit. They clung to each other.

Whatever Legate Kawaguchi was feeling, he didn't let it interfere with his interrogation. He said, "Could you please describe for me the torments performed upon you?"

Brother Vahan angrily turned on him. "Why are you trying to force Erasmus to reexperience the torments those murderers inflicted?"

"Because their nature may provide important information on the perpetrators," Kawaguchi answered. "The particular magics utilized will be clues to the backgrounds of those who performed them. I assure you, this is standard constabulary procedure in dealing with cases involving the Other Side, Brother Vahan."

"I pray your pardon," the abbot said; he was one of the rare people I've met who didn't find his manhood threatened by backing down. "You don't tell me how to conduct my affairs; I owe you the same courtesy."

"Erasmus?" Kawaguchi said.

The scriptorium spirit didn't look happy about recounting what had happened to him, but after a little while he nodded. "Let it be as you say, Legate, and may the truth bear out your hopes. First came fire: this would have been at 12:32, when my questioners decided I was and would remain obdurate."

"Fire wasn't reported in the monastery until after one," Kawaguchi said.

"Not the Fire of This Side, but that of the Other, which burns the spirit rather than the material," Erasmus replied. "Not for nothing, I can now tell you, do so many mortals fear the pangs of hellfire, for to endure such eternally would be anguish indeed."

Kawaguchi scribbled notes. I wondered how much good they'd do him. Counting the magics that don't have fire in them somewhere is a much easier job than reckoning up those that do. And the way Erasmus talked about what had happened to him suggested the fire sprang from Christian or Muslim sources; the former, especially, didn't lend itself to narrowing down the list of suspects.

The scriptorium spirit continued, "At 12:41, the invaders concluded fire was inadequate to persuade me. They resorted instead to the venom of sorcerous serpents, which coursed through my ichor and brought with it suffering different from, but not less intense than, that which the flames had produced."

"Snakes, you say?" Kawaguchi repeated with a now-we're-getting-somewhere air. "And of what nature were they?"

"With all respect, Legate, I must remind you that I am a scriptorium spirit at a monastery, not a herpetologist's establishment," Erasmus answered in a dignified voice. "I can state with authority that they were dissimilar to the one inhabiting the garden here, for which claim I have Scriptural authority behind me. Past that, fools may rush in but, while I am no angel, I fear to tread."

I found a question I thought Kawaguchi had missed: "Can you describe the men who tormented you, Erasmus?"

"Again, I fear not," the spirit answered. "They were masked against the sight of Your Side, and so cloaked around in sorcery that I have no notion of their true spiritual semblance, either, save that were it benign they would not have used me as they did."

I sighed. Kawaguchi sighed. Even Brother Vahan looked a little less saintly than he had. Nigel Cholmondeley and Madame Ruth shifted from foot to foot. They'd brought us all together here in virtuous reality, but for the amount of information Erasmus had given us, they might as well not have bothered.

"Very well, then," Kawaguchi said, sighing again. "What happened next?"

"I still refused to divulge the nature of the research Inspector Fisher had been conducting," Erasmus said. "At 12:48, the intruders again became discontented with their means of torment and shifted stratagems. I found myself tramped under the sharp hooves of an enormous cow."

That made me sit up and take notice: metaphorically, you

understand. Legate Kawaguchi leaned forward toward Erasmus till he was fell past the point where I thought he'd fall on his face. Maybe you can't do that in virtuous reality; I don't know. "A cow, you say?" he pressed. "Not a bull? Are you sure about that?"

"I am certain," Erasmus declared.

"Interesting," Kawaguchi said. I saw what he was flying toward. Bull cults are common. Straight Mithraism has never quite died, and there are modern revivalist sects trying to pick up supporters who don't get the spiritual charge they need from Christianity and Islam. Personally, I don't need to get drenched by the blood of a slaughtered bull to feel a union with the Godhead, but some folks evidently do.

But cows, now . . . two of the places where the cow is a focus of magic are India—home of the Garuda Bird—and Persia, from which sprang, among others in the case, Slow Jinn Fizz and Bakhtiar's Precision Burins (a place I hoped I'd get to before I died of old age).

Erasmus went on, "The hooves of the cow seemed sharp as whetted steel. They flayed me past any anguish I had previously imagined. And so, to my lasting shame, Inspector Fisher, at 12:58 I yielded to my inquisitors' torment and described in detail the records I had copied for you. Judge me as you will; the deed is done."

When a spirit talks about lasting shame, it means lasting forever unless it's a sylph or one of that flighty breed. I said, "Erasmus, you did the best you could. What you went through is more than I could have stood; I'm sure of that. You don't need to feel shame on my account."

"You are gracious," the scriptorium spirit said. Brother Vahan also inclined his head in my direction. That made me feel good; winning Brother Vahan's good opinion isn't easy, but it's worth doing.

"What happened after you finished providing the perpetrators with this information, after"—Kawaguchi glanced down at his notes—"12:58?"

"I finished betraying Inspector Fisher at 1:03," Erasmus said bleakly. "I hoped that would be the end of it, that the malefactors would take what they had learned and depart.

Instead, as you know, they forthwith kindled the fire which I gather resulted in the destruction of the Thomas Brothers monastery. As to that, I could not speak with certainty, for when the ground glasses in the scriptorium melted or shattered from the heat of the flames, I lost my interface with Your Side and, still in agony, awaited my own dissolution."

"The firecrew and constabulary rescued you," I said.

"Exactly so. At the time and since, I have doubted whether they did me any great favor, but, as with my betrayal of you, the deed is done and we now must proceed to act upon its consequences." The scriptorium spirit turned to Legate Kawaguchi. "Oh: there is one thing more. For some time after I was tormented, I lacked much of my normal awareness of self and surroundings. Were I flesh and blood, I gather you would say I was semiconscious. Only quite recently have I regained my full sensorium. When I did so, I found as part of my immediate surroundings—this."

I hadn't figured Erasmus for a sense of the dramatic. But from behind his back he pulled out a short green feather. Kawaguchi held out his had. "May I see it?" Erasmus gave it to him. He felt it, held it close to his face in a gesture that said he was nearsighted. He shrugged. "Just seems like a feather to the eye and the hand." He turned to Madame Ruth and Nigel Cholmondeley and asked, "Are magical forensic tests possible in virtuous reality?"

They both shook their heads. Madame Ruth said, "Remember, that isn't the actual feather you're holding, Legate, but its analog in this sorcerous space. And, like everything else in virtuous reality, it is imbued with special properties springing from this space and thus not a fit subject for testing."

"I should have thought of that." Kawaguchi clicked his tongue between his teeth, not so much in disappointment as in annoyance at himself. He turned to Brother Vahan. "Further questions?"

"I have one," I said. "How did the two men react when you finally yielded to the cow's hooves and told them what I'd been investigating?"

"One of them said to the other, 'He'll get his, too, I expect,'" Erasmus answered. It didn't surprise me, but it didn't delight me, either. If somebody was willing to burn down a monastery, the added burden of sin that would accrue from going after an EPA inspector couldn't have been heavy enough to worry him.

Brother Vahan said, "Old friend, how soon will you be able to manifest yourself normally on Our Side once more?"

"It shouldn't be much longer, holy abbot," Erasmus said. "The metaphysicians tell me I could do it now if my familiar haunts were restored. As it is, I'm given to understand it's a matter of days rather than weeks."

"Good," the abbot said. "I shall pray that the time will be soon, for purely selfish reasons: I find I miss you very much."

An undead who hadn't fed in a thousand years had infinitely more blood in him than Erasmus ever could, so when I saw the scriptorium spirit blush I just chalked it up to virtuous reality. And if we were out of questions, we didn't need to be there any more. I asked, "How do we get back to Interrogation Room Two?"

"You must return to awareness of the body you left behind there," Nigel Cholmondeley answered. "As soon as your hands leave contact with those of the persons to either side of you, the circuit will be broken and you—and all of us—will return to the mundane world."

My hands? I looked down, and of course I couldn't see them. From what my eyes reported, I might as well not have had any hands, or anything else—I was just there. Virtuous reality is an insidious kind of place: it so completely involves all the senses and seems so thoroughly real that leaving wasn't as easy as Cholmondeley made it sound. I wondered if early explorers had got stuck in it forever. If they had, I wondered if they'd realized it.

An intense look of concentration came over Brother Vahan's face. Presumably he couldn't see his own hands, either. But an instant later, I was sitting on a hard chair with a stifling helmet over my eyes and ears. I clawed it off. The grimy reality of the interrogation room was a long, long way from the Garden where I'd been a moment before.

Everyone else was taking off the masks, too. Now that we were back in the constabulary station, Nigel Cholmondeley was horsefaced again, Madame Ruth fat as any two people you want to name, and Legate Kawaguchi short and skinny and tired-looking. I suppose I looked the way I always do, too.

On the table in front of Kawaguchi, along with the cigarette burns and coffee rings, lay a note tablet full of scribbles. I didn't remember its being there when we sat down. I didn't think he could have brought it back from virtuous reality . . . but then I saw, right in the middle of the table, a bright green feather. Kawaguchi spotted it at the same time I did. He grabbed it and stuck it in a little transparent pouch made of spirit gum to keep it from being magically influenced.

"Remarkable," Nigel Cholmondeley said. "One seldom sees artifacts returning with participants in a virtuous reality experience."

"Officially, this is not and cannot be evidence," Kawaguchi said. "Its trail of provenance is severely tainted; any judge to whom it was presented would throw it out of court, and very likely the case with it. Unofficially, I shall convey it to the lab and find out what our forensics people make of it."

"Let me know, please," I said. If I'd snatched it first, I'd have taken it straight to Michael Manstein—assuming, of course, that Kawaguchi and half a dozen big constables with clubs hadn't started working out on me to make me give it back. Since they might have done just that, constables being demons for evidence, maybe it was for the best Kawaguchi got it instead of me.

Brother Vahan dipped his head to Madame Ruth and then to Cholmondeley. "Let me apologize to both of you for my previous doubts as to the nature of virtuous reality," he said; he was, as usual, nothing if not gracious. "I can see that it will become a valuable tool in thaumaturgic research."

"Thanks right back atcha for thinkin' fast and breakin' the circle." Madame Ruth sounded like herself again, too. Too bad. "That can be the tricky part, gettin' back here where we belong."

Nigel Cholmondeley put it more piously: "Mankind was ever reluctant to leave the Garden."

"So I thought," the abbot agreed. "But then I remembered I had no true right there, burdened as I was by the weight of Original Sin. After that, recalling my body to action in this actual world was easier."

The channeler and the medium looked at each other. "Let's talk about that some more, Brother Vahan, if you don't mind," Cholmondeley said. "The extraction technique you describe might well be incorporated into one of the helmets' ritual subroutines if we are able to isolate the symbolic essence of your thought sequence."

"It could make you a nice piece of change, and us, too," Madame Ruth said. "Like you said, virtuous reality is the coming thing, and if you was to get a piece of it—"

"Wealth means nothing to me," Brother Vahan said. I've heard a lot of people say that; he was one of the handful who made me believe it.

"As may be," Nigel Cholmondeley said, which meant he had his doubts, too. He also had a hook: "No matter how frugal you personally may be, have you not got a monastery to rebuild?" Brother Vahan stared at him.

I watched the hook snag the fish. The abbot said, "Let us discuss it, then, for the greater glory of God."

"Let's eat somethin' while we talk," Madame Ruth said, which struck me as more honest than *let's do lunch* and most of the other ways people try to combine business and food.

Despite my sausage, I was hungry, too, but not as hungry as I thought I'd be. When I asked my watch what time it was, I found out to my amazement that I'd been in the world of virtuous reality for only about five minutes. It had seemed like a couple of hours while I was there. Oneiromancers say dreams are like that: a lot of things going on but compressed very tightly in terms of time. Judy keeps up on the ins and outs of theoretical thaumaturgy better than I do; I made a note to ask her how virtuous reality simulated the dream effect.

I didn't have lunch with Brother Vahan and the medium and channeler; enough things were going on at the office that I wanted to put in as much time as I could there, trying to claw my way through the piles of junk on my desk. I wouldn't starve before dinner. So I went south through the pass into Westwood a little faster than a constable armed with a tracking demon would have approved of. Fortunately, I didn't spot any black-and-white carpets all the way back down St. James' Freeway.

After a good trip on the freeway, I got stuck in regular fly-way traffic on the way back to the Confederal Building. I peered around the carpets ahead of me, trying to figure out what had gone wrong this time."

The fellow on the rug next to me leaned over and called, "There's a demon stration up there at the corner."

Up there at the corner, of course, was where I was trying to go. I growled. "So what if there's a demonstration? There's a demonstration at that corner about three days a week." Then what he'd said really sank in. "A demon stration?" I didn't want to believe I'd heard that.

But he nodded. I wondered if I ought to turn my carpet around and get out of there as fast as the sylphs would take me. No wonder there was a traffic jam, if demons were out protesting Confederal policy. I hoped the building would survive. There'd be SWAT teams and God only knows what all else up there, trying to keep the irate Powers from turning the place into an inferno.

My sense of duty got the better of my sense of self-preservation. I kept going toward the Confederal Building. It took a while for me to inch close enough to find out what was going on. I'd been wrong in my first guess: the Powers at the demon stration weren't apt to turn violent, and they didn't need constabulary thauma-turges to hold them at bay. But as soon as I saw them, I understood why they stopped traffic. You see, they were all succubi.

Actually, that's not quite true. Some of them were incubi, and some of them—well, I'm not quite certain whose fancy some of them catered to, but whosever it was, I'm sure they met it.

As for me, I barely noticed those others. I was busy watching the succubi. I couldn't help myself. Some of the pictures up on Iosef's wall were pretty spectacular, but pictures don't begin to convey the essence of what succubi are all about. When you see them in the quasi-flesh, you can't help but think they're the creatures men were really designed to mate with; they make women look like clumsy makeshifts.

Phyllis Kaminsky, bless her heart, was down there arguing with some of them, trying to convince them to give up and go away. Phyllis is a nice-looking gal, several years younger than I am and in better shape, too. The company she was keeping made her seem a poorly jointed wooden puppet turned out on a lathe by somebody who didn't know how to run a lathe very well.

One little devil with a blue dress on happened to catch my eye. The promise on her face, the way she ran an impossibly moist tongue over unbelievably sweet, unbelievably red lips, the sinuousness (and you can turn that into a pun or not, just as you please—it works either way) of her hip action—put 'em all together and it's a minor miracle I didn't run into the carpet in front of me.

One of the reasons I didn't was that the gal flying that carpet wasn't exactly where she was supposed to be, either: instead of keeping her eye on the carpet in front of *her*, she'd been gaping at an incubus who was taller, darker, and handsomer than he had any business being.

When you think about it, you shouldn't be surprised our sexual demons are so strong. They've been evolving right along with us for as long as we've been human, proof of which is how strongly they manifest themselves on This Side. They're used to coming Across; they've been doing it for millions of years.

(You have a dirty mind, do you know that? Filtering out all the double entendres that come naturally [you see, there you go again] when discussing succubi is more trouble than it's worth.)

Unlike the Medvamp protesters, the succubi and incubi didn't carry signs or chant slogans. They just paraded; they were their own best message.

By then I'd got close enough to hear Phyllis as well as see her. She was saying, "—but the existence you lead degrades both you and mankind. Don't you see that sexual exploitation is wrong and damaging to the soul?"

"If this were a Muslim country, we'd be honored, not hunted," a succubus retorted. Though irate herself, she made Phyllis sound shrill and screechy by comparison: her voice brought to the ear the taste of Erse Creme liqueur. She went on, "We have no souls to worry about; we exist for pleasure. And since you humans endlessly prate about free will, surely you'll admit you can choose us or avoid us as you see fit."

Phyllis had been over that ground before. She said, "Part of your attraction comes from the Other Side, so it distorts free will. Besides, humans of unsavory sorts carry on their sordid affairs in areas you frequent because they know they'll find a lot of customers there. You don't just haunt neighborhoods—you blight them."

The succubus' shrug was magnificent. "This is your problem, not ours. We get we want from humans; they get what they want from us. We find it an equitable arrangement."

As I finally flew into the parking lot, Phyllis lost her temper and started shouting at the succubus. It's always a mistake to let Powers, even minor ones, get your goat. They have more patience than people anyhow; what with their far longer terms of being, they can afford it.

Besides, here I feared Phyllis was fighting a losing game. The succubus' knowledge of biology was empirical and extremely specialized, but she had a point: her kind and mankind were essentially symbiotes, and nobody was likely to make either turn loose of the other. If that hadn't happened all through recorded history, it wasn't likely to start in modern Angels City.

But Phyllis had a point, too. Because the people in our society who go to succubi and incubi are generally out for a cheap thrill, they're often the people who go after other thrills. Find a neighborhood with succubi on the streetcorners and you'll generally find it's not the kind of place where you'd want to bring up your kids if you had a choice. Keeping sexual demons of any flavor off the streets makes pretty fair sense to me.

I parked my carpet, got off, and went over to see if Phyllis wanted a hand from me. As I was walking up to her, that succubus in blue gave me the eye again. My breath went short. I couldn't help it: succubi have been perfecting the art of seduction probably since the days of the man-apes. Natural selection works on the Other Side no less than on this one—Powers that aren't adored perish, and others take their place. If my reaction meant anything, that particular succubus would stay around forever.

Phyllis saw me not quite slavering and made an exasperated noise. I suppose I can't blame her: I must have seemed more like part of the problem than part of the solution. She said, "What do you plan on doing, Dave? Will you whip out your little tin badge and run them all in?"

You don't want to get into a war of sarcasm with Phyllis, or at least I don't. I've been scorched often enough to keep that in mind at all times. So—please believe me—I was about to answer with something mild and soothing.

But before I could, the succubus in blue said, "I'm sure he'd rather whip out something else instead, dear." Just listening to her was enough to set my heart racing like a couple of laps around the track. But when she licked her lips again, I started sweating so hard I did the only thing I could (short of whipping out something else, I mean)—I fled.

Phyllis lost it. Again, I can't say I blame her—here she was, watching one of her own people turned into a bowl of quivering gelatin (I was definitely quivering, but at least part of me was a lot stiffer than gelatin) by one of the sexy little demons she was trying to control. She started screaming at the succubus. The succubus screamed right back, with invective from just about every language since primeval Indo-European. She'd had a lot of satisfied customers, all right.

Since I obviously wasn't going to be of any use at the demon stration, I went upstairs to work on other things. Rose had left a message on my desk: Professor Blank of UCAC had called while I was out.

Scratching my head, I took the message up to her. "Professor Blank?" I said, pointing. "Wouldn't he leave his name?"

Now Rose looked puzzled. "I think he said his first name was Harvey."

There I was, looking and feeling like an idiot twice in the space of ten minutes. Harvey Blank was chair of the Goetic Sciences Department at UCAC; he was one of the first people I'd phoned about investigating whether the Chumash Powers were still around. I slunk back to my desk and returned his call.

The telephone imps reproduced his voice even more blurrily than is their habit; he must have been eating something when he answered. After a sentence or two, he spoke more clearly: "Hello, Inspector Fisher. Thanks for returning my call. I wanted to get back to you about some preliminary results of the extinction investigation."

"Go ahead," I said, grabbing for a pencil and a scrap of parchment. "What have you learned?"

"Not as much as I'd like," he answered: yes, he was a professor. "The experiments I have conducted, however, do indicate that the Powers formerly venerated by the Chumash Indians are not currently manifesting themselves in the Barony of Angels."

"They're extinct, you mean?" I had curiously mixed feelings. Most of me was sorry, as I'm always sorry (well, almost always—I'd make an exception for Huitzilopochtli) to see the Other Side diminished. But that nasty, lazy piece everyone has lurking inside, the one Christians identify with Original Sin, let out a cheer because I wouldn't have to work as hard on the leprechauns if the Chumash Powers were gone for good.

"I didn't quite say that," Professor Blank said.

"That's what it sounded like to me," I told him.

"It was the first conclusion I drew from the thaumaturgic regression analysis," he admitted. "A more thorough evaluation of the data, however, leads to a different interpretation: it seems more likely that the Powers in question have not so much vanished as withdrawn from any contact with This Side. The withdrawal appears volitional."

"Are you sure?" I said. "I've never heard of anything like that." The general rule is that Powers will keep a toehold on

This Side if they possibly can: the more active they are, the more they show themselves in the world, the better chance they have of attracting and keeping worshipers to give them the veneration they need.

Professor Blank said, "No, I'm not sure. The void in the theological contours of the barony is certainly there. It is, however, if you will permit me to employ metaphorical language, more as if the Powers made the hole and pulled it in after themselves than as if they simply disappeared from spiritual starvation."

"They are gone, though?"

"They're gone," he agreed. "That much is indisputable. I have been unable to contact or detect them in any way, either by recreating the old Chumash rituals or through modern scientific sorcery."

"But they might come back?"

"If the situation is as I envision in the highest-probability scenario, that possibility remains open, yes. If on the other hand this is merely an unusually sudden extinction, as remains possible, they are indeed gone for good."

"Can you find out which more precisely?" The lazy part of me was still hoping to get away with running only one set of projections for the theological impact of leprechauns on the Barony of Angels. If I had to run two, all right. But if I had to run two and then *didn't know which one to use*—nightmares spring from such things. So do blighted careers.

"I'm working on that now," Professor Blank said. By the way he said it, he hadn't the faintest idea whether what he was working on would work, if you know what I mean.

"Let me ask you something else," I said: "Suppose the Chumash Powers *have* withdrawn voluntarily—in their terms, suppose the great eagle whose wings support the Upper World has flown away. Is it goetically even possible for them to reverse the process?"

"I don't know, just as I don't know why they've withdrawn," Blank answered. "My research team is still working on that, too. We're exploring various possibilities there."

"Such as?" I prompted.

"Speculation (and that's all it is at this point) ranges from withdrawal to maintain some level of survival—the Other Side's equivalent of fungi forming spores when the environment grows too hostile for normal growth—to an active protest against the thecological changes here over the past two centuries."

When I heard that, I wanted to bang my head on the desk. Protests about environmental issues are hard enough to deal with when they come from This Side. What was going on down on the sidewalk showed how much more complicated they could get when Powers started playing what had at first been a human game. Absurdly, I wondered whether the Chumash First People and Sky Coyote had gotten the idea from the parading succubi. After a moment, I realized that was impossible: the Chumash Powers had disappeared before the sexual demons went on the march.

"Hunger strike," I murmured, as much to myself as to Professor Blank.

"I pray your pardon?" he said.

"Maybe the Powers are starving themselves of recognition to force us to notice them and give them the veneration they require."

"Thank you, Inspector Fisher; that will go onto the list. And let me thank you again for involving me and my graduate students"—I presume that was what he'd meant when he talked about his research team before—"in this project. I am confident we shall eventually learn a great deal from it."

I didn't like the sound of that *eventually*. "When do you hope to have some results I can use to help plan policy, Professor? I think I ought to remind you that this isn't just a research project, but one where the answers will be put to practical use."

"I understand that, of course," he said, a little sulkily. He might have understood it, but he didn't like it one bit. *A professor indeed*, I thought. He went on, "We shall endeavor to be as expeditious as possible, provided that we remain consistent with appropriate experimental protocols."

"That's fine, sir, but I think I ought to warn you that if I don't have harder data than you've given by, hmm, three weeks from today, I can't guarantee that your report will become part of the decision-making process."

Was I playing fair? Of course not, not even slightly. Professors always claim they go into the university or take holy orders or whatever so they can devote their full attention to whatever they're interested in: Roman epigraphy or beekeeping or the thaumaturgical arts of a vanished Indian tribe. Sometimes they even mean it. But a lot more often, I've found that professors who see a chance to influence events outside academe will leap at it in spite of their alleged lack of interest. Truth to tell, I don't know if a savant of Roman epigraphy ever got that kind of chance (at least since the days when the Empire was a going concern), but my guess is that he'd grab it, too.

And so now Professor Blank said, "Three weeks, eh?" Even with two phone imps between his mouth and my ear, he sounded distinctly unhappy. Another phone pause followed. I understood the reason for this one: he was giving me a chance to say I'd made a mistake and the real deadline was three months—or three years—away. I didn't say any such thing. Blank sighed. "Very well, Inspector Fisher, I will attempt to meet the challenging timeframe you have outlined. God give you good day, sir."

"The same to you, Professor, and I'm grateful for your help. I look forward to seeing your detailed report; it will be most valuable both to me and to the Environmental Perfection Agency as a whole." As long as he was going to do what I wanted, I had no problem with letting him down easy. It worked, too; he seemed a lot happier by the time he got off the phone.

I spent the next several minutes making notes on the conversation, both as an *aide-memoire* for me and to let me have something to show Bea so she'd know I really and truly was working on all the cases that crowded my desk. In an ideal world, I wouldn't have had to waste my time with worries like that, but no one has ever claimed Plato would recognize the Confederal bureaucracy as an ideal world.

I asked my watch what time it was, found out it was almost half past four. A busy day. I was getting tired of not having the chance to get up to Bakhtiar's Precision Burins, but I had made one trip to St. Ferdinand's Valley. *Maybe tomorrow*, I told myself. I wrote a note reminding me to call Tony Sudakis tomorrow, too; the investigation had gone so many different ways lately that I hadn't done much with the Devonshire dump itself in quite a while. Sudakis probably figured I'd fallen off the edge of the world, not that he'd miss me if I did.

Instead of finding something constructive to do with the last half hour of my work day, I looked out the window to see if the succubi were still marching down below. They were, and traffic in the building rush hour on Wilshire Boulevard, always heavy, was becoming downright elephantine. Maybe I could duck south down side flyways to St. Monica's Boulevard and get on the freeway there.

It was a good plan. It should have worked, too; Veteran was crowded heading north because people couldn't turn onto Wilshire from it, but southbound traffic didn't look too bad. I felt pretty smug sliding down to the parking lot—this once, I figured, I had a fighting chance of beating the system.

Thaumaturgy hasn't found them yet, but there must be gremlins who sit around listening for thoughts like that. I was just strapping on my safety belt when a priest happened to fly down Veteran. In an instant, all the succubi who had been on Wilshire started running after his carpet, shaking everything they had (and believe me, they had plenty) and calling out blandishments that made my ears turn red—and they weren't even directed at me.

Succubi, of course, delight in tormenting priests: that's been obvious ever since Christianity began. And priests, being mortal, have been known to yield to temptation. Some of the temptation here was pretty tempting, too.

A normal rule in Westwood is that you can't find a parking space to save your soul. The priest, though, must have had the power of the Lord behind him, because he managed to slide his carpet into one. The succubi squealed with delight and jounced after him, sure they'd found another sinner in clerical collar.

They got a rude surprise. The priest hadn't stopped to dally with them, he'd stopped to give them a load of fire and brimstone to take the place of the sweet scents they were wearing: bitch wolves was the nicest thing he called them, and went on to things like haughty, vainglorious, lecherous betrayers, ready for every wickedness, and fickle in love (which, when applied to a succubus, is about like calling the ocean damp). He roasted them on both sides. Meanwhile, though, half the males on Wilshire tried to turn onto Veteran so they could keep ogling the succubi, which meant the traffic jam spread with them.

At first the succubi didn't believe the priest was serious. They had a thorough understanding of the way people work, and knew too many folks like to condemn in public what they do in private. So they kept on pressing themselves against the priest, rubbing their hands over him, kissing his cheek and his ear and the bare circle of his tonsure, paying no heed to his outraged bellows.

Then he pulled out an ampule of holy water. The succubi's squeals turned to screams. They ran, you'll pardon the expression, like hell. And the priest, his virtue intact even if his clothes were mussed, got back onto his carpet and flew away.

He flew away slowly. By then, that was the only way it was possible to fly on Veteran. Everyone else flew slowly, too, including me. I shouldn't have been thinking such uncharitable thoughts abut a man of the cloth, especially one who had just proved his faith against a challenge to which many would have succumbed . . . but I was. If he'd flown by five minutes later, I'd have had an easy trip to the freeway. Getting snarled in traffic instead would have tried the patience of a saint.

I made it home much later than I'd intended, and in a much fouler mood. These things happen. After a bottle of ale and a steak, my attitude improved a good deal. I know what would improve it more, too: I called Judy.

"I'm so jealous, I'm going to hit you the next time I see you," she said when I told her I'd been involved in using virtuous reality to contact Erasmus. "We were just talking about

that at the office today. The consensus in the business is that
it's the biggest advance in sorcerous technology since ectoplasmic cloning."

"I didn't think it was *that* important," I said. Look at the
ways having large numbers of identical microimps has
changed our lives: spellcheckers, telephones, ethernet sets,
all sorts of things our grandparents couldn't have imagined.
Thinking of that much change happening again—and probably happening faster, because it would be allied to the
developments that are already in place—made my head
spin.

But Judy said, "Oh, it is, David. The world will be a different place twenty years from now, because we'll have figured
out all the things we can do in virtuous reality. Think about
it: what's the biggest problem in sorcerous applications
today?"

"Ask me a hard one," I answered. "To accomplish everything people want to do these days, spells keep getting more
and more complex, and errors creep in." Some of the errors
are pretty ghastly, too, like the one at the Union Kobold
works in India a few years back, where a Raksha was mistak-
enly ordered to turn out wood alcohol instead of the more
friendly sort. Hundreds died from drinking it, and a couple
of thousand more were permanently blinded—all from one
small goof in translating a spell from Latin into Sanskrit so
the Hindu demon could understand it.

"You're right, of course," Judy said, which took my mind
off the contemplation of disaster. Just as well, too. She went
on, "But think what will happen when any old mage can go
into virtuous reality to develop his sorcerous subroutines.
Because of the nature of that space, the number of errors
should drop way down. Ideally, it should fall to zero, but I
think the fallibility principles will keep that from happening.
Still—"

"I hadn't thought of it in those terms," I admitted. "It just
seemed a handy way to reach a spirit who'd been too badly
damaged to manifest himself in this rough, rugged world." I
thought about some of the things the wizards had done to
poor Erasmus. Judy didn't need to know about those.

She said, "I'm just glad I'll have my master's and be out of the copy-editing and proofreading end of the business soon. Mark my words, the accuracy breakthrough that will come with virtuous reality is going to throw a lot of sharp people onto the streets."

"Change has a way of doing that: the more efficient the spells get, the more they do and the less anybody needs actual people," I said. One of the reasons the General Movers plant in Van Nuys is going under is that the Japanese have figured out a way to power the looms that make their flying carpets by *kamikazes*—divine winds.

"That does look to be the way it's going," she said, "but what do we do with all the people who lose jobs? Eventually nobody will need people for anything, and then where will we be?"

"The two answers that occur to me are *bored* and *broke*," I answered. "But those are for people in general. People in particular—us, I mean—will be married. We may end up broke, but I don't think we'll be bored."

"No, not bored," she agreed, "especially not with children in the house."

"Uh-huh," I said. I know children are usually one of the things marriage is about. I even looked forward, in an abstract sort of way, to being a father. But it didn't seem real to me; I had trouble imagining myself giving a baby a bath or helping a little girl with her subtraction problems.

Then I thought about the Corderos. They were nice kids who'd had every reason to expect a nice, normal baby. Instead they got Jesus, born without a soul. How were they handling it? How could I handle something like that if it happened to me? The very idea was nearly enough to put me off parenthood for good.

"You still there?" Judy asked when I didn't say anything for a while. "Relax—it's not as if you're going to have to start changing diapers tomorrow." The woman can read me like one of the grimoires she proofs. I suspect that, like them, I'll end up better for the editing, too.

Just to show her I had other things on my mind besides immediately turning into a daddy, I said, "Something else interesting happened today—or at least I thought it was." I told her about the demon stration outside the Confederal Building.

"I'll bet you thought it was interesting," she said darkly. Women take a particular tone when they talk about attractive competition that bothers them. They take a different—but not *very* different—tone when they talk about attractive competition that amuses them. Over the phone, I had a tough time telling which one Judy was using. She went on, "See anything you liked in particular?"

"Well—" The image of the succubus in blue leaped into my mind, as fully three-dimensional as the little demon had been herself. "As a matter of fact, yes." I did my best to sound sheepish, but I didn't know how good my best was.

Judy left me hanging for a couple of seconds before she started to laugh. "Good," she said between chuckles. "If you'd told me anything else, I'd have figured you were lying—succubi are made to be succulent, after all. I wish I'd been there; I could have leered at some of the incubi. Watching is fun, though I think men may be more apt to enjoy it than women."

"Maybe," I said. "It didn't seem to matter much to the traffic, though. Everybody was staring, men and women both."

"Oh, God, I hadn't even thought about that. It must have been awful." Commuting every day from Long Beach up into East A.C., Judy knows all about traffic tangles and loves them as much as anyone else who has to get on the freeway to go to work.

"It was worse than that." She laughed again when I told her how the strong-minded priest had foiled my effort to escape down Veteran. Thinking back on it, I decided it was funny, too. It certainly hadn't felt funny why I was sitting on my carpet twiddling my thumbs for an extra twenty minutes. "So how was *your* day?" I asked.

"Certainly not as interesting as yours," she answered. "Very much the usual: looking at sheets of parchment and making little marks on them in red. It keeps me out of the baron's Paupers' Home, but past that it doesn't have a whole lot to recommend it. I can't wait to finish my master's so somebody will hire me to work on the theoretical side of sorcery."

"Then you'll be working in virtuous reality all the time, if it turns out to be as important as you think it will," I said.

"It will, and I will. Then I'll come home and we can be less than virtuous together." Judy hesitated, just a beat. "But we'll be married, so it'll be virtuous after all. Hmm. I'm not sure I like that."

"I think it'll be fine any which way," I said. "And speaking—indirectly—of such things, do you want to have dinner with me tomorrow night?"

"Indirectly indeed," she said. "Sure, I'd love to. Shall we go to that Hanese place near your flat again?"

"Sounds good to me. You want to meet here after we get off work?"

"All right," Judy said. "It'll be good to see you. I love you."

"Love you too, hon. See you tomorrow. 'Bye."

Thinking of seeing Judy kept me going through a miserable Tuesday at the office. I did get some of the small stuff done. Lord, the things that show up on an EPA man's desk sometimes! I got a letter from a woman up in the high desert asking if the ashes of a coyote's flesh had the same anti-asthmatic effect as those of a fox's flesh when drunk in wine and, if so, whether she could set traps for the ones that kept trying to catch her cats. Just answering that one took a couple of hours of research and a phone call to the Chief Huntsman of the Barony of Angels (in case you're interested, the answers are yes and she had to buy a twenty-crown license first, respectively).

The environmental study on importing leprechauns, though, took a large step backwards. I got a very fancy-looking legal brief from an outfit that called itself Save Our Basin, which opposed allowing the Little People to establish themselves here. SOB put forward the fear that, once we had leprechauns here, all the Sidhe would henceforth pack up and move to Angels City. I'm condensing, but that's what the gist of it was.

Now on first glance this stuck me as one of the more idiotic environmental concerns I'd seen lately. The climate here, both literal and theological, isn't congenial to Powers from cool, moist Eire. But the Save Our Basin folks had so many citations in their brief—from the *evocatio* of Juno out of Veii and into Rome to the establishment of the Virgin at Guadalupe in what had been a purely Aztecan thecology—that I couldn't dismiss it out of hand. It would have to be countered, which meant more research, more projections—and more delay. I wondered how long leprechauns could stay in hiberniation. I hoped it was a long time.

I looked at the names on the letterhead of the Save Our Basin parchment. I didn't recognize any of them, but somebody in that organization was one clever lawyer. As far as I could see, none of the citations in the brief was precisely analogous to what would happen if we imported leprechauns into Angels City, but they were all close enough to being analogous that I (and, again by analogy, our legal staff) couldn't afford to ignore them. We'd have to examine every one of those instances, demonstrate that it was irrelevant, and withstand challenges from Save Our Basin trying to establish that the instances weren't irrelevant at all.

In a word, a mess. I figured the best way was to tackle their citations chronologically, so I started researching the Roman sack of Veii. I found out in a hurry that all the accounts of the sack are legendary, some more so than others. Legends are trickier to deal with than myths. Mythical material definitely has theological overtones; you know what the thaumaturgic content is. But in a legend you can't tell what's from This Side and what from the Other. A lawyer's paradise, in other words.

I'm sure Save Our Basin did it on purpose, too. Not for the first time lately, I had the feeling I was wading deeper into quicksand.

When quitting time finally rolled around, I breathed a heartfelt, "Thank God!" My spirits improved considerably as I left behind the spirits I'd been wrestling with at work and slid down to my carpet. I was looking forward to dinner with Judy, and to the rest of the evening being even more enjoyable than that.

On my way home, someone tried to kill me.

VII

Everything was fine till I got off the freeway at The Second. Traffic, in fact, had been a little lighter than usual, though on St. James' Freeway at rush hour a little light than usual isn't the same as light, or even close to it. Still, I was feeling pretty good about the world as I headed east up The Second toward my flat.

I had to wait for cross traffic at the corner of The Second and Anglewood Boulevard; a small church was being moved up Anglewood on top of a couple of extra-heavy-duty carpets. When at last it cleared the intersection, I tried to start across fast but couldn't because the little old lady on the carpet in front of me didn't. That probably saved my life, though I sent foul thoughts her way at the time.

A carpet had been idling in the parking lot of the fried

chicken place on the far side of Anglewood. I'd noticed it, and wondered what the two guys on it were thinking about. Most likely nothing, was my disparaging opinion; if they'd had any brains, they would have taken advantage of the hole in traffic the traveling church made and headed up The Second themselves.

They got moving fast enough after I went by. Too fast, in fact—if a black-and-white carpet had been anywhere nearby, they'd have picked up a ticket just like that. I saw in my rearview mirror that they didn't seem to like the way I was flying, either: they zoomed up above me to pass. That would have earned them another ticket from any constable who saw them.

I thought about signifying my opinion of the way they flew with an ancient fertility gesture, but I decided not to. As I've mentioned, Hawthorne is a tough town, and people have been known to get shot or have other unpleasant things happen to them on the flyways of Angels City. So I just did my best to pretend the louts didn't exist as they went up and over me.

As they did, though, one of them leaned out past the fringe of his carpet and dropped something down onto mine. They sped away . . . and my carpet didn't want to fly any more.

I had time for one startled squawk and the first two words of the *Shma* before the carpet, suddenly just a rug, hit the ground with a thump that made me bite my tongue and left my backside bruised for the next two weeks. If I hadn't been wearing my safety belt, if the carpet hadn't rolled up around me when I hit, or if I'd been going faster, I don't care to think what might have happened.

As things were, I wasn't badly hurt, but I had that weird sensation you get after an accident: I was pretty shaky, but I had almost total perception and recall of everything going on around me. Other carpets kept flying by a few feet overhead, the people on them intent on their own business and not caring at all about somebody who'd just had his carpet fail him.

But why had it failed? I couldn't figure that out. Did it

have something to do with whatever the punk had dropped on my carpet? I looked around for that, trying to find out what it was. I didn't see anything on the carpet itself, but something was stirring out on the weed-covered dirt just beyond the fringe.

I bent my head closer. The earth itself seemed to be writhing. For a second or two, I didn't understand what I was looking at. Then I did, and ice ran through me: it was a tiny earth elemental, busily digging itself back into its proper home.

Fire and water are the opposing elements we most commonly notice, but earth and air are opposites, too. Matt Arnold had talked about sylph-esteem and sylph-discipline, but if those two guys had tossed an earth elemental down onto my carpet, that was nothing short of sylph-abuse.

The elemental had gone now, though, back to its own proper home. I tried the starting spell. My carpet lifted off the ground as smoothly as if nothing had ever been wrong with it. Very carefully, looking every which way as I went and wishing for eyes in the back of my head, I flew on home.

All the way there, I tried to make some sense out of what had happened, the way theologians wrestle with God's will. Was it just a couple of hooligans out to have some sport with whoever drew the short straw? That's the sort of random violence that gives Angels City flyways a bad name, but this time I wished I could believe it. I couldn't, though.

Those two guys on that rug had been waiting for me in particular. I'd noticed them sitting a few feet off the ground in the parking lot while the church slowly flew by on Anglewood Boulevard. If they'd wanted to head up The Second, they'd had all the time they needed to do it. They'd just waited.

But why? Again, I didn't have much trouble coming up with an answer: it had to have something to do with the case of the toxic spell dump. I did my best to remember what the two punks had looked like. All I could come up with was swarthy and dark-haired. They might have been Persians or Aztecians. They might have been hired muscle, too: Israelites, Druzes, Indians from the Confederation or from India, even Hanese or Japanese. I hadn't got a real good look at then, and an awful lot of people in Angels City match up to the description swarthy and dark-haired.

I came to that dispirited conclusion about the time I set my carpet down in its parking space back at my block of flats. Somebody was going downstairs from his carpet as I was coming up from mine. He gave me an odd look as we passed on the stairs, but I didn't think anything of it past wondering what was haunting him that afternoon.

Then I turned the knob to my own flat. Judy sat curled up on the couch in the front room, reading a book on the Garuda Bird I'd picked up a few days before and hadn't got around to putting on a shelf yet. What started out as her smile of welcome turned into something else when her mouth sagged open in surprise. "Good God, David, what happened to you?"

A lot had happened to me, but I asked foolishly, "What do you mean, what happened?"

She sprang to her feet, grabbed me by the arm, and dragged me to the bathroom mirror as if I wasn't to be trusted to do anything that required rational thought on my own. "Look at yourself !" she commanded.

I mentally apologized to the fellow who'd stared at me while I was coming up to my flat. I looked like someone who'd been French-kissed by a vampire: streaks of blood ran from the corners of my mouth and had dripped down onto my shirt. Before I wore it again, I'd have to go visit Carlotta or somebody else with a vampster. All my clothes were disheveled, as if I'd been through a carpet crash in them. *Funny how that works*, I thought vaguely.

"What happened?" Judy said again.

So I told her, in as much detail as I remembered: pieces seemed blank, while others that happened only moments later were there in incredible perfection—I could have described exactly how every tiny clod of dirt wiggled and wavered as the earth elemental pushed its was through them after it rolled off my carpet. I started to, until Judy's face told me that wasn't something she needed to hear.

"You could have been killed," she said when I was through.

"That was the general idea," I said. "If I hadn't been wearing my safety belt, or even if I'd been going faster when they dropped the elemental on me—" I didn't care to think about that, much less talk about it. I turned on the cold water, splashed it onto my face. That, and then burying my head in a towel to dry off, gave me an excuse not to talk for a couple of minutes.

Then I tried to unbutton my shirt. That was when I discovered how bad my hands were shaking: I had a dreadful time making my fingers hold onto the smooth little buttons. After watching me struggle with the first two, Judy took over. As in everything she did, she was quick and deft and capable.

The feel of her fingers fluttering against my chest inflamed me as if she'd turned into a succubus. I've heard that living through a battle makes you horny. I didn't know about that, not firsthand; I hadn't been in a fight, let alone a battle, since I got out of primary school. But by the time Judy got to the last button, I couldn't wait any more. I grabbed her and kissed her—not quite as consumingly as I'd had in mind, because my tongue was still sore.

"Well," she said when she came up for air. Before she could say anything else, I kissed her again. "Well," she repeated a minute or so later, and this time she managed to go on: "It's a good thing I drank the cup of roots when I got here instead of waiting till after dinner."

It turned out to be a very good thing: for the next half hour or so, I forgot all about what had happened on The Second. The only problem with making to put aside your problems is that they're still there when it's over. Sitting up on the bed afterwards, I said, "You'd better be careful, too, honey. You've gotten yourself involved in this case. If they come after me—whoever *they* are—they're liable to come after you, too."

"That's non—" But it wasn't nonsense, and Judy must have known it, because she didn't finish the sentence. She sat up beside me. Her nod made her jiggle most pleasantly, but her voice was serious as she replied, "What have we gotten ourselves into here?"

I thought about Charlie Kelly and Henry Legion. "I don't know," I said grimly, "but I'm going to find out."

Dinner at the Hanese place was good. In fact, dinner was probably wonderful, but we were both too distracted to enjoy it as much as we should have—and, not meaning to be crude, my rear end hurt. And when we flew to the restaurant and then back again, I kept looking over my shoulder, wondering who was behind us . . . and why. I almost jumped out of my skin when a carpet zipped by closer than it should have, but it was just a couple of teenage kids with more machismo than brains.

When we got back to my flat—safe, sound, and overfed—Judy said, "I want you to do something for me." Like some people you may know, Judy has a Serious Voice. She was using it now.

"What is it?" I asked.

She said, "Before we went out, you said I should be careful from now on. Well, you should, too. I want you to start doing what they do in the thrillers: leave for work a few minutes early one day, then a few minutes late the next. Don't get onto the freeway at The Second every morning, or off it there every night. The same for Wilshire at the other end of your commute. Don't make yourself an easier target, I mean."

I started to laugh, to tell her that was all silly stuff. But it didn't seem silly, not after those guys had tried to do me in. "Okay," I said, and found myself nodding. "You do the same."

"I will," she promised.

I wondered if we ought to stop seeing each other for a while. If she'd said she wanted to do that, I wouldn't have let out a peep. But I didn't suggest it myself. Maybe that was selfish of me. In fact, I'm sure it was, a little. But the main reason I didn't was that I was pretty sure she was in too deep to turn invisible so easily.

"Do you want to stay the night, or do you think you'd be safer going home now?" I asked her.

"I'd intended to stay," she said. "I stuck a change of

clothes in your closet." She did some very visible thinking. "If they're interested in me—whoever *they* are—they have to know where I live. They could be waiting for me there as well as here. I'll stay." She made a face. "Oh, I don't like this! Having to think about everything before you do it—is it safe? is it risky? I don't like it at all."

"Me neither," I said. "But I'm glad you're staying. I wasn't what you'd call keen on being here by myself. I think I'd probably wake up every time a cat screeched or a dog barked." Was that selfish? Well, yes, probably. It was also very true.

I did something else then: I went into the hall closet, took out my blasting rod, and put it under the bed where I could get at it in a hurry. Judy watched without saying a word, but nodded soberly when I was done.

Judy and I woke up once in the middle of the night with a horrible start when the sylphs in somebody's carpet started screaming because the anti-theft geas was violated—or maybe because they thought it was, or maybe for no reason in particular. You never can tell with spirits of the air. Their nocturnal screams are a sound you hear fairly often in Angels City or any other good-sized town, generally when you least want to. At last whoever owned the carpet went down there and made them shut up, or maybe the thief flew away on it. Anyway, quiet returned.

"Jesus," Judy said.

"Or Somebody," I agreed. We both settled down and tried to go back to sleep. It took me a long time, and by the way Judy was breathing, she had as much trouble as I did. What had happened to me left both of us jumpy.

The horological demon in the alarm clock I'd bought at the swap meet caterwauled to get us up a little past six. The noise it made was so awful, I figured the Siamese exported its kind so they wouldn't have to listen to 'em. But at least it had the courtesy not to laugh as Judy and I woke up and untangled—we'd drifted together after we finally drifted back off, and were sort of sleeping all over each other.

Shower, shave (for me), dress, breakfast, coffee. We'd spent the night at each other's flats often enough that we had a routine for it. What wasn't routine was the way I walked Judy out to her carpet, looked around to make sure nobody was lurking nearby, and watched till she was out of sight. Then I went back to the garage, gave my own carpet a careful once-over before I got onto it, and finally headed for work.

I got there unscathed, shut the door to my office, and got on the phone. The first person I called was Legate Kawaguchi. He heard me out, then asked, "This occurred where? On The Second past Anglewood, you said?"

"That's right."

"This location, unfortunately, is not within the jurisdiction of the Angels City Constabulary Department, Inspector Fisher. I suggest you contact the Hawthorne constables and report it to them."

So I did, feeling foolish. People always say "Angeles City" or "A.C.," but the metropolitan area has lots of other municipalities, some large like Long Beach, others minuscule, but all of them jealously hanging onto as much autonomy as they can. The Hawthorne constables took my report and promised they'd look into it, but I didn't have any great faith in the promise. Unlike Kawaguchi, they had no feel for the kind of case in which I'd gotten myself involved. The decurion at the other end of the line asked if my flying could have angered the two men who dropped the earth elemental on my carpet. He wanted to keep things inside a simple framework.

When I finally got off the line there, I called Charlie Kelly in D.St.C. I listened to the imp at the far end squawk. It sounded very far away. I know you're going to tell me that's nonsense: thanks to the ether, no two points are more distant than any other two. I don't care; I'm telling you what I heard.

"Charles Kelly, Environmental Perfection Agency." *Took him long enough to answer his bloody telephone*, I thought.

"Good morning, Charlie," I said; it was still morning back in D.St.C., with half an hour to spare. "This is David Fisher, out in Angels City. A couple of men tried to kill me last night, Charlie. As far as I can tell, the only reason anybody would want to do that is the toxic spell dump case I'm working on—*your* toxic spell dump case. Don't you think it's about time you gave me the gospel truth, Charlie?"

"David, I—" There was a long, long silence on the other end, then a tiny sound, and then more silence. Even though it was reproduced through two phone imps, I recognized the sound: it was a handset, going gently back into its cradle. Charlie had hung up on me.

I didn't believe—no, I didn't want to believe—what that meant. Maybe, I told myself, Charlie'd had somebody important walk in and he'd get back to me later. Back in D.St.C., there were lots of important people, and even more who thought they were. I fooled with the parchment on my desk for fifteen minutes, then called back.

The phone squawked even longer than it had before. Finally I got an answer: "Environmental Perfection Agency, Melody Trudeau speaking." It was a woman's voice, all right, not the gravelly tones that made Charlie identifiable in spite of phone imps.

"Mistress Trudeau, this is David Fisher, from the Angels City EPA office. I'm looking for Charlie Kelly. I was on the phone with him a little while ago, and we got cut off." That was more than giving him the benefit of the doubt, but I still thought I might as well.

Then Melody Trudeau said, "I'm sorry, Mr. Fisher, but Mr. Kelly left for the day about fifteen minutes ago. Would you like me to take down a message for him?"

The kind of message I wanted to give him, I couldn't send over the phone. I said, "No, that's all right; thank you for asking," and hung up.

After that, I just stared at the phone for about five minutes. I needed that long for what had happened to soak in. As far as I could tell, Charlie Kelly had told me he didn't give a damn whether I lived or died. I know the Confederation has been only remotely feudal since not long after we broke away from England, but I still thought supervisors owed subordinates something in the way of loyalty, especially when they were the ones who'd got their subordinates into the mess in the first place. Go ahead, call me naive.

I started to go up front and dump my troubles on Bea, but

stopped about two steps away from my door. What was I supposed to tell her? "I'm sorry, boss, but I may not be in tomorrow because someone will have murdered me"? That didn't do the job, and what point complaining to her about Charlie Kelly? She couldn't do anything; she was junior to Charlie, too. She'd think he was contemptible, sure, but I already thought he was contemptible.

I stood there, halfway between my desk and the door, getting madder by the second. Then I turned around and stomped back to my chair. If Charlie wouldn't listen to me, Henry Legion would.

Seems logical, right? Getting hold of the CI spook wasn't as easy as I thought it was going to be. Central Intelligence wasn't in the D.St.C. telephone directory, apparently on the assumption that if you couldn't figure out how to reach them, you really didn't need to talk to them.

After I'd scratched my head for a minute or two, I called Saul Klein. He works for the Confederal Bureau of Investigation; his offices are a couple of floors above mine. I'd gotten to know him on the elevator and in the cafeteria. He's a good enough fellow. When he answered the phone, I said, "Saul? How are you? This is Dave Fisher down in the EPA. Can I pick your brain for a minute?"

"Sure, Dave," he answered. "What's up?"

"You know those little musical sprites they import from Alemania?"

"The minisingers? Sure. What about 'em?"

"I've heard some people express concern that they don't just learn new songs while they're here—that they might be picking up other things which could be useful for Alemanic intelligence." As far as I knew, there was nothing to that. Minisingers aren't spooks; you just take 'em to your *lieder* and turn 'em loose. A lot of taverns have them for background music, things like that. But my madness had method to it. Ingenuous as all get out, I asked, "Would that be CBI business, Saul?"

"Intelligence by foreign Powers? No, we don't touch that, Dave. You need to talk to Central Intelligence back at the capital," he said.

"Thanks. Do you happen to have their number?"

"Sure. I've got it right here," he said, and gave it to me. I wrote it down, thanked him again, and made my phone call. Sometimes the indirect approach is best.

Once I was actually talking with a real live human being (or so I presumed—you never can tell with CI), things went better. I got connected to Henry Legion faster than I'd ever been transferred before.

"Good day, Inspector Fisher," the CI spook said. His phone voice sounded more like his real voice than any natural person's. I wondered if that was because he, like the phone imps, was a creature of the Other Side, so they could pick up the essence of his voice as well as what he said. While I was wondering, he went on, "I thought I might hear from you again, but not so soon as this. What is the occasion of the call?"

"Somebody tried to kill me last night," I answered bluntly. "The only reason I can think of for anybody wanting to do that is the toxic spell dump case. I want to get to the bottom of that, and you're the only channel I have now."

No denying Henry Legion was sharp; he pounced on that last word like a lycanthrope leaping onto a roast of beef. "Now?" he said. "You previously had another source of information who has become inaccessible to you?"

"Inaccessible is just the word." I know I sounded bitter; I'd thought Charlie Kelly was a friend—oh, not a close friend, but somebody who wouldn't let me down if things got tough. He'd shown me what that notion was worth, though. Well, my loyalty to him stopped at the point where it was liable to get me killed. I told the spook, "You asked how I got wind of the danger of a Third Sorcerous War?"

"Yes?" Across three thousand miles, I could visualize his ectoplasmic ears springing to attention.

"Wait a minute," I said. "Before I tell you, I want your promise that you'll let me know what's going on. Everybody keeps saying that the more I know, the more dangerous it'll be for me. I can't think of anything a lot more dangerous than getting killed."

"I can," Henry Legion said. Maybe he really could; maybe

he was just trying to scare me. But I was past being scared of—or by—phantoms, and didn't answer. After a couple of silent seconds, the spook took another tack: "Why should you believe any promise I make? I am of the Other Side, and have no soul to stake on an oath."

"Promise on your pride in your own wits and I'll believe you," I told him.

Another telephone pause. When it was done, Legion said, "You're not the least clever mortal with whom I have dealt. Let it be as you say. By my pride in my wits, Inspector Fisher, I shall tell you what I know in exchange for your information—on condition that the secret go no farther than you."

"Uh," I said. I couldn't think of a condition better calculated to make Judy want to wring my neck. "My fiancée is also involved in this case, and has been just about from the start. She knows about the threat of the Third Sorcerous War. I can't promise not to tell her, but she doesn't blab."

Henry Legion let out a long sigh. "Sexuality," he said, as if he were cursing. "Very well, Inspector Fisher, I agree to your proposed amendment, provided she agrees to tell no one. Now speak, and withhold nothing."

So I spoke. I told him about Charlie Kelly, and about the bird Charlie kept being too coy to name. And I told him what Charlie had said about the risk of war—and about how Charlie had hung up on me and bugged out of his office.

"Ah, Mr. Kelly," the spook said. "Matters become less murky."

"Not to me, they don't," I told him.

"Although of low rank himself" (Charlie was several notches above me, but I let that go) "your Mr. Kelly is well-connected politically," Henry Legion said. "He is the close friend and familiar—I use the word almost in the thaumaturgical sense—of a Cabinet subminister whose name I prefer not to divulge but who, I think, is like to be the source of his, ah, sensitive information. That matter can be—and shall be—rectified, I assure you."

I didn't care for the way he said *rectified*. I wondered if the anonymous Cabinet subminister was about to have the fear of an angry God put into him . . . or if he'd have to suffer what they call an unfortunate accident. But that, for me, was a side issue. I said, "I told you what I know. Now you keep your end of the bargain."

At that point, much too late, I wondered how I was supposed to make him keep the bargain if he didn't feel like it. But he said, "Perhaps this conversation would be better continued face to face rather than through the ether. You are on the seventh floor of the Westwood Confederal Building, is that not correct?"

"That's right," I agreed.

"Hang up the phone, then. I shall see you shortly."

I dutifully hung up. Sure enough, a couple of seconds later Henry Legion materialized in my office—or rather, the top half of him did: the floor cut him off at what would have been his belly button if spooks had belly buttons. The sound-proofing in the Confederal Building is pretty good, but I heard the woman in the office right below me let out a startled squeal, so I presume Henry's legs end popped into being just below her ceiling.

The spook peered down at himself. He looked mistily annoyed, then said, "A three-foot error on a crosscountry journey isn't bad. It's not as if I were material." He sounded like someone trying to convince himself and not having much luck. He pulled himself up through the floor so his ectoplasmic wing-tips rested on the carpet.

It's a good thing he's not material, I thought. Two different sets of matter aren't designed to occupy the same space at the same time. The likeliest result of that would have been one big bang.

Once he was all in the room with me, his dignity recovered in a hurry. He draped himself over a chair, gave me a nod, and said, "By my pride in my own wits, David Fisher, I shall tell you what I can. Ask your questions."

His wits were still working pretty well, I noticed: if I didn't come up with the right questions, I wouldn't find out what I needed to know. Well, first things first: "Who's trying to kill me?"

Henry Legion's indistinct features distinctly frowned.

"Without further information, I cannot answer that with any more assurance than you possess yourself. I realize it is of the essence to you, but I trust you will understand it is not my primary concern."

"Yeah," I said grudgingly. Understanding didn't mean I had to like it. I tried something else: "If there is, God forbid, a Third Sorcerous War, who's going to be in it? And whose side will we be on?"

"God forbid indeed," the spook said. "As for who would begin the fighting if war came, again I cannot say with any certainty. The Confederation's place would depend on the patterns of other belligerents; as you may know, some of our alliance systems overlap others."

"As a matter of fact, I do know that." I was getting angry. "I also know that I gave you straight answers and you're giving me the runaround. I don't call that a fair exchange." I didn't know what I could do about that, unfortunately. If Henry Legion didn't feel like answering questions, all he had to do was disappear and ignore my phone calls from then on out.

But he didn't disappear. He held up a transparent but placating hand. Before he could say anything, Rose tapped on the door, then opened it and stuck her nose into my office. "I'm sorry, Dave," she said quickly. "I didn't realize you had someone in here." Then she got a good look at Henry Legion. Her eyes widened as she realized what sort of someone he was. But she closed the door and went away anyhow. Rose is a wonderful secretary.

"You were saying—" I prompted the spook.

"So I was," Henry Legion agreed. "I do apologize for appearing evasive, but the matter is more complex than most mortals, even those in high places, fully grasp. The turmoil that has marked this century—and that may yet precipitate the Third Sorcerous War—has roots that go back hundreds of years. It is an outcome of a fundamental shift in the balance of Powers that occurred with and as a result of the European expansion which began half a millennium ago."

"I do follow you," I said. "Remember where you are: this is the EPA. One of the things I'm working on that has nothing to do with the toxic spell dump case is whether the Chumash Indian Powers have gone extinct in the past few years."

"This is a trivial example of the phenomenon to which I refer," the spook said. "Powers have been reduced and displaced and others magnified on a scale unseen since the diminution and near-destruction of the Greco-Roman pagan deities and the rise of Christianity. And that impacted only Europe, North Africa, and western Asia; this is worldwide in scope. To give you some notion of what I mean, consider that Sarganatas and Nebiros, the one brigadier-major, the other field-marshal and inspector-general of the Judeo-Christian Descending Hierarchy, have for several centuries made their residence here in the Americas."

"I grant that they're wickeder than Huitzilopochtli, but are they any nastier?" I asked. The Aztecian war-god wasn't evil in and of himself the way the demon princes were, but his proper food was blood. My stomach twisted when I thought about the flayed human skin in the potion Cuauhtémoc Hernandez had sold to Lupe Cordero.

But Henry Legion said, "That is not the point. The point is that Huitzilopochtli has been displaced, and naturally resents it. The same is true of most of the indigenous Powers of the Americas, of Polynesia, of Australia. The Muslim expansion through the Southern Isles has reduced the range of the Hindu Powers, who still have their enormous Indian belief base upon which to draw. Ukrainian and Spanish conquests, on the other hand, have cut into the sphere where jinni and ghouls and other Muslim Powers can roam at will. And the horror that was Alemania two generations ago shows Christendom isn't immune to theological disaster, either."

"What you're telling me is that the whole world is going to hell," I said slowly. I wondered whether I was exaggerating for conversational effect or being perfectly literal.

"Central Intelligence prognostications put the probability of that outcome as less than ten percent in the next decade," Henry Legion said, his voice inhumanly calm. "A year ago, however, that same probability was assessed at less than three percent. Whether fully Judeo-Christian or not, Inspector Fisher, trouble is brewing beneath the orderly surface of our existence."

Since I'd had the door closed all morning, my office was warm and rather stuffy. I shivered even so. "Okay," I said. "There's trouble. What does it have to do with the Devonshire toxic spell dump?"

"As for a precise answer, I can only speculate," Henry Legion replied. "But consider this: the spell residues stored at that site are the worst and most potent yet devised. If they are leaking into the wider environment, they draw attention to the dump. That attention is liable to be extremely unwelcome if something undocumented but deadly is being disposed of at the Devonshire dump."

All at once, I remembered the Nothing I'd seen walking the path from the dump entrance to Tony Sudakis' office. I never had got around to asking him what that was. I hadn't called him Tuesday, either—too many other things going on.

"Have you any further questions?" Henry Legion asked.

"Yeah, I do," I said. "Okay, you don't know for sure which Powers or humans might touch off the Third Sorcerous War. You must have suspects, though. Isn't that what Central Intelligence is for—to be suspicious?"

"As a matter of fact, yes," the spook answered. "Suspects, you say? In order of probability, they are Persia, Aztecia, the Ukraine, and India."

That didn't help me much. Some sort of Persian connection seemed the most likely cause of trouble at the Devonshire dump, too, at least judging by what had happened to Erasmus, while I couldn't rule out the Aztecans, either, not with Huitzilopochtlism on the loose and the trail that had led me to poor soulless Jesus Cordero.

For that matter, I couldn't rule out the Powers of India, either, which meant Loki and the other aerospace firms were still suspects. Along with the cow, Erasmus had been tormented by sorcerous serpents, and the Garuda Bird is a great foe of such.

Complications, complications . . . I remembered that other serpent I'd seen, the one in the Garden of virtuous reality who hadn't had to crawl around on his belly. If the model for that serpent had behaved himself better, the world would be a more peaceful place today.

I said, "What you're telling me is that you don't know who's trying to kill me or who wants to start the war, but you want to use me to help you find out."

"In essence, yes," Henry Legion said. "Keeping you alive while the investigation proceeds would also be desirable."

"To me even more than to you," I assured him. The situation reminded me of an old riddle: how do you know when there are pixies around? The answer is, when you get pixilated. I never had found that riddle very funny. It was a lot less so now, when it was more like finding out who was trying to kill me by what happened when they did it.

Someone tapped on the door, then opened it: Rose again. She said quietly, "When I saw you had an important guest, David, I arranged for my phone imp to cover yours. Here's a message for you." Nodding as politely to Henry Legion as if she couldn't see through him, she went back outside again.

The spook said, "We here at Central Intelligence—and at other nations' equivalent services, I assure you—are generally less than delighted when an amateur like yourself gets stuck between the lines of the cantrip, so to speak: not only because of the danger to which you are exposed but also on account of your unpredictability, which may set off other unpredictable acts at a juncture when unpredictable acts have the potential to bring on what may for all practical purposes be Armageddon."

If Henry Legion had been a human being, he couldn't possible have said all that on one breath. As it was, Charlie Kelly had in essence told me the same thing. But Charlie had bugged out on me, while the CI spook was still on my side—I hoped.

"What do you suggest I do next?" I asked him.

"Carry on with your life and work as normally as you can," he answered. "If fate is kind—always an interesting question—you will eventually be able to work your way out of the center of interest you now occupy."

"And if fate isn't?" I said.

A human being, even one who worked for Central Intelligence, probably would have given me a soothing answer back. Henry Legion didn't. "If fate is unkind, Inspector Fisher, you will be killed. If fate is very unkind, the world will go with you. As I said before, the balance of Powers has been upset for a long time. Megasalamanders may be the least we have to worry about."

That much pessimism rocked me. "But a megasalamander can slag a whole city—" I felt absurd the second the words were out of my mouth. Was I bragging of how destructive our ultimate weapons were or complaining they weren't destructive enough?

"Yes, Inspector Legion, but although megasalamanders are of the Other Side, the devastation they create is confined to the material," Henry Legion said implacably. "Further, they do not launch themselves, but travel when and were ordered by the mages who control them. If the Powers seek to redress the balance on their own—"

He dematerialized then, leaving me an an empty office and cold dread in my middle. That's the trouble about arguing with a spook: if he wants it, he can have the last word. This time, though, I think he would have had it even if he'd stayed around.

I thought about what he'd just said. Suppose all the Powers that had seen their domains shrink over the past five hundred years or so got together and struck back at the Ones that had dispossessed them. A man mad for revenge is liable to take it no matter what it costs him and those he loves. If the Powers acted the same way, then heaven help the people over a big part of the globe . . . except it would more likely be hell on earth.

No wonder Henry Legion couldn't work up much concern about whether I individually lived or died. In a way, it didn't seem that important to me any more, either. But only in a way.

I stared down at my desk, trying to get back from contemplating Armageddon to doing my job. My eye fell on the note Rose had come in to give me. The message, I saw, was from Legate Kawaguchi. It said, in its entirety, "The feather is from a specimen of PHAROMACHRUS MOCINNO." It was written just like that; Rose had printed the formal name in block capitals so I couldn't possible misread it. Undoubtedly she'd had Kawaguchi give it to her letter by letter so she wouldn't get it wrong, too. Rose is a queen among secretaries.

Only one trouble: I hadn't the slightest notion what a *Pharomachrus mocinno* was. I called Kawaguchi back, but I didn't get him. He'd gone into the field—something horrible and gruesome had just broken. The centurion who took my call sounded so harassed that I didn't have the nerve to ask him whether he knew what kind of bird Kawaguchi had meant.

I went and checked our own reference library: not all environmental issues involve the Other Side. We had books about birds that dwell in the Barony of Angels. *Pharomachrus mocinno* wasn't one. A little information, but not much. I made a mental note to ask Kawaguchi about it the next time I talked with him, then went back to work.

A good rule I've developed and don't follow enough is *when in doubt, make a list*. Writing things down forces you to think about what's important to you. It works so well, it's almost magic. The first writing, I suspect, really was magic— magic against forgetting. It still serves that role if you give it half a chance.

So I wrote. When I was done, the top of the list looked like this:

① Checking around the Devonshire toxic spell dump.
② Bakhtiar's Precision Burins.
③ The Chumash Powers.
④ Importing leprechauns.
⑤ Chocolate Weasel.

Everything below ⑤, I figured, could wait. Most of the bottom of the list was day-to-day stuff where it didn't really matter whether the day was today, tomorrow, or next Tuesday. Some of the other items, like what had caused Jesus Cordero to be born apsychic, were important in and of themselves, but were also linked to high-priority items.

I also noticed I didn't really have five items up at the top: I

had two. Getting to Bakhtiar's Precision Burins and Chocolate Weasel sprang from trying to get to the bottom of what
was going on at the Devonshire dump, and of course the
Chumash Powers study and the one on leprechauns were
almost incestuously intertwined.

Armed with my list, I did go up front to see Bea. I wanted
to get her approval on it so I could carry on with a clear conscience and without having to worry about unexpected
thunderbolts from her. Rose waved me through into her
sanctum; for a wonder, Bea wasn't on the phone and she
didn't have anybody in there with her.

"Good morning, David," she said. One eyebrow went up.
"I hear you've been spending time with some high-powered
company. I'm very impressed."

I wasn't surprised Rose had told her; a secretary is supposed to keep a division head informed about what people
are doing. And besides, even a queen of secretaries is entitled to a little gossip.

But if Bea knew about Henry, I could take advantage of it
even though I wished I'd never met the CI spook. I said,
"The Devonshire dump case seems to be turning into a
national security affair. That's why I've put it at the top of my
to-do list." I shoved the parchment across the desk at her.

She looked at it, she looked at me, she shook her head
slowly back and forth a couple of times. In that church-choir
voice of hers, she said, "David, why do I get the feeling the
main reason you're showing me this list is to get my approval
in advance for what you intend to do anyway?"

With some bosses, wide-eyed innocence would have been
the best approach: *Me? I can't imagine what you're talking
about*. Try that with Bea and she'd rap your knuckles with a
ruler, maybe metaphorically, maybe not. I said, "You're right.
But I really think these are the things that *need* doing. I'll
handle as much of the rest of the stuff as I can, but I'm not
going to worry if I get behind on it while I'm settling the big
things." If I'd had to, I'd have told her about Charlie Kelly
then. That would have shown her I wasn't taking the spell
dump case too seriously.

But she looked at me again, nodded as slowly as she'd

shaken her head before. "David, part of being a good manager is giving your people their heads and letting them run with their projects. I'm going to do that with you now. But another part of being a good manager is letting people know you're not here to be taken advantage of."

"I understand," I said. And I did: if these cases turned out to be inconsequential, or if they were important and I botched them, she'd rack me for it. That was firm, but it was fair. Bea *is* a good manager, even if I do hate staff meetings.

"All right, David," she said with a faint sigh. "Thank you."

Rose gave me a curious look as I emerged from Bea's office. I flashed a thumbs-up, then waggled it a little to show I wasn't sure everything would fly on angels' wings. She made silent clapping motions to congratulate me. "Oh, David, what was that bird the constabulary legate called you about?" she asked.

"As a matter of fact, I still don't know myself," I said. "I went to the reference center to look it up, but I couldn't find it there. That means it's not local, whatever it is. I'll call Kawaguchi back this afternoon and find out. I'll let you know as soon as I do." One way to keep a secretary happy is not to hold out on her.

I went back to my office, dug through my notes, found the phone number for Bakhtiar's Precision Burins, and called. The way my luck had been running, I figured a thunderbolt would probably smite the Confederal Building just as I made the connection.

And I was close. The phone at the other end had just begun to squawk when a little earthquake rattled the building. I sat there waiting, wondering the way you always do whether the little earthquake would turn into a big one. It didn't; in a few seconds, the rattling stopped. Along with (I'm sure) several million other people, I breathed a prayer of thanksgiving.

The secretary for Bakhtiar's Precision Burins and I spent a little while going "Did you feel that?" and "I sure did" back and forth at each other before I confirmed my appointment and hung up. Then I got back on the phone—this morning I'd used it as much as Bea usually does—and called Tony Sudakis.

"Hello, Dave," he said. "I was wondering when I'd hear from you again. Thought maybe my file fell behind your desk or something." He laughed to show I wasn't supposed to take him seriously.

I laughed too, to show I didn't. "No such luck," I told him. "This is just to let you know that we will be doing a sorcerous decontamination check of the area around your site as soon as we can get the apparatus together."

"I appreciate the courtesy of the call, Inspector," he answered slowly—I wasn't Dave any more. "I have to tell you, though, we still deny any contamination. You'll need a show-cause order before you can start anything like that, and we'll fight it."

"I know," I said. "When your legal staff asks you, tell them the case is under the jurisdiction of Judge Ruhollah"—I spelled it for him—"since he granted me the original search warrant." If the EPA couldn't get a show-cause order out of Maximum Ruhollah, I figured it was time for us to fold our tents and head off into the desert.

"Judge Ruhollah," Sudakis repeated. "I'll pass it along. 'Bye." I didn't think he knew about Ruhollah. But the consortium's lawyers would.

I moved parchments from one pile to another on my desk, called Legate Kawaguchi again and found out he was still at the crime scene, then ate a rubberized hamburger at the cafeteria. I washed it down with a cup of hot black mud, slid down the parking lot, and headed up into St. Ferdinand's Valley again.

Normally I wouldn't go up there ten times a year. I'd been doing it so often lately that I was starting to memorize the freeway exits. I got off at White Oak and flew north toward Bakhtiar's Precision Burins. On the way, I passed a church dedicated to St. Andrew: actually, to San Andreas, because it was an Aztecan neighborhood. A line of penitents was filing in. I wondered why; St. Andrew's feast day isn't until November.

Then I remembered the morning's earthquake. No doubt they were calling on the saint to keep more and worse from happening. Their chants rang so loud and sincere, they made me sure that if another earthquake did strike, it wouldn't be San Andreas' fault.

I flew into the parking lot behind Bakhtiar's Precision Burins a couple of minutes early. The building that housed the outfit was four times the size of Slow Jinn Fizz's fancy establishment on Venture Boulevard, and probably cost about a fourth as much to rent. It had the virtue of absolute plainness—one more industrial building in an industrial part of town.

The receptionist who greeted me was about a fourth as decorative as the one at Slow Jinn Fizz, too. So it goes. But she was friendly enough, or maybe more than friendly enough. "Oh, you're Inspector Fisher," she said when I showed her my EPA sigil. "Did the earth move for you, too?" She giggled.

I didn't know what to make of that. If I'd been unattached, I might have been more interested in finding out. As it was, I figured the best thing to do was let it alone, so I did. I said, "Is Mr. Bakhtiar free to see me?"

"Just a minute, I'll check." She picked up the handset of the phone. Bakhtiar's Precision Burins wasn't in the high-rent district, but it used all the latest sorceware. The silencing spell on the phone was so good that I couldn't hear a word the receptionist said till she hung up. "He says he can give you forty-five minutes at the most. Will that be all right?"

"Thanks. It should be fine, Mistress Mendoza," I answered, reading the name plate on her desk: CYNTHIA MENDOZA.

"Call me Cyndi," she said. "Everybody does. Here, come on with me. I have to let you into the back of the shop because of the security system."

I followed her back down the hall. Bakhtiar's doorway wasn't hermetically sealed; as I've said, only really big firms and governments can afford that much security. But he did have an alarmed door: if anybody who wasn't authorized touched the doorknob, it would yell bloody murder.

Cyndi Mendoza took the knob in her hand and chanted softly from the Book of Proverbs: " 'She crieth at the gates, at the entrance of the city, at the coming of the doors,' " and then from the Song of Solomon: " 'I rose up to open to my beloved. I opened to my beloved.' " The knob turned in her hand. She waved me through ahead of her, then murmured something else to the door to propitiate it for having let me through.

"Do you know," she said as she led me through the burin works to Bakhtiar's office, "the same charm that persuades the alarmed door to open peaceably is also used sometimes as a seduction spell?"

"Is that a fact?" I said, though it didn't surprise me: nothing in the Judeo-Christian tradition blends sensuality and mystic power like the Song of Solomon.

She nodded. "It doesn't get tried as often as it used to, though—it only works on virgins." This brought forth more giggles.

She couldn't have made it more obvious she was interested in me if she'd run up a flag. A man always finds that flattering, but I wasn't interested back. I said, "Is that a fact?" again. It's one of the few things you can safely say under any circumstances, because it doesn't mean a thing.

"Well, here we are," Cyndi said, stopping in front of a door that had ISHAQ BAKHTIAR, MARGRAVE painted on it in black letters edged with gilt. She tapped on the door—which mustn't have been alarmed, since it didn't scream—then headed back toward her own desk. I'm afraid she gave me a dirty look as she went by.

Ishaq Bakhtiar opened his own door, waved for me to come in. He didn't look like a corporate margrave; he looked—and dressed—like a working journeyman wizard. By stereotype, Persians come in two varieties, short and round or long and angular. Ramzan Durani of Slow Jinn Fizz had been of the first sort. Bakhtiar exemplified the second. Everything about him was vertical lines: thin arms and legs, his big, not quite straight nose and the creases to either side of it, the beard worn short on the cheeks and long on the chin that made his face seem even narrower than it was.

Like Ramzan Durani, he wore a white lab robe. Unlike Durani's, his didn't give the impression of being something he put on to impress visitors. It wasn't what you'd call shabby, but it had been washed a good many times and still bore faint stains that looked like old blood and herbal juices.

When we clasped hands, his engulfed mine—and I'm not a small man, nor one with short fingers. But if he hadn't gone into sorcery, he would have made a master harpsichordist; those spidery fingers of his seemed to reach halfway up my arm.

"I am pleased to meet you, Inspector Fisher," he said with a vanishing trace of Persian accent that did more to lend his English dignity than to turn it guttural. "Please take a seat."

"Thank you." I sat down in the chair to which he waved me. It wasn't very comfortable, but it was the same as the one behind his desk, so I couldn't complain.

"Will you take mint tea?" he asked, pointing at a samovar that must have come from a junk shop. "Or perhaps, since the day is warm, you would rather have an iced sherbet? Please help yourself to sweetmeats, also."

Since he poured tea for himself, I had some, too. It was excellent; he might not have cared how things looked, but how they performed mattered to him. The sweetmeats sent up the ambrosial perfume of almond paste. Their taste didn't disappoint, either.

He didn't linger over the courtesies, nor had I expected him to, not when he'd blocked out only forty-five minutes for me. As soon as we'd both wiped crumbs from our fingers, he leaned forward, showing he was ready to get down to business. I took the hint and said, "I'm here, Mr. Bakhtiar, because you're one of the major dumpers of toxic spell byproducts at the Devonshire site, and, as I said over the phone, the dump appears to be leaking."

His dark brows came down like thunderclouds. "And so you think it is my byproducts that are getting out. You think I am the polluter. Allah, Muhammad, and Hussein be my witnesses, I deny this, Inspector Fisher."

"I don't know whether you're the polluter," I said. "I do know from your manifests that enough sorcerous byproducts come from this business to make me have to look into the possibility."

"Get the burin-maker—he is always the polluter."
Bakhtiar scowled at me, even more blackly than before. "In
superstitious Persia, I could understand this attitude though
I know how foolish it is. Here in the Confederation, where
reason is supposed to rule, my heart breaks to hear it. Taken
over all, Inspector, Bakhtiar's Precision Burins reduces the
sorcerous pollution in Angels City; we do not increase it.
This I can demonstrate."

"Go on, sir." I thought I knew the argument he was going
to use, but I might have been wrong.

I wasn't. He said, "Consider, Inspector, if every wizard
had to manufacture his own sorcerous tools, as was true in
the olden days: not just burins but also swords, staves, rods,
lancets, arctraves, needles, poniards, swords, and knives with
white and black handles. Because the sorcerers of the
barony would be less efficient and more widespread than we
are here, far more magical contamination would result from
their work. But that does not happen, because most
thaumaturges purchase their instruments from me. They
cause no pollution because they are not doing the work. I
am, and because of it, Bakhtiar's Precision Burins draws the
attention of regulators like yourself."

I've heard that single-source argument many times. It
generally has an element of truth to it: doing things in one
place often is more efficient and better for the environment
than scattering them all over the landscape. And Bakhtiar
was right when he said single-source providers do stand out
because they still pollute and the people who use their services don't. But all that doesn't mean single-source providers
can't pollute more than they should.

I said as much. Bakhtiar got to his feet. "Come with me,
Inspector. You shall see for yourself."

He took me out onto the production floor. It was as ef-
ficiently busy as most other light industrial outfits I've
seen. A worker wearing asalamandric gloves lifted a rack
of red-glowing pieces of steel out of a fire, turned and
quenched them in a bath from which strong-smelling
steam rose.

"That must have been the third heating for the burin

blanks," Bakhtiar said. "Now they steep in magpie's blood and the juice of the herb *foroile*."

"Ergonomically efficient," I said; the factory hand had been able to transfer them from the flames to the bath without taking a step. As they soaked up the virtues of the blood and the herb, he prayed over them and spoke words of power. Among the Names I caught were those of the spirits Lumech, Gadal, and Mitatron, all of whom are potent indeed. I asked, "How do you decontaminate the quenching bath after you've infused the Powers into it?"

"The usual way: with prayer and holy water," Bakhtiar answered. "Inspector, I do not claim these are one hundred percent efficacious; I am aware there is a residue of power left behind. This, after all, is why we dispose of our toxic spell byproducts at the Devonshire facility, as mandated by the laws of the barony, the province, and the Confederation. If leaks have occurred, surely that is the responsibility of the dump, not of Bakhtiar's Precision Burins. We have complied with the law in every particular."

"If so, you don't have a problem," I answered. "My concern is that someone has been disposing of byproducts that aren't listed on his manifest, things vicious enough to break through the protection setup, even if in only minuscule amounts, and to sorcerously contaminate the surrounding environment."

"This I understand," he said, nodding. "As manufacturers of burins and other thaumaturgical tools, however, we operate with a limited range of magic-engendering materials, as you must know. Here, come with me. See if you find one tiny thing in any way out of the ordinary for an establishment such as ours."

I came. He was right; I didn't find anything out of the ordinary. The knives with the black handles were steeped in cat's blood and hemlock and fitted with handles of ram's horn. Interesting that Bakhtiar, a Muslim, conformed to common Judeo-Christian usage there; I'm given to understand the affinity goes back to the *shofar*, the ram's-horn trumpet which commemorates the trumpets that toppled Jericho's walls.

Another technician was inscribing magical characters onto
hazelwood wands and cane staffs. The scribing instrument
was a burin, presumably one of Bakhtiar's precision burins.
He also inscribed the seals of the demons Klippoth and Fri-
most onto wands and staffs, respectively. I could feel the
power in the air around him.

The sorcerous and the mundane mingled in the production of the silken cloths in which Bakhtiar's burins and other
instruments were wrapped. The firm did its own weaving
in-house; three Persian women in black *chadors* and veils
worked clacking looms, turning silk thread into fine, shim-
mering cloth. I wondered how long it would be before the
automated looms of the Japanese made that economically
impractical. They'd taken much of the flying carpet business
from Detroit, and they were skillful silkworkers. As far as I
could see, the combination made it only a matter of time.

Bakhtiar said, "The red silk is for the burins, the black, fittingly, for the knife with the black handle, and the green for
the other magical instruments. For those others, the proper
color is less important, so long as it be neither black nor
brown."

A calligrapher with a goose quill dipped in pigeon's blood
wrote mystic characters on a finished silk cloth. Around him,
a dozen other goose quills, animated by the law of similarity,
wrote identical characters on other cloths. I asked Bakhtiar,
"Why are you using automatic writing for this process and
not that of inscribing the wands and staffs?"

"As we have the opportunity, we shall, *inshallah*, do the
latter as well," he answered. "But the silks are merely protective vessels for the instruments, while the instruments
themselves are filled with a thaumaturgic power which as yet
overcomes the automating spells. But we are working on it,
as I say. In fact, I read recently that a sorceware designer up
in Crystal Valley has had a breakthrough along those very
lines."

"Was he using virtuous reality, by any chance?" I asked.

"As a matter of fact, he was." Bakhtiar sounded surprised.
Up till then, his expression had said I was an unmitigated
nuisance. Now my nuisance value was at least mitigated. He

said, "You are better informed on matters sorcerous than I should have expected from a bureaucrat."

"We don't spend all our times shuffling parchments from one pile to the next," I said. "Too much of our time, yes, but not all."

He stared at me out of black, deep-set eyes. "I might even wish you spent more time at your desk, Inspector, provided that time was the period you have instead set aside for harassing legitimate businesses such as mine."

"Investigation is not harassment," I said, and stared right back. Persians of the lean variety tend to look like prophets about to call down divine wrath on a sinful people, which gave Bakhtiar what I thought of as an unfair advantage in that kind of contest, but I held my own. "And we can't afford to take a spill from this dump lightly. In aid of which, may I see the decontamination facility you mentioned?"

"I shall take you there," he said. "I expected that would be your next request."

Sensibly, Bakhtiar kept his decontaminators off the main shop floor and in a chamber of their own. That both minimized any corruption that might interfere with their work and made sure their procedures wouldn't weaken the sorcery that went into the instruments.

"Inspector Fisher, allow me to present Dagoberto Velarde and Kirk McCullough, the decontamination team for Bakhtiar's Precision Burins," Bakhtiar said. "Bert, Kirk, this is David Fisher of the EPA. They think we're responsible for a leak at the Devonshire dump."

I didn't bother denying that any more; I'd seen I wasn't going to convince Bakhtiar and his crew. The decontaminators glared at me. Velarde was short and copper-brown, McCullough tall, gaunt, and red-haired, with the light of religious certainty shining in his hard gray eyes. "Just carry on, gentlemen," I said. "Pretend I'm not here."

By their expressions, they wished I wasn't. They made an odd team, one you wouldn't find everywhere, but they worked smoothly together, as if they'd been doing it for years. They probably had. One of the guys from the shop floor—no, I take it back, it was a woman in hard hat, overalls, and boots—wheeled in a vat on a dolly. She slid it off, nodded to the decontaminators, and headed back out.

Bert Velarde broke open an ampule of holy water, sprinkled it over the vat to neutralize as much of the goetic power in there as it could. Holy water is efficacious if applied by any believer, and, while you can't always tell by looking, I would have bet two weeks' pay he was Catholic.

But prayers by Catholic layfolk aren't as potent as those from priests. Velarde didn't pray. That was Kirk McCullough's job. He had a deep, impressive voice and a thick Caledonian burr. He hardly bothered looking at the Book of Common Prayer he held in his big hands; he knew the words by heart. That didn't mean he was just reciting by rote, though—he put his heart into every word.

"Kirk is an elder of the Church of the Covenant," Bakhtiar told me quietly. "The diversity of Angels City has its advantages."

"I'll say," I agreed. Ishaq Bakhtiar was one sharp operator. The distinction between clergy and laity is much less in Protestant churches than in Catholicism; the prayers of an elder, who presumably was among the elect, were as likely to be heard as a minister's. And Bakhtiar could hire two laymen for less than he'd have had to pay one who was consecrated. Like I said, a sharp operator.

He was also sharp enough to say, "And if you have any doubts whatsoever, Inspector Fisher, as the whether the decontaminators are fully employed, come back to my office with me now and I will show you complete records of their activity since we moved into this building."

I had no doubts, but I went with him nonetheless. He rummaged through his files, plopped a handful down in front of me. I looked through them. They showed me what he'd said they would. This left me unsurprised: how often will the head of a business voluntarily show documents that don't paint him in the best possible light?

But if anything was wrong at Bakhtiar's Precision Burins, you couldn't have proved it by me. All his procedures were what they should have been; his decontamination team might have been unorthodox (in the nontheological sense of the word), but it was effective.

"Anything else, Inspector?" he asked when I'd worked my way through the last folder. Rather pointedly, he asked his watch what time it was.

The little horological demon's answer showed I'd already devoured fifty-five of his precious and irreplaceable minutes, where I'd promised to make do with a mere forty-five. I guess I was supposed to wail and abase myself and swear never to sin in that particular way again. Living in a large city, though, has a way of coarsening you. When I said, "I'm sorry I took up so much of your time," I put just enough bureaucratic indifference into my voice to let him know I wasn't the least bit sorry.

He glared at me again. This time, I didn't bother glaring back, which only irked him more. I got up. "I think I can find my own way out."

"No, you mis—" He caught himself. If he was really rude to me, who could guess how much trouble I'd cause him? Persians understand about revenge. He tried again: "No, Inspector, you forget the door. It is active in both directions."

So, no matter how much he didn't care for me, he had to escort me out so I wouldn't alarm his door (and in case you're wondering, I hadn't forgotten). He gave me some insincere parting pleasantries and let me walk up the hall by myself.

Cyndi Mendoza hit me with a dazzling smile when I came out to her desk (I'd forgotten about her—Bakhtiar could have won the exchange if he'd called her back to his office to bring me out, but that would have cost him an extra couple of minutes of my presence, and I suppose he was too efficient to think of it). She said, "Do you remember that opening spell?"

Which was, no doubt, intended to get around to asking if I thought it would work on her. I forestalled that, though: I said, "I'm sorry, no—I make it a point never to remember anything." I walked out while she was still staring.

When I got back to the Confederal Building and went up to my office, I found on my desk a note from Rose in big red letters: *David, come up to Bea's office immediately*. Wondering what sort of trouble I'd managed to get into while I was gone, I went up to Bea's office.

In the anteroom sat Rose—the real ruler of the domain— and a fussy-looking little fellow with a big nose and a loud cravat. He was looking through one of Rose's stationery catalogues, which meant he was either madly meticulous or bored stiff: the latter, if a couple of little faint spots on his shirt meant anything.

"Hello, Dave," Rose said to me, and then, "Here he is, Mr. Epstein."

The little man bounced to his feet. "You are David Fisher, Inspector, Environmental Perfection Agency?" he asked, running my name and job title together.

"Yes," I said. "Who are you?"

"Samuel Epstein, subclerk of the courts, Angels City, Barony of Angels." From under the stationery catalogue he drew out a piece of parchment so splendid with calligraphy (it's mostly done by automatic writing these days, as with the quills inscribing symbols on the silk instrument covers at Bakhtiar's, but it still looks mighty impressive) and gaudy with seals. "I hereby deliver unto your person this summons to appear in the court at the day and hour indited hereon in the matter of *The Constabulary of Angels City* vs. *Cuauhtémoc Hernandez*." He presented it to me with such a gorgeous flourish that I half expected to hear a ruffle of drums.

I read the parchment. It was what Epstein said it was. "I'll be there," I told him. "Sorry to keep you waiting here so long. Couldn't you just have left this on my desk?"

"Not in cases involving thaumaturgy in the commission of a first-degree felony," he answered. "In such cases, the chain of transmission of summonses must be as tightly controlled as that concerning the transmission of evidence."

"Okay," I said, shrugging; he undoubtedly knew the arcana of his own field. "But you must spend an awful lot to time just sitting and waiting. Why don't you bring along something more interesting to read than that?" I pointed at the catalogue.

But he recoiled with as much horror as if I'd offered him a bacon cheeseburger. "Anticipating idleness would constitute moral turpitude on my part. Good day to *you*, sir." He edged around me and fled.

Rose and I looked at each other. She said, "If I spent a lot of working time waiting, I'd bring something interesting, too." That relieved my mind; if Rose doesn't think something involves moral turpitude, you can take it to the bank that it doesn't.

All the way home, I thought about what had gone on at Bakhtiar's. It was of a piece with everything else connected with the Devonshire dump case: as far as I could tell on a quick visit, everything there was on the up and up, and the boss loudly denied doing anything that could possibly make toxic spell byproducts get out of the containment area and into the environment. Somebody was lying, but who? Not knowing was devilishly frustrated.

I was going to call Judy after I finished dinner, but she called me first. "Want to do something perverse?" she asked.

I know a straight line when I'm handed one. "Sure," I answered. "Do you want to fly up here, or shall I go down there?" Besides, the very male part of me panted, there was always the outside chance that was what she had in mind.

The snort she gave me said it wasn't—and also said she'd fed me the line on purpose. Maybe she wanted to see what I'd do with it, or maybe she'd already guessed what I'd do with it and wanted to see if she was right. She said, "I was thinking more along the lines of a Monday night date."

"That's perverse, all right," I agreed. "Why Monday night?"

"Because I read in the *Independent Press-Scryer* that a new Numidian restaurant is opening up Monday night about six blocks from here. Feel like coming down and trying it with me?"

"Numidian, eh?" Jews often go to Muslim-style restaurants, and the other way round, too; no need to worry about pork on the menu or back in the kitchen. And Aside from that, I like North African food. Couscous, *salata mesh-wiya*—tuna salad with chili pepper, eggs, tomatoes, and peppers, dressed with olive oil, lemon juice, and salt—chicken with prunes and honey, the lamb soup called *harira souiria*, with onions, paprika, and saffron . . . my stomach rumbled just thinking about it. "Sounds wonderful. Only thing is, how crowded will it be?

"We can find out. Of course, if you don't want to—"

"I said it sounded wonderful." I really had, too, so I got points for that. "What time do you want me down there?"

"What time do you want to come?"

"Listen, Mistress Adler, this is your date, so you tell me what to do."

"Hmm," she said. "Is that how it's supposed to work? Okay, I'll play along—is a quarter to eight all right?"

"Sure—by the time we get there, I'll be hungry enough to do proper damage to the menu. And afterwards—always assuming I don't fall asleep on your couch because I'm so full—maybe we can do something perverse."

She snorted again.

VIII

Monday shaped up as a very good day. Not only did I have a date with Judy, but Maximum Ruhollah had come through with the show-cause order that would let me—Michael Manstein and me, actually—go up and examine the area around the Devonshire dump to see what was leaking and, God willing, find out why. That happened Thursday. He spent Friday quashing appeals from the Devonshire Land Management Consortium.

The order was still good when I got to the Confederal building Monday morning. Had one of the appeals succeeded, the words would have faded right off the page. They tell stories about officials who go out to conduct their business, open up their briefcases, and pull out a blank sheet of parchment. Nobody dies of embarrassment, but sometimes you wish you could. I reminded myself to check my document before I handed it to Tony Sudakis. If there was anybody I didn't want laughing his head off at me, he was the guy.

I met Michael Manstein up on the seventh floor. He was packing vials of this, jars of that, silk bags full of other things and tied with elaborately knotted scarlet cords into his little black bag. I scratched my head. "Why not just take a good spellchecker?" I asked.

He glanced up from what he was doing. "I am operating under the assumption that we will be searching around the walls for leaks, David," he said, as patiently as if I were a kiddygarden pupil. "The containment spells would degrade the performance of the microimps in a spellchecker."

That had certainly happened when I used my own portable to run an unofficial scan of the dump: it hadn't picked up anything but the containment cantrips. I'd figured a more sensitive model would overcome the interference, but the reason I had Michael along, after all, was that he knew more of such things than I did. "You're the wizard," I told him. "Shall we go? Your carpet or mine?"

We ended up taking his; he'd had a special option package installed to insulate his sylphs from the potent magics he often flew with. I didn't care to risk having my carpet break down and strand me in the middle of nowhere (for which, as detractors of Angels City will tell you, St. Ferdinand's Valley is an excellent substitute). As we slid down to the lot, I grinned—no staff meeting for me today.

Michael Manstein flew exactly as you would expect: exactly at the speed limit, exactly where he ought to have been, every change of height or direction signaled at exactly the right time. *Exact* fits Michael exactly, as you will have gathered.

He parked his carpet in the same lot I'd used when I first came up to the Devonshire dump. We got off and started across toward the dump. I'd taken maybe three steps when I said, "Didn't you forget to activate your anti-theft geas? You ought to go back and do it; this isn't a saintly neighborhood."

His thin, rather pallid face took on an expression I'd never seen there before. If you can believe it, Michael Manstein looked smug. He said, "What's sorce for the geas is sorce for the gander."

Sometimes magicians are irritating people. All right, so Michael had better theft protection on his carpet than the usual geas woven into the fibers while it's still on the loom. All right, so even if someone succeeded in beating that protection, he'd still be able to tell where his rug had gone. But was that excuse enough for making bad puns about it? I didn't think so, especially not early in the morning.

The security guard sitting in his glass booth was a different fellow from the one who'd been there the last time I went up to the dump, so he didn't recognize me. Two EPA sigils and a show-cause order prominently displayed (yes, it still had writing on it) were plenty to get his attention, though. He picked up his phone, called Tony Sudakis, then came back out to us and said, "He'll be here in a minute."

Sudakis took longer than that, but not much. The guard set the insulated footbridge over the barrier so Tony could come out and talk with us. He gave me a bonecrusher handclasp, made Michael wince with another one, and said, "Okay, let's see the order."

I gave it to him. He read it carefully, handed it back to me. "This says you're authorized to search 'the surround of the aforementioned property.' " He made a face. "Lawyer talk. Anyway, this doesn't say thing one about coming inside."

"That's right." I nodded. "We're trying to see what's leaking out, after all."

"Okay," Sudakis said again. "I am directed by our legal staff to provide no more cooperation than what the order demands. That means that if you need to take a leak, you've got to do it across the street. You can't come into the containment area for anything." He gave me an apologetic shrug. "I'm sorry, Dave, but that's what my orders are."

"Since we'll be sniffing around your wall, maybe I'll just stand up against it if I need to whizz," I told him. He gave me a funny look; bureaucrats aren't supposed to talk like that.

Michael Manstein said, "I'm going to get to work now."

He opened up his little black bag and started taking things out of it.

Sudakis watched him setting up. I watched Sudakis. After a minute or so, I said, "Walk around the corner with me, Tony."

"Why? You gonna whizz on my shoes?" But he walked around the corner with me.

As soon as we were out of sight of Michael—and, more to the point, the security guard—I gestured as if I were pulling out an amulet. Tony Sudakis might be a bruiser, but don't ever think he's dumb. He went through his little pagan ritual with the chunk of amber he wore in place of a crucifix.

When he nodded to me, I said, "Okay, we can't go inside the dump. I understand your position. But I still want to ask you about something I saw, or thought I saw, when I was in there before. I'd have done it sooner, but I keep forgetting."

"What is it?" His voice was absolutely neutral; I couldn't tell whether he wanted to help, was angry at me, curious, or anything. He just set the words out in front of him as if they'd been printed on parchment.

I described as best I could the Nothing I'd seen in the dump, the way, just for an instant, the containment wall seemed to recede to an infinite distance from my eyes. "Did you ever notice anything like that?" I asked him. "It was—unnerving."

"Sounds that way," he agreed, and now he let life creep back into his words. He shook his big fair head. "Nope, can't say I ever did see anything of that sort." He quickly raised a hand. "Don't get me wrong, Dave—I believe you. You spend as much time as I have inside that containment area and you'll see all kinds of strange things. Like I said before, you get all those toxic bits of not-quite-spent sorcery reacting with each other and you *will* see funny things. You'd better believe you will. But that particular one, no. Sorry."

"Okay, thanks anyhow." I didn't know whether to believe him or not; as usual, he was hard to get a spell on. I wondered if it was because he worshiped Perkunas. In a mostly Judeo-Christian country (and the same goes for Muslim lands, too), followers of other Powers often seem difficult to fathom. On the other hand, Tony probably would have been tricky if he'd been a Catholic, too.

"Anything else—anything else short—you want to talk about while the charm's still on?" he asked.

I shook my head. We went back around the corner to the containment area entrance. The security guard looked moderately entranced himself, watching Michael set up. Tony Sudakis didn't give Manstein even a glance; he positioned the footbridge, motioned for the guard to pick it up again, and marched in toward his office.

Maybe working in the toxic spell dump for so long had dulled Tony's sense of wonder. Lots of strange things undoubtedly happened in there, most of the sort you wouldn't want to see outside a stout sorcerous barrier. But for me—and evidently for the security guard, too—nothing is more interesting than watching a skilled thaumaturgical craftsman at work. And Michael Manstein is one of the best.

If you're looking merely to detect the presence of most substances and Powers, you don't need fancy sorcery. Suppose you want to find out if someone's spilled sugar under a rug, for instance. Get out some sugar of your own and apply the law of similarity. If you get a reaction in your control bowl, it was sugar under the rug all along (ants everywhere are a good clue, too).

But if you're trying to see whether the influence of, say, Beelzebub is leaking out of a toxic spell dump, you don't go about summoning up Beelzebub to see if the law of similarity applies—not if you're in your right mind, you don't, anyhow. Byproducts from spells that invoke Beelzebub are contained within warded dumps for good reason: you don't want them getting out into the environment. And if you summon the Lord of the Flies outside the containment area, that's just what's going to happen.

And so Michael Manstein attacked the problem indirectly. I mention Beelzebub because that's Whose influence he was checking for when Tony Sudakis and I came back from our *sub rosa* (or should I say *sub sucino*?) chat. Instead of even thinking about invoking the demon, he pulled out a jar full of every thaumaturge's friend, the good old common fruit fly.

Because fruit flies are very simple—and very stupid—creatures, they're exceptionally sensitive to magic. Apprentices practice spells with them; if you can't make your charms work on fruit flies, you're better off in another line of work.

And when that magic has anything to do with Beelzebub, of course, their sensitivity increases even more. Just by watching the way they flew from the jar, Michael could tell whether the demon's influence had leaked out where it didn't belong. It was as elegant and low-risk a test as you could imagine.

Since I'm not a mage myself, to me that just looked like little brownish flies coming out of a bottle. When Michael screwed the lid back on, I figured I could safely interrupt him, so I asked, "Any sign of Beelzebub?"

"None apparent to me," he answered. "The Lord of the Flies is renowned for his trickery, but I do not believe him capable of evading the fruit-fly test; it draws them even more strongly than spoiled plums."

"Good to hear," I said, "because I know there are spell byproducts with his influence on them inside the dump."

"Yes, that is to a certain degree reassuring," Michael agreed. "If a Power so corrosive as Beelzebub cannot break free of the containment area, that augurs well for its chances of holding in other, less aggressive, toxic spells."

"Who after Beelzebub?" I asked.

"I had thought Huitzilopochtli," he answered. "He is at least as dangerous as Beelzebub, and we have seen through the case of that wretched *curandero*'s nostrum that he is active—and seeking to become more active—in the Angels City area."

Again, he didn't try to invoke the Aztecian war god: after all, we were doing everything we could to keep Huitzilopochtli from manifesting himself around Angels City. Instead, he performed another indirect test, this one using flayed human skin substitute. It looked like parchment, but it made my flesh creep all the same.

Michael chanted in a clucking, gobbling language. It wasn't Poultry; it was Nahuatl. Spanish is the dominant tongue in Aztecia today, but many people still use Nahuatl in their day-to-day lives, and it's as much the language of the native Powers as Arabic is for jinni. I hadn't known Michael knew it, but I wouldn't bet against Michael's knowing any particular thing.

The chant ended. Michael looked down at the square of flayed human skin substitute. It seemed just the same as it had when he took it out of his bag. He grunted softly. "What's the matter?" I asked.

"I would have expected to observe some reaction there," he answered. "Huitzilopochtlic contamination is as likely an inducer of apsychia as any I can think of. But there appears to be no external seepage, at least not as measured by this test."

"What were you expecting to see?" I asked.

"The influence of Huitzilopochtli was brought into the Devonshire toxic spell containment area by means of flayed human skin substitute. Had that influence spread beyond the containment area, the sheet of the substitute material I have here would have demonstrated it by beginning to bleed."

I gulped; I was sorry I'd asked. "Would it be—real blood?" I asked.

"In thaumaturgy, 'real' is a word almost without meaning," Michael said sniffily. "It would look, feel, smell, and taste real. Whether it could be successfully removed from the flayed human skin substitute and impplanted in the veins of someone who had suffered a loss from injury or vampirism . . . Truth to tell, I do not know. It might be worth determining. An interesting question. Yes."

He pulled a pencil out of the pocket of his lab robe, peered around for something on which he could jot a note. For one dreadful second, I feared he was going to scribble on the piece of flayed human skin substitute. I don't think my stomach could have stood that. But at the last minute he fished out a parchment notebook instead, and did his jotting on that.

He spent the rest of the morning and the whole afternoon on tests of that sort. To my amazement and distress, he came

up empty every time. No, I take that back: he did find one
leak. After four in the afternoon, when both of us were fed
up and frustrated enough to try something silly, he tested for
stardust, and sure enough, the tip of the wand he was using
glowed for a minute.

"Undoubtedly deposited here, along with more unsavory
items, by one of the Hollywood light-and-magic outfits in
search of a hit," Michael said.

"But even if stardust is leaking, it's not toxic," I said. "The
most it could possibly do would be to make somebody popu-
lar who doesn't deserve to be."

Michael Manstein looked at me as if I were a schoolboy
who'd added two and two and come up with three. Not five,
but definitely three—I'd fallen short of what was expected of
me. Like a good schoolmaster, he set me straight: "The problem is not stardust outside the containment area, David. As
you say, that is trivial in and of itself. The problem is that
stardust could not possibly get out of the dump if it were not
leaking. We have, therefore, established that the leak exists.
What we have not established is which serious contaminants
are emerging from it."

"Oh," I said, feeling dumb. Odds were awfully good that
he was right. Still, though— "You tested for all the dangerous Powers whose influences are likely to be in the dump,
and came up with zip. Stardust is pretty elusive stuff; even
the light-and-magic people don't know for sure where it'll
stick. Maybe it did leak out by itself."

"Indeed," Michael said. "And maybe you could find a
mineral able to create blasts to rival those of megasalamanders, yet I would not lose sleep fretting over the probability
of either event. I will take oath upon any scripture you care
to select that something—and something malevolent, at
that—created the breach through which the stardust
emerged. That is my professional judgment."

You work with experts to get their professional judgment.
If, having got it, you then choose to ignore it, you'd better
have a real good reason. I not only didn't have a real good
reason, I thought Michael was right. But if he was, what had
gone wrong?

I said, "What bothers me most about detecting the star-dust and nothing more serious is that the dump operators will be able to claim that the dust didn't really come from inside, even though we know it was dumped there."

"The neighborhood will make it hard for them to substan-tiate that." Michael waved to show what he meant. I had to nod. If ever a neighborhood remained conspicuously untouched by stardust, the one around the Devonshire dump was it.

"Why haven't we found any nastier influences leaking, then?" I asked.

"The most obvious reason is a failure in our testing tech-nique," Michael answered. "I must confess, however, that at this moment I cannot tell you where the flaw lies. All my procedures have in the past shown themselves to be more than satisfactory."

I asked my watch what time it was. When I found out it was twenty to five, I said, "Let's knock off for the day and see if we're more brilliant in the morning." I wanted to get back to my own carpet so I could go down to my place, pack an overnight case, and then head for Judy's.

Most days, Michael Manstein's impressive integrity wouldn't have let him contemplate taking off early, let alone doing it. When he said, "Why not?" I confess I blinked. He added, "We certainly aren't accomplishing anything here at the moment with the possible exception of entertaining the security guard." Maybe he was trying to justify leaving to himself, or maybe to me. At that point, I didn't need any jus-tifying; all I wanted to do was head south.

Michael must have talked himself into it, because he started sticking tools and substances back into his little black bag. I stood there waiting, hoping he wouldn't get an attack of conscience. He didn't. As soon as he was through, we walked across the street to his carpet and headed for Westwood.

Traffic was its usual ghastly self. So many carpets on so many flyways meant there was so much lint and dander in the air that the famous Angels City sunshine turned pale and washed-out; a lot of people were rubbing their eyes as they flew. That pollution usually seems worse in St. Ferdinand's Valley than other parts of town, too; they don't get the sea breeze there to clear it out.

What they're going to have to do one of these days is design a flying carpet that isn't woven from wool. People have been trying to do that for years; so far, they haven't managed to come up with one the sylphs like. But if they don't succeed before too long, Angels City isn't going to be a place anybody in his right mind would want to live.

I breathed easier—literally and figuratively—when we got out of the Valley and back into Westwood. Michael pulled up beside my carpet in the parking lot. "Are you going to go back up to your office and see what awaits you?" he asked.

"Nope," I said. "What's that New Testament line? 'Sufficient unto the day is the evil thereof'? Something like that, anyhow. Tomorrow will have troubles of its own. I'm not really interested in finding out about them in advance."

"As you will," Michael said. Since it was nearer six than five, he didn't have any trouble finding a parking space—most people who work at the Confederal Building had gone home. He headed on in anyhow; now that he was here, he'd do some more work. Maybe he was feeling bad about his fall from probity.

Me, I didn't feel bad at all. Hungry, yes, but not bad. I jumped onto my carpet and headed home. I got off at Imperial instead of The Second, just in case more earth elementals with my name on them were waiting for me.

If they were, I evaded them—I got home unscathed. I stayed just long enough to use the plumbing and toss tomorrow's outfit into an overnight case. Then I was out the door, down the stairs, back on my carpet, and on my way to Judy's.

Going down St. James' Freeway into Long Beach in the evening is a gamble. When it's bad, the carpets might as well be sitting on your living room floor. I could have got there at nine as easily as a little before eight. But I was lucky, and so I pulled up in front of Judy's place right on time.

I used the talisman to let her building's Watcher know I belonged there, then went up the stairs two at a time to her flat. I knocked on the door. When she didn't come right away, I figured she was using the plumbing herself or something, so I let myself in.

I took one step in the front room and then stopped, staring. For a second, I thought I'd gone into the wrong flat. It took me a while to realize Judy's spare key wouldn't have let me into any place but hers.

But Judy, as befits a copy editor, is scrupulously neat. The flat had been trashed. Books were scattered all over the floor, knickknacks strewn everywhere. Some of them were broken. *Earthquake*, I thought, and then, more sensibly, *burglars*.

I ran into the bedroom, calling Judy's name as I went. Nobody answered. On the bed, lying exactly parallel to each other, just the way Judy would have set them there, were a green silk blouse and a pair of linen pants: the right kind of outfit to wear to the opening of a nice new restaurant.

The bedspread was white. I am, you will have gathered, familiar with Judy's bed and its bedclothes. The red stain next to the blouse was new. It wasn't a big stain, but seeing even a little blood is plenty to make your own blood run cold.

"Judy?" My voice came out as a frightened croak. No answer again. I hadn't really expected one.

The bathroom door was open. The air in there felt humid, as if she'd taken a shower not long before. She wasn't in there now, though, not anywhere—I yanked back the curtain to be sure.

Burglars faded from my mind. I wished the word would have stayed; stuff, after all, is only stuff. You can always get more. But an uglier, more frightening word took its place: *kidnappers*.

I didn't want to think it, let alone believe it. After what had happened to me on The Second, though, what choice did I have? I ran back to the bedroom, where the phone was. I snatched up the handset.

Nothing happened. The phone was dead. Ichor dripped from the little cages that held the ear and mouth imps. The front mesh on both cages was pushed in. Whoever had snatched Judy had taken the time to impplode the phone before he left with her.

I hurried out to the walkway, went to the flat next door. I

knocked, hard. "I need to use your phone to call the constabulary," I said loudly. Someone was home; St. Elmo's fire glowed through the curtains and I could hear little noises inside. But nobody came to the door.

Cursing the faintheart to a warmer climate than Angels City's, I ran downstairs and pounded on the manager's door. He answered; opening the door was part of his job. He'd seen me going in and out often enough to recognize me. As soon as he got a good look at my face, he said, "What's the matter, son?"

I didn't take offense; that's how he talks. Besides, he's old enough to have fought in the Second Sorcerous War (and he has a bad limp, so maybe he did), so he's old enough and then some to be my father. I said, "May I use your phone, please? I think Judy's been kidnapped." As with any magic, saying the word made it real.

"Judy? Judy Adler in 272?" He gaped at me, and then at the door I'd left open, I suppose to confirm that that was the flat I was talking about. He stood aside. "You'd better come in."

His flat could have been furnished from the St. Ferdinand's Valley swap meet; the operative phrase was essence of bad taste. From the couch, his wife gave me a fishy stare. That was the least of my worries. But he took me to the phone and let me use it, so his carp-eyed wife could stare all she liked.

Even through two phone imps, the Long Beach constabulary decurion sounded bored when he answered my call. *Kidnapping*, though, is a word to conjure with when you're talking to constables.

"Don't go back into the flat," he told me. "Stand out in front of the building and wait for our units. It won't be long, Mr., uh, Fisher."

I stood out in front of the building. It wasn't long. Two black-and-whites pulled up, red and blue lanterns flashing. Right behind them were a couple of plainweave carpets that carried plainclothes constables.

Everybody swept up to Judy's flat and started doing constabulary-type things: physical searches, spells, what have you. One of the plainclothesmen grunted when he saw the imploded phone. "Looks like a professional job," he said. "We aren't likely to come up with anything much."

They hadn't bothered asking me for a statement yet. I said, "This isn't just an isolated case. I can guarantee you that."

"Oh? How?" The plainclothesman sounded—skeptical is the politest way I can put it.

As with the bored decurion at the phone desk, I had the words to rock him. I spoke them, one by one: *attempted murder, Thomas Brothers fire, Central Intelligence*. "You'd better get hold of Legate Shiro Kawaguchi, up in St. Ferdinand's Valley," I added. "He can fill you in on the details."

"All right, sir, we'll do that," the plainclothesman said—he was a tall black fellow named Johnson. "Jesus, what kind of mess are we walking into the middle of?"

"A bad one," I said. "But you're not in the middle of it; you're just on the edge. *I'm* in the middle—and so is my fiancée."

A fellow wearing forensics crystal balls on his collar tabs came up to Johnson and said, "I ran a similarity check between the blood on the bedspread and the razor I found in a bathroom drawer. They match, so that's probably Adler's blood."

I moaned. That's a word you hear every so often, but you hardly ever use it, let alone do it. This was one of those times. I felt as if I'd been kicked in the belly. Judy, bleeding? Judy, maybe dead?

I must have said that out loud (though I don't remember doing it), because the forensics man put a hand on my shoulder and said, "I don't think she's dead, sir. There's evidence of some funny kind of fast-dissipating sleep spell in the flat. My best guess is, she put up a fight, they slugged her, she kept fighting, and they knocked her out so they could get her away from here."

I liked him, and believed him, too. He didn't try sounding like somebody who knew everything there was to know; no pseudo-learned drivel about analyses and reconstructions. His best guess was what he had, and that's what he gave me. I thought it seemed likely, too.

The constables in uniform had been knocking on doors through the block of flats. People opened doors for them—even the louse who lived next to Judy and had pretended I didn't exist. But there's a difference between getting doors to open and learning anything once they have. The constables came back to Judy's flat empty-handed: nobody had seen anything, nobody had heard anything.

"That's insane," I exploded. "They take an unconscious woman downstairs and out of a block of flats at a busy time of the evening and nobody noticed?"

"Must have been magic," Johnson said. "If they used it to knock Mistress Adler out, they probably used it to aid the getaway, too."

"I'll check that," the forensics man said, and he bustled out onto the walkway.

"What do I do now?" I said, as much to myself as to anyone else. Half of me wanted to make like a light-and-magic show mercenary and go out slaughtering all the bad guys. The other half, unfortunately, reminded me that not only did I not know how to get my hands on the bad guys, but that if I went after them—whoever *they* were—alone, they'd dispose of me instead of the other way round.

Johnson's answer showed that, as suited a constable, he had a thoroughly practical mind: "What you do now, Mr. Fisher, is come down to the station with us so we can get a sworn statement from you."

I didn't know where the Long Beach constabulary station was; I had to follow one of the plainweave carpets back there. It turned out to be almost on the ocean, in a fancy new building. Legate Kawaguchi would have killed for Johnson's large, bright, efficient office. Come to that, I wouldn't have minded having it myself.

Like constables anywhere in the Barony of Angels, the Long Beach crew had a regular library of scriptures on which the people with whom they dealt could swear truthfulness: everything from the *Analects* to the *Zend-Avesta*. They pulled out a Torah for me; I rested my hand on the satin cover while I repeated the oath Johnson gave me.

Then he called up their scriptorium spirit to take down

my words. I repeated everything I'd said in Judy's flat, and added detail to go with it. After a while, I paused and said, "What time is it, anyhow?"

Johnson asked his watch. It said, "Nine forty-one."

"Could you get me a sandwich or something?" I asked. "I came down here for a dinner date with Judy, and I haven't eaten since lunch. We were going to try that new Numidian place—"

"Oh, Bocchus and Bacchus?" Johnson said. "Yeah, I've seen it advertised. I wouldn't mind trying it myself. Hang on a minute, Mr. Fisher; I'll find out what I can round up for you."

Instead of couscous and lamb, I had a greasy burger, greasier fries, and coffee I drank only because it would have been an environmental hazard if I'd poured it down the commode. Then I finished giving my statement, and then I said, "What do I do now?" This time I was asking the plain-clothesman.

"Try to live as normally as you can," he said. I'd heard that advice before; I was sick of it. How are you supposed to live normally when people are trying to kill you and they've abducted the person who matters most to you in the world? Johnson must have understood that. He raised a light-palmed hand and went on, "I know it's a tall order. What we're going to have to do now is wait for contact: wait for either your fiancée or the people holding her to get in touch with you. Whatever their demands are, say you'll comply and then let us know immediately."

"But what if they—?" I couldn't say it—*absit omen* and all that—but he knew what I meant.

"Mr. Fisher, the only consolation I can give you is that if they'd intended to commit homicide, they could have done it. They must have some reason for wanting Mistress Adler alive."

"Thanks," I said from the bottom of my heart. It made sense. Now all I had to do was pray the kidnappers were sensible people. But if they were sensible people, would they have been kidnappers?

Johnson came around his desk, set a big hand on my

shoulder. "You just go on home now, Mr. Fisher. Try and get some rest. Do you want one of our black-and-whites to fly up with you, make sure you're not walking into a trap yourself?"

After a couple of seconds, I shook my head. He looked relieved, as if he'd regretted the offer as soon as he made it. I suspected the Long Beach constables were stretched as thin as any other force. It's an ugly world out there. I'd just had my nose rubbed in how ugly it can be.

He walked out to my carpet with me. "We'll be in touch, sir. And we'll also get in touch with that Legate Kawaguchi of yours, and with Central Intelligence, and with the CBI, too, because it's a kidnapping . . . What's funny, sir?"

"I can get in touch with the CBI," I said. "I work two floors under their Angels City office." I wondered if Saul Klein would get involved in the case. Nice to have one *landsman* around, anyhow. He'd certainly be more comfortable to work with than the CI spook; Henry Legion was unnerving.

Johnson patted me on the shoulder again, sent me on my way. I remember very little about flying back to Hawthorne—too much else on my mind, too little of it good. I propitiated the Watcher for my block of flats, glided into the garage, got off my carpet, and headed for the stairway. Once I was inside the building, I didn't worry about how late it was, or how dark. Stupid, I know, especially after what had happened to Judy. I suppose *you've* never done anything stupid, eh?

A vampire stood grinning at the bottom of the stairs.

Modern medicine can do a lot for vampires: periodic blood implants to stifle their hunting urge, heliotrope baths to let them go abroad between dawn and dusk (never on Sunday; the correspondence between real and symbolic sun is too strong then), sun-spectacles to keep them from being blinded when they do fare forth by day. Those who choose to—and, I admit, those who can afford to—take advantage of such techniques can lead largely normal lives.

Not all do. Some would sooner follow their instincts and prowl. I hadn't heard of vampires in Hawthorne, but I wasn't shocked to encounter one. For one thing, I think I was beyond shock; for another, as I've said, this is a pretty rough little town.

Just for an instant, I wondered if he was connected with the bastards who'd taken Judy. I had my doubts. Vampires, if I can mix a metaphor, are usually lone wolves. Odds are, this one was just trying to keep himself fed. Random street crime, however, is just as dangerous to its victim as one that targets him in particular.

The vampire's eyes glittered. I knew that if I looked into them for very long I'd be fascinated, and then the blood-sucker could do whatever it wanted with me. I reached under my shirt, pulled out something on a chain round my neck.

The vampire must have thought it was going to be a crucifix. Its fanged mouth opened in a scornful laugh. A lot of vampires, especially the ones that survive for very long in Christian countries, are of Balkan Muslim blood, and so immune to the sign of the cross.

But I didn't pull out a cross. What I wore instead was a mystic Jewish amulet, a seven-by-seven acrostic prepared by the same Mage Abramelin Works that made my blasting rod. I yanked it off over my head and threw the kaballistic missile at the vampire.

He had quick reflexes—he caught it before it hit him in the face. But that didn't do him any good. His cry of pain turned to an anguished howl. The Hebrew term for vampires is *kepiloth*—"empty ones"—and it's a good description. Because they've lost so much humanity, they're extremely vulnerable to magical countermeasures. When the acrostic based on the Hebrew word for "dog" hit this one, he had no choice but to transform.

"Get out of here, you son of a bitch!" I yelled, and drew back my foot to give him a good kick. He fled, yelping, tail between his legs.

I picked up the amulet, hung it back around my neck, and trudged upstairs to my flat. Only later, when I was lying down and trying to sleep, did it occur to me that if I hadn't been emotionally drained from what had happened to Judy, the vampire might have made me panic and drained me in the literal sense before I thought of the amulet. As it was, I just took him in stride and did the right thing without even thinking about it.

Every so often, lying there, I'd ask my watch what time it was. The last answer I remember getting was 2:48.

Going to work on three hours' sleep is one of those nightmares everybody has once or twice. A lot of the time, a new baby in the house is the reason. Not for me. Thinking about a baby made me think about Judy. We'd had so many plans— I didn't want to think about throwing them all away.

A cup of coffee with breakfast. Another cup of cafeteria mud the minute I got in, and another one right after that. One more half an hour later. I felt myself wind tighter and tighter. By God, I'd get through the day. If tonight ever came, I'd probably be too buzzed to sleep then. One things at a time, though. Get through the day first.

That meant more phone calls. I didn't feel the least bit guilty about using my office; my personal affairs and those of the toxic spell dump case had become inextricably intertwined. First I called Saul Klein upstairs.

"Saul, this is David Fisher down in the EPA again," I said. "I want—no, I don't want to, but I have to—report a kidnapping."

"This is the report that we received from the Long Beach constabulary last night?" he asked. When I said yes, he went on, "Is this connected with the minisingers case you were telling me about a little while ago?"

I'd forgotten the minisingers. I discovered that, along with tired and worried, I could be embarrassed, too. "No, it doesn't have anything to do with that. If you've received that Long Beach report, Saul, does that mean you'll be on the case?"

"I'll be involved, yes," he answered. "Is it convenient for you that I come down and discuss matters now? You're on the seventh floor, is that right?"

"Yes, and sure, come on down. Can you stop at the cafeteria and bring a couple of cups of coffee? I'll pay for them."

He came; we drank coffee; he asked all the same

questions Johnson had the night before. Numbly, I gave the same answers. He scribbled notes. When I was done, he said, "We'll do everything we can for you, David, and for Mistress Adler. I promise you that." I noticed he didn't promise they'd get her back alive and unhurt; he must have known better than to make promises he might not be able to keep.

When he left, I called Henry Legion. The spook said, "I shall be there directly." He was, too, faster crosscountry than Saul Klein had been from two floors up. Of course, Henry Legion hadn't had to stop for coffee.

I told my story for the third time. Repetition made it feel almost as if it had happened to someone else—almost, but not quite. The CI spook said, "This is disturbing. Events are moving faster than crystal-ball projections had indicated. My opinion is that your scanning around the toxic spell dump may well have been the precipitating factor."

"But except for a little stardust, we didn't find anything," I said, nearly wailing, as if I were I kid who got caught and walloped for peeking in a bedroom window without even seeing anything interesting.

"You may know that," the spook said. "I would doubt the perpetrators do." Then he disappeared on me. I hate that. It always gives him the last word.

Two down. My next call was to Legate Kawaguchi. I wondered if he'd still be off on his other case, but no, I got him. "This is in relation to the kidnapping of Mistress Adler whom I met at the Thomas Brothers fire?" he asked when he heard it was me, so the Long Beach constables must have already talked with him.

"That's what this is in relation to, all right," I said heavily. "I can't imagine any other reason for kidnapping Judy, especially when whoever did it also tried to kill me a few days ago."

"I can imagine other reasons," Kawaguchi said. Before I could start screaming at him, he went on, "I admit, however, that your scenario appears to be of the highest probability. As you will have surmised"—and as I had surmised—"I have discussed this matter with the Long Beach force. I would, however, also be grateful for your firsthand account."

I gave it to him. *One more repetition*, I thought: one more movement out of the realm of reality and into that of discourse. In a way, it was a sort of anti-magic. Magic uses words to realize what had only been imagined. I was using them to turn tragedy and horror into memory, which is ever so much easier to handle.

When I was through, Kawaguchi said, "Did you learn from the forensics man what sort of sleep spell he detected at your fiancée's flat?"

"You know, I didn't," I answered. "The plainclothesman—Johnson—and I went down to the Long Beach station so I could make my sworn statement there, and the forensics fellow didn't stick his head into Johnson's office while I was giving it."

"I shall inquire," Kawaguchi said. His words were spaced a little too far apart, as if he was writing and talking at the same time.

I said, "I wanted to check with you, too, Legate, to see if you have any new answers that would help clear up who did this to Judy." Whoever it was had also undoubtedly arranged to have the earth elemental dropped on my flying carpet. At the moment, that seemed utterly unimportant to me.

"New answers, no," he said. "I have some new questions, however: there has been vandalism relating to the Garuda Bird project at the Loki plant in Burbank, vandalism behind a hermetic seal."

"That's supposed to be impossible," I said, now speaking slowly myself—I was scrawling a note to call Matt Arnold.

"Many things once supposed impossible have come true," Kawaguchi said. "Take virtuous reality, for example."

"Thank you," I exclaimed. "That reminds me of something else I wanted to ask you: what's the more usual name for *Pharomachrus mocinno*?"

Kawaguchi actually laughed; I hadn't been sure he could. "My apologies, Inspector; I should not have read the name to your secretary straight off the laboratory report. The common name for the bird in question is the quetzal."

"Quetzal?" I slammed into that head on, as if my carpet had run into a building. "Are you sure?"

"Confirmed by an ornithologist and an Etruscan ornithomancer," Kawaguchi said.

"You're sure," I admitted. "But that's crazy. Michael Manstein—he runs the sorcery lab here—and I went around the Devonshire dump yesterday, and we found no trace of Aztecian sorcery leaking. He even tested with flayed human skin substitute for Huitzliopochtlism."

"I have told you what I know," Kawaguchi said. "The possibility remains that the feather was somehow altered in its translation from virtuous reality into our own merely mundane space and time; as I noted at the time, if would not be accepted as evidence in a court of law. Another alternative is that the feather is indeed derived from a quetzal, but was deliberately placed within range of the scriptorium spirit Erasmus' sensorium for the purpose of misleading us."

"Yeah," I said. "Or it might be real—whatever that means in connection with something out of virtuous reality."

"Exactly so," Kawaguchi said. "Ockham's Razor argues for that interpretation, although the others cannot be ignored."

I shave my data with Ockham's Razor, too; it's the most practical tool to use in preparing baseline data for projections and such. But, like any other razor, it will cut you if you're not careful with it.

"Thanks for the information, Legate Kawaguchi," I said. "Would you do me one more favor, please. Would you call a spook named Henry Legion at Central Intelligence back in D.St.C."—I gave him the number—"and tell him what you've just told me? It's something he needs to know, believe me. Use my name; it'll help you get through to him."

"I shall do as you suggest," Kawaguchi answered slowly. "The implications, however, are—troubling."

"I know." When I'd first heard Charlie Kelly reluctantly admit the possibility of the Third Sorcerous War, it chilled me for days. Now, as far as I was concerned, it was old news. Judy bulked ever so much larger in my thoughts. I couldn't worry about the whole world going up in smoke; that's too much for any mere man to take in. But when some damned—I hope—bastard kidnaps the woman you love, you understand that real well.

Kawaguchi and I said our goodbyes. He promised again that he would call Henry Legion. Me, I called Loki, and eventually got connected to Matt Arnold. "I just got off the phone with Legate Kawaguchi of the ACCD," I told him. "He said you had a break-in and some vandalism on the Garuda Bird project."

"That's right," he answered. "One of our people was critically injured, too."

"Kawaguchi didn't say anything about that," I said. "What happened?"

"He was bitten by a snake." Even over the phone, I could hear Arnold's voice turn grim. "Some clever sorcerer found a way to beat a hermetic seal. Did the constable tell you about *that*?"

"He mentioned that it had been done, but not how," I answered. "You sound like you know."

"I do, yes," Arnold said. "There'll be some sleepless nights up in Crystal Valley until they can bring their sorceware up to date."

"You don't need a crystal ball to predict that," I agreed. "How was it done? Everyone's always claimed hermetic seals are proof against just about anything." I heard the silence that meant he didn't want to tell me. Quickly, I added, "Remember, I have a professional interest in this. Any magic that can beat such a powerful seal has to have serious consequences for the environment."

"All right," he said grudgingly. "I guess I can see that. But don't go spreading the word to all and sundry, you understand?"

"I'm not a reporter or a newsman for the ethernet," I replied with dignity.

"Okay," he said. "What happened was, the bastards used one of Hermes' own attributes to break the seals he was supposed to oversee. It was a very clever application of the law of similarity, I'll say; I wish whoever came up with it would have put as much energy into something legitimate."

"Go on," I said.

"The snakebite has something to do with it."

He paused again. I realized I was supposed to figure out

why. Some other morning, I might have enjoyed playing intellectual games. That particular day, I just didn't have it. "I'm sorry; I must be dense," I said—my troubles weren't any of his business. "Can you explain it for me?"

A sniff conveyed across the ether by two phone imps carries an impressive weight of scorn. Matt Arnold said, "Think about the *kerykeion* Hermes carries."

"The what?"

He made another impatient noise. As far as I was concerned, lucky for him he was at the far end of a phone connection. The EPA doesn't have the money—or the secrets—to get hermetic seals, so I had no reason to be familiar with the minutiae of Hermes' cult. Maybe he realized that, or maybe he just wanted to get me off the phone so he could go back to whatever he'd been doing before I called. He said, "The Latin term for the *kerykeion*—not really proper, you know, for talking about a Greek Power—is the caduceus."

That I did understand. "The staff with the . . ." My voice trailed away. "Snakes," I said in an altogether different tone of voice. "No wonder you said the bite had something to do with it."

"That's right," he said, as if there might be some hope for me after all. "They used the affinity of all snakes to the ones of the caduceus to weaken the seal and let them get into our secure areas."

"Sneaky." I added, "I hope you told Legate Kawaguchi about that. If one set of bad guys figures out a stunt, everybody will be using it two weeks later." Then something else occurred to me. "How did your vandals get to the hermetically sealed areas, anyhow? You had some tough-looking guards out front when I was there."

"They got lulled to sleep." Arnold sounded as if he didn't like to admit that. "Some kind of spell or other—Kawaguchi's forensics people haven't got back to me with the data."

Excitement ran through me: it sounded a lot like the way Judy's kidnappers had operated. I wrote that down so I wouldn't forget it, and promised myself I'd call Plainclothesman Johnson as soon as I was off the phone with Arnold.

While I still had him on the ether, though, I asked, "What kind of snake bit your man?"

"It was a fer-de-lance," Arnold answered. "Nasty thing— the venom makes you bleed internally as if you had a vampire gnawing you from the inside out. Lucky it's a relative of our local rattlesnakes; the antivenin spells for the one were efficacious enough—we hope—against the other. Like I told you, Jerry's still on the critical list, but they think he'll pull through."

"I'm glad to hear it," I said. "But why a fer-de-lance in the first place? Why not use our rattlers?"

"For one thing, it's more poisonous, if that's what the bastards were after. And for another, if the sorcerers were Aztecians, they'd be more familiar with their native serpents than ours."

"And if they weren't, they could throw suspicion on Azteca by planting snakes native to that realm." I was thinking about the quetzal feather. Till now, I'd suspected the Persians more than anyone else. I wondered if I'd have to change my mind. I also remembered Persians' deviousness; if they could hide their schemes by implicating someone else, they'd do it. And I remembered I still hadn't visited Chocolate Weasel.

Matt Arnold said, "Forensics ought to let us know before too long."

"I hope so," I said. "Thanks for your time."

"I've already wasted so much on this miserable business, a little more doesn't matter now." With that encouraging word, Arnold hung up on me.

I called Johnson. When he answered, my ear imp yelled into my ear, so I suppose he was yelling at his mouth imp: "Did the kidnappers call you? Or your fiancée?"

"I'm sorry, no." How sorry I was! I explained what I'd heard from Matt Arnold, then asked, "Has your forensics man been able to identify the sleep spell that was cast in Judy's flat?"

"Hold on," he said. "That's in my notes—I saw it. Let me look." The imps reproduced the noise of shuffling parchments. Then I heard Johnson say, "Yeah, here it is," more as if to himself than to me. After a few more seconds, he must have put the handset up to his mouth again, because his voice came back loud and clear: "I've got it, Mr. Fisher. Forensics says it's an Aztecian spell, summoning the Power named the One Called Night, the one from the Nine Beyonds, to cast sleep on the victim. There's a note here that it's not generally used with good intent. I'm sorry to have to tell you that, sir."

"Not half as sorry as I am to hear it," I answered. But I wasn't surprised, or not much. Either Aztecians really were behind this or somebody was putting on one hell of a bluff— and I mean that literally. The higher the evidence mounted, the more I doubted it was a bluff.

From its own point of view, after all, Aztecia has owed the Confederation a big one for a long time. Angels City used to be Aztecian territory, after all. So did St. Francis, up north. So did the Arid Zone and New Aztecia further east, and Snowland, and Denver and all the rest of Ruddy. With them, Aztecia would be a great nation. Without them, the Confederation wouldn't be.

And that's just in the sphere of mortal politics. I thought about what Henry Legion had said about the shift in the balance of Powers. It was already plain that Huitzilopochtli wanted his own back. And if that green feather meant what it seemed to, so did Quetzalcoatl. The two Powers had been rivals before the Spainish came. If they'd composed their differences . . . if that was so, then Heaven help the Confederation. Heaven had better help, anyhow.

I called Legate Kawaguchi back. When I got him, I asked, "What kind of sleep spell knocked out the guards at the Loki plant in Burbank?"

"That's in my notes," he answered, just as Johnson had. He was quicker to find the answer than the Long Beach constable had been. "Here we are. The report indicates that it was an Aztecian spell, one invoking the Power variously called the Page and the Crackler, sending the spirits of the victims to the Nine Beyonds."

"The Nine Beyonds!" I said. "Is this Power also known as the One Called Night?"

"I don't see that name here. Let me check with forensics and call you back." He did, too, inside of five minutes. "Inspector Fisher? The answer to your question is yes. Forensics wants to know how you knew; this Power is not commonly invoked in Angels City."

"I just got off the phone with Long Beach. The One Called Night is the Power that put Judy to sleep."

Kawaguchi was nobody's fool. "I shall consult immediately with Plainclothesman Johnson," he declared. "This link must be explored to the fullest extent possible."

More goodbyes. After they were through, I sat staring at the phone, wondering whether to call Henry Legion again or give Tony Sudakis a piece of my mind. Before I could do either, Rose stuck her head into my office and said, "Bea would like to see you and Michael up front, please. You weren't there for staff meeting yesterday, so she wants to catch up on what you've been doing."

"No," I said. It came out utterly flat, as if—ridiculous notion—somebody built a mechanical that could talk.

Rose stared. She knows I'm not fond of staff meetings, but when the boss says come unto this one, he cometh; and when she says go unto that one, he goeth, at least if he knoweth what's good for him. "But, David—" Rose began, trying to bring me to my senses.

"No," I said again. "Can't. Too busy. I was just going out into the field when you came in." It wasn't true, but I could make it so. I got up from my desk, started for the door. If Rose hadn't got out of the way in a hurry, I'd have walked right through her.

"David, are you all right?" she called after me as I trudged down the hall.

"No," I answered. Being very tired is kind of like being drunk; it makes you say the first thing that pops into your head. You often regret it later. I wondered if I'd still have a job to come back to even as I was sliding down to the parking lot.

It's a good thing I'd come to know St. Ferdinand's Valley well over the past few weeks: I could fly up to the Devonshire dump without having to think about where I was going.

I wasn't real good at thinking, not then. When I'd told Rose I was about to go out and do field work, I hadn't had the slightest idea where I'd go and do it. Grilling Tony Sudakis face to face instead of over the phone was the closest thing to a good idea I'd had.

This time, the security guard didn't need to see my EPA sigil before he got on the phone with Sudakis. A minute later, he set up the footbridge and I went into the containment area. As I walked up the warded path toward Sudakis' fortress of an office, I looked for the patch of Nothing I'd seen a couple of times before. Rather to my relief, I didn't notice it, not then.

Sudakis opened the outer door himself. He probably started to say something pleasant and meaningless, but one look at my face made him change his mind. "You all right, Dave?" he asked.

I gave him the same answer I'd given Rose: "No." To him, though, I amplified it. "I was supposed to go out to dinner with my fiancée last night after I got back from examining this place. I didn't get to do that. When I went down to her flat, I found she'd been kidnapped."

"That's terrible," he exclaimed, a comment I could hardly disagree with. He started to take me inside, then stopped in his tracks. Say what you like about Antanas Sudakis, he's plenty sharp. He looked back at me. "Wait a minute," he said slowly. "You think there's some kind of connection between us and that, don't you? Listen, Dave, I'm here to tell you that—"

I overrode him: "You bet your sweet ass I think there's a connection, Tony. I've thought there was a connection ever since the Thomas Brothers monastery burned down. I really thought there was a connection when a couple of louts tried to kill me after I got off the freeway one afternoon—"

"When *what*?" Now he interrupted me.

I realized I hadn't told him about that, so I did. Then I went on, "And now, the day after the EPA wizard and I scan this place, Judy gets snatched. What am I supposed to think, Tony? What would *you* think?"

"I don't know," he said, hardly louder than a whisper.

He was shaken—I could see that. His left hand reached for the little amber amulet he wore under his shirt. He made it go down by what looked like a deliberate effort of will. I decided to shake him up some more: "And just so you know, Tony, you do have a leak in your containment setup. Michael Manstein and I found Hollywood stardust all around your walls."

"Stardust is harmless," he said, rallying as gamely as he could.

"Yeah, but if stardust is leaking, what else is getting out with it?" Michael had had to make that obvious point for me; now I took malicious pleasure in hitting Sudakis over the head with it.

He was tough. I'd known that already. "You didn't find anything else, did you?" he demanded.

"No, but we will. It's only a matter of time and thaumaturgy, and you know it as well as I do." I took a deep breath, tried to calm down. "Anyway, that isn't what I came up here for. I wanted to find out who you called when Michael and I got to work out here. Whoever it is either did the kidnapping themselves or else called somebody to arrange to have it done."

"The only call I made was to the Devonshire Land Management Consortium office," he said. "I had to let them know so—they—could—" He ran down like a mechanical watch as he realized what he was saying. He kicked at the cement under his feet. "Oh, shit."

"Them or somebody connected with them," I said. "It just about has to be."

I thought he'd give me more arguments, more denials, but he didn't. "Yeah," he said in a voice like ashes.

"So what are you going to do about it?" I said, pushing hard. "Be a good little consortium soldier and pretend none of this has ever happened? You can. It would be legal. You'd probably even get promoted. But could you look at yourself in the mirror whenever you went into a men's room?"

"Fuck you, Dave," he said evenly. I did try to hit him then. He caught my fist before it connected. I'd known he was stronger than I am, but not how much. If he'd hit me back, somebody else would be telling you this story. But he didn't. He just hung onto me for most of a minute, then said, "You done being stupid?"

I nodded. He let me go. "Good. You don't want to try preaching at me again. It won't push me in the direction you want me to go. You got that?" He waited until I nodded again before he went on, "Okay. Now that you've got that straight, I'd do everything I can to help you get your lady back. For my reasons, mind you, not yours. We're wasting time here."

"I don't think I understand you at all," I said.

"I don't think you do, either." It wasn't pejorative: more as if he was stating a law of nature. Maybe he was. As I've said, I'd never dealt with anybody of European origin who still clung to his people's old gods, not in an artificial cult like that of Hermes, but as part of a tradition as old and serious as my own. *Balance of Powers*, I thought, and then wondered Whose side Perkunas was on. After enduring umpty hundred years of Christianity, the Lithuanian Power might be as eager as Huitzilopochtli to get his own back.

But no matter where his god stood, I thought Tony stood with me. Almost dragging me in his wake, he started down the walk toward the exit. I happened to look back toward his office at just the right time. "Wait!" I exclaimed, and grabbed his arm.

It was like taking hold of the Juggernaut's car; once he got moving, he didn't want to stop for anything. "Look back there," I said in a tone heading toward desperate. "That's what I was talking about before."

Grudgingly, he turned around. "I don't see anything," he said.

"I don't see anything, either," I answered. "I see Nothing. Here, stand right where I am now." I moved off the spot, he moved onto it. He shook his head, started to go. Now I was desperate. "Stand on tiptoe," I suggested; I'm several inches taller than he is.

He gave me a look that would have wilted me under any other circumstances. When I stayed crisp, he shrugged and went up on his toes. A second later, he said something in

Lithuanian that I didn't understand. Then he dropped back into English: "You were right after all, Dave. I don't know what that is."

Neither did I. At the moment, I couldn't see the Nothing; the dump just looked like a weedy vacant lot. But when I'd stood where Tony was now, the wall beyond that point seemed to recede into infinite space. And yet, at the same time, it was obviously right where it belonged. I don't know how to explain it any better than that; I got the feeling I wasn't sensing it entirely through normal vision.

Tony Sudakis came down off tiptoe. He was, as usual, briskly decisive. "When you see something you don't understand in a toxic spell dump, you'd better start trying to find out what it is just as fast as you can," he said. "Why don't you call your wizard—his name was Manstein, right?—and have him get up here? The sooner he can find out what's going on over there, the sooner we can start trying to deal with it."

"Aren't you the same fellow I heard yesterday talking about how if Michael or I set so much as a toe inside the confines of the dump, your people would sue us until the vulture let Prometheus' liver alone?"

"Go ahead, rub it in," he said. "Yeah, I'm that guy. But I'm also the guy you've finally convinced. So come on back to my office."

I was never so happy to turn around in my life. As we headed back toward the squat, ugly fortress, I asked, "Do you know what got dumped in that area? The more I can tell Michael, the quicker he'll be able to identify what's going on."

"Makes sense," Sudakis said. He looked over toward where we'd seen that Nothing. It wasn't there now, of course, because we weren't in the right spot. "That'd be about, hmm, Area 37. I'll check for you."

He pawed through the files, muttering all the time: "No, can't be that one—that one was exorcised two years ago . . . Maybe this one? No, forget it—I know everything roc's eggshell can do . . . Hah!"

"Hah?" I echoed.

"Gotta be this one, Dave. Three-four months ago, one of

the Baron's Watchers of the Shore found the remains of what sure looked like a major conjuration out on Malibu Beach. They tested the junk for thaumaturgical activity, but it came back negative—and I mean real negative, like there'd never been any magic around it since time began. Nobody believed that, not from the way the stuff was laid out, so they brought it here and dumped it in spite of the tests."

"I remember that one," I said. "There were letters in the *Times* complaining about the waste of taxpayers' crowns."

"That's it," Tony agreed. "You ask me, the only thing worse than the government spending money when it doesn't need to is *not* spending it when it does need to."

I started to pick up the phone, then stopped. "You said 'stuff' was laid out. What kind of stuff?"

He looked down at his parchments. "Funny stuff—like nothing I've ever seen before. Staffs with stone disks mounted on one end, others with those shells called sand crowns instead. If I had to guess, I'd say the stones were carved flat to look like the sand crowns. And there were other staffs, long and short, topped with feathers. Looked like some kind of Indian ritual, maybe, but not one I know."

"Okay." I got on the phone and called Michael. While I waited for him to answer, I worried some more: *balance of Powers*. Indian magic would not be well-inclined toward what I thought of as peace and order, not now.

"Environmental Perfection Agency—Michael Manstein speaking."

"Michael? Hi, it's David Fisher. Listen, I've got a new job for—"

Michael interrupted, something he hardly ever does: "David, where are you. What on earth are you up to? Bea is quite vexed"—a word only he would come up with—"with you and Rose is practically in tears."

That made me feel bad, but it would have made me feel worse if I didn't feel pretty bad already. In words of one syllable, I explained where I was and what I was up to. I also told him about Judy, which explained why I was up to it.

"Good heavens, David," he said, about as big an outburst

as you'll ever hear from him. "No wonder your behavior was so anomalous."

"Yeah, no wonder at all," I grunted. *Anomalous* wasn't the word for it; *shitty* was. I could blame it on endless worry, no sleep, and too much coffee, but in the end it came back to me. If you're not responsible for what you do in this world, who is?

"Have you discovered anything of import in your return to the Devonshire toxic spell containment area?" Michael asked, graciously not saying anything more about what sort of beast I'd been.

"As I matter of fact, I have." I told him about the Nothing, then put Tony Sudakis on the phone so he could confirm it.

Tony gave the handset back to me. Michael was saying, "—shall fly there forthwith to investigate. Your description strikes me as extremely urgent." He hung up.

"He's on his way," I said to Sudakis.

"Okay," he answered. "I'd better stay here, then, to make sure he can get in and do what he needs to do. What about you? You gonna wait here with me?"

I thought about it, shook my head. "I've got to get back and mend my fences. Listen, do you have a telephone at home?" I waited till he nodded, then said, "Would you give me your number? I may need to get hold of you any time. Like it or not—and I'm *not* saying you're liable; please understand that—you're in the middle of this, too—and they've got Judy, whoever *they* are."

He scrawled it on a scrap of parchment. "Here you go. Call when you need to."

"Thanks." I went out the door, down the warded path (I didn't even look back for the Nothing this time), over the footbridge, and out to my carpet. On the way back to St. James' Freeway, I passed a florist's shop. I stopped and bought Rose some roses. Sometimes words aren't contrition enough.

Rose's eyes went wide when I set the vase on her desk. She pointed to the closed door to Bea's office. "She's in a meeting right now, but she'll want to see you when she gets out. And thank you, David. You didn't have to do this. Michael told me what your trouble was. I'll pray for you."

Rose is one of the good people. If God was in a mood to listen to anybody, He'd listen to her. "I did have to do this," I said. "It's the stuff before that I shouldn't have done."

She waved that aside and started to say something more, but I was already on the way back to my office. No matter how much of a big, hairy thing I'd been, I found she'd faithfully taken my messages while I was out. One was from Henry Legion. I'd have to call him back, I thought.

Then I looked at the next one. It was from Judy.

IX

I don't know how long I stood there staring at the little piece of parchment in my hand. Every feeling you can imagine ran through my mind—joy that Judy was alive, fear that she was in *their* clutches, hope, worry, rage, all of them jumbled together at once in a way that would have made me dizzy even if I hadn't been running on no sleep and too much coffee.

Eventually I started thinking as well as feeling. The message, not surprisingly, left no return number. I ran back down the hall (I almost ran into Phyllis Kaminsky, too) to Rose, threw it on her desk. "I meant to tell you about this, David," she said, "but what with the flowers and all, it went right out of my mind. I'm sorry."

So even Rose could make mistakes. I hadn't been sure it

was possible. But it didn't matter, not right then. "Never mind," I said. "How did she sound? What did she say?"

"She just asked for you and hung up when I told her you were out of the office," Rose said. "I didn't know anything was wrong then." She gave me a reproachful look; if I'd told her earlier, she might have been able to do more. "You have to remember, I've only spoken with her the couple of times she's come up here and occasionally taken messages for you—and no one ever sounds like herself on the phone."

Miserable phone imps— But no sooner had that thought crossed my mind than I ran up the hall (and almost ran down Phyllis again; she let out an indignant squawk) back to my office.

I wished Michael were still here instead of up at the Devonshire dump. I'd read that a good wizard could sometimes trace a phone call even after the etheric connection between the imps at the opposite ends was broken.

Phone imps are nearly identical, one to another—that's what ectoplasmic cloning is all about. Nearly, but not quite. As Bacon's *Prosciutto* puts it, "There's a divinity that shapes our ends/Rough-hew them how we will." Tiny imperfections get into the cloning process—macro identical, but micro different. That's why the phone switching system works so well: because the imps are so like one another and spring from the same source, the laws of similarity and contagion make establishing contact between any two of them easy. And because they aren't quite identical, each can be assigned its own place in the telephone web.

"God, I'm an idiot!" I exclaimed a moment later. God, I presume, already knew this. Michael Manstein was a good wizard, sure, but he wasn't the only good wizard involved in this case—the CBI had plenty of skilled mages, just two floors up. I called Saul Klein, told him what had happened.

"I'll send someone right to you," he said as soon as I was through. Henry Legion might have got down to my office faster than the wizard did, but I don't think any mere mortal could have. She was a Hanese woman who came up just past my elbow, but she seemed smart and businesslike as all get-out. She introduced herself as Celia Chang.

"What time would this telephone call have been placed?" she asked.

I looked down at the parchment. Rose, bless her efficient soul, had made a note of it. "Ten twenty-seven," I answered.

"And it's now"—she paused to ask her watch—"five minutes past twelve. A little more than an hour and a half. The etheric trail should not be impossibly cold. Let me see what I can do, Mr. Fisher."

From the efficient way she went about things, I gathered this wasn't the first time she'd traced phone calls—probably not the fifty-first, either. If anybody had to use that particular thaumaturgy a lot, it would be the CBI. I felt easier; I'd been wishing she were Michael, but now I decided I didn't need to worry about it.

She opened her little black bag, took out what looked like a telephone handset but wasn't (I'd never seen a blue porcelain phone, anyhow), and set it on the desk next to my phone. "Does the telephone consortium know you have gear like that?" I asked.

"Officially, no," she said. Her smile made her look much younger and prettier than she had without it. "Unofficially—ask me no questions and I'll tell you no lies." Like anybody else with an ounce of concern for the world to come, she was hesitant about being forsworn.

"Never mind," I told her.

She took a copper cable from one pocket of her lab robe, used it to connect her blue box to the real telephone. As she did so, she made a face. "Properly, this should be silver," she said. "It's a better conductor of sorcerous influences than copper—but it's also more expensive, and so it's not in our thaumaturgical budget. If I were in private practice—" She shook her head. "If I were in private practice, I'd be less useful. I'm sure you have to manage on fewer resources than you find ideal, too."

"How right you are," I said.

She was making small talk while she could, just to put me at my ease. When the need for serious conjuration came, she started ignoring me. That was all right; I hadn't expect anything different. Wizards dealing with the Other Side don't need their elbows joggled, even metaphorically.

Mistress Chang might have been Hanese by blood, but she used standard Western sorcerous techniques, ones that date back to the *Species* of Origen and some of them even farther. No reason she shouldn't have; for all I knew, her ancestors might have come to the Confederation a couple of generations before mine. After censing the copper cable (and stinking up my office), she took two metal plaques, each inscribed with a demon's seal, and affixed them to the cable.

"I don't need a full manifestation from either Eligor or Botis," she explained, "but I do require the application of some of their attributes: Eligor discovers hidden things, while Botis discerns past, present, and future. Now if you will excuse me—"

The first gesture of her elegantly manicured hand was a wave to get me to move back a couple of steps. The next was a pass that accompanied her conjuration. Calling up demonic attributes without getting raw demon, so to speak, is a tricky business; I watched quietly and respectfully while she did what she had to do.

It was more like coaxing than commanding: no impressive circles or pentagrams, no *manifest thyself or eternal torment shall overwhelm thee*. At the climax of the incantation, she just said, "Help me, please, you two great Powers." I tell you, modern sorcery lacks the drama it had in the good old days.

But we can do things now that our ancestors never dreamt of trying. When Celia Chang pointed to the plaques on the cable, the seals that bound Eligor and Botis, which had been black squiggles on silver metal, began to glow with a light that outshone the St. Elmo's fire on the ceiling.

The light started to fade, then grew again. "They're searching through time for the etheric connection," Celia Chang said. Just then, Botis' seal blazed for a moment; I had to blink and turn my head aside. The CBI wizard softly clapped her hands together. "We have the fix in time. Now to see whether Eligor's allegory algorithm can uncover the missing phone number."

I didn't know what we were waiting for—probably for Eligor's seal to flare up the way Botis' had. That didn't happen; its squiggles continued to shine as they had before. I don't know if you're familiar with Eligor's seal: it looks rather like an open mouth with a rubber arrow threaded through its upper lip.

Arrow or not, though, that sort of a mouth up and spoke like the old Roman godlet Aius Locutius: one number after another, until there were ten. Celia Chang and I both wrote them down as Eligor gave them to us. By the time we'd recorded the last one, the lines on both plaques had stopped glowing.

"Let's compare them," the wizard said. I handed her the scrap of parchment on which I'd taken down the numbers. She held out the one on which she'd written them. We'd both heard the phone number the same way. She asked, "Is this number familiar to you?"

"No." I shook my head. "It's not Judy's; it's not any phone number I've seen before."

"I expected as much, but you never know," she said. "We'll have to go to the telephone consortium, then, and learn to whom the number belongs—if anyone, of course. It might be a public phone."

"I hadn't thought of that," I said in a hollow voice. Hard for me to imagine kidnappers having a victim make a call from a pay phone in the middle of the morning, but it was possible, especially if they knew of one that couldn't be easily seen from the street.

Mistress Chang said, "We'll be in touch with you as soon as we learn anything, Mr. Fisher." She packed up her sorcerous impedimenta, nodded to me—still businesslike, but with, I thought, some sympathy, too—and strode out of the office.

My stomach growled, fortunately a couple of seconds after that. What with all the coffee I'd poured down there, it had been growling on and off for a while now, but this was a different note. It wanted food. No matter what your mind tries to do to you, your body has has a way of reminding you of life's basics.

I went over to the cafeteria and bought myself a vulcanized hamburger—as a matter of fact, it was cooked so hard that Vulcan, had he been of a mind to, could have carved the battle reliefs that he'd put onto the shields of Achilles and Aeneas right onto the surface of the meat. I ate it anyhow; at the moment, I didn't much care what I fed my fire, as long as it filled me up. And I washed it down with more coffee.

The stuff was starting to lose its power to conjure up my demons. I found myself yawning over the last of my fries. But no rest for the weary; I plodded back to the office to see what I could accomplish.

In short, the answer was *not much*. Part of the reason was that I jumped halfway to the ceiling every time the phone yarped, hoping it would be Judy again. It never was. None of the calls I got was of any consequence whatsoever. Every one of them, though, broke my concentration. In aggregate, they left me a nervous wreck.

Along with hoping one of the calls would be from Judy, I also kept hoping one *wouldn't* be from Bea. I just didn't have it in me to play staff meeting games right then, and I wasn't real thrilled about having to bear up under sympathy, either. Atlas carried the whole world, but right now I had all the weight on me I could take.

But Bea, to my relief, didn't call. Except for relief, I didn't think anything of it at the time. Looking back, though, I think she didn't call precisely because she knew I couldn't deal with it. Bea is a pretty fair boss. I may have mentioned that once or twice.

The phone squawked yet again. When I answered it, Celia Chang was on the other end. "Mr. Fisher? We have located that telephone whose number I traced a little while ago. It is, unfortunately, a public phone up on the corner of Soto's and Plummer in St. Ferdinand's Valley."

"Oh," I said unhappily.

"I am sorry, Mr. Fisher," she said, "but I did think you would want to know."

"Yes, thank you," I said, and hung up. I never have figured out why you thank someone who's given you bad news—

maybe to deny to the Powers that it's really hurt you, no matter how obvious that is.

After Celia Chang's call, the phone stopped making noise for a while. I tried to buckle down and get some work done, but I still couldn't make my mind focus on the parchments in front of me. I'd write something, realize it was either colossally stupid or just pointless, scratch it out, try again, and discover I hadn't done any better the next time. All I could think about was Judy—Judy and sleep. In spite of all that coffee, I was yawning.

About half past three, someone tapped on my door. Several people had been in already; news of what had happened was getting around with its usual speed in offices. I knew they meant well, and it made them feel better, but it just kept reminding me of what Judy had gone through and might be going through now. Still, once more couldn't make me feel much worse than I did already. "Come in," I said resignedly.

It was somebody I worked with, but somebody who already knew what was going on. "Hello, David," Michael Manstein said. "I trust I am not intruding?"

"No, no," I said—someone else would have been, but not Michael. "Here, sit down, tell me what that thing—that Nothing—I mean—in the Devonshire dump is."

He folded his angular frame into a chair, steepled his long pale fingers. "First tell me if you have any word of your fiancée," he said. So I had to go through that again after all. He listened attentively—Michael is always attentive—then said, "I am sorry you were out of the office when Judith called. I wish I could have been here when the CBI wizard traced the call, as well. I have had occasion to attempt that twice, but succeeded in only one instance. An opportunity to improve my technique would have been welcome."

I had the feeling he was more interested in the magic for its own sake than the reason it had been used, but I couldn't get angry about that—it was Michael through and through. I tried again to make the carpet fly my way: "So what was that Nothing? Did you analyze it?"

"I did," he answered. "As best I could determine, it is— Nothing."

"What's that supposed to mean?" I know I sounded peevish—nerves, exhaustion, coffee again.

Michael didn't notice. What he'd found intrigued him too much for him to pay attention to details like bad manners. He said, "It is, in my experience, unique: an area from which all the magic has been removed, not externally, as would be normal, but internally. Whatever Powers are involved are still contained within the barrier established around them, but have in effect created that barrier to shield them from the surrounding world—or *vice versa*. I have no idea how to penetrate the barrier from This Side."

"Could whatever's in there burst out from the Other Side?" I asked.

"It is conceivable," Michael said. "Since I am of necessity ignorant of what lies inside the barrier—think of it as an opaque soap bubble, if you like, although it is almost infinitely stronger—I cannot evaluate the probability of that possibility."

I worked that through till I thought I understood it. Then I said, "Why does the, the Nothing make everything behind it look so far away?"

"Again, I cannot give a precise answer," Michael said, "I believe I do grasp the basic cause of the phenomenon, however: the barrier is in effect an area where the Other Side has been removed from contact with This Side. The eye naturally attempts to pursue it in its withdrawal, thus leading to the impression of indefinitely great distance behind it."

"Okay," I said. That made some sense—certainly more than anything I'd thought of (which, given my current state, wasn't saying much). But it raised as many questions as it answered, the most important of which was, how do you go about separating This Side and the Other? They've been inextricably joined at least since people and Powers became aware of each other, and possibly since the beginning of time.

Michael said, "If your next question is going to be whether I have a theoretical model to explain how this phenomenon came to be, the answer, I regret, is no."

"I regret it, too, but that's not what I was going to ask you," I said. Michael raised a pale eyebrow; to him, finding a theoretical model ranked right up there with breathing. My mind was on simpler things: "I was going to ask if you'd come with me to inspect Chocolate Weasel tomorrow morning." I explained how more and more of the evidence was pointing toward an Aztecian connection.

"Beaten a hermetic seal, have they?" Michael murmured; again, the thaumaturgy interested him more than anything else. He went on, "We'll be seeing learned articles on that for some time to come. But yes, I will be happy to accompany you to Chocolate Weasel. Where is the facility located?"

"In St. Ferdinand's Valley, near the corner of Mason and Nordhoff," I answered. That wasn't a part of the Valley I'd learned yet; the Devonshire dump was north of it, while the businesses and factories I'd visited were farther south and east. I figured Michael or I could find it, though.

He said, "Shall we take my carpet again, and meet here as we did yesterday?"

"All right," I answered. I was just as glad that he'd fly us up into the Valley; at the moment, I wondered whether I'd be able to get myself home tonight.

Michael headed for the lab, no doubt intent on catching up on whatever he'd had to abandon when I called him from the Devonshire dump. I asked my watch what time it was—a little before four. Not quite soon enough to go home, but too late to do anything useful (assuming I could do anything useful) to the parchments on my desk.

I decided to try to call Henry Legion. I realized there was an advantage in dealing with a spook rather than a person (the first I'd found, so I treasured it): even though it was just about seven back in D.C., he was likely to be on the job. At least, I didn't think spooks had families to go home to.

And sure enough, I got him when I called. "Inspector Fisher," he said. "I was hoping I would hear from you. What have you learned since this morning?"

So I told him what I'd learned: the hermetic seals, the quetzal feather, the fer-de-lance, the One Called Night, the Nothing. It took a while. Until I told him what all I'd found out in the course of the day, I hadn't realized how big a forest it made; one tree at a time had been falling on me. But, to shift the figure of speech, I had a lot of pieces. I didn't have a puzzle.

"I shall convey your information to the appropriate sources," he said when I was through. "Inspector Fisher, the Confederation may well owe you a large debt of gratitude."

"I'm sorry," I said, "but right now that doesn't matter much to me. All I want to do is get Judy back, and I don't think I'm much closer than I was." Maybe fitting some of the pieces together would help. I asked, "Is it the Aztecians that we've bumped up against here?"

"Your information makes that appear more likely," he answered, maddeningly evasive and dispassionate as usual.

I was too tired to get angry at him. I just pushed ahead: "If it was the Aztecians, why did they attack the Garuda Bird?"

The CI spook hesitated—I must have asked the right question. "The answer which immediately springs to mind is that the Garuda Bird is the great enemy of serpents, being the representative of birth and the heavens, while serpents are in the camp of death, the underworld, and poison."

"The great enemy of serpents." For a second, it didn't mean anything—I *was* beat. Then an alarm clock started yelling inside my head. "Quetzalcoatl."

"This though had occurred to me, yes," Henry Legion said.

"What do we do?" I demanded.

"Prayers come to mind," the spook answered, which, while sensible, was not what I wanted to hear. He added, "Past that, the best we can. Call if you require my assistance, Inspector Fisher; I shall do what I can for you."

"Thanks," I said. I was talking to a dead line; he'd hung up.

Someone tapped on the door. I looked up. Now, as the day wound down, it was Bea. I gulped. She wasn't the person I wanted to see right then. Or at least I thought she wasn't, until she said quietly, "I just want you to know, David, that my prayers will be with you tonight."

From Henry Legion, the suggestion of prayer had had the

undertone that even that probably wouldn't help the mess we were in. Bea, though, sounded calmly confident it would make everything all right. I liked her attitude better than the spook's. But then, Henry Legion knew more about what all was wrong than she did.

"I'm sorry I didn't come see you," I muttered. I wasn't just sorry; I was ashamed of myself. But that's not something you can casually say to your boss.

I guess she was good at reading between the lines. She said, "If you like, we can talk about it more tomorrow. Why don't you go home and try to get some rest now? You'll be better for it." She made shooing motions, then smiled. "My mother used to do that to chase chickens off the back porch. I haven't thought about it in years. Go on home now."

"Thank you, Bea," I said humbly, and I went on home.

I don't remember what I cooked for supper that night, which is probably just as well. I thought about going to bed right afterward, but if I did that, I knew I'd wake up at three in the morning and stay up. So I rattled around in my flat instead, like a pea in a pod that was much too big for it.

The quiet in there felt very loud. I wished I had an ethernet set to give myself something to occupy my ears and maybe my mind. Being alone with yourself when you're worried is hard work. I tried to work, but I couldn't concentrate on the words.

The phone yelled. I banged my shin on the coffee table in the front room as I sprang up and dashed off to answer it. It was some mountebank selling microsalamander cigar lighters. I'm afraid I told him where to put one before he let the salamander loose. I limped back out front after I hung up.

I picked up my book again. I should have been reading something useful, maybe about the Garuda Bird or Quetzalcoatl. But no, it was a thriller about thirteen guys on a spy mission to Alemania during the Second Sorcerous War. I was at the exciting part—the Alemans were trying to drive them into the alkahest pits still bubbling from the First Sorcerous War. Even so, I kept losing track of what was going on.

The phone again. I almost hoped it was another huckster; I'd taken savage, mindless pleasure in baiting the first one. Too much had happened to me, with no chance for me to hit back at anyone. If a miserable salesman chose that moment to inflict himself on me, it was his lookout.

"Hello?" I snapped.

"David?" The progressive distortion from two phone imps couldn't mask the voice. All my rage evaporated even before she went on, "It's Judy."

"Honey," I whispered; just hearing for sure that she was alive took my breath away. I made myself talk louder: "Are you all right?"

"I'm—fair," she said, which made me fearful all over again. She hurried on: "Don't ask questions, Dave. You have to listen to me. They won't let me talk long. They say you have to stop messing around with things that aren't your business, or else—" I waited to hear what the "or else" was, but she'd stopped. I was afraid I could figure it out for myself.

"Tell them I say I'll do whatever they want," I answered. I hoped she'd get the distinction: just because I said it didn't mean I would.

"Be careful, Dave," she said. "They aren't joking. They—" Her voice cut off. Faintly, as if the imps were reproducing the words of someone farther from the phone, I heard, "Come on, you."

"Honey, I love you," I said. While I was talking, though, somebody hung up the phone. I don't think Judy heard me.

I spent a while wishing damnation on the wretches who'd snatched her, then pulled myself together and called the Long Beach constables. Plainclothesman Johnson had the night off; I got some other worthy, name of Scott. He heard me out, then said, "Thanks for passing on the information, sir. We'll do what we can with it."

Which meant, as I knew only too well, they weren't going to do much. It did tell them, as it had me, that Judy was still on This Side. That did count for something to them, and it had counted for a lot more than something to me. I had fresh hope.

I called the CBI. Saul Klein had gone home, but the fellow who answered the phone knew what was going on with the case. I asked him, "Can you send someone down to try to trace the call? Your Mistress Chang managed to do it earlier today."

"Well, why not?" the CBI man said after he thought it over. "Can't hurt to try." He read me back my home address to make sure he had it right, then said, "We'll have someone there in half an hour or so."

It was more like forty-five minutes, but that didn't surprise me. I drive St. James' Freeway every day; I know how things can be down there. When the rap on the door came, I opened it with my left hand. My right hand was holding the blasting rod: after what had happened to Judy, I wasn't taking any chances.

The weedy little fellow outside gave back a pace when he saw I was carrying a rod, which meant he almost went ass over teakettle down the stairs. He rallied fast, though. "Can't say as I blame you, sir," he said, and flashed a CBI sigil that said he was an intermediate thaumaturgic analyst—by which I learned the CBI has silly job titles, too—named Horace Smidley. I lowered the rod right away. He might not have looked like the light-and-magic show version of a CBI man, but he sure did look like a Horace Smidley.

I led him to the phone. He went through the same tracing ritual Celia Chang had used earlier in the day back at the office. He wasn't as smooth as she had been—he was only an *intermediate* thaumaturgic analyst, after all—but he got the job done. The quasi-mouth that formed Eligor's seal spoke its series of digits, then fell silent once more.

"That's the same number they used when they called before," I said.

"Is it? Careless of them." Smidley made a clucking noise in the back of his throat; I got the idea that he disapproved of carelessness no matter who perpetrated it, even if it made catching the bad guys easier. He went on, "I'll take the information back with me."

"What do you think it means?" I asked. "Are they holding

Judy somewhere close to there and using that phone because it's convenient to them?"

"That is most probable," he said; he and Michael Manstein would have got on well together. "The other possibility is that they are deliberately transporting her a long distance to mislead us. Possible, as I say, but risky: any accident or flying violation that a constable happens to observe destroys what up to now has appeared a well-organized scheme."

Again, you could tell he liked organization, no matter who was using it or for what purpose. I worry about people like that; the Leader of Alemania had had a lot of them behind him. Horace Smidley, though, was on my side, for which I was duly grateful. I thanked him for taking the trouble to come down at night.

"My pleasure," he said, and then, to my mind, weakened the answer by adding, "And my duty." He headed down the stairs—intentionally this time—and then, I presume, on back to Westwood.

Me? I shut the door after him, brushed my teeth, and went to bed. I don't remember another thing until the alarm clock scared me awake the next morning.

It was going to be a hot one. I could tell as soon as I got out of bed. Even after a long night's sleep, I still felt tired, but out my bedroom window I saw that the wind stirring the eucalyptus tree next door was some from out of the northeast: what they call St. Ann's wind. That always strikes me as rude, or don't you think naming a wind after the Virgin's mother implies she talked too much?

The wind swirled hard enough to shake my carpet as I headed for the freeway. When I flew past a vacant lot, I watched the dust devils spinning tumbleweeds around and tossing them up into the sky. There are more dust devils these days than there used to be; I've always said cutting the budget for meteorological exorcists was a mistake. One day the devils will join forces and blow down a building or three, and fixing things will end up costing a lot more than we're saving now.

But what politician looks to the future? I wondered why I

was bothering myself, come to that. If the Third Sorcerous War broke out, dust devils would be the least of my—and everyone else's—worries.

Michael was waiting for me in the parking lot. "Have you received any news?" he asked as I walked up to his carpet.

"They made Judy call me last night," I said, nodding. "Whoever they are, they want us to stop investigating anything that has anything to do with the Devonshire dump—or else."

Michael gave me a curious look. "Yet you are still here." He turned on to Wilshire to get to St. James' Freeway for the trip up into the Valley.

"Yeah, I'm still here," I said. "I don't believe stopping would really make them turn Judy loose. And besides . . . the deeper we get into this case, the more important it looks." God help me, I was starting to think like Henry Legion. Saving the world, not just one person, looked bigger all the time.

We got off the Venture Freeway at Winnetka and headed north, Michael flying, me navigating. It was a mixed kind of neighborhood, first a business block, then a row of homes, then some more businesses. Once we flew past what looked half like a school, half like a farm. I glanced down at my map. "That's the Ceres Institute of St. Ferdinand's Valley." In spite of everything, I laughed. "Angels City *is* an ecumenical place."

"Another artificial cult," Michael said; his business is keeping up with such things. "They say the goddess really does improve agricultural productivity."

"I wonder how much maintaining her cult adds to the price of produce, though." Cost-benefit analysis again. You can't get away from it in our society: it was the same kind of thing I was doing to see whether the Chumash Powers would be worth preserving if they did still happen to exist. That reminded me I'd have to call Professor Blank one of these days and see what more he'd harassed his graduate students into finding out.

"We should be getting close," Michael said.

"We are," I answered, after a check of where we were. "The next major cross street is Nordhoff. You'll want to turn left there. Mason is the next fair-sized street that will cross it, about half a mile west of Winnetka."

"Very good." Michael swung into the leftmost flight lane at Winnetka and Nordhoff. We had to wait for all the south-bound carpets to go past before we could turn, though. Strange how rules of the road that were codified for horses in Europe long before anyone outside the Middle East was flying carpets still govern the way we handle traffic. Sorcery, of course, maintains anything old and curious because being old and curious makes it powerful in and of itself. I'd never thought of traffic rules falling into that category, though.

The north side of Nordhoff was a light industrial park, with one big rectangular box of a building following another. The south side was mostly houses, though the corner with Mason boasted a liquor store, a Golden Steeples that probably did a land-office business from all the working types across the street, and also a Spells 'R' Us.

Chocolate Weasel was in the industrial park, a couple of buildings past Mason. Michael let his carpet down in an open space near the front door. As I undid my safety belt and stood up, I noticed that a lot of the carpets in the lot were old and threadbare. People didn't work here to get rich, that was obvious.

Michael picked up his little black bag. We walked over to the entrance side by side. The first thing that hit me when we went inside was the music. There were minisingers involved in the case after all—I'd have to tell Saul Klein. But they weren't playing *lieder*—oh my, no. The inside of Chocolate Weasel sounded like an Aztecian bar in East A.C.—or maybe like one down in Tenochtitlan—both in style of music and in volume. I must confess I winced.

All the chatter inside was in Spainish, too. No, I take that back: I heard a little clucking Nahuatl, too. No English, not until people noticed us. I got the idea people who didn't look Aztecian didn't pop into Chocolate Weasel every day. The Aztecian community in Angels City is big enough to be a large city of its own, and doesn't have to deal with outsiders unless it wants to.

By the looks they gave us, we were outsiders they didn't

want to deal with. Those looks got darker when we pulled out our EPA sigils, too. Suddenly everyone in the place developed a remarkable inability to understand English. Michael foiled that ploy, though, by asking for the head of the firm in fluent Spainish.

I wondered if the secretary would fall back into Nahuatl; she was one of the people I'd heard using it. If she did, though, Michael would give her another surprise. I wondered how many pale blonds spoke the old Aztecian language. *Not many* seemed a fair guess.

But, rather to my disappointment, she didn't. In fact, hearing Michael use Spainish made her unbend enough to remember she knew some English after all, which put me back in the conversation. She took us down the hall to the consortium markgrave's office.

Jorge Vasquez looked at us with about as much enthusiasm as a devout Hindu confronted with a plate of blood-red prime rib. He was a handsome fellow in his early forties, and doing quite well for himself: unless I missed my guess, his suit would have run me close to two weeks' pay.

He shoved our sigils back across the desk at us, then leaned forward to glare. "I am sick and tired of harassment by the EPA," he said. "You people have the attitude that our spells must be perverse because they are based on the authentic rituals of our people. It is not true; our procedures are no more wicked than the thaumaturgy the Catholic Church works through transubstantiation." He pointed to the crucifix on the wall behind him.

"That's a matter of opinion," I answered. "Myself, I'm Jewish." I didn't elaborate; what it meant was that I found any ritual of human sacrifice, no matter how symbolic, on the unpleasant side.

Vasquez didn't say anything, but his nostrils flared. So he wasn't real fond of Jews, eh? Well, that was his problem, not mine.

I went on, "In any case, this visit has nothing to do with the merit of your rituals, only with the way you're preparing your toxic spell byproducts for disposal. The Devonshire dump is leaking, and leaking something noxious enough to cause an outbreak of apsychic births in the neighborhood. Considering some of the materials and cantrips you use, I hope you can understand how we might be concerned."

"I tell you again, Inspector Fisher, this is bigotry in action," Vasquez said. "We run a clean shop here. What do you think we are doing, attempting to bring about the dominion of Huitzilopochtli over Angels City?"

That was one of my major concerns, but telling him so didn't seem politic. I just said, "Why don't you take us over to your flayed human skin substitute processing facility? That's the likeliest source of thaumaturgic pollution here, I think."

"It is a legitimate sorcerous substance, permissible under the laws of the Confederation," Vasquez said hotly. "I repeat, you are harassing Chocolate Weasel by singling us out—"

"Bullshit," I said, which made him sit up straight in his chair: not the first time lately I'd surprised somebody by not talking the way an EPA inspector was supposed to. I didn't care. If he was hot, I was steaming. I went on, "You are not being singled out, sir. I've been visiting businesses that dump at Devonshire for weeks now. You're not being discriminated against because you're Aztecian, either—I've hit Persian places, aerospace firms, what have you. But even you won't deny flayed human skin substitute is a dangerous substance, I hope? Now we can do this politely on an informal level or I can go out, get a warrant, and turn this place inside out. How do you want to play it?"

He calmed down in a hurry. Somehow I'd thought he might. He said, "What sort of tests do you have in mind?"

I looked at Michael—he was the expert. He said, "I intend to use the similarity test with my own piece of skin substitute to see if uncontrolled Huitzilopochtlic influences are present." He was going to try the same test he'd used back at the dump, in other words.

I didn't know what Vasquez would say about that—maybe start complaining about theological discrimination. But he didn't; he just got up and said, "Come with me, gentlemen." I concluded he was a lot like Ramzan Durani of Slow Jim Fizz: plenty of bluster when he was excited, but a reasonable man underneath. Fine with me; I'd had it up to here with arguments.

As soon as we left the office, the racket from the mariachi minisingers came back full force. That kind of music has its enthusiasts. Unfortunately, I'm not any of them. And the minisingers, true to their Alemanic *Ursprung*, gave it a slight oompah beat that did nothing to improve matters.

The workers on the factory floor glared at Michael and me as we went by. Not everybody loves the EPA. Too bad. The Confederation would be contaminated a lot worse than it is if we weren't around.

Squares of flayed human skin substitute lay at the bottom of vats. Even though the stuff was legal, it turned my stomach. Michael said, "Take one out for me, please." Vasquez translated his request into Spanish. One of his men reached in and fished out a dripping sheet.

"It's darker than the substitute you have in your kit," I remarked.

Vasquez said, "This is the residue of the tanning baths. Proper cleansing will restore the usual shade."

Michael Manstein raised an eyebrow at that, but he didn't say anything, so I let it ride. I said, "I trust you have proper import certificates for the flayed human skin substitute?"

"I shall fetch them immediately," Vasquez said. "Please do not let my absence delay you in your tests." He headed back toward his office.

Michael got to work with his sheet of human skin substitute and the one the worker had pulled out of the vat. I clutched my kabbalistic amulets. I was ready for anything from his sheet of substitute starting to bleed to all hell breaking loose. I was ready for what might have been worse than hell breaking loose: I was ready for Huitzilopochtli alive and in Person and in a bad mood. I wasn't sure I'd get out of Chocolate Weasel in one piece if that happened, but I had a chance.

Jorge Vasquez came back while Michael was still incanting. He handed me the certificates I'd asked for. Sure enough, they showed he was bringing in flayed human skin substitute produced by the law of similarity, as certified by some high sorcerer down in Tenochtitlan, the point of origin of the stuff. The certificate had Aztecian export stamps and Confederation import stamps right where they belonged. On parchment, Chocolate Weasel was as legal as could be.

"Thanks very much, Mr. Vasquez," I said. "You maintain excellent documentation."

"I have to," he answered, his tone bitter. "It is the only way I can protect myself from harassment because I am an Aztecian businessman serving my people on Confederation soil." He was back to that song again. I let it alone; nothing I could say was going to make him change his mind.

Michael spoke a last couple of magical words, lifted the wet sheet of flayed human skin substitute from the one he'd taken out of his little black bag. "No sign of bleeding," he said, sounding as surprised as he ever did—which is to say, Vasquez, who didn't known him well, wouldn't have noticed any change in his voice. "I must conclude that the specimen from the vat is thaumaturgically inactive with respect to Huitzilopochtli."

"I could have told you as much," Vasquez said. "In fact, I did tell you as much, but you chose not to listen. Are you satisfied?"

I nodded, reluctantly. I'd thought we'd surely find the pot of gold at Chocolate Weasel (which reminded me I'd have to do something one of these days about the study on naturalizing leprechauns). Michael said, "The data we have obtained leave us no reason to be dissatisfied," which struck me as damning with faint praise. He must have been disappointed, too.

"I presume you will have the courtesy to mention this in your written report," Vasquez said with icy, ironic politeness. "I also trust you will be making that report soon."

I knew a hint to get out of there when I heard one. I'd have liked to stay and snoop some more, but after Michael failed to find any trace of Huitzilopochtlic influence on the flayed human skin substitute, I didn't see how I could. I waited for Michael to finish packing the tools of his trade, then dejectedly followed Vasquez back to his office.

In front of that office, he sank another barb: "I hope you

gentlemen can find your own way out. Good day." He went inside and closed the door after him.

We found our own way out. Once again, nobody up front took any interest in us except to speed us on our way. I was ready to go, too. I'd had such high hopes everything would break open at Chocolate Weasel. But what did we get there? Nothing, the same as we'd got everywhere else. It wasn't just a case any more, either. Judy's life lay on the line.

"Damnation," I said as we scuffed our way across the lot toward Michael's carpet.

"No sign of it there, not so far as I could prove," he said, "although, so far as I know, flayed human skin substitute, unlike the authentic product, comes in only one color and is merely toughened, not darkened, by the tanning process."

"Really?" I said. "That's interesting, but if you found no sign of Huitzilopochtli, it's nothing more than interesting."

"My thought exactly," he said, sitting down and reaching for his safety belt.

A tattered old carpet on its last fringes flew slowly into the lot, settled into a parking space maybe fifty feet from us. The two guys on it were talking in Spanish, and paid us no attention whatever. One of them wore a red cap, the other a blue one.

That rang a vague bell in my mind, but no more. Then the fellow in the blue cap turned his head so I got a good look at his face. You don't soon forget the looks of a guy who's tried to bounce your balls—it was Carlos, the charming chap from the swap meet. And the man with him was Jose. They got off their carpet—they didn't bother with safety belts—and went on into Chocolate Weasel.

I stood there staring after them. "Come on," Michael said, a little querulously. "Having failed here, we may as well return to the office and more productive use of our time."

"Huh?" He snapped me back to myself. "We haven't failed here—your test may have, but we haven't." He looked at me as if he had no idea what I was talking about. After a moment, I realized he didn't. I explained rapidly, finishing, "Those are the two who sold Cuauhtémoc Hernandez his poison, full of real human skin and the influence of

Huitzilopochtli. What are they doing at Chocolate Weasel if it's really as legit as your test showed?"

"A cogent question." But Michael was frowning. "Yet how could the similarity test I employed on the flayed human skin substitute be in error? It was conducted under universally valid thaumaturgic law."

A dreadful suspicion was growing in me. I didn't want to speak it out loud, for fear of making it more likely to be true—or maybe it was more the worry that comes out in the phrase, *Speak of the devil*. I did say, "I'm not questioning supernatural law, just the assumptions you made the test under. And I think I know how we can find out if I'm right. Come on."

"What are you doing?" Michael said, but he unbuckled, got off his carpet, and, little black bag in hand, followed me across the street.

A salesman came up smiling when we walked into the Spells 'R' Us store, me still a couple of paces in front of Michael. "Good morning, sir—sirs," he said, amending things when he realized we were together. "What sort of home thaumaturgics can I interest you in today?"

I showed him my EPA sigil. A couple of seconds later, Michael got his out, too. He still didn't know what I was up to, but he'd back my play. The salesman—he looked like a college kid—stopped smiling and looked real Serious.

"As you see, we're from the Environmental Perfection Agency," I said. "We're in the middle of an investigation and we urgently need a spellchecker. I'd like to borrow one from you and activate it for a few minutes."

The kid gulped. "I can't authorize that myself, sir. I'll have to get the manager." He fled into the EMPLOYEES ONLY section of the store to do just that.

The manager looked like what his salesman would turn into in about ten years: he'd added a mustache to the mix, and lost his zits and some callowness. He listened to my story, then asked, "Are you investigating us?" I got that one real quick: if I said yes, he'd say no.

But I could say no with a clear conscience. When I did, the manager led Michael and me over to the display of spellcheckers against one wall and waved to show us we could help ourselves.

Since money was no object, I chose a fancy Winesap from Crystal Valley. Then I asked the fellow, "Does that liquor store next door carry Passover wine, do you think?"

"You use that ritual, do you?" He looked interested, as if he wanted to talk shop but knew it wasn't the right time or place. "Yes, I think they would, sir. This part of the Valley has a fairly large Jewish population."

"Thank you, sir," I said. "May we use this unwrapped one here? I don't want to inconvenience you any more than I have to. Believe me, I appreciate your cooperation." I turned to Michael. "You can wait here, if you like. I'll bring back the wine." At his nod, I trotted out of the Spells 'R' Us.

Sure enough, the liquor store had what I was after: big square bottle with a neck long enough to use as a clubhandle in a pinch, label with a white-bearded rabbi, a fellow who looks like the Catholic conception (excuse me) of God the Father peering out at you. Because it's specially blessed, Passover wine is thaumaturgically more active than your average enspirited grape juice, so it's available all year round. I bought a bottle of sweet Concord—just picking it up brought back memories of childhood Seders, when it was the only wine I got to taste all year—and took it back to the home thaumaturgics emporium.

Michael said, "If you plan to go back inside, David, and if your conjecture is accurate, there is a significant probability that the staff will make a sizable effort to disrupt your activity."

My feeling was that there was a significant probability the Chocolate Weasel staff would make a sizable effort to disrupt *me* if I was right, and never mind my activity. But I said, "If they're doing what I think they're doing in there, I don't think we'll need to go back inside."

While we talked back and forth, the salesman and Spells 'R' Us manager stood off to one side, listening so hard I thought they'd grow asses' ears the way King Midas did in the Greek myth. At another time or place, it might have been funny.

I went outside, Michael following again. The two guys
from Spells 'R' Us watched through their plate-glass window.
I could figure out what they were thinking when they saw
me point a spellchecker probe at Chocolate Weasel—something on the order of, *What's been across the street from us
for God knows how long?* It was a good question. With luck,
I'd have a good answer soon.

The rich, fruity smell of the Passover wine came welling
out of the bottle when I broke the seal. I poured a capful
(they make the cap just the right size to hold the usual acti-
vating dose—good ergonomics) into the spellchecker
receptacle and chanted the blessing. No sooner had I finished the *boray pri hagofen* and added *omayn* than the
screen lit up with a smile. The microimps inside were happy
and ready.

But, even though I aimed the probe at the Chocolate
Weasel building, the spellchecker didn't pick up anything
from it. It identified the magic associated with the flyway,
and also the crosswalk cantrips, not all of which, as I've
noted, are Christian by any means. I said something unfortunate and added disgustedly, "You'd think they didn't work
any magic at all in there."

"Which we know is not the case," Michael said. "This sug-
gests to me that the building is shielded against probes from
outside."

"You have to be right," I said. "But what can we do now?
Go on in? Like you said, if we do that, we're liable not to
come back out again."

"I am of the opinion that we have sufficient information
to seek a warrant and let the constabulary deal with the
matter from here on out," Michael said. "The staff of
Chocolate Weasel are consorting with criminals, and the
building's being so tightly sealed is suspicious in and of
itself. The blanking of the sorcery within goes far beyond
any that would be required to prevent industrial
espionage."

Just then the front door to Chocolate Weasel opened and
a couple of women came out. No matter how good the
place's shielding was, I'd already found out it wasn't

topologically complete like the Devonshire dump's: I hadn't had to cross over an insulated footbridge to get in. That meant influences could go out through the opening, too.

I looked down at the ground glass on the spellchecker. The microimps saw something across the street, all right, something they didn't like one bit. Words started forming: UNIDENTIFIED—FORBIDDEN. I felt as if someone had poured a bucket of ice water down my back. The door to Chocolate Weasel closed quickly and the damning words disappeared from the ground glass, but they remained imprinted on my mind. I'd hoped never to see their like again, but here they were.

"That's the same spellchecker reaction I got when I probed the potion that *curandero* gave Lupe Cordero," I said. "Now I know why your similarity ritual failed, Michael." I was glad I hadn't had lunch yet; I might have thrown up right on the sidewalk in front of Spells 'R' Us.

Michael shook his head. "I'm afraid your logical leap went past me there."

"You were testing for similarity to flayed human skin substitute," I said. "I don't think that's substitute in there—I think that's real flayed human skin."

"Yes, that might conceivably throw off the accuracy of the test." Sometimes Michael is almost off in a virtuous reality of his own. I suppose I shouldn't have been surprised he thought about the testing first, but I was. Still, he does connect to the real world. After a couple of seconds, his eye got wide behind his spectacles. "Dear God in heaven, there are thousands of square feet of flayed human skin substitute in those vats. If it is the genuine material rather than the substitute—"

"Then a lot of people have ended up dead, Huitzilopochtli is well fed, and the whole stinking world may come down on our heads." I didn't realize I'd started spouting doggerel till the words were out of my mouth.

"It is now imperative—no, mandatory—that we notify the authorities forthwith," Michael said.

Since he was right, I shut down the spellchecker (no doubt to the microimps' relief) and took it back into Spells

'R' Us. "Thanks very much, gentlemen," I said. "We appreciate the help. Now can you tell us where the nearest pay phone is?"

"There's one outside the Golden Steeples," the manager answered, "if it hasn't been vandalized."

The salesman blurted, "But can't you tell us what's going on?"

"I'm sorry," I said, "but it's against EPA policy to reveal the results of an ongoing investigation. As I say, you've helped, though."

Leaving them frustrated, we headed across Mason toward the Golden Steeples. The closer we got, the less optimistic I was about finding the phone in working order. The local street gangs had vandalized the building, scrawling tags like HUNERIC and TRASAMUND on the wall in big, angular letters. Graffiti are an environmental problem, too, one for which we don't have a good answer yet.

And sure enough, when we came up to the pay phone, I saw that somebody—presumably the punk who went by that monicker—had carved the name GELIMER into the base of the phone and used either a tweezers or a little levitation spell to get the coins out through the narrow slits he'd cut. Of course, once he violated the integrity of the containment system, the coin-collecting demon was also able to escape, and pay phones are rigged so their imps stay dormant unless he collects his fee. The phone, then, might as well not have been there.

Unless— I turned to Michael. "Are you a hot enough wizard to get around Ma Bell?"

"Possibly—with time and equipment we lack at the moment," he said. "Finding another pay phone would be more efficient."

Ergonomics again. Whether it's what size to make the cap on a bottle of wine or deciding to spell or not to spell, you can't get away from it. "Let's go back to the carpet, then," I said. "We're sure to pass one as we fly back to the freeway."

We crossed over to the Chocolate Weasel parking lot. Me, I wasn't what you'd call enthusiastic about setting foot there again, but I didn't feel too bad because I was doing it only to leave the place for good.

Though I didn't really need to, I picked up the map to check the route south. We could either head back to Winnetka the way we'd come and then down, or else we could fly west to . . .

"Michael," I said hoarsely, "I know where we can find a pay phone."

"Do you?" He glanced over to me. "I did not think you were overly familiar with this section of St. Ferdinand's Valley."

"I'm not," I said. "But look." I pointed to the map. The next major flyway, a couple of blocks west of where we were, was Soto's. And the next decent-sized street north of Nordhoff was Plummer. "I know there's a pay phone there because that's where Judy called me from."

"Good heavens," Michael said. "The concatenated implications—"

"Yeah," I said. "Chocolate Weasel is involved in something really hideous, they're doing their best to hide it, it leaks out of the Devonshire dump, we find out about it (I find out about it, I mean), somebody tries to get rid of me, somebody does kidnap Judy, and then they make her call me from a phone just around the corner from Chocolate Weasel."

"Since there is a phone at that location, and since it was undoubtedly working as recently as last night, I suggest we use it," Michael said. He lifted the carpet off the Chocolate Weasel parking lot, eased onto Nordhoff, and flew west toward Soto's. Just getting away from Chocolate Weasel felt good, as if I were escaping cursed ground. Considering what I thought was going on inside the building, that might have been literally true.

Michael turned right onto Soto's and flew up to Plummer. The corner there had a bunch of little shops. I didn't see a pay phone in front of any of them. I wondered if Celia Chang and Horace Smidley had screwed up. But what were the odds of their both screwing up the same way? Astrologically large, I thought.

"When a solution is not immediately apparent, more

thorough investigation is required," Michael said, a creed which for the research thaumaturge ranked right up there with the one hammered out at Nicaea.

He parked the carpet in front of a place whose sign had two words in the Roman alphabet—DVIN DELI—and a couple of lines in the curious pothooks Armenians use to write their language. I don't read Armenian myself, but I've seen it often enough to recognize the script.

Sure enough, the fellow behind the counter in there looked like Brother Vahan's younger cousin, except that he sported a handlebar mustache and had a full head of wavy iron-gray hair.

"God bless you, what can I do for you gentlemen today?" he said when Michael and I walked in. "I have some lovely lamb just in, and with yogurt and mint leaves—" He kissed the tips of his fingers.

Even if mixing meat and milk wasn't kosher, it sounded good to me. I hated to have to say, "I'm sorry, we're just looking for a pay phone."

"Across the street, behind the *carniceria* next to the Hanese bookstore," he said, pointing. "I don't know why they didn't put it out front, but they didn't. And when you've made your call, why don't you come back? I have figs and dates preserved in honey, all kinds of good things."

He was a salesman and a half, that one. I got out of the Dvin Deli in a hurry, before I was tempted into spending the next hour and a half there, buying things I didn't need and half of which I wasn't permitted to eat.

The Hanese bookstore also had a two-word English sign—HONG'S BOOKS—and the rest was in ideograms. For a couple of seconds, I didn't see the pay phone back of the Aztecian meat market. It was on the far side of a very fragrant trash dumpster; nobody flying casually down the street would have noticed anything going on while whoever had Judy made her call me. The *carniceria*'s back door didn't have a window, either, so people in there might not have spotted anything amiss, either.

I dug in my pocket, found change, and fed it into the greedy little paw of the pay phone's money demon. I called

Plainclothesman Johnson, Saul Klein, and Legate Kawaguchi, in that order. Johnson and Klein weren't altogether convinced that Chocolate Weasel was involved in Judy's kidnapping, though they both said the evidence was better than anything else they had. Kawaguchi said I'd handed him enough so he could give Chocolate Weasel a good going-over.

"Don't just send constables," I warned him. "That place is major sorcerous trouble. If you don't call out a hazardous *materia magica* team for it, you'll never, ever need one."

"I appreciate your concern, Inspector Fisher," Kawaguchi said, "but I assure you that I shall make all necessary arrangements. Good day." *Shut up and let me do my job*, was what he was saying. I just hoped he knew the kind of trouble his people were liable to walk into at Chocolate Weasel.

After that, I had to cadge some more change from Michael. I called Bea to let her know what was going on. Instead of Bea, I got Rose, who told me the boss was at a meeting away from the Confederal Building and couldn't be reached no matter what for the next couple of hours.

"Wonderful," I said. "Listen, Rose, things are liable to start falling on your head any minute now." I explained how and why.

She just took it in stride. I would have been surprised at anything less. Whatever needed doing, she'd take care of it as if Bea were standing behind her giving orders. We're unbelievably lucky to have her, and we know it.

When I was done, she said, "I have two important phone messages for you. One is from Professor Blank at UCAC and the other is from a Mr. Antanas—is that right?—Sudakis at the Devonshire dump."

"Yes, Antanas is right. Thank you, Rose. We'll be back at the office soon, and I'll attend to the calls then. 'Bye," I said, and hung up. I'd been meaning to call Blank, and I wasn't all that surprised to hear from him first. But I wondered why he said it was urgent for me to call him back—nothing about his investigation of the Chumash Powers had been urgent up till now. And I wondered what had bitten Tony on the backside.

Just my luck to be out of the office when two important calls came in.

Michael said, "Before we leave this site, I suggest that you examine it most carefully. I would be willing to wager the CBI has tried already, but if you find anything here which you can identify as belonging to Mistress Adler, the law of contagion may enable us—or the constabulary, or the CBI— to trace her present whereabouts. No guarantees, of course, sorcerous countermeasures having become so effective these days, but a chance nonetheless."

So I looked. God, did I look! Leaving something behind was just the sort of thing Judy would have done if she got the chance—anything to give us a better shot at finding her. I went down on my hands and knees and pawed through weeds and pebbles like a wino after a lost quarter-crown, hoping, praying, she'd managed to drop a button or something.

No luck. All I got was the knees of my pants dirty. Finally I admitted it, even to myself. "Sorry, Michael, but there's nothing here. In the adventure stories, people always manage to leave a clue while the bad guys aren't watching. I guess it doesn't work that way in real life."

"It would appear not to," he agreed. "This is my first encounter with a situation which might reasonably fall into that category, so my experience is as limited as yours. I suspect, however, that if real criminals made as many errors as those in adventure stories, virtue would triumph in the real world more often than it does."

"I suspect you're right," I said glumly, brushing at my trousers. Some of the dirt looked to be there to stay. I sighed, feeling useless and also, irrationally, as if I'd let Judy down. "Let's head back to the office, then—we're wasting time here. From what Rose said, I've had a couple of calls that need answering right away."

"I also have other work upon which I could be usefully engaged," Michael said. That made me feel bad all over again; I hadn't even asked him what I was disrupting by dragging him up to the Valley again and again. But he went on, "Seeking information which will aid in the rescue of your fiancée necessarily takes priority over other concerns."

"Thank you, Michael," I said as we walked back to his carpet. His glance over at me was puzzled, as if he wondered what I was thanking him for. Maybe he did. He thinks so well that I sometimes wonder about the rest of his spirit.

I noticed that he flew down Soto's to the freeway instead of going back to Winnetka. With Michael, I think it was gust for the sake of greater efficiency. I'd have done the same thing, but not on account of that: I just wouldn't have wanted to swing back any closer to Chocolate Weasel than I had to.

When we got back to the Confederal Building, I bought something allegedly edible from the cafeteria; while I fought it down, I kept thinking about lamb with yogurt and mint leaves—sinful as bacon for me, but it sounded delicious all the same—and candied dates. Then, with my fireplace full of fuel—and with a heartburn to prove it—I went to my office and picked up the phone.

Professor Blank sounded blurrier than phone imps could normally account for when he answered the phone, so I figured I'd caught him at lunch twice running, and probably a brown bag one. UCAC boasts better eateries than we have here, which meant he was either tight with a crown or else dedicated to what he was doing.

I'd been willing to give him the benefit of the doubt even before he said, "I'm so glad you returned my call, Inspector Fisher. I've been waiting here at my desk, hoping you would."

"I just now got in," I answered, starting to feel guilty because I'd eaten lunch before I called him back. "Rose, our secretary, said it was urgent, so you're the first call I've made." That, at least, was true. "What's up?"

"I trust you will recall," he began, which meant he didn't trust any such thing, "that when we last spoke I was uncertain whether the Chumash Powers were extinct or had, so to speak, encysted themselves on the Other Side, abandoning all contact with This Side for an indefinite period, perhaps in the hope of being lured back Here should more worshipers appear to propitiate them."

He hadn't said all that when we talked before; some of it he must have worked out since then. But he had said enough of it to let me answer, "Yes, I remember that. Do you know which is true now?"

"The latter, I'm afraid," he said, "and I mean that in the most literal sense of the word."

I'd figured it was the latter; having learned that the Chumash Powers were in fact extinct wouldn't have been news urgent enough for him to haunt his office waiting for me to call back. But I hadn't though even finding them active would be frightening. "What's to be afraid of?" I asked.

"The Powers are indeed encysted; new regression analysis establishes that beyond any statistical or theological doubt," he said. "But it's a topologically unusual spherical encystment. Are you aware, Inspector, that the surface of a sphere can be continuously deformed until it is inside out?"

"Well, no," I said. "What does that have to do with the Chumash Powers?"

"It's a good approximation of what those Powers seem to have done on the Other Side," he answered. "As I said in our earlier conversation, they seem to have taken a hole and pulled it in afterward, apparently leaving nothing behind." Something he said there made a bell toll in my mind, but before I could figure out what it was, he went on, "The problem, from our point of view, is that the Powers, if my calculations are correct, can reverse their encystment and burst out violently at any time they choose."

"Violently?" I echoed. "How violently?"

"Crystal-ball prognostications vary; the scenario is unique and so many of my parameters are uncertain," he said. "If, however, they release maximum magical energy, the effects on the surrounding area will be somewhere between those of a megasalamander ignition just above it and an earthquake, oh, approximately on the order of magnitude of the one that hit the city of St. Francis in the early years of this century. The effects will be different, you understand, because they'll be primarily thaumaturgic rather than physical, but the size of the event will be more or less in that range."

"Jesus," I said, which shows how acculturated I am. Foolishly, I added, "No wonder they didn't want to bother making rain."

"No wonder at all, Inspector," Professor Blank said. "Neither I nor my staff have been able to determine where the interface between the Chumash powers' encystment and This Side is presently located. We would have expected it to be in the extreme northwest of the Barony of Angels, for that was formerly Chumash territory, but, as I say, we have not succeeded in detecting it. I hope that, with your greater resources, the Environmental Perfection Agency will do what we have not accomplished. Good day."

He hung up on me. I wanted to kill him. "Hello. Here comes a catastrophe. I've found out it's on the way, but I can't deal with it. All up to you, Dave. Good luck, pal." That's what was left at the bottom of the alembic. In my nose, it smelled like old catbox.

Instead of committing murder, I called Tony Sudakis. He didn't sound as if I'd caught him at lunch, but he had something in common with Professor Blank anyhow: he sounded scared. "Dave? It's you? Perkunas and the Nine Suns, I'm glad to hear from you! You know that thing—I mean, that Nothing—you spotted in the containment area? It's going through some changes, and I don't like 'em even a little bit."

"Changes? What kind of changes?" I asked, thinking I didn't need one more thing to worry about on top of everything Professor Blank had just dumped on me.

"Well, for one thing, you can notice the effect from anywhere along the safety walk now, and I can see it from the roof of my office, too. Eerie, if you ask me. But there's worse. I can *feel* something starting to build over there, even through the wardspells, like the world's gonna turn inside out any minute now. It's bad. I don't even know if the outer containment wall will hold this one. And if it doesn't—"

He let it hang there. I gulped. I didn't like the way it sounded, not even slightly. "What have you done so far?" I asked.

"I've called for a SWAT team, but a lot of those are busy somewhere else," he answered. I had a hunch I knew where, too: they were taking down Chocolate Weasel. Tony went on, "I called you for two reasons. You were the guy who spotted the Nothing in the first place, and the wizard you had with you seems pretty sharp. Man, I tell you, I think I need all the help I can get on this one."

"I'll get Michael. We'll be there as fast as we can fly," I promised. Then something Sudakis had said really hit me. I echoed it: "Inside out."

"What's that?" Tony said. "Listen, if you and your buddy Manstein don't get here in a hurry, there may not be any here to get to, you know what I mean?"

"Inside out," I repeated. "Tony, didn't you say the stuff in that zone came from the beach up in Malibu?"

"Yeah," he said. "So?"

"Way up at the northwest edge of the Barony of Angels, right?"

"Yeah," he said again. "What are you flying at, Dave?"

"Get a hazmat team there *right now*," I said, fear knotting my belly: I thought I knew why Professor Blank's grad students hadn't found the Chumash Powers' encystment site where they thought it was supposed to be.

"I've been trying to," Tony protested. "They won't listen to me."

"Tell 'em the guy who tipped 'em to Chocolate Weasel says this is liable to be a thousand times worse. Tell 'em that. Use my name. They'll come, all right."

"You know what's going on." Even through the phone imps, he sounded accusing.

"I'm afraid I do. I'm coming anyway." I hung up on him for a change. Then I ran down the hall, yelling for Michael like a man possessed. He listened to me for fifteen seconds, tops, grabbed his black bag, and sprinted for the slide, me right behind him. We piled onto his carpet and hightailed it back to St. Ferdinand's Valley. Knowing what we were heading for, I wished we were flying the other way.

X

"Balance of Powers," I said as Michael guided the carpet up onto St. James' Freeway for the return trip to the Valley.

He waited until he was sure a bigrug hauling crates of tomatoes wouldn't catch up with us, then turned his head my way. "I beg your pardon?" he said. "The term is not one with which I am familiar."

I wondered if Henry Legion had broken Central Intelligence Security to pass it on to me. The spook hadn't said not to use it, though, so I explained it to Michael.

He listened thoughtfully till I was done. People who listen to you are so rare that when you find one, you'd better cherish the novelty. After he saw I'd finished, he thought some more. Some people, their tongues wag miles out in front of their brains. Michael, you will have gathered, isn't like that.

When he was good and ready, he delivered his verdict. I mean it just like that—he really sounded magisterial: "There is, I believe, much truth in the view you express. The great European theological and economic expansion of the past five hundred years, coupled with the enormous growth of thaumaturgic knowledge that spearheaded, among other things, the Industrial Revolution, has indeed had a profound impact on both the politics and thecology of the rest of the world. I can hardly be surprised to learn that long-established Powers, chafing under the pressure of European-imposed belief structures imposed by superior military and magical force, are actively seeking to overwhelm that force."

"You mean you approve?" I stared at him.

"That is not what I said," he answered, more sharply than usual. "I said I am not surprised that the Powers and, presumably, the peoples who reverence them, seek to regain their former prominence. I did not say I wished them success in that effort. Such success would be the greatest disaster the world has ever known, or so I believe, at any rate."

"You get no argument from me," I said.

"I had not expected you to disagree," he said. "You have a reasonable amount of sense, by all appearances."

I wanted to reach over and pat him on the knee. "Why, Michael, I didn't know you cared," I said. From his point of view, he'd just given me the accolade, and I knew it.

"Facetiousness aside," he amended. I just grinned. He ignored that and went on, "Let us take the Americas, for instance, they being the most clearcut examples of a massive human and thecological transformation in the past semimillenium."

"Okay, take the Americas," I said agreeably, gesturing to show he was welcome to them. Truth was, as long as I was schmoozing with Michael, I didn't have to think (as much) about either Judy or the likelihood that Armageddon was liable to come bubbling out of a toxic spells dump.

Michael gave me a severe look. "Facetiousness aside, I said."

"Sorry," I told him. "You were saying?"

"Nothing of great complexity; nothing, in fact, that should not be obvious to any reasonably objective observer: that we immigrants have done more and better with this land in the past five hundred years than its native peoples would have accomplished during the same period."

"Nothing that isn't obvious, eh?" I said, grinning wickedly. "Plenty of people, natives and immigrants both—I'll use your phrase; why not?—would say you've just committed blasphemy, that we've done nothing but slaughter and pollute in what was, for all practical purposes, paradise on earth."

"I find only one technical term appropriate to use in response to that viewpoint: bullshit." Michael delivered his technical term with great relish. "I am not saying that slaughter did not take place; I am not denying that we pollute—working as I do for the Environmental Perfection Agency, how could I? I do deny, however, that this was, in a manner of speaking, government work for the earthly paradise."

"Careful how you talk, there," I said. "You work for the government yourself, remember?"

Michael refused to be distracted. "Leaving aside the habits of the natives of the islands off the coast, whose tribal name gave English the word 'cannibal,' the two most prominent cultures in the Americas five hundred years ago were the Aztecs, also cannibals, who fueled themselves both theologically and in terms of protein through human sacrifice, and the Incas, whose theology was benign enough but who regimented themselves more thoroughly than the Ukrainians would have tolerated before their latest crisis."

"You're hitting below the belt, talking about peoples who didn't live in what's now the Confederation," I protested. "What about the noble warriors and hunters of the Great Plains?"

"Well, what about them?" he asked. "The culture they now revere and think of as ancient did not exist and could not have existed before the coming of the Europeans because their own ancestors had hunted the American horse to extinction—hardly good environmental management, in my opinion. And the firearms they used to defend their territory—bravely—against encroaching whites were all bought or stolen from those same whites, because they did not know how to make them for themselves."

"Whoa, there." I held up a hand. "Blaming people for not having skills isn't fair. And the whites who took the land away from the natives weren't what you'd call saints. Conquest by firewater, deliberately spread smallpox, and mass exorcisms of the native Powers isn't anything to be proud of."

"You're right," he said. "But if Europeans had not found the Americas until, for example, the day before yesterday, they would not have found them much different from the way they were five hundred years ago. And that is precisely the point I am trying to make. Thanks to modern thaumaturgy, our present culture supports far more people at a higher level of affluence and greater material comfort than any other in the history of the world."

"Is that all you judge culture by?" I asked. "Seems to me there should be more to life."

"Oh, no doubt. But make note of this, David: as a general rule—not universal, I concede, but general—the people who show the greatest contempt for material comforts are those lucky enough to have them. The Abyssinian peasant starving in his drought-stricken field, the Canaanite cobbler suffering under a plague of gnats because no local sorcerer knows enough to properly control Beelzebub, the slum-dweller in D.St.C. aching with a rotten tooth because her parents hadn't had the crowns to go to an odontomagus to affix the usual invisible shields to her mouth . . . they will not speak slightingly of the virtues of a full belly and a healthy body, things we take for granted despite their being historically rare."

"Wait a minute, Michael. You just cheated there. You were talking about how wonderful our culture is, and then one of your suffering examples comes straight out of our own slums. You can't have it both ways."

He didn't answer for a few seconds; he was getting the carpet off the freeway. Once he'd done that, though, he said,

"I fail to see why not. I never claimed we were perfect. Perfection is an attribute of the divine, not the human. I said that, on the whole, we do better for more people than anyone else has. Our flaws notwithstanding, I hold to that position."

I thought about it. The only times I'd ever been hungry were at Yom Kippur fasts, and those I undertook for the sake of ritual, not because I had no food. I slept in a flat on a bed; I was protected against diseases and curses that had lain whole nations waste in ancient times. I said, "You have a point."

The other thing was, the Chumash Powers and the Aztecians wanted to restore the unpleasant old days. The trouble with that was that most of the millions of people in the Barony of Angels liked the new days better. What would happen to them? My limited acquaintance with the Chumash Powers didn't make me think they were that ferocious, but Huitzilopochtli—

The Chumash Powers must have cut a deal with the Aztecian war god, I realized. I tried to imagine the secret dealings that must have happened on the Other Side. Huitzilopochtli was a much bigger fish than the Sky Coyote, the Lizard, or the demons of the Lower World, but they were extra powerful here because the Barony of Angels was their native territory. The combination could prove deadly.

I reached that unpleasant conclusion about the time Michael pulled into the parking lot across the flyway from the Devonshire dump. To my relief, three or four black-and-whites were already there, their synchronized salamander lanterns flashing red and blue.

People were standing on the sidewalk rubbernecking the way they always do when something goes wrong. Over on the dump side of the street, a couple of constables were laying down the ritual yellow tape that keeps rubberneckers from getting too close to the action.

Michael and I hurried across. The constables saw our EPA sigils and demystified a stretch of tape so we could cross the line. "Did you get a hazmat team here?" I asked one of them.

"Yeah, we did," he said. I thought they had; there were more black-and-whites in the parking lot than constables outside the dump. But while his partner put the magic back into the line, the fellow went on, "The guy who runs the dump tried to get an EPA hazmat team, too, but it was already on an urgent call, worse luck."

Luck had nothing to do with it; I'd told Kawaguchi he was liable to need that team at Chocolate Weasel. And he was, God knows. But Tony Sudakis was liable to need it here, too. No magic yet has made people able to be two places at the same time. They're working on it, I understand, with thau-matechnology based on what they've learned with ectoplasmic cloning, but so far it happens only in light-and-magic shows and sorcerous fiction stories. Too bad. Boy, could we have used it.

The security guard recognized Michael and me. Without being asked, he brought out the footbridge so we could cross into the containment area. As soon as we did, he yanked it away as fast as he could. In principle, that was smart; you didn't want to weaken the magical containment scheme in any way. In practice, I was afraid it would do about as much good as sunglasses under the megasalamander blast Profes-sor Blank had mentioned.

About three steps down the warded path that led to Tony Sudakis' office, I stopped dead in my tracks. Tony hadn't been kidding—you could see the Nothing from anywhere on the walkway now. You felt that if you leaned forward, you might fall straight toward it forever. And he'd been right about the feeling that pervaded the dump, too; it was as if the Nothing were an egg quivering on the verge of hatching.

But that wasn't the only thing that made me stop and stare. The constables from the hazardous *materia magica* team weren't working only from the warded path—they'd actually gone into the dump itself to come to grips with the Nothing.

Sure, they knew what they were doing. Sure, they were draped with so many different kinds of apotropaic amulets that they looked like perambulating Christmas trees. Sure, their shoes had cold-iron soles to insulate them from the thaumaturgic vileness that littered the place. All the same, they put their souls on the line, not just their soles. I wouldn't have gone out there for a million crowns.

For Judy? Yes, without a second thought. If you don't know what really matters to you, why bother living?

Tony Sudakis was up on the roof of his office. He saw Michael and me, waved, and disappeared. A minute later, he came pounding down the path toward us. He had a hard hat on his head, his cravat was loosened and his collar open. He was a foreman again, not an administrator, and looked as if he loved it.

"Glad you got here," he said. "Dave, on the phone you sounded like you know more about this shit than maybe anybody. You want to brief Yolanda there?" He pointed up ahead to one of the hazmat team people.

Up till then, I hadn't noticed the boss of the team was a woman. She was black, slim, maybe my age—not half bad, though she looked both too smart and too tough to be model pretty.

I told her what I knew about the Chumash Powers, and what I'd heard from Professor Blank not an hour earlier. When I was through, she crossed herself. "What are we supposed to do, then?" she said. "This is worse than we're really set up to face. Maybe a military team would be a better bet to resist."

"I doubt that," Michael put in. "Military teams are configured against specific security threats—Persian, Aztecian, Ukrainian. But the Chumash, till this moment, have never posed a danger to the Confederation. Warrior priests and the like will not be able to help us."

Yolanda scowled; you could tell she was the kind of person who wanted to get right in there and do things, then worry about consequences later. "What do the two of you recommend, then?" she demanded.

Do as well as you can, was the answer that immediately sprang to mind. If the Chumash Powers remanifested themselves with the burst of thaumaturgic energy Professor Blank had feared, there was nothing else to do, and even that wouldn't help. But you always have to play the game as if you think you're going to win—which, when you get down to it, is also part of dying well.

So I said, "Delay. Every second we keep that Nothing encysted buys us time to evacuate the neighborhood. It may not help, but then again, it may. Tony, I presume you have procedures in place for an emergency evacuation?"

"Sure," he said.

"You'd better implement them, then. EPA orders, if you like."

"You got it, boss." He went back to his office on the dead run. If his procedures were like most people's, he'd have a bunch of spells completed but for the last word or pass or whatever, so he could but them into effect one after another, bang, bang, bang.

Sure enough, maybe thirty seconds later we heard a dreadful cacophony from the cacodemons mounted at each corner of the containment fence. It reminded me, fittingly enough, of the air raid warnings that would help mark the start of the Third Sorcerous War.

After they'd screeched for a while, the cacodemons started yelling, "Evacuate the area. Evacuate the area. Contamination may escape from the Devonshire containment site. Evacuate the area." Then they shouted what I think was the same thing, only in Spainish.

They were loud enough to be heard for miles. That was why they were there, but they made talk inside the containment area just about impossible for anybody who wasn't an accomplished lip-reader. I was sure my ears would ring for the next couple of days—assuming I was still around in a couple of days.

Michael stuck his head next to mine, bawled in my ear, "Delay is all very well, but in the end futile. Sooner or later—probably sooner—the Chumash Powers will succeed in breaking free of their encystment and returning to This Side, with the accompanying energy release you have described."

He turned his head so I could yell into his ear. It was my turn, after all. Yell I did: "I know, but we'll get some people away, so when the Great Eagle and the Lizard and rest get out, they won't do the damage they want to."

I turned my head. Michael shouted, "Possibly not. The damage they do inflict, however, will be more than adequate to satisfy anyone not—" I'm sure he kept talking after that, but I stopped hearing him. I was running for Tony Sudakis' office as fast as my legs would carry me.

He was coming out as I dashed in. He might as well have been Phyllis Kaminsky—I almost bowled him over. "Phone," I said, panting. Inside the blockhouse, the noise from the ca-codemons was just too loud, not deafening.

"Sure, go ahead." He followed me back up the hall. I made my call, talked for maybe a minute and a half, hung up. When I was done, Tony stared at me, big-eyed. "You think that'll work?" he asked, unwontedly quiet.

"Let me put it this way," I answered. "If it doesn't, do you think these concrete blocks are going to save us?" He shook his head. I went on, "I don't, either. The hazmat mages out there will delay all they can, but how long is that. Sooner or later, probably sooner"—I realized I was echoing Michael—"the Chumash Powers *will* break out. And when they do—"

"Bend over and kiss your bum goodbye. Yeah," Sudakis said. "How much time do you think they need to buy?"

"I just don't know," I answered. "Burbank isn't far, but I don't know how much prep they have to do first. All we can do now is wait and hope."

We walked back out into the unbelievable din together. I bawled into Michael's ear; Tony yelled into Yolanda's (no question he got the better half of that deal). Michael shouted back at me, "Not the best chance, but I see none better." Then he walked over to scream, presumably, the same thing at Tony.

"I wish I had your connections," Yolanda shouted at me.

"I wish I *didn't* have them," I answered, "because that would mean this miserable case never happened."

She nodded grimly. We all stared toward the east, like the Kings of Orient with somebody extra thrown in for luck. Trouble was, all the luck in this case had been bad.

I thought about poor little Jesus Cordero. Seeing if the

Slow Jinn Fizz jinnetic engineering techniques could make him a soul hadn't seemed urgent. He was just a baby, after all; years and years would go by before he had to worry about forever vanishing from the scheme of things. That's what I'd thought. But if the Chumash Powers burst forth, he'd be gone for good. Not even Limbo. Just gone.

Out in the dump, one of the hazmat mages crumpled like soggy parchment. I couldn't tell whether the toxic spell residues had overcome him or whether he'd just broken under the burden of delaying the burst. Yolanda leaped off the warded path and dragged him back toward its very tenuous safety.

One he was back on the path, he pulled himself into fetal position and lay there shivering: sorcerous shock of some kind, sure enough. He was breathing, and he nodded his head when Yolanda shouted at him, so he wasn't critical. Since he wasn't, the rest of us kept looking eastward. Either we'd be saved, in which case we could treat the hazmat mage later, or we wouldn't, in which case nothing we did for him now would matter anyway.

I preferred the first choice, but wouldn't have bet anything big on getting it.

Suddenly, Tony Sudakis' finger stabbed out. "Isn't that—?" He didn't go on, maybe for fear his words would induce it not to be.

"I don't think it is," I yelled—hard to sound bitter when you're yelling, but I managed. "More likely to be a big cargo carpet on the landing approach toward Burbank airport."

We all watched for another couple of seconds. Tony shook his head. "A carpet heading into Burbank would be getting smaller. This is getting bigger."

"So it is," Michael said. He forgot to yell, but I read his lips. When Michael forgets to do something he should, you know he's under strain. We all were. I didn't want to think he was right, just because that would have made getting my hopes dashed all the crueler.

But after another few seconds, there could be no doubt. The speck in the air we were watching swelled out of speck-dom far faster than any carpet could have, and it didn't have a carpet's shape, either. I saw great wings beat majestically. "The Garuda Bird!" I shouted—with all my heart and with all my soul and with all my might, as the Bible says.

The Bird came on unbelievably fast. Two or three more flaps and it was hovering over the dump. Of course, it didn't need to work its wings the way a merely material creature of flesh and feathers would have. The Other Side suffused it; it was, after all, an avatar of Vishnu. As Matt Arnold had said back at the Loki works, it couldn't have flown—or existed at all—as a material creature; when it hovered above the dump, its wings spanned the entire width of the containment area and more, and cast the ground into shadow almost as deep as night.

It looked much like the poster in Arnold's office—those incredible wings supporting a huge-chested body that didn't look birdlike at all to my mind. Nor was its head anything like that of a natural bird, but for the hooked beak that took the place of nose and mouth. The rest, especially the eyes, looked more nearly human, and the feathers on top of its head, instead of being peacock-brilliant like those of the body and wings, were black and soft like hair.

The wings beat again, right over our heads. The blast of wind from a flap like that should have blown walls down, and blown dust motes like us into the next barony, but it didn't. After a moment, I realized why: since it flew more by magic than with its wings, their flapping was just a symbolic act, not quite a real one. And thank God for that; it wasn't something I'd worried about when I called Matt Arnold.

The Garuda Bird threw back its anthropomorphic head and let out a bellow that sounded like a tuba about the size of a city block played by a mad giant who'd quit halfway through his first tuba lesson. Let me put it like this: by comparison, the squalling cacodemons were quiet and melodious.

One thing, or rather two sets of things, thoroughly ornithomorphic (ah, Greek!) about the Garuda Bird were its talons. In fact, it was the most talonted bird I'd ever seen: those enormous gleaming claws could have punctured the Midgard Serpent, by the look of them. I would have paid a good many crowns to watch that fight—from a safe distance, say the surface of the moon.

Now, as the Bird hovered over the Devonshire dump, its left foot closed on the Nothing. The hazmat mages pelted back out of the way. I found I was holding my breath. This was something else I hadn't had figured when I called Arnold: was the Garuda Bird's magic strong enough to penetrate the encystment the Chumash Powers had thrown up around themselves? If not—well, if not, I told myself, we weren't any worse off than we would have been without the Bird.

When the Garuda Bird's talons struck the Nothing, sparks flew, but the talons didn't go in. I was praying and cursing at the same time, both as hard as I could. The Garuda Bird bellowed again, this time in fury. I staggered, wondering if the top of my head would fall off and whether I'd ever hear again.

The muscles in the Garuda Bird's monster drumsticks bunched. That's what I saw, anyhow, though I knew it was only a quasi-physical manifestation like the Bird's flapping wings. What it meant was that, on the Other Side, the Garuda Bird was gathering all its thaumaturgic force.

Its claws closed on the Nothing once more. More sparks flew. The Bird cried out yet again, but its talons still would not penetrate. I thought we were doomed. But then, ever so slowly, the needle tips of those immense claws began sinking into the Chumash Powers' shell of withdrawal.

Tony's mouth was wide open. So were Michael's and Yolanda's and mine. We were all shouting for all we were worth, but I couldn't hear any of us, not even me.

The Garuda Bird's feet disappeared into Nothing. You couldn't see them. They were just—gone. I stopped shouting. My heart went into my mouth. The Garuda Bird wasn't a power that had had to hide itself away to keep from going extinct; the belief of hundreds of millions of people fueled it. Never in my most dreadful nightmares had I imagined that it wouldn't be able to overcome the Chumash Powers that hid inside the Nothing if once it broke their shell.

The Bird's next roar carried a note of pain. It flapped its

wings again: almost a real flap this time, for dust rose in a choking cloud from the dry dirt of the dump. Through the dust, I saw more of the Garuda Bird's leg than I had before. "It's coming out!" I cried, coughing.

Another flap, more dust, still another wingbeat. Then, with a *pop!* in my head that felt like the psychic equivalent of the one you'd make by sticking your finger into your mouth against the inside of your cheek, its feet came all the way out of the Nothing. In its claws writhed the Lizard.

Yolanda grabbed me and kissed me on the cheek. A good thing she did, too, because Tony Sudakis slapped my back so hard, I might have staggered off the warded path and into the dump if she hadn't been holding on to me.

No matter how joyful he was, Michael Manstein didn't do things like slapping people on the back. He shouted, "Brilliantly reasoned, David! The similarity between lizards and snakes *was* enough to touch off the Garuda Bird's instinctive antipathy."

"Yeah," I said, which I admit wasn't a fitting response to praise like that. But I was too busy watching the fight above my head to get out more than the one word.

The Chumash Lizard was an alligator lizard the size of the biggest anaconda you ever saw. If you live in Angels City, you know about alligator lizards. They're the most common kind of lizard around here. The material ones can get more than a foot long, with yellowish bellies and dirt-brown backs striped with black. For critters their size, they have large, sharp teeth. The ones on the Chumash Lizard looked to be a couple of inches long, and it had a whole mouthful of them.

Alligator lizards also have little short legs, which makes them look even more ophidian than most lizards (they're related to glass snakes, which aren't snakes but lizards with no legs at all). My guess—my hope—was that that would just make the Garuda Bird madder.

The Lizard made horrible hissing noises and bit at the Garuda Bird's legs. However huge and fierce it was, though, it had no more chance against the Bird than an ordinary alligator lizard would have against an eagle that decided to have a reptilian lunch.

Crunch! With a noise like a monster cleaver biting into a side of beef, the Garuda Bird bit off the Lizard's head and about the front third of its body. Ichor spattered down all over the dump. Luckily, it didn't splash any of us—talk about your hazardous *materia magica*.

The Chumash Lizard's body convulsed and thrashed even more wildly than before. Even material lizards are hard to kill. Lizards that are also Powers . . . But all the thrashing didn't stop the Garuda Bird from gulping down the rest of the Lizard.

Michael tapped me on the shoulder. "I believe you may now definitively declare one Chumash Power extinct," he yelled.

"You know what?" I yelled back. "I don't miss it a bit. Dreadful thing for an EPA man to say, isn't it?"

"I find myself less scandalized than I might be under other circumstances," Michael said.

With another earsplitting bellow, the Garuda Bird tried to poke its clawed feet into the Nothing. Again, it was hard work. But the Bird didn't have to back up and make a second effort: slowly but surely, talons, toes, and feet sank into the Chumash Powers' sphere of encystment and disappeared.

The Bird let out a pain-filled screech like the one it had made when (I guess) it seized the Lizard. It started flapping its wings again in that half-material way it had used to force itself out of the Nothing. Feet, toes, talons reemerged—and then, with another of those psychic *pop!*s, the Garuda Bird was free once more.

It didn't come out of the Nothing empty-footed, either. Its claws held what the Chumash called the Great Eagle. I will admit, a golden eagle with a body the size of a Siberian tiger's is pretty Great—under other circumstances, as Michael had put it. Up against the Garuda Bird, the Chumash Eagle might as well have been a sparrow.

The Eagle, unlike the Lizard, didn't try to fight. It wriggled, twisted, broke free, and streaked for the sky. I feared it would get away: it seemed so much more graceful in the air than the ponderous Garuda Bird. But the contest wasn't only, or even mostly, bird body against bird body. It was magic against magic, too, and the Garuda Bird had not only its native Indian potency but also all the souping up the Loki Kobold Works had given its sorcerous systems. It didn't just fly—it was destined for space. It shot after the Eagle faster than the eye could follow.

High in the sky, the Eagle tried to dodge—if it couldn't flee the Garuda Bird, maybe it could outjink it. But no. One of those immense feet closed on it, and this time there was no escape. I heard a despairing shriek fade and die. Hovering above the dump, the Garuda Bird devoured its prey. A couple of big feathers came spiraling down into the containment area—all that was left of the Chumash Eagle.

"We'll have to decontaminate those," Yolanda said.

"As soon as you do, there's another Chumash Power that won't show up in the Barony of Angels again," I said. As an EPA inspector, I felt bad about that. As somebody who was wondering whether he'd still be alive five minutes from now, I figured I'd worry about the long-term consequences of the Great Eagle's demise later, if there was a later.

High overhead, the Garuda Bird let out a roar that made all its earlier cries seem like whispers. It folded its wings and stooped like a hawk onto the Nothing. I braced myself—uselessly, I knew. When that bulk hit, the earth wouldn't just shake, it would quake, San Andreas notwithstanding.

A split second before the Bird's talons seized the Nothing, another psychic *pop!* sounded in my head, this one bigger than the other two put together. The talons closed on empty air—the Nothing was gone. Somehow—sorcerously, of course, but don't ask me about the Kobold Works' proximity spells, because I don't know from nothin'—the Bird stopped in midair without touching the ground.

I looked out at the far wall of the Devonshire dump, and it seemed only as far away as it should have. The sense of the imminent immanence of something eminently dreadful's becoming dreadfully evident was gone, too. I looked over at Tony Sudakis. "I think you can tell the cacodemons to shut up," I yelled at him.

He flipped me a salute—casual but, I thought, not faked—and trotted back toward his office. As he did so, the

Garuda Bird rose into the air (without a single flap) and headed east, back toward Burbank. That took more weight off my mind: my guess was that the Bird would have stayed around had it sensed any remaining trouble.

Just the same, I walked over to the spot on the path from which I'd first noticed the Nothing, a million years ago: that's what it felt like, anyhow. I wasn't quite there yet when the cacodemons closed their mouths. Sudden silence hit me as hard as the squalls of alarm had before.

I knew just where that spot was now. I looked out across the weed-strewn dirt toward the Nothing and saw—nothing. I was never so glad not to capitalize an "n" in my whole life.

"I think they're gone," I said, words which ranked right up there with the first time I told Judy, *I love you*.

"I believe you are correct," Michael said. "What we sensed, in my opinion, was the Chumash Powers abandoning any contact with This Side to keep the Garuda Bird from reaching into their encystment, dragging them out one by one, and destroying them. Thaumaturgic analysis will eventually confirm or refute this, but it is a tenable working hypothesis."

"I'm with you," Yolanda said. "If they went away like that, they won't be back." She wiped her forehead with a sleeve. I'm not sure she really grasped just how bad a hazmat she'd helped hold at bay, but none of what her team did for a living was easy.

"Perkunas and the Nine Suns, I hope not." Tony Sudakis clutched his amber amulet in one beefy fist.

"Let me use your phone one more time?" I asked him. "I'll call Professor Blank at UCAC; he's been running a study for me to find out whether the Chumash Powers really have become extinct. I think we can safely say two of them have, but he'd be the best fellow to evaluate what's become of the others."

"Be my guest." Sudakis waved me toward the blockhouse. It wouldn't have done a bit of good against what had almost come forth from the dump, but suddenly it looked strong and secure again.

I got hold of Blank. He was still in his office, wondering, I suppose, whether the building was going to collapse around him. When I told him what had happened at the dump, he let out a sigh of relief so heartfelt even phone imps couldn't spoil it, then promised to send his research team out as fast as carpets could get from UCAC to Chatsworth. Since it was heading into late afternoon, that wouldn't be any too fast, but the urgency level had gone down, too.

Then I called Legate Kawaguchi to see how the constables were doing at Chocolate Weasel. Him I didn't get; instead, some other constable bawled in my ear, "You can't talk to him, bud, whoever you are. He's down at the war, and I'm headin' that way myself." He hung up with a crash that that phone imps did an uncanny job of reproducing.

That sent me out of Tony's office on the run. I filled him in on what Blank had said, then passed on the rest of the word to Michael. "The only thing that can mean is Chocolate Weasel, I think," I said. "We'd better get over there as fast as we can."

"I concur," Michael said.

Yolanda—her last name, I finally had the chance to notice on her badge, was Simmons—said, "Where's this Chocolate Weasel place? Sounds like we might do some good there, too."

"Your team is welcome to follow my carpet," Michael said. "Will the health of the gentleman who collapsed suffice for the venture?"

"I'm okay," the gentleman said, and sat up to try to prove it. He still didn't look okay, but he was game, anyhow. "All the stuff in here just overloaded my protective systems for a minute there."

"It's liable to be worse at Chocolate Weasel," I said, but he shook his head—he didn't think it was possible. I envied him his innocence.

The security guard put down the footbridge for us, and we trooped out. Then the fellow took off his uniform cap and bowed, which made me feel great. The guard might not have know who'd done what, but summoning the Garuda Bird wasn't something you could ignore.

Thanks to the cacodemons' announcing an emergency

evacuation, traffic around the dump was unbelievably snarled. We passed Chocolate Weasel's address on to the hazmat team and followed them instead of the other way round: they had constabulary lanterns on their carpets, which helped move people out of their way.

About halfway to Chocolate Weasel, we met head-on a rush away from that area. I gulped, remembering what the constable who'd answered Kawaguchi's phone had said about a war. Maybe he hadn't been exaggerating.

A constable in full combat gear, material and thaumaturgic, was turning back traffic heading in Chocolate Weasel's direction. The hazmat team's lanterns got them through; Yolanda's shouted encouragement and our EPA sigils did the job for us.

"You know, Michael," I said, "just once today, I'd like to fly *away from* the scene of a disaster."

"I have considerable sympathy for this point of view," he answered. "However—"

"Yeah," I said. When duty calls, you'd better do it. Doing it and liking it, though, were not the same critter.

When Yolanda asked another constable exactly where we were going, he directed her to a command post at the corner of Nordhoff and Soto's. The reason that was the command post, I discovered when we followed her there, was that it was as close to Chocolate Weasel as you could get without being in immediate danger of getting yourself messily killed.

Sure enough, Legate Kawaguchi was there, in uniform and helmet—not Constabulary Department standard issue, but samurai-style, with the *mon* of his clan affixed to the forehead to help protect him against malignant magic.

He didn't act surprised to see me. "Good afternoon, Inspector Fisher. I must admit, you were not in error concerning the nature of that building ahead." He pointed east.

I looked that way myself. A thin column of smoke rose from the Chocolate Weasel facility. "Tell me that's not what I'm afraid it is," I said to Kawaguchi.

"I wish I could," he answered. "They are tearing the hearts from victims and kindling fires in their chests. We face the apparition not only of Huitzilopochtli but also of Huehueteotl, the fire god."

"In proper Aztecian ritual, that practice occurs only at the completion of the Five Empty Days between the end of one year and the start of the next," Michael said, as if objecting not so much to the slaughter as to its taking place outside canonical limits. Sometimes he can be quite exasperating.

Kawaguchi said, "My guess is that they're going outside the usual pattern to try to bring the Powers to full potency outside their native land."

Michael said, grudgingly, "Yes, I suppose such a procedure might be efficacious. It remains most irregular, however." You see what I mean?

"Where are they getting their victims?" I asked; to me, that was more important than whether they were following all their own rules for the sacrificial rites. I thought about the two guys at the Spells 'R' Us place who'd let me borrow the spellchecker. I thought about them spreadeagled on an altar with their chests hacked open. I wanted to be sick.

"Resistance backed by thaumaturgy of a high order began as soon as our first units responded into the parking lot," Kawaguchi answered. "My best guess is that several employees volunteered to become the initial victims to trigger their Powers' presence here."

"Again, this seems likely," Michael agreed.

I nodded, too. Kawaguchi probably had the right of it, despite his curiously bloodless way of describing sacrifices of the bloodiest sort. But constables, who see so much blood in their work, need to ward themselves from the reality of what they do with mild-seeming words. After all, words have power, too.

Then something else occurred to me. "You said those were the *initial* victims. Have there been more?"

"Unfortunately yes, an unknowable but large number," Kawaguchi said. "Because of the strength of the Powers evoked within the Chocolate Weasel building, we have been compelled to draw back our lines several times. The perpetrators have taken advantage of this to raid surrounding businesses and homes. We do not know the precise status of all individuals captured, but some will almost certainly have been employed to nourish Huitzilopochtli and Hue-hueteotl."

I thought about some poor lunk whose stomach decided to growl while he was flying up Nordhoff. He'd spot the Golden Steeples, pull in, grab himself a burger . . . and end up with his still-beating heart torn out of his body, just for being in the wrong place at the wrong time. You'd have to be a very thoroughgoing Calvinist to find the mark of divine plan in that.

Then I had a worse thought. Much worse. I'd been acting on the assumption that the people from Chocolate Weasel had something to do with kidnapping Judy. If she was hidden away somewhere in the building when the constables flew into the lot . . .

"God forbid," I whispered. I tried not to think about it, to tell myself it was impossible, but I knew too well it wasn't.

Just then, the roof of the building that housed Chocolate Weasel started burning a lot brighter. It wasn't an ordinary flame; it wasn't even like the flame from a salamander, which is powered from the Other Side but manifests itself here. This flame you didn't just see; you felt it in the place where prayers come from. I close my eyes, but that didn't help. My soul still felt scorched.

"Huehueteotl," Legate Kawaguchi and Michael said in the same breath. Quietly, Michael added, "One must conclude that the sacrifices within the building have reached a critical mass, allowing him to manifest himself fully in Angels City."

"I wonder how long we have to wait for Huitzilopochtli," I said numbly.

"He being a greater Power, more sacrifice will be necessary to bring him onto This Side," Michael answered. "Huehueteotl's manifestation, however, will only speed his translation from the Aztecian gods' realm on the Other Side to our present location."

"Thanks for the encouragement," I said. Michael gave me a puzzled look, then recognized irony and nodded.

The flames on the roof leapt higher. After some delay,

thick smoke began to rise as real flames joined the spectral ones emanating from Huehueteotl. I wondered how the people inside the Chocolate Weasel building were faring now that it burned around them. Maybe Huehueteotl protected them from the flames so they could go on sacrificing. Or maybe they'd just keep doing what they were doing until they burned to death. Every faith has its martyrs willing, even eager, to die for the greater glory of the Powers they reverence.

I wished the Aztecians would have shown their piety another way.

Kawaguchi was shouting into a constabulary-model eth-ernet set. It held two different imps, so he could both send and receive messages. He looked toward the burning build-ing, then to Michael and me. "Are you gentlemen familiar with the Hanese ideogram for the term 'crisis'?"

"I am," Michael said; I might have guessed he would be. He went on, "It combines the ideograms for 'danger' and 'opportunity.' "

Kawaguchi looked surprised and maybe a little disap-pointed that a pale blond chap had stepped on his lines. But he nodded and said, "Exactly so. And developments here have now reached the crisis stage. If in the next few minutes Huitzilopochtli succeeds in manifesting himself as thor-oughly as Huehueteotl has—"

That was the danger, all right. If it happened, Angels City was in more trouble than it had ever known. The only prob-lem was, I didn't see any sign of the opportunity.

"I have been in touch with the archdiocese of Angels City," Kawaguchi said. "They will do what they can for us."

"An acute strategic move, Legate," Michael said, nodding in approval. "The Power based at Rome successfully over-came those centered on Tenochtitlan almost five hundred years ago; with luck, it will do so again."

"*Alevai,*" I said, a most un-Catholic endorsement of his sentiment. But I didn't stop worrying, or even slow down. The Spanish who'd brought Christianity to Aztecia were fanatics, nothing else but; they had to be, or else they never would have tried it. But over the years, the Church has turned fat and lazy and rich and comfortable. The fanatics were in the Chocolate Weasel building now, doing their best to fuel the revival of the old Aztecian gods.

Balance of Powers, I thought, and shivered.

"What are we waiting for?" I asked Kawaguchi. "Exorcists to come and try to drive Huitzilopochtli back to the Other Side before he can fully establish himself here?"

The constable, you will have gathered, was a worn, dour fellow. Now he surprised me with a wall-to-wall smile. "The response the cardinal offered me was nowhere near so half-hearted."

I wished he hadn't said halfhearted, not when you thought about how Huitzilopochtli and Huehueteotl were being summoned into Angels City. But the cardinal, that stiff-necked Erseman—I'd thought he was on the fanatical side when he refused to grant the burned Thomas Brothers monks a dispensation for cosmetic sorcery. Most of the time, I still thought that kind of fanaticism out of place in our century.

But right this minute, it might end up saving all our asses—and maybe our souls, too.

Kawaguchi kept watching the sky. Had Quetzalcoatl shown any sign of manifesting himself along with the other Aztecian Powers, I would have tried to get hold of Burbank again to see what the Garuda Bird could do against the Feathered Serpent. As things were, though, I didn't see how the Bird could help.

I wondered what Kawaguchi was waiting for. Whatever it was, I hoped it would be good—and powerful. Something nasty—something *else* nasty, I mean—was going to happen inside that building any minute now. I could feel it coming, in the same part of the inner me that felt the growing presence of Huehueteotl like a bad sunburn.

Suddenly, Kawaguchi pointed. I spotted a flying carpet, way above the usual flyways and ignoring their traffic grid as if it didn't exist. Maybe it had a constabulary clearance that overcame all the anti-flying invocations that gave people and business their privacy . . . or maybe it was under the control of a higher Power.

As it got closer, I saw it was a big carpet, a freight hauler, and heavily loaded. It was gold, with a white cross—the colors of the Vatican flag. I knew the Vatican rug would also bear a woven-in legend in white—IN HOC SIGNO VINCES—but it was too high and too far away for me to be able to read that.

It was heading straight over the Chocolate Weasel building. Huehueteotl's magical fire flamed up to meet it. I was afraid the flames would burn down the carpet and everybody on it.

But one thing I give the Catholic Church—it has a saintly hierarchy in charge of looking out for more different things than all the bureaucrats in D.St.C. put together. St. Florian watches specially over those who must contend with fire. I have no idea whether his power would have been enough to overcome Huehueteotl down inside the Chocolate Weasel building, but it sufficed to keep the god from crisping the carpet.

One of the monks riding the carpet (I could see his bare pate shining in the late afternoon sun) tipped a big earthenware urn down onto the roof of the Chocolate Weasel building, then another and another and another, methodical as if he were on a carpet bombing run over Alemania in the Second Sorcerous War.

Those urns and whatever they held were heavy—I could hear them smashing on and maybe through the roof from several blocks away. And whatever was in them was spectacularly efficacious. The constant heat on my soul that radiated from Huehueteotl went away, as if my spirit had suddenly dived into a clear stream. *He maketh me to lie down in green pastures: he leadeth me beside the still waters. He refresheth my soul* ran through my head.

I turned to Kawaguchi and Michael Manstein and asked, "What are they dropping on them?"

They both stared at me as if I were an idiot. Then Michael said, "That's right, you are Jewish," as if reminding himself. Very gently, he went on, "It's holy water, David."

"Oh." All right, I was an idiot. In fact, I was doubly an idiot: not only was the stuff thaumaturgically potent in and of itself, it was also perfect symbolically—what better to oppose fire of any sort than its opposite among the elements?

Once Chocolate Weasel took all the punishment it had urned from the carpet, Kawaguchi blew a long, shrill blast on a whistle. SWAT teams, Yolanda's hazmat crew, and the EPA hazmat outfit swarmed toward the Chocolate Weasel building. Ordinary constables, the guys with mostly passive sorcerous gear and merely physical weapons—the grunts—followed in their wake.

"They were thrown back twice before," Kawaguchi said, more to himself than to me or Michael. "This time—"

This time they moved forward. The SWAT team wizards carried holy water sprinklers like the ones the Loki guards in Burbank packed. Those hadn't been enough to protect them against the growing might of the Aztecian Powers before. Now those Powers had been reduced by bombardment from On High, so to speak. And now the SWAT teams advanced cautiously toward the parking lot in front of Chocolate Weasel, then toward the building itself.

I got distracted at that point: the archdiocesan carpet floated down and landed just a few feet from me. "Good afternoon, Inspector Fisher," one of the monks on it said. "I wondered it I might see you here today. Somehow it seems fitting."

"Brother Vahan!" I exclaimed. "It certainly does." I trotted over to shake his hand. "Were you the bombardier up there?"

"I was indeed," he said with a sober nod. "God moves in a mysterious way, His wonders to perform. Not scriptural, but in this case accurate."

A curate? No, you're an abbot, my mind gibbered. I forced myself back to the here-and-now: "What do you mean?"

"I mean that I was in the cardinal's office, beseeching him on bended knee to reconsider his prohibition against my brethren's use of cosmetic sorcery to restore their appearance, when Legate Kawaguchi's communication reached His Eminence. He thought me an appropriate agent for the task requested, and I was pleased to obey him in this instance."

Brother Vahan was stubborn to the point of being bull-headed, if he kept after the cardinal to change his mind once he'd decided to do something. You don't do that if you're in monastic orders; you are, after all, sworn to obedience along with poverty and chastity. My guess was that Brother Vahan wouldn't have said a word about the cardinal's decision had it affected him. For his monks, though, he'd argue—a good man.

And I could see why the cardinal would have wanted him on that carpet: who would have more strength of purpose going up against the probable destroyers of the Thomas Brothers monastery than its abbot?

"As to the other, I gather His Eminence told you no again?" I said.

His thick eyebrows—virtually the only hair he had on his head—twitched upwards. "From what do you infer that?"

"You said you were happy to obey him 'in this instance,' " I answered. "I took it to mean you weren't happy about the other."

"Most Jesuitically reasoned." His thin smile said he was teasing me. It went away too soon. "I'd rather he had refused me this and granted the other. Many could have done what I just did, but who except me will speak for my brethren?"

I didn't know what to feel: pleased with myself for understanding the way Brother Vahan's mind worked, angry at the cardinal for sticking to his refusal like a prickleburr, or pleased His Eminence had the gumption to commit his best to a crisis. Those last two were inextricably mixed, which only complicated things more.

Faint across a couple of hundred yards came shouts from the constables and then pops of pistol fire. Normally pistols are nothing to scorn—they're about the most dangerous mechanical hand weapons around. After everything I'd been through that day, those pops and the clouds of gunpowder smoke I saw rising from the parking lot seemed about as consequential as the firecrackers whose cousins they were.

Kawaguchi pulled out his own pistol, cocked it, checked his flint, and then trotted down Nordhoff toward Chocolate Weasel. Michael and I started after him, but a constable

about the size of both of us put together shook his head and
rumbled, "That wouldn't be smart." He stepped in front of
us and spread his arms wide to make sure we listened to him.
Since he was doing a pretty good impression of the Great
Hanese Wall, I stopped. So did Michael.

That meant we had to wait. Waiting is harder than doing.
When you're doing, you don't have time to worry. When
you're waiting, if you're anything like me, you think about all
the things that could go wrong. I'd waited for the Garuda
Bird. I'd waited for the carpet from the archdiocese. I was
waiting again. I was sick of it. I waited anyhow, peering down
Nordhoff to see what I could see.

Not too much, not for a while. Then I heard more pistol pops, and then people started coming back up the
street. Some of them were constables, some prisoners
with their hands in the air. As they got closer, I saw that
several sets of those upraised hands were red, with drips
running down toward the elbows. I heard someone make
a sick, gulping noise, and realized a moment later it was
me.

One of the SWAT team wizards was carrying an obsidian
knife. Another one walking beside him kept spraying it with
holy water. I gulped again. That knife, I had no doubt,
belonged in the Devonshire dump. If ever spells were
guaranteed harmful to the environment, they're the ones
that go along with human sacrifice.

I recognized one of the prisoners—Jorge Vasquez. He saw
me at about the same time I saw him. I thought about
making some crack about his getting shut down for EPA
violations along with everything else, but I kept my mouth
shut. Even captured, he looked too smart and tough for me
to want to twit him.

Behind him came Legate Kawaguchi, who was busy loading another charge of powder and ball into his pistol as he
walked along. Brother Vahan called to him: "Do any within
that building require my services?"

Kawaguchi finished ramming home the ball before he
looked up. "For last rites and such, you mean, Brother?" He
shook his head. "Just corpses in there."

"Martyrs," Brother Vahan said, his voice grim. "Their reward shall surely come in heaven."

I wondered about that: was somebody who got caught in the wrong place at the wrong time a martyr in the same sense as a person who deliberately invited death for the sake of his faith? I'm neither Catholic nor theologian, so I can't tell you what Brother Vahan should have been thinking by the standards of his church.

That was the least of my worries, anyhow. I lunged for Kawaguchi in a way that almost made him level his newly loaded pistol at me. "Did you—" I choked on fear and had to force myself to go on: "Did you find Judy in there?"

To my relief, he slipped the pistol back into its holster. Then he said, "Inspector Fisher, I neither searched extensively through the Chocolate Weasel building nor closely examined the bodies of the victims around the altar." *Something else to be decontaminated*, I thought. Kawaguchi was continuing, "So long as you understand these limitations, sir, I can state to you that I did not see a corpse matching the description of your fiancée in that—that abbatoir."

Kawaguchi talks like an upper-level constable: as if every word he says is going to show up in a written report or as courtroom testimony Real Soon Now. For him to pick a word like abbatoir . . . all at once I was glad the very large fellow in the blue uniform hadn't let me follow the legate.

I was also gladder than I could say that—subject to his careful limitations—he hadn't found Judy. If I chose to believe that she wasn't there because he hadn't found her, can you blame me?

Michael said, "Legate, can we lend any further assistance?" We hadn't lent Kawaguchi much assistance before that I'd noticed. Michael is usually too precise to make a slip like that, but after everything that had happened during the day, can you blame him, either?

"Thank you, sir, but I think not," Kawaguchi answered. He turned to me. "Inspector Fisher, you did your best to warn me of the magnitude of this threat. I must concede that at the time of our telephone conversation I did not have a full appreciation of it. My apologies for that error."

"Who would have believed this?" I said. My guess was that Kawaguchi still didn't have a full appreciation of what he'd been part of today. Put what happened here together with our desperate struggles back at the Devonshire dump, let both containment efforts fail, and Angels City goes right off the map. And who could say what was happening elsewhere in the Confederation, or would have followed Aztecian success here? Maybe we'd put a spike in the wheel of the Third Sorcerous War.

"David, I shall take you back to Westwood now," Michael said in a tone that brooked no argument. I wasn't in a mood to argue, anyhow; now that the terror which had kept me hopping most of the day was easing, I could feel myself subsiding into something with all the crisp decisiveness of a bowl of tapioca pudding. More boneless with every step, I walked over to his carpet. We headed down toward the Venture Freeway. I told myself I never wanted to see St. Ferdinand's Valley again.

When we got to the Confederal Building, Michael got off the carpet and headed for the entrance instead of going home. He gave me a bemused look when I fell into step beside him. "I may as well keep working," I told him. "The more I have to do, the less time I have to worry."

"Ah," he said, "The anodyne of distraction." Which is what I'd just said, but I hadn't managed to boil it into four words.

If I didn't have anything urgent on my desk, I figured I'd write up what I'd been through today. The EPA, like any government agency, thrives on documentation, and I must confess that I've been indoctrinated to the point where I sometimes don't believe something is real until it's committed to parchment. On the other hand, if Moses had had to fill out all the EPA forms parting the Red Sea would have required, the Bible would be written in Egyptian.

Only one message waited for me, from a woman named Susan Kuznetsov. I frowned, trying to remember who she was. Then name and face matched: the no-nonsense gal from the Barony's Bureau of Physical and Spiritual Health who'd reported little Jesus Cordero's apsychia to me.

I asked my watch the time: going on six. Mistress

Kuznetsov had impressed me as the hard-working type, so I called her back. Sure enough, I got her. "Inspector Fisher!" she said; I thought she sounded pleased. "I'd expected you'd be gone for the day."

"I just got back in," I told her. "What can I do for you?"

"Inspector, the Cordero family has been contacted by a consortium styling itself Slow Jinn Fizz," she answered. "This consortium mentioned the possibility of instilling a soul into the infant, something they had been given to believe was impossible. Unlike too many poor and poorly educated families, the Corderos called me for advice instead of allowing themselves to be taken in by probable charlatans. My preliminary investigation, however, indicates that Slow Jinn Fizz may perhaps be able to deliver on some of its claims. I called you to learn whether it's yet come under EPA scrutiny yet."

"As a matter of fact, I was out there myself, right around the time Jesus Cordero was being born," I said.

When I didn't go on right away, Susan Kuznetsov said, "And? Are they flimflam men like so many outfits with impressive claims?"

"You know, I don't really think so," I answered. "I think they're right on the edge of making psychic synthesis possible, and I think the procedure may well have important benefits for apsychic patients and give them at least a chance at life after death."

"Really?" She sounded surprised. "You recommend the procedure, then?"

"I didn't say that," I told her, and then explained: "I don't knew where or from whom the pieces of soul the jinni are synthesizing come from, or whether Slow Jinn Fizz is solving one problem now at the expense of widespread psychic depletion years, maybe even generations, down the line. It's certainly a tempting technology, but you know who the Tempter is."

"I certainly do," she said. "So you'd suggest the Corderos stay away from it?"

If she'd asked me that the day before, I would have said yes. Thanks to modern medicine, Jesus Cordero had every chance of living to a ripe old age, and psychic synthesis would be investigated and refined until people understood all the gremlins in the process. That would be the right time for him to have a soul implanted.

But after what had happened at the Devonshire dump and then at Chocolate Weasel, I felt less easy about that wait-for-developments approach. Just because the odds said you were likely to lead a long life didn't mean you would: a big piece of Angels City had almost gone up in flames. If you were an apsychic, could you afford to take a chance like that? Would you want to, knowing extinction awaited?

"Mistress Kuznetsov," I said carefully, "the EPA hasn't taken a position on Slow Jinn Fizz and what it does. Before we do, we'll have to weigh short-term benefits against lower-grade long-term risks. My guess is that the technology won't be allowed out of the experimental stage and into general use for many years."

"I know that much already," she answered. "The people from Slow Jinn Fizz said as much to the Corderos, and I give them credit for it. What I'm really asking is, what would you do if that were your kid?"

"If it's my kid, I worry about saving him first and everything else later," I said. "Isn't that what being a parent's all about? But just because that's what I'd do doesn't mean it makes good public policy."

"That's fair," she said. "Let me put it a different way, then: would the EPA have kittens if the Slow Jinn Fizz experimental protocol expanded to include Jesus Cordero?"

"Right now, the answer to that is no," I said. Too much else—bigger stuff—was going on for us to worry about Slow Jinn Fizz right now, but I didn't tell that to Susan Kuznetsov. I hoped that one day (one day soon, God willing) things would slow down to the point where we'd be able to worry about the problems synthesized souls present. No doubt they were important, but they weren't world-threatening, so for now they'd just have to wait.

And besides, I told myself, how much environmental damage on the Other Side would manufacturing a soul for one little boy cause? Not much, surely, and it would do so much good for Jesus Cordero.

You know, of course, which road is paved with good intentions. So do I. So does the EPA. The real question wasn't what would happen when one apsychic kid got a soul. The real question was what would happen when jinnetic engineering and jinn-splicing techniques began stirring up the psychic material of the Other Side on a large scale.

I didn't have any answers for that. Neither did anybody else. The EPA's job was to make sure we found those answers before exploiting those techniques got us into trouble, not afterwards. But to give Jesus Cordero, a series of one case, a chance at life after life—why not?

Mistress Kuznetsov said, "Inspector, I want to thank you for being flexible; you're going to make the Corderos very happy, and as for Jesus—he won't understand what's happened for a long time yet, but when he does, he'll be eternally grateful."

"I hope so, anyway," I said. "The technique is experimental and, from what Ramzan Durani told me, it hasn't yet undergone the test of mortality. But when you're in that position, you have to grasp at straws, don't you?"

"That's my view as a public health officer, certainly," Susan Kuznetsov said. "I wasn't sure how the EPA would view the matter."

"If you'd said you wanted to add a thousand people to the experimental list, I would have given you a different answer. But one little boy, and one I've met—"

"Yes, the law of contagion does remind us of how important personal contact is, doesn't it? I was just afraid you'd be working against contagion, as I often have to do, rather than allowing it full scope."

"Not this time," I answered quietly. Letting Jesus Cordero have a chance to beat apsychia wasn't as big a thing as thwarting the Chumash Powers or keeping Huitzilopochtli and his fiery friend from establishing themselves in Angels City, but it felt just as good. Maybe better—as Susan Kuznetsov had said, this was personal.

I only wished the rest of my personal worries were doing as well. No word of Judy, none at all.

To keep myself from thinking of that and what it might

mean, I plunged into the environmental impact report on what importing leprechauns into Angels City was liable to do to the local theology. I made more progress in an hour and a half than I had in the past two weeks. No wonder: now I could make my prognostications secure in the knowledge that the Wee Folk weren't going to have any adverse effect on the Chumash Powers. I'd taken care of that myself, in spades.

Eventually, I supposed, I'd get around to feeling bad about siccing the Garuda Bird on them. An EPA man, after all, is supposed to protect endangered Powers, not exterminate them. From their point of view, I couldn't really blame the Lizard and the Great (but not Great enough) Eagle and the rest for wanting to overturn the balance of Powers and twist things back to the way they'd been before the first Europeans touched the New World.

But, along with a couple of hundred million other people, I live in the world that's sprung from the European expansion. And, as Michael Manstein said, we'd done more and better with this land than its original inhabitants would have in the same length of time. So while I figured I'd eventually get round to feeling bad, it wouldn't be any time real soon.

Speaking of Michael, he poked his head into my office about then. "I'm going home now," he said. "Perhaps you should do the same." He clearly wasn't used to me working longer hours than he did.

He was right. I went home. I ate something (don't ask me what), then went to bed. Worries or no, I slept almost as soundly as if I'd been in Ephesus: the aftermath of nearly dying a couple of times during the course of a day. If my alarm clock hadn't screamed me awake, I might be snoring yet.

No sooner had I got to the office than the phone started yelling. I came this close to knocking over my cup of cafeteria coffee grabbing for it. "Environmental Perfection Agency, David Fisher."

"Inspector Fisher, this is Legate Shiro Kawaguchi, Angels City Constabulary Department." Kawaguchi spoke as if he were introducing himself for the first time. "Inspector

Fisher, interrogation of the suspect Jorge Vasquez has led us to your fiancée, Mistress Judith Adler."

I let out a whoop that rattled my windows. "That's wonderful, Legate! When can I see her?" He didn't answer right away. My joy crashed into dread. "Is she—all right?"

"Unfortunately, Inspector Fisher, I must tell you she is not," Kawaguchi answered. "You will perhaps remember that an Aztecian Power, variously called the Crackler, the Page, and the One Called Night, was involved in the abduction of Mistress Adler."

"Yes, of course," I said.

"From what our forensics man has to say, Inspector, it appears that the One Called Night, to use the name with which you appear to be most familiar, has carried Mistress Adler's spirit into the realm known as the Nine Beyonds. We have recovered her body. She appears to be physically unharmed; she will eat or drink if food or water is placed in her mouth. But as for anything more than that . . . I'm very sorry, Inspector Fisher, but at present it is just not there."

"What do we do, then?" I asked hoarsely.

"Our preliminary and tentative thaumaturgic efforts to restore her to herself have failed; she does not seem as responsive to certain rituals as we had hoped." Kawaguchi paused. "I believe you are Jewish. Is Mistress Adler, also?"

"Yes."

"That may account for part of it, then. Most rituals designed to counter the Crackler assume a Catholic victim, and would be less efficacious in rescuing one from a different faith. While we continue to do our utmost, I suggest you also pursue every flyway that occurs to you. Otherwise, Inspector, I can offer no guarantee that Mistress Adler's body and spirit will ever be reunited."

XI

I took my troubles down to Madame Ruth—you know, that medium with the gold-capped tooth. She had an office down on 34th and Vine. I hoped she could help with a problem like mine. When Erasmus had been so dreadfully hurt as the Thomas Brothers monastery was torched, she and Nigel Cholmondeley managed to access him where everyone else had failed. I was praying she'd be able to do the same for Judy.

In her green silk dress and the matching scarf she used to cover her hair, she put me in mind of nothing so much as an enormous watermelon wearing too much makeup. But her looks didn't matter, not to me they didn't. She and her English partner were the local experts on virtuous reality, and from what I'd seen of the technique, I figured it offered the best chance of rescuing Judy's spirit and bringing it back to This Side where it belonged.

Madame Ruth heard me out, then slowly shook her head back and forth. "I dunno, Inspector Fisher," she said. "This ain't gonna be as easy as gettin' hold of what's-his-name, the scriptorium spirit, was. You don't just wanna access your fiancée's spirit, you wanna download it, too. That's one fresh problem."

"If you say that's one, you mean there are more," I said. "What are they?"

"Two good ones, offhand," she answered. "One's in the spiritual realm. We were able to build our own kinda place to meet the spirit—Erasmus, that's what he goes by—in. If your girlfriend's already stuck in the Nine Beyonds, we're gonna hafta go in there and haul her out. Like I said, that ain't gonna be easy."

I wondered what walking through a simulation of the Nine Beyonds would be like. Could even virtuous reality pretty up something with a handle like that so anyone except a Power named the One Called Night would want to go there? I had my doubts, but I also had no choice, not if I wanted Judy back. I asked, "What's the other problem?"

Madame Ruth coughed and looked down at her desk, an elephantine effort at discretion. "It's not spiritual," she said. "It's more material-like, if you know what I mean." She stopped there.

After a couple of seconds, I figured out what she was flying at. "I'm sure Judy's medical insurance will cover your fees," I said. "It's one of the Blue Scutum plans, and it has an excellent thaumaturgy benefits package."

"That's okay, then," she said, nodding briskly. I understood that she had to show a profit, but what would Judy have done without insurance? Got stuck in the Nine Beyonds forever because no one would come after her without crowns on the barrelhead? Or ended up bankrupting herself to pay the fees afterwards? Nothing's simple these days.

"Will you try to help her?" I asked.

"Lemme talk with my partner. This is gonna take both of us," she said, and got up to go next door. I didn't age more than eight or ten years in the few minutes she was gone. She came back with Cholmondeley, tweedy as ever, in her wake. She must have read my face, because she said, "It's okay, Mr. Fisher. We'll give it a try."

I started gasping out thank-yous, but Nigel Cholmondeley cut me off. "Time for all that later, old chap, if we succeed. Meanwhile, where is Mistress, uh, Adler now located?"

Kawaguchi had told me that. "Her body's at the West Hills Temple of Healing," I said. Where the rest of her was . . . Well, Cholmondeley and Madame Ruth already knew about that.

Madame Ruth was looking through her appointments scroll. "We're on for this afternoon and tomorrow morning, too," she said. "We can work her in tomorrow afternoon, though, if that's okay wit' you?" She looked at me. I nodded. I wanted them to drop everything and rush right out to take care of Judy, but everybody else they were working for felt his case was the most important one in the world, too. Madame Ruth said, "It's okay, Mr. Fisher, maybe even better than okay. This gives us a chance to square things with the constables and with the West Hills place, so as we can be all set up and ready to go."

I nodded again. Cholmondeley unrolled his own scroll, inked a quill, and scribbled a note. "We shall see you there, then, at half past one." He stuck out a bony hand. I clasped it, then walked out of Madame Ruth's office. I wanted to get back to my own shop as soon as I could: I was using vacation time for this visit. Crazy how you keep track of the little things even when the big ones in your world are falling every which way.

There was a rack of news stands outside Madame Ruth's building. I stuck a quarter-crown into the waiting palm of one of the little vending demons, took away a copy of the *A.C. Times*. I figured yesterday's goings-on would be page-one stuff, and so they were: the flight of the Garuda Bird across St. Ferdinand's Valley isn't something you can easily ignore. Neither is the emergency evacuation of the neighborhoods surrounding the Devonshire toxic spell dump.

Sure enough, both of those got plenty of ink, though the

reporters seemed confused about just what had happened. That didn't bother me; the whole truth here probably would have set off a panic we didn't need, especially since (I hoped) things were back under control.

One of the reporters quoted Matt Arnold out at the Loki works. He gave the impression he'd turned the Garuda Bird loose as a preorbital flight test, then went on about the next step in the space program after the Bird got us into low orbit: Loki was designing new sorceware to work the Indian Rope Trick from some spot on the equator 22,300 miles straight up to geosynchronous orbit, from which mages could project sorcery over big parts of the globe day and night.

Nobody asked me, but I thought Loki ought to work on a new rope, too.

The mess at Chocolate Weasel made page one, too, but only as a big industrial accident. Not a word about the sacrifices, not a word about any connection to the mess at the Devonshire dump.

What really got me, though, was the rest of the headlines. The Aztecian Emperor had ordered his entire cabinet executed. It was, the *Times* said, the first general cabinet massacre since the time when Azteca almost joined the First Sorcerous War on the Alemanian side. The new ministers were supposed to be "more inclined toward improving relations with the Confederation than their predecessors had been."

Or else, I read between the lines.

There'd also been some sort of disaster outside D.St.C., but I didn't even glance at that story. I just headed over to Westwood to go back to work.

When I got up to my floor, Bea was coming down the corridor as I stepped out of the elevator shaft. She asked about Judy and gave me her best in a way that sounded as if she really meant it. I'm sure she did, too; Bea cares about people. Sounding as if you care, though, isn't so easy. Then she said, "You and Michael have done some very important work lately, and under extremely trying circumstances. I want you to know I know it, and I couldn't be more pleased."

"Thank you," I said. "But you know what? I think I'd rather have spent all that time in a nice, dull staff meeting."

Her head went to one side; I realized I'd stuck my foot in my face. "I'm going to understand that the way I hope you meant it," she said, to my relief more in sorrow—and in amusement—than in anger.

She let me escape then, so escape I did, to the smaller problems left behind after the spectacular collapse of the bigger ones. I plugged away at the leprechaun study, lining up values for my variables so I could get rolling on the crystal-ball prognostications maybe next week. I had to call the Angels City archdiocese for some of the data I needed; the Catholic Church has lived side by side with the Wee Folk on the Emerald Isle for the past fifteen hundred years, and knows more about 'em than anybody these days.

Try as I would, though, I didn't get a whole lot done. People kept coming in to congratulate me and wish me the best—Phyllis, Rose, Jose. Even if the papers were being coy, the folks I work with knew what I'd done. Maybe Michael had talked with them; I don't know. It's not that I didn't appreciate their dropping by, but they kept distracting me from what I was trying to do. And when I got distracted, I had a hard time pulling my mind back where it was supposed to be.

I also kept trying to crystal-ball it in my head, to work out where in the big picture the events in Angels City really fit. What did thwarting the Chumash Powers have to do with the liquidation of the Aztecian cabinet, for instance? Something, sure, but what?

As with the leprechaun study, I was missing data. Here, though, the Catholic Church wasn't the place that had 'em. I called Central Intelligence back in D.St.C. and asked for Henry Legion.

I listened to a long silence on the other end of the ether. Then the CI operator asked, "Who's calling, please?"

"David Fisher, from the EPA out in Angels City."

"One moment, sir." If that was one moment, you could live a long lifetime in three or four of them. At last, though, someone came back on the line—a new voice, but not

Henry Legion's. "Mr. Fisher? I'm sorry to have to tell you that Henry Legion's essence has undergone dissolution. He gave his country the last full measure of devotion; his name will go up on the memorial tablet commemorating our agency's heroes and martyrs. He shall not be forgotten, I assure you."

"What happened?" I exclaimed. "And to whom am I talking?"

"I'm afraid I can't answer either of those questions, sir: security," the new voice said. "I'm sure you understand. Good day. Thank you for your concern." The phone imps reproduced the sound of a handset clunking into its cradle.

I hung up, too, and stared at the phone for a while. Whatever Henry Legion had been doing, it cost him everything. I knew I'd never learn all the answers I wanted, not with him gone. I was back to my own guesses, for better or worse—probably worse. After seeing a little ways into his secret, secretive world, I was blind again.

I wondered if his passing had anything to do with the extermination of the sitting Aztecian cabinet, or perhaps with the disaster outside D.St.C. the *Times* had mentioned. Did some sort of war try to start there, too, and get suppressed as it had in Angels City? More things I'd never know, not without Henry Legion to ask.

Since I'd never know, sitting around wondering was just a waste of taxpayers' crowns. I buckled down and tried to do my job, but things came slow, slow. Maybe I suddenly needed a crisis breathing down my neck like a hungry werewolf to make myself perform.

Lord, what a horrid idea!

I flew into the parking lot of the West Hills Temple of Healing about ten past one the next afternoon, then flew around inside the lot for the next ten minutes looking for a space for my carpet. I wouldn't have been late, not for anything.

When I told the receptionist who I was and for whom I was looking, she said, "Go up to the fifth floor, Mr. Fisher. Mistress Adler is in 547, right across the hall from the

Intensive Prayer Unit. Just follow the IPU signs and you can't go wrong."

Famous last words, I knew. Well, this time the gal was right; the signs took me straight to 547. I didn't know what to think about Judy's being where she was. Should I have been glad she was so close to intensive prayer in case she needed it, or worried she was there because they were afraid she *would* need it? Being me, I worried.

When I opened the door to 547, I discovered a constable sitting in one of the uncomfortable-looking chairs in there. He carefully checked my EPA sigil and said, "You're fine, Mr. Fisher, but we have to be sure," before he went back to his book.

By then I'd forgotten all about him. Seeing Judy again took everything else out of my mind. She didn't look bad, but then she always looks good to me, so I wasn't in any real position to judge. Her color was good, her eyes were open, she was breathing normally: to that much I can objectively attest.

But I soon noticed that, even if her eyes were open, they didn't track. I walked across her field of vision a couple of times, but she took no notice of me. She didn't say anything. When she moved on the bed, she didn't adjust the covers afterwards. Her body lay there, but not the rest of her. That was off in the Nine Beyonds, the realm of the One Called Night.

Madame Ruth and Nigel Cholmondeley came in just then, accompanied by a fellow in a white lab robe who introduced himself to me as Healer Ali Murad. "I look forward to learning to apply virtuous reality to healing situations," he said. "This will be an excellent opportunity for me to enhance my knowledge."

Wonderful. Somebody who saw Judy as a guinea pig, nothing more. I wondered how he'd like enhancing his knowledge of what getting flung out a fifth-floor window felt like. He looked pretty sharp—maybe he could learn to fly before he hit the ground.

I made myself relax. By his lights, Hr. Murad was only doing his job. What he learned from Judy might help him treat somebody else. But that didn't mean I had to like him, and I didn't.

Nigel Cholmondeley was carrying a case large enough that he had to be stronger than he looked. He set it on the empty bed next to Judy's, flipped open the brass catches, and took out four of the big-eared virtuous reality helmets I'd last seen in the constabulary station.

He looked at the setup in the room, fretfully clucked his tongue between his teeth. "Forming a circle under these circumstances will be rather difficult," he said, making the *a* in *rather* so broad I thought he'd never finish pronouncing it.

Madame Ruth was bluntly practical. "We'll just turn her around," she said. "It'll be easy if her head end's at the foot of the bed." Hr. Murad took care of that, moving Judy with a practiced gentleness that said he might have a bedside manner after all. Madame Ruth rounded on the constable. "Hey, you, be useful—move some chairs around for us." She gestured to show what she wanted.

The constable gave her a dirty look but did as she asked him: he put one chair at the foot of the bed, close by where Judy's head now rested, and one more to either side at that end of the bed. While he was taking care of that, Nigel Cholmondeley set a virtuous reality helmet on Judy. She didn't react at all as it covered her eyes and ears.

When he was done, Cholmondeley turned to me and said, "You sit here." *Here* was the seat right across the footboard from Judy. Cholmondeley and Madame Ruth took the other two seats. Grunting, Madame Ruth got up from hers and arranged Judy's arms so her wrists and hands dangled off the sides of the bed. "Oh, capital," Cholmondeley said as she sat back down. "Now we shall be able to maintain the personal contact so essential in this exercise."

He handed me a virtuous reality helmet. I put it on. The world went black and silent. From my earlier experience, I knew I was supposed to take the hands of the people to either side of me. I groped for them. At first, I didn't find them. I wondered what was wrong until I realized Madame Ruth and Cholmondeley needed to put on their helmets, too.

I wished I were holding one of Judy's hands, but that wasn't how the medium and the channeler had set things up, and I had to assume they knew what they were doing. No sooner had that thought crossed my mind than Nigel Cholmondeley's left hand caught my right. A moment later, Madame Ruth's right hand took my left in a warm, damp, fleshy grasp.

And a moment after that, the psychic circle complete, we were on the Other Side. Madame Ruth had warned me we wouldn't be going back to the garden where we'd questioned Erasmus, so I'd been braced for worse. I wasn't braced for what we encountered.

"We're here, sure enough," Nigel Cholmondeley said; as soon as he spoke, I could see his virtuous image.

"But where is *here*?" I asked to help him see me.

"A bad place," Madame Ruth said, springing into apparent being. "Very bad."

As in my earlier venture into virtuous reality, they both appeared idealized to my second sight: Cholmondeley handsome, with more meat on his scrawny bones; Madame Ruth minus about half of her corpulent self and her screechy tough-guy accent. As before, I couldn't see myself at all.

I couldn't see any sign of Judy, either.

Not as before, I couldn't see anything but my spirit guides. The Nine Beyonds were dark as an underground cave at midnight. My sight had been totally obscured when I slipped the virtuous reality helmet over my eyes. What I was sensing now felt darker than totally obscured. I don't know how, but it did.

It was just dark like a cave; it didn't feel as if we were inside one. If we'd been in a garden before, my guess was that we were in jungle now, jungle on a moonless, starless night a million miles—or maybe farther—from anything of man's. Though I knew my body was back in a cool room at the West Hills Temple of Healing, the air that seemed to be around me felt hot and wet and smelled as if things I didn't want to know about were just beginning to rot somewhere not far enough away.

Things were moving there, too, and I didn't know what

they were because I couldn't see them. Whatever they were, I didn't think they meant us well. This was not a place where we were meant to be. A sudden sharp noise made the self I didn't have start in alarm: it sounded as if something had stepped on a dry twig, although where you could have found a dry twig in that stifling humidity, I couldn't tell you.

I remembered the One Called Night was also known as the Crackler. Having remembered, I wished I could forget again.

I turned to Madame Ruth. "How are we supposed to find Judy in all this?" We were somewhere in one Beyond; even if we somehow went over every inch of it (and I was afraid it had a lot of inches), that left eight more to search. We were liable to be there forever, or maybe twenty minutes longer.

The Emperor Hadrian's death poem ran through my mind: *Animula vagula blandula . . . Little soul, wandering, gentle guest and companion of my body, into what places will you go now, pale, stiff, and naked, no longer sporting as you did?* If I'd perceived myself as embodied in that dreadful place, I would have burst into tears. The image fit only too well what I feared was happening to Judy's spirit.

"We'll do the best we can, Mr. Fisher," Madame Ruth answered. "Beyond that, I don't know what to tell you. This domain is not shaped by us alone; the Power who dwells here influences our perceptions. We must attempt to move, and hope we find ourselves guided toward Mistress Adler."

She'd warned before we set out that this wouldn't be as easy as contacting Erasmus had been. She hadn't warned how bad it would be. Maybe she didn't know till we tried it; virtuous reality is a technology that's just opening up, which means one of the things its practitioners are still discovering is what can go wrong.

I got the feeling that if anything went seriously wrong in the Nine Beyonds, Hr. Ali Murad would learn some things he hadn't expected—and some new intrepid explorers of virtuous reality would have to try to rescue three more spirits lost in this suffocating place.

Would they have any better fortune than we did?

Madame Ruth had said we had to try to move, to explore

the Nine Beyonds and hope we found Judy. Move we did, but it wasn't easy. The Nine Beyonds resisted every metaphysical motion we made. We cried out, but everywhere in vain. It was as if we were drunk, as if the Nine Beyonds themselves were having sport with us, mocking our search. We might as well have been wading through mud, through quicksand, through hot clinging slime.

And it felt as if the area in which we stood and moved was growing smaller all the time. With everything perfectly black all around us, with Madame Ruth and Nigel Cholmondeley the only things my second sight could perceive, I don't know how I got that impression, but I did. That led me to another interesting question (if *interesting* and *horrible* are synonyms): what would happen if it closed real tight around us?

Some experiments you'd rather not see performed, especially on you.

No sooner had I thought that than I discovered I wasn't the only one feeling the invisible closing in. Voice tight with concern, Nigel Cholmondeley said, "I think we had best withdraw, lest we be overwhelmed by that which lurks in darkness here."

"How do we get away?" I asked.

"Break the circle; free your hands," Madame Ruth said. "Quickly!"

That hadn't been easy even when we were leaving the virtuous reality garden. Remembering you had an actual physical body that could do things was tough; making it do those things tougher.

And not for me alone—I watched the virtuous images of Cholmondeley and Madame Ruth twist in concentration as they struggled to make their bodies respond to their wills. No doubt my own virtuous image bore a similar grimace in their second sight.

Madame Ruth had been right; we needed to hurry. Something was breathing down the neck I hadn't brought along to the Nine Beyonds. I didn't know what the One Called Night could do to me, but I was very conscious of operating on the Power's turf—or rather, muck. If it took hold of me . . .

Just then, one of us (to this day, I don't know who)

managed to get a hand loose and break the circle. Coming back wasn't like returning from the garden; I seemed to be falling and falling in a forever compressed into maybe a second and a half. Worse still, I thought the One Called Night was falling after me, falling faster than I was, reaching out with black, black hands in which never a star would shine.

Under the virtuous reality helmet, my eyes flew open. I saw only darkness there, too, but it was a darkness I knew, the familiar darkness of This Side. Unlike the blacker than black of the Nine Beyonds, I knew what to do about this. I yanked the helmet off my head and sat blinking in the mellow afternoon sun.

I got my helmet off just ahead of Nigel Cholmondeley and Madame Ruth. Their faces—their real, everyday faces, not the idealized images they bore in the realms of virtuous reality—were pale and haggard, as yours would be, as mine surely was, after such a narrow escape.

Cholmondeley leaned forward, pulled off Judy's virtuous reality helmet. Her face showed nothing, just as it had before the helmet went on. Her spirit hadn't been in there to experience what we'd gone through.

Madame Ruth wiped sweat from her forehead with one sleeve. I didn't think the sweat had anything to do with wearing the helmet. "Jesus," she muttered. "It tried to follow us back."

"Too bloody right it did." Cholmondeley also sounded shaken to the core. "I think it used Mistress Adler as its conduit: it controls her spirit, after all."

"I never heard of that," I said.

"Nor had I," Cholmondeley answered. "Nor, so far as I know, has any practitioner of virtuous reality. Of course, there is the *caveat* that anyone encountering the phenomenon at full strength, so to speak, is unlikely to remain a practitioner of virtuous reality, or, indeed, of any trade thereafter." He essayed a laugh; it came out as a series of nervous little barks.

"The procedure was unsuccessful?" Hr. Murad asked. He hadn't been there with us. Lucky him.

"Buddy, you're lucky—we're lucky—it's us sittin' here

talking to you, and not the One Called Night," Madame Ruth said. Nigel Cholmondeley's nod in support of that was as herky-jerky as his laugh had been.

I stood up. I felt as if I'd been away from my body for a long time, slogging through the steaming, lightless swamps of the Nine Beyonds. The physical part of me, though, the part that hadn't left the chair, rose now so smoothly that I knew virtuous reality had fooled me again.

Before Hr. Murad could turn Judy the right way around on her bed, I leaned over the footboard and looked down into her face. Her eyes were open, and looking back at me. Nothing showed in them, any more than it had before: no recognition of me, no awareness of where she was.

I kept looking, down into the blackness of her pupils. Was the One Called Night hiding in that blackness, peering back at me through those portholes into This Side while it held her spirit trapped in the Nine Beyonds? I had no way to tell.

When I stepped back, the healer did put Judy back where she belonged. Nigel Cholmondeley was glumly packing the virtuous reality helmets back into their travel case. He set a hand on my arm. "Terribly sorry, old man, I truly am. I'd hoped for better results."

"So did I." I looked at Judy again. If we couldn't get her spirit back from the Nine Beyonds, she was going to stay in that bed for the rest of her life, eating when they fed her, drinking when they gave her water, wiggling every now and then for no reason at all. And what would happen when she died? Could her spirit break free of the One Called Night even then?

I shivered all over, and the room wasn't *that* cool. In a way, she was even worse off than Jesus Cordero. With no natural soul of his own, he at least had hopes of getting an artificial one from Slow Jinn Fizz. But what could Ramzan Durani do for Judy, whose spirit was stolen rather than absent?

What could anyone do?

Hr. Murad stepped in front of Madame Ruth as she was about to go out the door. "Wait, please," he said in the tone of somebody trying—not too hard—to be polite about giving an order. "We have not yet fully examined the etiology of your treatment's failure."

Madame Ruth looked down her nose at him. She was taller than he was, as well as wider. "If you don't get out of that doorway, sonny, I'm gonna squash you flat. You ask nice, maybe we'll talk about it later. Right now I need a drink or two a whole lot more than I need you." She advanced. Hr. Murad retreated. Nigel Cholmondeley followed in her massive wake.

I followed, too. Leaving Judy was a knife stuck in my heart, but staying there, with her like that, hurt even worse. I felt another sleepless night coming up. I'd had too many of those lately, and earned every one of them.

"Excuse me," I called to Cholmondeley and Madame Ruth as they were about to step on the slide back down to the lobby.

They both paused. "Sorry like anything we couldn't help ya, Mr. Fisher," Madame Ruth said. "I'm just glad we got ourselves back to This Side in one piece. Too bad we couldn't bring your girl friend with us."

"Most unfortunate," Nigel Cholmondeley agreed.

"For Judy especially," I said, at which the two of them had the grace to nod. That gave me the nerve I needed to go on: "If I can come up with anything that would give us a better chance, would you be willing to take another try at rescuing her from the Nine Beyonds?"

They looked at each other. I didn't like the look; it said, *Not on your life, bud.* Madame Ruth opened her mouth to answer, and I'd bet a big pile she was about to say that out loud. Cholmondeley raised a finger to stop her; he was the smooth man of the pair. What he said was, "It would have to be something quite extraordinary, Mr. Fisher." Which was also *no*, but sugar-coated so it went down sweeter. Besides, he wouldn't want to drive away business by coming right out and saying virtuous reality just couldn't do some tricks.

So he let me hope—a needle-eye's worth, maybe, but hope. The last thing at the bottom of Pandora's box, and generally running too many lengths behind trouble ever since. But it was all I had, so I clasped it to my bosom.

What I didn't have was any idea of what I might come up with that would give us a better chance in the Nine Beyonds. The One Called Night seemed to rule the roost there. Why not? It was his roost.

If we could make him confront us on neutral ground, so to speak, we'd have a better chance of making him release Judy's spirit. But how? The Nine Beyonds were his home on the Other Side. I didn't see any way to force him out. Beat him on his home ground, then? We'd tried that already, with no luck.

That left—nothing I could see.

Madame Ruth and Nigel Cholmondeley had already slid away. I stood by the slide, doing my best to come up with the brilliant idea to save the day. It's always easy in the adventure stories. I'd even done it myself, when I summoned the Garuda Bird to the Devonshire dump.

Not this time.

Another sleepless night. This time I mean it literally. When it got to be about one in the morning, I just gave up and made myself a cup of coffee. If I was going to be awake, I might as well be *awake*, I figured. Somehow I'd stagger through the next day and somehow, after that, I'd sleep. Meanwhile . . .

Meanwhile, I prowled around my flat. For want of anything better to do, I cleaned it cleaner than it had been since just before the High Holy Days the year before. When I moved the couch and chair to clean under them, I found close to a crown and a half in loose change, so I even turned a profit on the deal.

I read an adventure story, paid some bills, wrote some letters, all the things you do in slack time. I wrote to people who hadn't heard from me in so long, I hoped the shock wouldn't send 'em on to the Other Side.

Every so often, I'd get up from the kitchen table—which doubled as desk—and go back in the bedroom. Not to try to go to sleep: I'd given up on that. I'd push back the curtain and look out at the night. It was very dark out there, no moon, just a couple of stars I could see. I might have thought it looked really black if I hadn't almost been trapped in the Nine Beyonds that afternoon. Next to that place, Angels City night was high noon in the desert.

Back out to the kitchen for another cup of coffee. As I had once or twice before, I wished for an ethernet set to give me some noise to be lonely with. With quiet all around me, I couldn't keep from thinking, and none of my thoughts were ones I wanted.

I went back to the bedroom again. Still night outside. What a surprise. My alarm clock told me it was half past four. Maybe I was imagining things, but I thought the horological demon sounded slightly worried at having me awake and prowling around at that hour. Maybe I alarmed it for a change.

I sat down on the bed. The state I was in, that proved another mistake. It made me remember all the times Judy and I had lain there together, and how unlikely we were to do it again. My eyes filled with the easy tears that can come when you're half underwater with exhaustion. An effect of the law of contagion? I don't know.

Out to the kitchen again, this time for breakfast. You stay up all night, you get hungry. I was washing the dishes when a pigeon landed on the tile roof above me with a noise like a flying carpet crashing into the side of a hill in the fog. There have been times when that kind of predawn racket's bounced me out of bed in a fright. If I'd been asleep, it might have happened again. As things were, I welcomed the noise—it showed something besides me was alive and moving.

I finished washing the dishes, dried them (a prodigy), and put them away (a bigger prodigy). Then I took a shower, and after that I went back into the bedroom and got dressed to face the new day.

Facing the day, in fact, was easy: when I opened the bedroom drapes, the eastern sky was brilliant pink, shading toward gold at the horizon. It got brighter by the second as I watched. Finally the sun crawled up into sight. Another day had started. I didn't feel too bad, not physically. Mentally, spiritually . . . a different story.

The sun rose higher, as the sun has a way of doing. What

had been a black mystery out past my window was revealed as—what a surprise!—romantic Hawthorne, a not particularly exotic suburb of Angels City.

I started to turn my back on the too-familiar panorama, then stopped with one foot in the air. Before I fell over, I spun around and ran for the little book by my phone. I was just about sure I had that number, but not quite. I checked. I had it. I called it.

"Hello?" Through two phone imps, I recognized that groggy tone. I'd had it myself, the too early in the morning when Charlie Kelly called me and got me and Judy and maybe the whole world into the mess we were in. I didn't care. I started to talk.

I found a parking spot right at the corner of Thirty-Fourth and Vine, settled my carpet into it, and settled me down to wait. I'd got there twenty minutes before I was supposed to meet him. He'd promised he'd come. He'd even sounded eager to help, which to my way of thinking only proved he didn't fully understand the situation.

That corner wasn't one of the swankier ones in Angels City, and it wasn't an angel who sauntered past and gave me the eye. It was a succubus, swinging her hips fit to make the Pope sweat. But my mind was on other things. She muttered something I was lucky enough not to catch and walked on down the street.

Two spaces in front of me, a carpet pulled out and headed up Vine. Within half a minute, another one slid into the space. "Tony!" I exclaimed gladly; promises or no, I'd feared he'd find some reason not to come. Before six in the morning, you're liable to promise anything, just to get a pest off the phone.

But here he was, grinning like a man who's had some sleep, anyhow. "Let's go, Dave," he said. "I've read a lot about virtuous reality; you think I'm gonna throw away a chance to check it out from the inside?"

If he'd had any sense, he would have. He must not have had sense; he gave me a shot in the ribs with his elbow and went into the office building ahead of me. He was singing something in Lithuanian. I caught Perkunas' name, but that was all. Before I'd met Tony, I wouldn't have understood that, either.

My legs are longer than his. By the time we got to Madame Ruth's office, I was a couple of strides in front of him. I opened the door and went in, Tony on my heels. If I told you Madame Ruth looked delighted to see me, I'd be lying.

"Mr. Fisher," she said, as patiently as she could (which wasn't very), "we told you yesterday we couldn't do anything more for you."

"No, that's not quite what you said," I answered. "Nigel Cholmondeley said you couldn't do anything unless I came up with something extraordinary. Well, here he is—Mr. Antanas Sudakis." I wasn't making all the sense I might have; more than a day without sleep will do that to you.

Tony grinned. "Something extraordinary, hey? I like that."

Madame Ruth did *not* look amused. "Why is he extraordinary?" she asked. *Why is he extraordinary, wise guy?* was what her tone said.

So I told her why, in detail and probably repeating myself more than a little. I watched her eyebrows, or rather the painted lines that showed where they used to live. They'd ridden high and skeptical on her forehead when I started, but the longer I talked, the lower they got.

When I finished, she just said, "Wait here, both of youse." She walked out, came back a minute later with Nigel Cholmondeley. "Okay, buster, tell him what you just told me."

So I did. I doubt I was any smoother the second time around than I had been the first. By the time I was through, Cholmondeley was rubbing his long, horsy chin in speculation. When he spoke, it wasn't to me but to Tony Sudakis: "My principal objection, sir, is doubt that Perkunas is a Power sufficiently powerful (please forgive the play on words) to achieve the effect desired in the Nine Beyonds."

"The Thunderer not powerful enough?" Tony was a man of direct action. I was afraid he'd take some now: pitching Cholmondeley through a wall, for instance. But he didn't; he just said, "Listen, once upon a time not so long ago a farmer invited the Devil to his daughter's wedding. He didn't really want him there, so he said the Christian God, the Virgin, and a bunch of saints were coming, too. The Devil didn't care. Then the farmer told him he'd invited Perkunas, and the Devil stayed away—he remembered how the Thunderer had beaten the tar out of him the last time they met. If he can do that, you think he can't handle something like the One Called Night?"

Madame Ruth and Cholmondeley looked at each other. I'm no psychic, but I could read their minds anyhow: Perkunas had to be one tough, smart Power to have survived so long in the predominantly Christian thecosystem of Europe. I wouldn't have wanted to run him up against Huitzilopochtli or Huehueteotl, but the One Called Night wasn't a Power on their order of magnitude himself.

The other variable in the equation was that Perkunas hadn't gone down to hell to beat the tar out of the Devil. Could he do it in the Nine Beyonds, even with the advantage I'd outlined to the virtuous reality practitioners?

I had no idea. I did know I wasn't going to bring it up if the medium and the channeler didn't. I was willing to take any chance at all to go after Judy again; I wanted to persuade them to try again, too, because I couldn't reach the Nine Beyonds without 'em.

"Gentlemen, do please excuse us," Nigel Cholmondeley said. "We shall have to consult with each other on the proper course of action to take."

They went over into the next office, which was Cholmondeley's. Last time they'd done that, I hadn't heard a thing. Now, Madame Ruth's screeches came right through the wall. A moment later, so did Cholmondeley's shouts. I was glad they'd identified what they were doing as a consultation. If they hadn't, I'd have called it a brawl.

But everything was sweetness and light when they came back into Madame Ruth's office. Madame Ruth glared at me, scowled at Sudakis, glared at me again. Then she said, "Let's go."

I gaped. "Just like that?"

"Just like that," she said. "We've got nothing calendared

till late this afternoon, and either we'll be able to bring this off by then or else we'll end up stuck in the Nine Beyonds and we won't gotta worry about it. So come on."

On we came. Tony and I flew to the West Hills Temple of Healing each on his own carpet. That sort of thing adds to Angels City's traffic nightmares, but it was more convenient for both of us because we'd be going home in opposite directions. Besides, I didn't want to endanger anybody but me if I fell asleep at the fringe.

We got into the West Hills parking lot within a couple of minutes of each other, then stood around waiting for Cholmondeley and Madame Ruth. I figured they'd be a little while; they had to pack up their gear before they flew over. Tony smoked a cigarillo while we waited. He'd just ground it out under his heel when their carpet settled itself a couple of spaces over from mine.

"We can go straight up," Cholmondeley said as he hauled the case toward the doorway. "I called ahead to make sure Mistress Adler isn't undergoing any other spiritual therapy at the moment." He was more efficient than I'd given him credit for.

"Good," I said, from the bottom of my heart, for it also meant they hadn't had to transfer Judy to the IPU or anything like that. They were supposed to call and let you know when they did that, but I'd been away from home all morning. She hadn't got worse, then. Where she was struck me as bad enough.

We went up to the fifth floor together. Waiting for us in Judy's room, along with the constable, was Hr. Murad. He and Madame Ruth exchanged unfriendly looks. I felt like reminding them they were on the same side, but they remembered by themselves. Murad arranged the chairs for the virtuous reality circle before anyone asked him to, and he remembered that circle would have an extra member today.

This time I shifted Judy to the foot of the bed. However much I'd hoped it would, it didn't feel as if I were touching the woman I loved. Her flesh might have been there on the bed, but her essence wasn't.

Nigel Cholmondeley slid the virtuous reality helmet onto her head. As before, he and Madame Ruth took the seats to either side of her. I sat on the other side of Madame Ruth, with Tony between me and Cholmondeley.

From his case, Cholmondeley passed us virtuous reality helmets. The room went black as I slipped mine on. Again as before, a few seconds' undignified fumbling followed, with all of us trying to find our neighbors' hands.

And then we were back in the Nine Beyonds: blacker than black, hot, wet, fetid. Somehow I got the idea the One Called Night knew we were there faster than he had before. I couldn't see anything, but the space around me already felt tight and strained, as if my spirit was trying to fit into a pair of pants a couple of inches too small for it.

"Boy, this may be the Other Side, but it's sure not the high-rent district," Tony Sudakis said. When he spoke, he became visible to me in the midst of the darkness. When I met him, I thought he looked like somebody who'd been a good football player till the competition got too big for him to handle. Well, his virtuous reality image was about seven feet tall and maybe four feet wide through the shoulders: big enough to make a good football team, not just a player. Other than size, though, it looked like Tony.

"This is what I warned you about," I said, mostly to make myself known to him. Madame Ruth and Nigel Cholmondeley spoke up, too, and appeared in my second sight as they did so. No trace of Judy. I hadn't expected one, but you never give up hope.

Cholmondeley turned to Tony Sudakis. "If this is to work, it had best work soon: the advantage of surprise, don't you know?" he said. "The longer the One Called Night has to gather his resources against us, the worse our likely plight."

"Okay." Tony's virtuous voice was nearly an octave deeper than the one he really had. He reached inside the shirt that had grown with his torso, pulled out the little amber amulet I'd seen him use the first time I walked into his office.

Here, though, it didn't seem like just amber. It shone like a tiny piece of the sun, and shed real light through the gloom of the Nine Beyonds. Looking at trees and mud and stagnant water wasn't much, but it beat looking at hostile, smothering black nine ways from Sunday.

In that rumbling, thunderous voice, Tony Sudakis called, "Perkunas, Thunderer, hear your loyal subject. Do for us, trapped here in the Nine Beyonds, as you did for the Morning Star at her wedding: give us, I pray you, the Nine Suns in the sky!"

He'd sworn by Perkunas and the Nine Suns a couple of times, enough to make me think his god might have some power in the Nine Beyonds that the One Called Night wouldn't expect. If ever a Power seemed ideally suited to influence another's home environment, this was the time.

I waited for what felt like forever, though I knew time was, to say the least, arbitrary in the realm of virtuous reality. Then that glowing bit of what had been amber flew off the chain around Tony's neck and streaked for the black sky. Surely you've wished on a falling star. There in the Nine Beyonds, I wished on a rising one.

Up and up the shining spark flew. No matter how high it rose, it didn't get any dimmer. Its progress halted directly over what would have been my head if I could have sensed myself in virtuous reality.

Another pause, and then a great explosion of light, enough and more to dazzle the eyes I didn't have here. The sky stayed black, but suddenly nine suns blazed there, in the most beautiful ring I'd ever seen.

"By Jove," Nigel Cholmondeley murmured.

"No," Tony said smugly. "By Perkunas."

Light spread over the Nine Beyonds for the first time since the One Called Night shaped his realm from the raw stuff of the Other Side. I could see what was around me and, in a different way, I could perceive the whole domain at once.

I could be wrong, but I thought each of the Nine Suns illuminated a different Beyond. I sensed all Nine Beyonds. All I'll say about them is that, even illuminated, each was less attractive than the next. If the One Called Night had designed this place for his personal comfort, well, if you ask me, he should have hired a decorator.

And there, off in the distance and yet at the same time close enough to reach out and touch, I saw something that didn't belong in this dark jungle. "Judy!" I cried. The One Called Night might have tried to hide her, but he couldn't, not with Perkunas' Nine Suns blazing down from the black sky.

No sooner had I called her name than she stood there beside me. As I've said, virtuous reality images have a way of improving on mundane reality. Not, you understand, that I ever thought Judy needed improving on, but seeing her there made me understand all at once how Beatrice must have looked to Dante.

Dante hadn't needed virtuous reality to see that way, but Dante was an artist and a genius. Me, I'm just an EPA man. However it had come to me, I knew I'd cherish Judy's virtuous image the rest of my days.

You know what else? By her expression, I didn't look half bad to her, either.

She said, "Thank you, David. I was beginning to be afraid I'd never get out of this dreadful place. I never lost hope, but I was worried. When the One Called Night hid me from you the last time you came here, whenever that was, I wondered if anyone could sense me. But you found a way."

"I never lost hope, either," I said. "I—" The light that filled the Nine Beyonds got dimmer. I looked up into the sky. The Nine Suns were still there, but they seemed to fade more with every apparent second I watched.

"We have to escape at once," Madame Ruth said urgently. "This is the domain of the One Called Night. Perkunas and the Nine Suns may have taken him by surprise, but Perkunas is not the ruling Power here."

"My colleague is correct," Nigel Cholmondeley said. "We must break the virtuous reality circle. Remember your fleshly forms; will them to separate one from the other, to loose the hands you are now holding. Quickly!"

I concentrated on the body I'd left behind at the West Hills Temple of Healing. Remembering I had hands, let alone moving them, took more effort than I thought I had in me. And all the while, the Nine Beyonds got darker and darker and darker. I felt the power of the One Called Night closing in around us.

And then I was back in room 547 again. I was still holding hands with Tony Sudakis and Madame Ruth, so I hadn't been the one to let go. That was the first thing I noticed as I did turn loose of my companions and snatch the virtuous reality helmet off my head. Only then, as I blinked against light that seemed much too bright, did I realize the One Called Night hadn't tried to chase us as we left his domain this time.

You have to understand—all that passed through my mind in a fraction of a second, and a small fraction to boot. Then I stopped caring about it, because Judy had taken off her helmet, too. She was sitting up in her bed, looking over her shoulder at me, and smiling bright as all Nine Suns put together.

I smiled back. So did Tony, Nigel Cholmondeley, Hr. Murad, and the constable who'd been keeping watch on her: she wasn't wearing her own clothes, just a pure white healing gown of virgin linen, and all it had in back was a couple of ties that didn't do much to hold it together.

When Judy figured that out, she squeaked and wiggled around so the part of the gown that actually covered her was frontways to us. Then she said to me, "David, I think you'd better introduce me to these people. You got to me through virtuous reality, didn't you?"

"That's right," I said, and did as she'd asked. After the hellos and thank-yous, I went on, "You told me you wanted to get involved in the new technology. I don't suppose you wanted to see it from the inside out, though."

"No." She shook her head so her hair flew every which way, a Judy gesture I'd seen since the day I met her. It made any tiny doubts I'd had disappear: she was back on This Side, fully and completely. "It was still interesting," she added. "I'd recognize all of you from the way I saw you in the Nine Beyonds, but you, David, you looked just the same to me."

Cholmondeley and Madame Ruth gave me an odd look. I didn't understand for a second, and then I did: you need to be a person of unusual virtue—Brother Vahan, say—to keep your normal appearance in virtuous reality. My ears got hot. "Must be love," I muttered.

"Very likely," Nigel Cholmondeley said. "After all, were it not for the love you bear for Mistress Adler, she would still be trapped on the Other Side."

That only made my ears hotter. Back in the Nine Beyonds, I'd idealized Judy into an image I'd cherish all my life, while she'd seen me just as I am. Which was the greater compliment? I couldn't begin to tell you.

The constable pulled out a sheet of parchment and a pen. Where the rest of us were exalted, he stayed businesslike. "Can you describe the motivations of the alleged perpetrators who caused your spirit to be projected into the realm on the Other Side termed the Nine Beyonds, Mistress Adler?" he asked formally.

"You mean, why they sent me there?" Judy said—sure enough, a copy editor to the core. She shook her head again. "They didn't tell me much, which was probably sensible from their point of view. I think they just didn't want to have to worry about my escaping for a while. They had some sort of big plans afoot, though; I know that much. They kept saying they'd deal with me properly once this other thing, whatever it was, happened."

That reminded me she didn't know what had gone on at the Devonshire dump or Chocolate Weasel. It also explained why she hadn't been at the Chocolate Weasel building, but I didn't want to think about what those people had intended to do to her once they got the power they'd sought.

As fast as I could, I filled her in on what had been happening on This Side while she was Elsewhere. She nodded soberly, saying, "That fits in well with what we were talking about before they kidnapped me. I'm just glad we managed to foil it."

"Not 'we,' Mistress Adler," Tony Sudakis said. "Him." He pointed right at me. "If he hadn't thought to summon the Garuda Bird, we'd all have been in the soup."

"Somebody had to do something," I said. Seeing the admiring look Judy was giving me, I added, "What I think I'll do is hire Tony to do my advertising for me. The other thing you have to remember is that if it hadn't been for his Perkunas and the Nine Suns, we couldn't have rescued you."

"Yeah, but you were the one who thought of that, too, and made Madame Ruth and Cholmondeley here go along with it even when they weren't what you'd call enthusiastic," Tony said. The virtuous reality duo nodded vigorously.

"Well, if you insist on giving me the credit, you know what?" I said. "I'm gonna take it." Everybody laughed and clapped hands.

Judy said, "Do I have any clothes here besides this peepshow of a gown? Now that I'm living in my body again, all I want to do is check myself out of here . . . where exactly am I, anyhow?"

"This is the West Hills Temple of Healing, Mistress Adler," Hr. Murad said. He opened the closet, pointed to a tunic and trousers. "These are the garments in which you were discovered. They have been laundered subsequent to their detailed examination by the constabulary."

I dare say they'd needed laundering, too; I wondered how long Judy's body had worn them and soiled them while her spirit was trapped in the Nine Beyonds. She must have been thinking the same thing, for she said, "They'll do to get me out. Then I think I'll burn them."

"As you wish, Mistress Adler," Hr. Murad said. "One formality yet remains before you can be released." Judy gave him a classic make-it-snappy look. It took effect. Hastily, he went on, "I must certify you as sound before sending you down to the business office."

"Go ahead, then," Judy said, visibly composing herself. As one who worked with magic, she knew the importance of adhering strictly to rules and procedures.

To give Hr. Murad his due, he made the examination the formality he'd told Judy it would be. He took her pulse and blood pressure, then said, "Please recite the creed of your faith."

"*Sh'ma yisroayl, adonai elohaynu, adonai ekhod,*" Judy said, and then for good measure repeated it in English: "Hear, O Israel, the Lord our God, the Lord is one."

Hr. Murad made cryptic notes on her chart. When he was

through scribbling, he said, "I have the pleasure of pronouncing you physically and spiritually sound."

"Then please leave, all of you, and let me get dressed," she said, adding, "David, when I'm done with their business people, will you take me home?"

"Sure," I said. "We'll have to let the Long Beach and Angels City constables know you're well; they'll both want to talk with you. But," I went on—quickly, to keep her from throwing the bud vase on the night table at me, "we don't have to do it right now."

"I'll take care of that," the A.C. constable on guard duty said. He grinned. "I'll give you a little while, though."

"Thanks," Judy said. We all trooped outside. Hr. Murad went off to see another patient. Nigel Cholmondeley and Madame Ruth headed for the slide. So did the constable.

I turned to Tony Sudakis. "Thanks more than I can say."

"No problem." He brushed it aside. "I'm just glad everything worked out. Listen, I gotta get back to work. I hope I see you around—long as you're not investigating my dump."

"They'll send somebody else out there from now on," I told him. "I've got a conflict of interest."

He grinned, slapped me on the back, and took off. I waited in the corridor. Right across from me was a sign with big red letters: INTENSIVE PRAYER UNIT. ALL VISITORS MUST BE BLESSED BEFORE ENTERING. I just looked at it, gladder than I can say that Judy hadn't had to pass through those portals.

She came out of her room. I had to show her where the business office was down on the ground floor; she knew nothing of how she'd come here but what I'd told her. The business people were inclined to be huffy with her until she said the magic words: Blue Scutum. Then suddenly everything was easy, though she did have to spend a while filling out the BS forms.

At last we went out to the parking lot and buckled ourselves onto my carpet. Before we took off, I leaned over and gave her a kiss. She grabbed me. We hugged for a while. Before I puddled up, I started flying her home. I took everything slow and easy, keeping in mind how tired I was.

It was the middle of the day, so traffic was easy. Practically everybody at her block of flats had gone to work. We had to use my entry talisman; she didn't have hers.

"Oh, God, it's good to be here," she said when we went in. The curtains were open; she shut them. Then she went into the kitchen and opened the icebox. I heard her cluck in distress: "Have to throw most of this stuff out. But oh, good—there's still some beer in here."

"Beer?" I echoed.

She clucked again, this time at my foolishness. "For the cup of roots," she explained, as if I weren't very bright (and at the moment, I wasn't). She came back into the front room, where I was standing like a lost soul. She did her best to remedy that; this kiss she gave me . . . well, if my eyelids were window shades, they'd have been flapping on their spindles from being yanked up too hard.

"Here's what I'm going to do," she said, ticking off points on her fingers, neat and organized as usual: "I'm going to drink the cup of roots. I'm going to get out of these clothes, never ever put them on again, and take a shower to help me forget I was wearing them. Then I'm going to put on something I hope you'll think is more interesting and try and thank you properly for getting me back from the Nine Beyonds. How does all that sound?"

"Wonderful," I said hoarsely.

"Good. It sounds wonderful to me, too." She gulped down the cup of roots, then took off her clothes right there in the middle of the living room. When I tried to grab her, she skipped back away from me. "Go sit down," she said. "I *do* want to get clean. I won't be long, I promise. All right?"

"All right," I said, and went over and sat down to prove it. She nodded in approval and headed off toward the bathroom. The water in there started to run.

I fell asleep on the couch.

Judy eventually forgave me, though she hasn't let me forget about it. All I ever wanted, from the minute I landed in the Devonshire dump case, was to get things back to normal again. Brushing the edge of Armageddon is for saints and heroes, not a working stiff like me.

I have to say I'm making progress. Judy and I set our date, and I solemnly promised to stay awake for the wedding and the night after, too. "You'd better, or I'll have it with somebody else," she told me. But we were both joking and we both knew it, so that was all right.

I still haven't caught up on all my work. I'm gaining, but I've spent so much time in court lately that I haven't been at my desk as much as I'd need to dig out from under the backlog. But helping give the people who kidnapped Judy and almost wrecked Angels City (plus God knows how much of the rest of the Confederation) just what they deserve has its own satisfaction.

And, for that matter, I won't be out of court even after those trials are done. One thing I did manage to accomplish was the report on the environmental impact of introducing leprechauns into Angels City. I didn't see any problems with it, especially after the Chumash Powers became irrelevant to the prognostication. After Bea read the report, she said nice things about me in Monday staff meeting (or so I'm told; I wasn't there at the time—somehow I bear up under the disappointment).

But Save Our Basin decided to contest my findings, so that case should drag on more or less into eternity. My guess is that any possible damage the Wee Folk might cause would cost less to fix than all the litigation about them, but I'm just a dumb inspector; they don't pay me to make policy.

And I've been working on one other thing. Not long after all the commotion I've been talking about here, I happened to notice a tiny item in the *Times* to the effect that one Charles Kelly, an assistant administrator with the Environmental Perfection Agency back in D.St.C., had resigned and been replaced by a chap named Gupta Singh.

Did Charlie jump or was he pushed? I didn't know then and I don't know now. I looked at the little story and thought about how much trouble had come about—and how much more *could* have come about—from the way he'd handled the Devonshire dump case. Not only had he given it to me informally, he'd been coy about feeding me information I needed like anything, and then he'd fled like an exorcised demon when I counted on him most.

People had died in part because Charlie didn't handle his job the way he was supposed to. Even more to the point as far as I was concerned, I'd almost lost the most important person in my life. I know that on a cosmic scale my priorities there are skewed, but I don't weigh myself on a cosmic scale.

And what had happened to Charlie because he'd screwed up and chickened out? He'd left his job, and he might not even have been forced out of it. That was all. It didn't seem enough, somehow.

I know what you're thinking: you're thinking I took out a compact on him. Sorry, no—bloody vengeance isn't my style. Besides, I don't know any mages who know that kind of demon, and I didn't care to go looking for one. Charlie wasn't worth jeopardizing my soul for, either. But still—

I left it in the back of my mind, the place where things stew while you take care of more immediate concerns. Finally, just before I got called to the witness box one day, I had an idea I liked.

Unfortunately, doing something about it didn't prove as easy as I'd hoped. The first time I called back to D.St.C., I couldn't get the information I needed. Frustrated but not, I resolved, beaten, I put the idea back into the stewpot and let it simmer while I went on with the rest of my life.

A couple of days later, while I was gulping down a burger at the courthouse cafeteria (better than the one at the Confederal Building, but not much), I knew where I could get my answer. Once you've made connections, you're a fool if you don't use them.

So I called Central Intelligence, identified myself, and asked to speak to the fellow who'd let me know Henry Legion had shuffled off this mortal coil. I didn't have a name with which to identify him, but I hoped CI would be able to get around that. Sure enough, inside a minute he was saying, "Good day, Mr. Fisher. I'm glad everything worked out well for you and your lady."

Well, I shouldn't have been surprised that Central Intelligence knew about such things. "Thanks," I managed.

"What can I do for you today?" he asked.

I told him what I wanted and why I wanted it. "I'll only use it the once," I promised. "If you like, I'll take a formal oath on that."

"No need, Mr. Fisher," he said. The phone imp in my ear reproduced a curious scratchy noise I identified as a chuckle. "Just between you, me, and the wall, I'd say you've earned the right to use it any way you like. Don't stay on the ether now; I'll call you back in a couple of minutes with what you need."

I hung up. Pretty soon, just as promised, the phone yarped. I answered it, wrote down what the chap from Central Intelligence gave me, thanked him again, and hung up.

Then all I had to do was wait. Since I was doing this for my convenience, not Charlie's, I waited till Saturday night: my Sabbath was over, so I could use the phone without the slightest sin, and I didn't have to get up early and go to work the next morning. That counted, too, for what I had in mind.

I was yawning when I picked up the phone at my flat, but I didn't care. I called the number I'd gotten from Central Intelligence: Charlie Kelly's home phone. I listened to the racket it made.

"Hello?" Even with phone imps between us, Charlie sounded drowned in sleep.

"Hello, Charlie," I answered brightly. "This is Dave Fisher, out in Angels City. How are you this morning?"

"Jesus," he said, his voice a little clearer. "Do you have any idea what time it is?"

Since I'd asked my alarm clock, I knew down to the minute. "Your time, it's 5:07," I said: "Just the same time when you called me here to get me into the Devonshire toxic spell dump case. It turned out all right, no thanks to you."

He started to splutter. I hung up.

You know what? Phones aren't so bad after all.

There Are Elves Out There

An excerpt from

Mercedes Lackey
Larry Dixon

The main bay was eerily quiet. There were no screams of grinders, no buzz of technical talk or rapping of wrenches. There was no whine of test engines on dynos coming through the walls. Instead, there was a dull-bladed tension amid all the machinery, generated by the humans and the Sidhe gathered there.

Tannim laid the envelope on the rear deck of the only fully-operated GTP car that Fairgrove had built to date, the one that Donal had spent his waking hours building, and Conal had spent track-testing. He'd designed it for beauty and power in equal measure, and had given its key to Conal, its elected driver, in the same brother's-gift ceremony used to present an elvensteed. Conal now sat on its sculpted door, and absently traced a slender finger along an air intake, glowering at the envelope.

Tannim finished his magical tests, and asked for a knife. An even dozen were offered, but Dottie's Leatherman was accepted. Keighvin stood a little apart from the group, hand on his short knife. His eyes glittered with suppressed anger, and he appeared less human than usual, Tannim noticed. Something was bound to break soon.

Tannim folded out the knifeblade, slit the envelope open, and then unfolded the Leatherman's pliers. With them he withdrew six Polaroids of Tania and two others, unconscious, each bound at the wrists and neck. Their silver chains were held by some-*things* from the Realm of the Unseleighe—inside a limo. And, out of focus through the limo's windows, was a stretch of flat tarmac, and large buildings—

Tannim dropped the Leatherman, his fingers gone numb. It clattered twice before wedging into the cockpit's fresh-air vent. Keighvin took one startled step forward, then halted as the magical alarms at Fairgrove's perimeter flared around them all. Tannim's hand went into a jacket pocket, and he threw down the letter from the P.I. He saw Conal pick up the photographs, blanch, then snatch the letter up.

Tannim had already turned by then, and was sprinting for the office door, and the parking lot beyond.

Behind him, he could hear startled questions directed at him, but all he could answer before disappearing into the offices was "Airport!" His bad leg was slowing him down, and screamed at him like a sharp rock grinding into his bones. There was some kind of attack beginning, but he had no time for that.

Have to get to the airport, have to save Tania

from Vidal Dhu, the bastard, the son of a bitch, the—

Tannim rounded a corner and banged his left knee into a file cabinet. He went down hard, hands instinctively clutching at his over-damaged leg. His eyes swam with a private galaxy of red stars, and he struggled while his eyes refocused.

Son of a bitch son of a bitch son of a bitch. . . .

Behind him he heard the sounds of a war-party, and above it all, the banshee wail of a high-performance engine. He pulled himself up, holding the bleeding knee, and limp-ran towards the parking lot, to the Mustang, and Thunder Road.

Vidal Dhu stood in full armor before the gates of Fairgrove, laughing, lashing out with levin-bolts to set·off its alarms. It was easy for Vidal to imagine what must be going on inside—easy to picture that smug, orphaned witling Keighvin Silverhair barking orders to weak mortals, marshaling them to fight. Let him rally them, Vidal thought—it will do him no good. None at all. He may have won before, but ultimately, the mortals will have damned him.

It has been so many centuries, Silverhair. I swore I'd kill your entire lineage, and I shall. I shall!

Vidal prepared to open the gate to Underhill. Through that gate all the Court would watch as Keighvin was destroyed—Aurilia's plan be hanged! Vidal's blood sang with triumph—he had driven Silverhair into a winless position at last! And when he accepted the Challenge, before the whole Court, none of his human-world tricks would benefit him—theirs would be a purely magical combat, one Sidhe to another.

To the death.

* * *

Keighvin Silverhair recognized the scent of the magic at Fairgrove's gates—he had smelled it for centuries. It reeked of obsession and fear, hatred and lust. It was born of pain inflicted without consideration of repercussions. It was the magic of one who had stalked innocents and stolen their last breaths.

He recognized, too, the rhythm that was being beaten against the walls of Fairgrove.

So be it, murderer. I will suffer your stench no more.

"They will expect us to dither and delay; the sooner we act, the more likely it is that we will catch them unprepared. They do not know how well we work together."

Around him, the humans and Sidhe of his home sprang into action, taking up arms with such speed he'd have thought them possessed. Conal had thrown down the letter after reading it, and barked, "Hangar 2A at Savannah Regional; they've got children as hostages!" The doors of the bay began rolling open, and outside, elvensteeds stamped and reared, eyes glowing, anxious for battle. Conal looked to him, then, for orders.

Keighvin met his eyes for one long moment, and said, "Go, Conal. I shall deal with our attacker for the last time. If naught else, the barrier at the gates can act as a trap to hold him until we can deal with him as he deserves." He did not add what he was thinking—that he only hoped it would hold Vidal. The Unseleighe was a strong mage; he might escape even a trap laid with death metal, if he were clever enough. Then, with the swiftness of a falcon, he was astride his elvensteed Rosaleen Dhu, headed for the perimeter of Fairgrove.

He was out there, all right, and had begun laying a spell outside the fences, like a snare. Perhaps in his sickening arrogance he'd forgotten that Keighvin could see such things. Perhaps in his insanity, he no longer cared.

Rosaleen tore across the grounds as fast as a stroke of lightning, and cleared the fence in a soaring leap. She landed a few yards from the laughing, mad Vidal Dhu, on the roadside, with him between Keighvin and the gates. He stopped lashing his mocking bolts at the gates of Fairgrove and turned to face Keighvin.

"So, you've come to face me alone, at last? No walls or mortals to hide behind, as usual, coward? So sad that you've chosen *now* to change, within minutes of your death, traitor."

"Vidal Dhu," Keighvin said, trying to sound unimpressed despite the heat of his blood, "if you wish to duel me, I shall accept. But before I accept, you must release the children you hold."

The Unseleighe laughed bitterly. "It's your concern for these mortals that raised you that have *made* you a traitor, boy. Those children do not matter." Vidal lifted his lip in a sneer as Keighvin struggled to maintain his composure. "Oh, I will do more than duel you, Silverhair. I wish to Challenge you before the Court, and kill you as they watch."

That was what Keighvin had noted—it was the initial layout of a Gate to the High Court Underhill. Vidal was serious about this Challenge—already the Court would be assembling to judge the battle. Keighvin sat atop Rosaleen, who snorted and stamped, enraged by the other's tauntings. Vidal's pitted face twisted in a maniacal smirk.

"How long must I wait for you to show courage, witling?"

Keighvin's mind swam for a moment, before he remembered the full protocols of a formal Challenge. It had been so long since he'd even seen one. . . .

Once accepted, the Gate activates, and all the Court watches as the two battle with blade and magic. Only one leaves the field; the Court is bound to slay anyone who runs. So it had always been. Vidal would not Challenge unless he were confident of winning, and Keighvin was still tired from the last battle—which Vidal had not even been at. . . .

But Vidal must die. That much Keighvin knew.

From Born to Run *by Mercedes Lackey & Larry Dixon.*

* * *

Watch for more from the SERRAted Edge:
Wheels of Fire by Mercedes Lackey & Mark Shepherd

When the Bough Breaks by Mercedes Lackey & Holly Lisle

MAGIC AND COMPUTERS DON'T MIX!

RICK COOK

Or . . . do they? That's what Walter "Wiz" Zumwalt is wondering. Just a short time ago, he was a master hacker in a Silicon Valley office, a very ordinary fellow in a very mundane world. But magic spells, it seems, are a lot like computer programs: they're both formulas, recipes for getting things done. Unfortunately, just like those computer programs, they can be full of bugs. Now, thanks to a *particularly* buggy spell, Wiz has been transported to a world of magic—and incredible peril. The wizard who summoned him is dead, Wiz has fallen for a red-headed witch who despises him, and no one—not the elves, not the dwarves, not even the dragons—can figure out why he's here, or what to do with him. Worse: the sorcerers of the deadly Black League, rulers of an entire continent, want Wiz dead—and he doesn't even know why! Wiz had better figure out the rules of this strange new world—and fast—or he's not going to live to see Silicon Valley again.

Here's a refreshing tale from an exciting new writer. It's also a rarity: a well-drawn fantasy told with all the rigorous logic of hard science fiction.

69803-6 • 320 pages • $4.99

THE BEST OF THE BEST

GRAND ADVENTURE
IN GAME-BASED UNIVERSES

With these exciting novels set
in bestselling game universes,
Baen brings you synchronicity at its
best. We believe that familiarity with
either the novel or the game will
intensify enjoyment of the other.
All novels are the only authorized
fiction based on these games and
are published by permission.

THE BARD'S TALE™

Join the Dark Elf Naitachal and his apprentices in
bardic magic as they explore the mysteries of the
world of The Bard's Tale.

Castle of Deception
by Mercedes Lackey & Josepha Sherman
72125-9 * 320 pages * $5.99   _____

Fortress of Frost and Fire
by Mercedes Lackey & Ru Emerson
72162-3 * 304 pages * $5.99   _____

Prison of Souls
by Mercedes Lackey & Mark Shepherd
72193-3 * 352 pages * $5.99   _____

And watch for **Gates of Chaos** by Josepha Sherman
coming in May 1994!

BUG YOUR BOOKSTORE

We've said that a sure-fire way to improve the selection of SF at your local store was to communicate with that store. To let the manager and salespeople know when they weren't stocking a book or author that you wanted. To special order that book through the bookstore, rather than order it directly from the publisher. In order to encourage you to think about these things (and to satisfy our own curiosity), we asked you to send us a list of your five best and five worst reads of the past year. And hundreds of you responded.

So we got to thinking, too. Below you will find what we think are our top fifteen reads on our current list (in alphabetical order by author). If your bookstore doesn't stock them, it should. So bug your bookstore. You'll get a better selection of SF to choose from, and your store will have improved sales. To sweeten the deal, if you send us a copy of your special order form and the book or books ordered circled on the coupon below, we'll send you a free poster!